"From the infant stages of the romance genre Ann Major has been a significant contributor. Her name on the cover instantly identifies the book as a good read."

—Sandra Brown,

***New York Times* Bestselling Author**

"Ann Major expertly combines the elements of romance to create an unforgettable love story."

—Bestselling author Mary Lynn Baxter

"Ann Major understands the captivating power of love. She writes with persuasion."

—Cindy Bonner, author of *Lily*

"Whenever I pick up a novel by Ann Major, I know I'm guaranteed a heartwarming story."

—Bestselling author Annette Broadrick

"No one provides hotter emotional fireworks than the fiery Ann Major."

—Melinda Helfer,

Romantic Times Magazine

More Praise for Ann Major

"Engaging characters, stories that thrill and delight, shivering suspense and captivating romance. Want it all? Read Ann Major."
—Nora Roberts, *New York Times* Bestselling Author

"Ann Major's *Secret Child* sizzles with characters who leap off the page and into your heart.... This one's hot!"
—Bestselling author Lisa Jackson

"Ann Major's CHILDREN OF DESTINY series sizzles, steams and touches the heart with its emotional intensity."
—Harriett Klausner, *Affaire de Coeur*

"Ann Major is a top-notch writer who conjures up well-paced plots that consistently deliver to her readers."
—Bestselling author Pamela Morsi

"Compelling characters, intense fast-moving plots and snappy dialogue have made Ann Major's name synonymous with the best in contemporary romantic fiction."
—*Rendezvous*

ANN MAJOR

SECRET CHILD

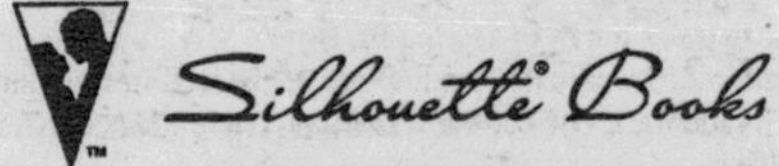

Published by Silhouette Books
America's Publisher of Contemporary Romance

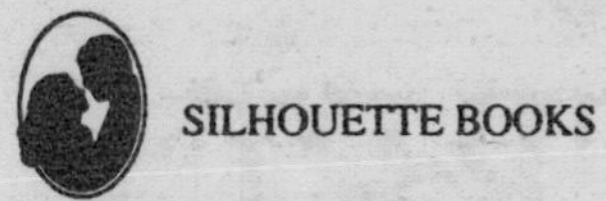

SILHOUETTE BOOKS

SECRET CHILD

ISBN 0-373-48356-2

This edition published by arrangement with Harlequin Books S.A.

Printed in U.S.A.

I am grateful to my editor, Tara Gavin, and to her colleagues and staff for their hard work and encouragement; to my late agent, Anita Diamant, for her years of encouragement and friendship; I am grateful to my new agent, Robin Rue; to my late colleague, Sondra Stanford, and to Mary Lynn Baxter, as well.

Many other people helped me. Kay Telle invited me to Vail, where inspiration for this novel struck. Morgan Thaxton, Chili Robinson, Elizabeth Stowe, and Ann and Dick Jones gave generous interviews and advice. Robert Lund, Tad Cleaves, David Cleaves, Kim Cleaves and Jason Nichols helped correct several drafts. I am also grateful to my talented secretary, Patricia Patterson, and to my housekeeper, Ella Mae Lescuer.

Last but not least, I thank Ted.

Prologue

Bronte felt a raindrop hit her cheek. Involuntarily her fingers tightened on the metal clasp of her purse.

A second drop splashed her prim, white collar.

The urge to run was almost overwhelming.

But it was nine long blocks back to her hotel.

Bronte Devlin hated big cities.

But this one should have been different.

She preferred wide-open spaces and big blue skies. She preferred men who wore jeans and Stetsons and lived outside to stuffy, pale-skinned businessmen in suits and ties.

She had been standing on Fifty-fourth Street for thirty minutes, trying without success to hail a cab during the evening rush hour.

It was October, but it felt like July.

The sky was so black she thought it could start raining any second. She felt lost and forlorn, almost fainting in the thick, humid heat.

Not that New York City wasn't bustling with an endless stream of cabs. Buses, too. Not that the air wasn't dense with their exhaust fumes. But the cabs were full. Just as the sidewalks were jammed. People of all races, ages, classes, shapes and sizes jostled past her, hurrying toward jobs, restaurants, hotels and homes.

Thunder reverberated through the air. Suddenly, she was a thousand times more anxious as she imagined these strangers having what she didn't—purposeful lives, marriages. And children.

They had somewhere to go. And someone who loved them.

They still believed in something.

She had to get out of this city that had once been home—and fast.

As soon as she got back to her hotel, she would throw her clothes into her suitcase and leave. She had no idea where she'd go, certainly not back to Wimberley, Texas, where she had stood in her principal's prison-green office and torn up her teaching contract. She'd sold her clothes in a garage sale, given away her cat, Pogo, to a friend. She had no home now.

Kindergarten would be starting soon, but she had known she couldn't face teaching the children another year. She couldn't bear the way she saw Jimmy's face every time another long-lashed, little boy with copper-colored curls looked up shyly from his coloring book or raised his hand to ask a question. A kindergarten teacher needed illusions. She had lost hers.

Her Jimmy was dead.

With his pale skin, fiery hair and constant grin, he had been the joy of her life. Light boned and hyperactive, Jimmy had loved his dog, his cat, his horse, his skateboard, his chocolate-chip cookies with ice-cold milk and his three best friends. She had loved the hectic job of raising him, and entertaining the children who were always dashing in and out of their house. She hadn't even minded if they used their outdoor voices indoors or slammed the screen door a hundred times a day. And then suddenly one rainy afternoon, with no warning, he was gone.

When they had buried Jimmy in his boots and cowboy hat, Bronte had died, too. So had her marriage to her cowboy husband and her dreams of other children—although more gradually. So had her belief in life.

Bronte had tried to go on as Bryan—dear placid, staid, unimaginative Bryan, who had never seemed to be as deeply touched by life as she—had so wisely pontificated she should. She had tried to live with the rage and then the hollow pain of their loss. Even after Bryan had walked out, she had kept teaching kindergarten, struggling to go on, hoping that something would happen to renew her faith. Then suddenly, a month ago, she had torn up her contract and fled back to New York, her childhood home. She had even taken her maiden name back.

Running away was as hard as teaching. The overwhelming emptiness inside her seemed to be expanding. Sometimes she just wanted to give up and die.

But she hadn't.

Not yet, anyway.

Who had said, "Everywhere I go, there I am"?

She didn't know anyone in Manhattan anymore. Still, she had gone to West 69th Street, where she'd lived as a child. Where her beautiful mother had practiced arias in between screaming matches with her equally famous father.

But the street had felt every bit as strange and alien

as it had when Bronte had been a child. Only it was alien in a different way.

Her mother's handsome brownstone mansion was divided into a dozen fashionable apartments. Strangers raised canaries on the second floor, where her mother had lavishly entertained movie stars and dictators. The fourth-floor balcony where their cook had kept pots of red geraniums, where their black cat had sunned and where Bronte had hidden from her mother's rages, was now jammed with bicycles.

A young career woman in black, chewing gum, had rushed out of the front door. When she saw Bronte staring up at the building, the girl had demanded to know whether she was looking for somebody or just lost.

"I think I am...a little of both," Bronte had admitted. Then she added shyly, "Did...did you know that this used to be Madame Devlin's house?"

"The diva who ran off with the Brazilian shipping tycoon? Wasn't there some tragedy?" The girl paused. "Her picture is in the foyer. She was very beautiful."

"Back then they said she was the most beautiful woman in the world. There was this huge cult surrounding her. She...she was my mother."

"Really? Well, you don't look much like her," the girl said. "Too bad." Then someone shouted to her and she waved and dashed off down the street with her friend.

Yes. Bronte had been the ugly duckling and her mother, the swan, had been so ashamed of her.

All that had once been a problem. Until Bronte had rebelled against the beauty god. And the success god. Until she'd realized the world was filled with ordinary people. Until she had become a teacher and had married easy-going Bryan, who had said she was pretty; Bryan who hadn't gone to college, who hardly knew there was such a thing as opera. They'd had Jimmy, and Bronte had made a whole new life for herself—a laid-back, ordinary life her attention-seeking mother, who had been driven by inner demons to excel and cause scandal, would never have approved of nor understood.

Bronte had failed at that life, too.

She had wanted to come back to her mother's house. To remember how her life had been. To try to see where she had gone wrong.

She remembered herself as a child parading up and down the staircase in long, glittering robes, and her mother's rage later when she'd found the costume torn. Bronte remembered all the other rages, too. Rages over dirty fingernails, over clumsy curtsies when Bronte was introduced to somebody her mother had wanted to impress at one of her soirees.

Bronte had been so...so ordinary. Unable to sing even the simplest melody. And so plain.

Suddenly, she didn't want to remember that first life, which had been such an immense burden to her once. She still wanted to keep that time far away and unreal.

Too late Bronte realized that this was not a city to offer comfort to one with profound grief and loss and guilt. So here she was, all alone on busy Fifty-fourth Street. Hadn't her mother pitied her and told her she was nothing special, that she would fail at whatever she tried?

Despite her striking red hair, slim figure and her almost-pretty, sweet face, which had an appeal all its own, Bronte might as well have been invisible on that crowded street corner. Nobody noticed her.

Suddenly two large men sprang from a shop door and charged after a teenager like a pair of stampeding bulls.

"Thief!" a bull bellowed as rain pelted the sidewalk.

"Get him!"

Bronte barely got a glimpse of the boy. She'd been looking up, panicked by the dark sky with its keening wind and huge raindrops.

The biggest man lunged, ripping the bundle of money out of the boy's arm.

The brown paper sack burst.

Fifty-dollar bills exploded everywhere. A gust from the storm caught the money and sent green bills drifting over the crowd. Everybody started pushing and grabbing and jumping to catch them.

The tough-faced store owner slugged the boy hard in the stomach and then in the jaw, sending him reeling backward into Bronte, whose leather-soled flats slid on the slick sidewalk. She careened backward off the curb just as the light turned yellow and the downpour really began. Just as a speeding taxi driver stomped on his accelerator to make the light.

While money and rain flooded the street, Bronte held up her hands helplessly—in a vain attempt to signal the taxi to stop.

A woman saw her and screamed.

"Get out of the street, girlie!" a bystander yelled.

Terror froze Bronte's raised hands as the taxi driver braked too late, and the blur of yellow and chrome kept hurtling toward her.

Funny how she hardly felt the blow, how there was only an odd, numbing warmth as she was lifted into the air. Then she was falling. Still, she felt nothing as black asphalt rushed up to meet her face.

While she lay on the street, a vast dome seemed to close over the skyscrapers and encase her lifeless body like a huge jar. Only there weren't any holes punched in the lid, and she had to fight for every breath. The ferment of people and taxis and buses were all on the other side of the glass. Even the rain couldn't touch her.

The cabdriver got out and screamed at her in some foreign language she didn't understand. Others were screaming as well, but their babble seemed to come from a long way away.

High above her, against a liver-colored skyscraper, a huge matinee sign with the bold image of her favorite movie star, Garth Brown, floated. He had dark skin, dark hair and an incredibly fierce demeanor. How many nights had she stayed up late watching his old movies, and fantasizing after Bryan had walked out that she'd fall in love again and start over? But it hadn't happened. Now it never would.

Someone knelt and touched her face with fingertips she couldn't feel. A white-haired lady called 911.

In the absolute silence and aloneness inside her jar, Bronte felt the beating of her heart. She tasted blood. She watched fluttering green bills sift slowly down on top of her.

Shadows began to darken.

Garth's face dissolved.

Was she dying?

Her fierce moan of denial was so loud it startled her.

Jimmy was dead.

Bryan had needed more attention than she could give him and had left her for a younger, more cheerful woman who adored him, a woman who was not haunted by ghosts.

Bronte had lost everything.

But suddenly, miraculously, she knew that she wanted to live.

When she heard sirens, the pain in her chest began. First it was only pressure, deep and constricting, holding her down.

As she gasped for every breath, the wall of brown buildings seemed to move together. The sky darkened. Then everything dissolved in a rush of black.

Jimmy. Jimmy. Jimmy.

Bronte felt her little boy's rowdy presence as she'd dreamed so many times of feeling it.

Happiness filled her.

He was all right. He was all around her.

The doctors had lied to her. Bryan had lied to her.

She hadn't failed.

Jimmy wasn't dead.

He wasn't.

She'd been right all along. God couldn't be that cruel.

She tried to open her eyes and see her son.

But her eyelids were as heavy as lead.

She didn't have the strength to move even the tiniest muscle.

Still, his presence instilled a wonderful peace as well as a belief that she had to live....

When Bronte regained consciousness, she was lying on a gurney in a crowded emergency room. Someone was squeezing her hand.

She could barely feel the firm, blunt fingers of the stranger who probed expertly for her pulse. All she could feel was the searing pain every time she tried to breathe.

"God Almighty!" a young nurse behind him said. "What happened to her face?"

"She was hit by a cab," a sterner, older voice said.

"Hey—shut up!" the doctor said. "I'm getting a pulse!"

"Poor thing. Who'd want to live looking like that?"

"Bronte Devlin?" Webster's heart was racing as he thumbed through the young woman's chart.

He had noticed her red hair when he'd seen her staring at her mother's home.

He hadn't been sure who she was, but he had followed her. But before he'd had a chance to speak, she'd been hit by that cab.

Coincidence?

Synchronicity was the current buzzword. Webster Quinn was used to blessings from the gods.

Any other plastic surgeon might have blanched at the sight of the young woman in the blood-smeared, white dress, but the notorious, silver-haired Dr. Webster Quinn, famed for his bizarre genius and immense ego, thrived as both a rebel and an outcast. At fifty, he had three passions—work, the opera and a mysterious woman.

Professionally, nothing turned him on more than achieving the unachievable. His successes had dazzled the world. Secretive by nature, he rarely shared his innovative methods and aggressive procedures with colleagues. Naturally, he did not advertise his failures.

Awestruck, Webster knelt low, fingering a matted lock of the girl's hair with a trembling hand.

Even in his blue scrubs, he looked more like a television actor playing a doctor than a real doctor. His keen blue eyes, which were usually so cold, blazed with an almost fanatical light.

Incredible.

He couldn't believe his good fortune.

Madame Devlin's daughter.

Her hair, as bright as spun flame, was a perfect match.

When he probed the young girl's eyelids, she made a small, whimpering sound. But it wasn't compassion for her obvious discomfort as she struggled for every breath that made his heart stop. It was the vivid green hue of one swollen eye.

Her eye color was an exact match, too.

She was slim and tall.

Like the *other.*

And the bone structure…

She was the *original*'s daughter. Closer to the genuine article than the *other.*

His palms grew sweaty. His heart raced faster.

He felt like Michelangelo stumbling upon a perfect piece of Carrara marble.

Finally, Webster studied the mangled face of Bronte Devlin.

Instead of pity or revulsion, he felt an excitement he imagined to be like that of the elation of a gifted sculptor who saw what other fools could not see.

This poor, broken creature would be the raw material for his second masterpiece.

The damage wasn't nearly as extensive as it might appear to those less talented and less sure.

As soon as the other doctors patched her ribs and saved her life, he would spirit her away to his clinic in Costa Rica. Although it was perfectly legal for any simpleminded goose with a medical degree to perform the most complex sort of plastic surgery in the

United States, Webster preferred to do his highly innovative procedures out of the country, as far as possible from the prying eyes of his critical colleagues. Not that he couldn't make a few basic repairs here while she was healing from her other, life-threatening injuries.

Webster, who had left California and moved east under a cloud of scandal ten years ago, was the most controversial plastic surgeon in the state of New York. Yet his credentials were impeccable. He had a wall full of diplomas. He had graduated first in his class from UCLA Medical School. He had operated on some of the most famous movie stars in Hollywood. One of cinema's oldest and most glamorous stars, who was over sixty but looked twenty on the screen, had made Quinn a household name by proclaiming on national television that he had magic fingers.

Everybody agreed that he was a creative genius who routinely worked miracles. But since Webster played by his own rules, his creativity and genius were considered his most dangerous liabilities. His few admirers in New York cited that he had donated as much of his time and expertise to charity cases as he had to the rich.

But neither his admirers nor his enemies would have suspected his motivations as he studied the injured young woman on the gurney.

For a moment Webster remembered another tall, slim redhead who had slipped inside his office after hours five years ago.

He had given her a new face, which had been her key to wealth and fame. She had become his lover. And his obsession.

He had shown her into a suite of offices called the

Magic Rooms. The walls had been painted black, and his magic paraphernalia and memorabilia had been on display in lighted, glass cases.

"You have to change my face," she had said in a desperate whisper. "It's a matter of life and death." She had picked up a pair of dice and rolled them.

A pair of sixes lay on his desk.

"Whose?"

If only he had not stared straight into her green eyes.

"Terrible people...you cannot imagine how terrible have forced me to do this, or I would never... You must make me beautiful. Very beautiful. The most beautiful woman in the world."

"Plastic surgeons are not magicians. The idea that I am a sculptor of the flesh who can transform an ordinary woman into a magnificent goddess is fantasy."

She stroked a case that contained a top hat and a black velvet cloak lined with red satin. "You underestimate us both. I am no ordinary woman. You are no ordinary surgeon."

He had started to argue, but she had exerted such an incredible power over him that he was dumbstruck. He had noticed that her perfume smelled of gardenias.

A framed portrait of Madame Devlin, the diva, whose voice and beauty had electrified him for as long as he could remember, had graced the wall behind the mysterious woman in his office.

He had felt a sudden shocking rush of inspiration as he had compared Madame's slender face to the real woman's pale, triangular features. A stillness had descended upon him as he began to wonder if he could perform such a miracle.

She would believe it to be *her* miracle.

But it would be *his*.

"Can you do it?"

"It will be risky and expensive."

"I'm not afraid. Money is no object. Neither is...this...." She loosened his tie and jerked his top two shirt buttons apart.

Pushing her hands away, he gasped, "I live with someone."

"Not any longer."

She had undressed him before he could protest. She had begun to touch him, and the moment he'd felt her talented fingertips stroking his bare skin, an electric stillness had descended upon him.

Then his flesh had started to burn, and a meteoric burst of lust had overpowered his will. Forgetting his rigid code of medical ethics that forbade sex with a patient, he had torn off her black dress and pushed her down on the floor, falling on top of her like a heavy animal. All that had mattered was to shove himself savagely inside her again and again, to plunge deeply, to know the fierce ecstasy of her long limbs writhing under his. Their bodies had been fluid and electric, like two snakes on a dark forest floor, as graceful as eels in a dark undersea world.

When it was over, there had been red marks on his back and purple bruises on her breasts. He had never hit a woman before, and he had felt cheap and dirty. He had sworn to himself that the new perversions she had introduced him to would lose their appeal, and her hold on him would soon be over.

He hadn't known then that the well-ordered pattern of his life had shifted into something obscene, that even then she was already a dangerous obsession.

He thought of his secret mistress constantly, of the things she did to him when they were alone. Of the things she did with other men when she was away. It had been a mistake to give her the face of a goddess. Sometimes he fancied she was the devil and that she'd stolen his soul.

She was a cruel master.

She had used him and abused him. Not that she didn't rationalize everything she did.

Sometimes he hated her.

Sometimes he wanted to escape.

Sometimes he wanted revenge.

Most of the time he did as she ordered.

He had waited for this moment.

He had a plan.

He would make another one.

The wretched young woman on the stretcher, whom he'd believed to be unconscious, moaned. Startled, he came back to the present and to the gravity of the matter at hand.

He felt shaken by a twinge of conscience. What would this young woman think and feel when she found out what he had done? It didn't matter.

He leaned down and whispered very gently, very soothingly in his much-practiced, movie-star doctor's voice against her ear.

She opened her eyes, and he noted with relief that the peculiar frightening aspect in the *other*'s eyes was absent. This woman could never hold him in thrall. She would be easy to manage.

"Go away!" the girl said as she grew aware of his presence.

"Do you want to live or die?" he whispered kindly.

"Without my face?" She turned away from him with a thready sob. "My son is dead. Everybody's dead. I'm all alone. I have failed at everything. I thought I wanted to die before this happened..."

"Your parents?"

"Dead."

He felt a wave of unwanted pity for her. "I'm a plastic surgeon. I can leave you as you are...or I can make you into the most beautiful woman in the world. I can give you paradise on earth. You will be the envy of every woman, and every man will desire you."

Every man but me.

He told himself this rather too forcefully. He would have other uses for her.

"Your injuries are not as terrible as you believe them to be. But I must get started at once if we are to have even a chance at success. Do you want to live or die?" he repeated.

His deep, melodious voice was soothingly hypnotic. His cool blue eyes were tender.

Of the evil in his soul there was no trace.

Part 1
WILD CHILD

Chapter 1

The siren was shrill, cutting the eerie silence like a knife.

Jack West awoke with a start, his black gaze as alert as a cat's as he glanced fiercely about his cheap, San Antonio motel room. He half expected to find himself back in cell block C, a knife-tip against his throat, a murderer's legs straddling his waist.

He was alone.

Safe.

Even so, his heart pounded a few seconds longer, his senses having been honed by the constant danger.

He felt the familiar loneliness close over him. It was deep and dark, but he surrendered to it.

The name Jack West once had meant something in south Texas. He'd been rich and famous.

No more.

Jack West. Crisp, prison-cropped black hair. Indian dark eyes with long bristly lashes, brooding eyes that could flame with hate as hot as tar-tipped torches or go as cold as black ice and stare straight through his enemy.

Before prison he'd been tough.

His carved face and tall, muscular body were harder and leaner than ever. Scars crisscrossed his broad back from the night he'd gotten drunk on smuggled gin with a black inmate named Brickhouse.

When Jack had sobered up he'd been in lockdown. He'd been badly beaten and slashed. The bulging muscle of his left forearm had throbbed almost as much as the deeper cuts on his hands and shoulders. He'd had vague memories of being held down while Brickhouse used a ballpoint pen and a sewing needle to tattoo matching hunting knives onto their forearms. There had been even cloudier memories of the fight when they'd been jumped by six inmates with knives.

Jack's once healthy, dark skin was sallow, and the scars on his back were nothing compared to the ones on his soul. He couldn't forget that even before his conviction, Theodora had thrown him off the ranch, seized his daughter and cut him off from his old life forever. Once he had almost believed his life might count for something, after all.

No more.

Jack West wasn't much different than a dead man.

He was even worse off now than when he'd started as a beggar and a thief in Matamoros, Mexico. His mama had been a cheap Mexican whore, his father an Anglo ranch foreman who'd paid for his five minutes with her. He'd known his father's name only because his mother had stolen his wallet.

Jack had spent his earliest years in a small shack in a dusty Mexican barrio, where he'd had to steal or starve. He'd lived on the fringes even there. He'd lived the second half of his life like a cowboy prince in the big, white, stucco house on El Atascadero, one of the grandest of the great, legendary ranches in south Texas. But he'd existed on the fringes there, too. Because nobody forgot where he'd come from and what his mother had been, least of all him.

Jack owed his Anglo looks and height and his ranching talent to his father, but on the inside he was more Mexican than Anglo. He knew that because when they'd locked him up, his soul had left him. He'd watched it go.

His mother would have said he had the *susto.*

Whatever. His soul hadn't come back yet—even though they'd let him out. He didn't want it back, either.

What he wanted was a drink.

But he hadn't let himself touch the stuff.

He'd decided to stay sober for at least one full night.

Outside in the sweltering dark, an ambulance raced north on San Antonio's Loop 410, its scream dying as if suffocated by the Texas heat.

Jack blinked, forcing himself to relax when he didn't hear the sound of boots racing toward his cell. Instead of blue uniforms and fists bulging with brass knuckles or spoons sharpened into clumsy knives, he saw the rosy rectangle of light behind thin drapes and heard the muted roar of traffic. The lumpy pillow he'd used to cover the phone because he'd taken it off the hook when the reporters kept calling still lay across the telephone on the nightstand.

There were drapes on the windows. Instead of bars.

The soft mattress and clean sheets were real, too.

The five-year nightmare in an eight-by-six cell was over.

He was free.

Whatever that meant.

Bastard from a barrio. Ex-con. Starting over at the bottom again.

When he laughed harshly, his neck began to ache, so he pulled the pillow off the telephone and bunched it under his head. Gently he replaced the receiver on the hook.

He couldn't sleep; he hadn't slept through a night in years. Still, he lay back and closed his eyes, dreading the dawn.

Yesterday he'd been in solitary, his ankles shackled, his hands cuffed to his waist. His toilet had been overflowing, permeating his narrow cell with a foul stench. When he'd asked for something to clean up the mess with, the fat guard had laughed and told him to wallow in the rot like the pig he was.

Then this morning the same guard had yelled at him to grab his bedroll; he was moving.

Jack had been stunned when they'd handcuffed him and driven him to San Antonio and then set him free.

Nobody, not even his lawyer, had bothered to inform him about the serial killer who'd made headlines all over Texas when he'd confessed to one of the murders Jack had been locked up for.

Jack hadn't been prepared to deal with reporters demanding to know how freedom felt when he'd been shoved out the gate into blinding sunshine and sweltering heat.

Since he had nowhere to go and there was no one to care, freedom had only changed the nature of his fears. He'd blinked and rubbed his wrists, stalling, keeping his eyes on his cheap, prison-issue running shoes, not knowing what to say. Not wanting to say anything. Five years ago the press had crucified him. So when reporters had pestered him with calls after he'd checked into the motel, he'd taken the phone off the hook.

To survive the violence, he'd shut off his emotions. He'd learned to keep his thoughts to himself, to trust no one. He'd learned regimentation. He'd obeyed his jailers with curt grunts and nods.

He was little better than an animal. Guards and inmates alike had beaten him and taught him how to cower like a dog and to hate deeply.

He was free...but he was embittered and unfit company for most decent folk. Maybe that wouldn't have mattered if he'd had a family who'd stood by him.

But Theodora had made her feelings clear right from the first. Never once had she written or come to see him. After his conviction, he'd lost custody of his daughter, Carla.

All his letters to Carla and to Theodora had come back. *Return to sender.* The guards had chanted that line aloud when they'd thrown his letters through the bars of his cell.

To hell with Theodora. To hell with the whole damn world. He'd started alone; he might as well end alone. Never again would he let anybody get close to him. He'd take some low job and drink till he found oblivion.

If Jack hated thinking about Carla and Theodora, he hated thinking about Chantal, his wife, even more.

For she had betrayed him in every way that a wife could betray a husband. He had put up with her abuse and then her absences and infidelities for years. Then one day, she had pushed him too far.

When had the deeply rooted hatred between them gotten its start? Had the seeds of it been between them even on that first day Theodora had brought him home to El Atascadero?

As a small boy growing up in Mexico, Jack had dreamed of *el norte,* the United States.

But the reality hadn't been like his dream.

He had dreamed of a mother who could feed him. Of a world where children had homes and clothes. Of a father who'd claim him.

Instead Chantal had been swinging on the ranch gates, waiting with a seething heart for Theodora's limousine to rush up the palm-lined drive with the ten-year-old boy from Mexico.

Theodora had rolled down the car window and let in the blistering heat. Not that he'd felt it. He was used to heat. Besides, he'd been too pop-eyed from his first glimpse of the big house.

Then the girl had snickered, and he'd seen her. Oh, but she'd been a marvel to behold. She had charmed a whip snake. Dozing, its monstrous head dangling, its thick body had been coiled around her arm. The girl and the snake had been so still they'd seemed like enchanted creatures. Then he had looked into Chantal's eyes—strange green eyes that looked out at him but did not allow him to look inside her. Snake's eyes in the pale, unusually pretty face of a redheaded little girl.

Even then she had been blaming him for her problems and waiting there with that snake of hers to attack him.

She had known his mother had just died—his father, too. But she hadn't minced her words. "Go home, you son of a Mexican *puta.* If your father had wanted you here he would have come for you himself."

Chantal had smiled, and her white teeth had been pretty. But her icy eyes had despised him as if he were something less than human, less than nothing.

Still, his voice had been as tight and cold as hers. "You may be a *puta,* too, someday. You're meaner than one right now."

"You two are going to live like brother and sister," Theodora had said. "Say you're sorry and be polite." When he'd only stared sullenly at the girl, Theodora had scolded him.

Chantal had been a skinny thing then in her jeans and cowboy hat. She'd jumped off the gate with her dangling snake and spat at the ground in front of his feet. "I'm not sorry! Catch this, *basura.*" Before Theodora could stop her, Chantal had uncoiled the snake, shaken it and thrown it straight at his face. Trying to ward off fangs, flicking tongue and writhing coils, he'd lunged for Chantal, who had leaped on her pony. Flying hooves spewed dirt and rocks into his face as she raced away.

The snake had wrapped around his shoulders, and as he'd screamed, it had coiled tighter.

"Shut up, boy. It's just a whip snake."

Finally, Theodora had untangled the snake and tossed it gently into the high brown grasses, where it slithered away.

"It's not poisonous. It can't hurt you."

Maybe the snake was harmless. But the girl wasn't.

Chantal had made him feel dirty and low and cowardly, too, but he'd been right about her. When she'd grown up, she'd been the sexiest, hottest girl anybody in three counties had ever seen.

Everybody had had her. Lots of times. Including him.

But he'd been the only one fool enough to marry her.

He hadn't wanted to marry anybody so young.

But she'd tricked him. And he'd felt sorry for her. Sorry for the kid, too.

He still wasn't sure the fair-skinned, delicate-looking Carla was his.

Jack's jaw clenched.

Chantal was dead.

He'd best forget her.

There was no way now ever to even that score.

He wanted to lock his memories of her deep inside him and throw away the key.

But memories like he had weren't so easily bottled.

Not till he knew she was dead for sure.

Her body had never been found.

Her lover's killer, Nick Busby, the gas-station attendant with the thin face and the scrawny goatee, had become an instant celebrity that night two weeks ago when he'd confessed to a dozen murders all over Texas, that night when he'd told a bunch of Houston cops that he'd met Chantal and her young lover in a bar and followed the two of them back to El Atascadero. Busby had bragged that he'd watched them have sex and had then shot the boy for kicks.

But he hadn't confessed to killing *her*.

What Jack wanted to know was where the hell she had gone that night.

How could a woman just vanish without a trace? If she were alive, why would she have stayed away?

For five damn years? Without a thought that her husband was rotting in prison for her murder? Without a thought for her daughter, whom she loved, even in her own bizarre and highly destructive way? Without a thought to the immense inheritance that was her birthright?

Not that Chantal, who wasn't normal, had ever given a damn about him once she'd tricked him to the altar and given birth to Carla seven months later. With lightning speed, she'd moved to Houston and into the bed of her less-than-discriminating brother-in-law, Martin Lord.

Jack's lawyer, Bobby Doyle, kept telling him to forget about her, that she had to be dead. To make a fresh start of it.

But it wasn't that easy.

Jack lay in the dark awhile longer, wishing he could turn off his mind and go back to sleep.

Half an hour later his mind was still festering with uneasy memories about Chantal when the phone rang.

He let it ring.

Six. Eight times.

Persistent devil.

Who the hell could be calling that he'd want to talk to?

Nobody. Curiosity would be the sinking of him yet, he decided as he grabbed the phone, expecting a stranger.

A familiar, raspy, bourbon-slurred tone made his chest knot with a poignant rush of rage, regret and bitter anguish.

Theodora.

When his eyes filled with quick, hot tears, he savagely brushed his fingers across his lashes. He was so upset, he almost slammed the phone down.

"I've been trying and trying to call you, boy," she snapped, as full of venom and vigor as always, never for a second thinking he might not know her, nor caring that he might not want to hear from her. "I've been up half the night dialing this damned phone, trying to get you. As if I don't have a ranch to run come dawn. Like always, you don't mind a bit putting me to trouble."

"You've been drinking while you dialed, I reckon." His voice was deceptively soft and very cold.

"Maybe. A little."

"More than a little. I'd say half a bottle."

"Maybe so. You'd know. Well, it's been a long night, Jack."

"A long five years," he muttered.

She laughed huskily. "You haven't changed."

"I have. You haven't." It cost him to make his tone so low and hard.

"I've been watching your half brother's old movies tonight. Got me thinking...about you."

People said Jack could double for his world-famous half brother, who'd made it big in Hollywood playing cowboys and tough guys. Raised by different mothers, the siblings had never even met. Some cowboy. But Jack had damn sure had Garth thrown up to him all his life. The actor had never set foot on the ranch. Jack didn't think much of his brother's shallow movies. He didn't much like the attention he'd received because of their resemblance, either. Guys in prison had gotten ticked off about his pretty face. They'd called him Hollywood and had wanted to beat him up because of it. Still, he'd always envied his brother because everybody loved him.

"What the hell do you want, Theodora?"

"I've been thinking about things. About what you've been through. About the ranch. I want you to come home, boy."

"Home?" He hated how the word made his voice shake. "You never once wrote me or came to visit. Only Mario and Caroline did."

And Cheyenne. At least she'd written.

Every time Mario had come, he'd glanced around the prison mournfully and complained that Caesar, his oldest son, had fallen in with a wild crowd and was going bad.

Caroline, Theodora's beautiful, classy sister-in-law from the East Coast, had visited him once. She'd sat across from him as cool and pale as ivory. Always a perfectionist in dress and decorum, she'd sat straight backed and frozen in a beige silk, designer suit, too upset by the violent prison setting to ask more than if he was getting enough to eat. He had been too ashamed to tell her starvation was the least of his worries. Still, he'd been touched that she'd come. He'd always envied Maverick having such a sweet, pure woman as a mother. Caroline had been good to Jack, too. If it hadn't been for Caroline Jack might not have known that such a woman could exist.

Why the hell had he brought up Theodora's not coming? He didn't give a damn about her or anybody now.

"I expect I had my reasons for not visiting you."

"I didn't kill her."

"I wasn't the only one to think you did. A jury convicted you."

"I didn't kill anybody. I couldn't—not ever, no matter how much—" Damn. How could he care what she thought.

"I believe you—now."

"No. You believe some lying, psychopathic, serial killer! You believe that damn perverted stranger bragging to a bunch of federal marshals up in Houston so he could show them how stupid they all were for not catching him sooner."

"No. I believe what he showed me. They brought the skinny bastard down here, you know. He killed somebody down in Val Verde. They were taking him there for questioning, you see. The ranch was on their way, so they stopped off here, marched him all around the place. In jangling leg shackles that made him trip over every cactus. But he knew stuff he couldn't have known if he hadn't been here that night. They let me talk to him private like. He told me he heard all those things you accused Chantal of doing. The same things I heard. He quoted you word for word. He's got a scar from a bullet in his shoulder. He says Chantal shot him."

"I told you five years ago—I'm innocent." Jack had been drunk that night. Too drunk to remember much or know for sure what he'd done or hadn't done. Without an alibi, without even his own memory, he'd found nobody had believed him.

Theodora made no apology. As far as Jack knew, she had never said she was sorry to a single soul in her whole damned life. She was into controlling people and land; she was like a steamroller. Heaven help you if you got in her way. So he wasn't surprised when nothing more came from her but a deep and brooding silence.

Her silence wrapped around Jack.

He lay in the dark, his heavy, unwanted emotions suffocating him.

He wanted to feel nothing.

He should hang up.

"You think you can just dial me up, and I'll come running back to you like I did when I was a half-starved kid and you were the grand queen of El Atascadero? Maybe I was once your number-one charity case," he muttered bitterly, "but not anymore, old woman. You don't have anything I want."

"So, what will you do? El Atascadero is the only home you've ever known. You spent every dime you had on lawyers. I'm the closest thing you've got to family."

"I used to think so. I took a lot from Chantal—because of you. But you turned on me." That had hurt way more than anything Chantal had ever done.

Silence.

"As if you have so many better offers," she said at last. "At minimum wage, you won't be much better off than you were in Mexico."

"I guess I can survive on the bottom. What the hell do you want, anyway?"

"I want you to find my daughter and bring her home."

Jack's heart sank.

So—Theodora wanted Chantal.

Not him.

Like always.

Not that he gave a damn. Not that he gave a damn about a living soul now.

"Hasn't she caused you enough grief, old woman?"

"She's my daughter. Then there's...Carla."

"I don't want to hear about Carla!"

Again there was silence.

"You called the wrong man, Theodora. I don't want to find Chantal. I want to forget her. To be free of her. I lost five years and everything I ever cared about. Hell, six guys beat me so bad one night, I damn near died because of her. As for Carla, my daughter's better off without an ex-con for a father."

He lowered the phone, intending to hang up.

But Theodora wasn't about to let him off that easy.

She knew all of his buttons.

Which ones to punch. Which ones not to.

She zeroed in on the right ones and rammed her gnarled and blue-veined fist on them fast and hard.

"Oh, you're a fine one to say Carla's better off with no daddy. A fine one. You with that boulder-size chip on your shoulder ever since you were a boy because your daddy never claimed you, and I did. You were always wishing I'd go easier on you and treat you with kid gloves like Caroline treated Maverick. You never have forgiven me for taking you in, and you can't forgive the world. Poor Jack. Or do you want to be Mocho now? You gonna feel sorry for yourself the rest of your life—Mocho?"

He was surprised that she brought up his birth name. Mocho.

"No. I'm not going to feel a damn thing. I'm going to hang up on you and get as roaring drunk as you. And I'm going to stay that way—till I die."

Chapter 2

"Go ahead. Drink yourself to an early grave. Nobody cares about you. Nobody ever tried to give you a chance. Who's going to care if your little girl needs her daddy when her own daddy doesn't care?" Theodora persisted in a soft slur.

"I don't want to hear about her." His voice sounded oddly choked.

"Damn right, you don't. What father in his right mind would want a kid that won't go to school half the time? She runs away, too. Her friends ain't much to write home about, either. Sometimes she retreats into deep, scary silences—just like Chantal did. She draws terrible pictures. She's so lonely, Jack. The kids at school...she has the same kinds of problems there you used to. When the other kids won't play with her she acts so proud, closes herself off...."

"Aren't you done yet, old woman?"

"Hell no...!" she drawled, Texas-style. "I'm just

getting started. Next there's Maverick's running the ranch into the ground the same way he's done Caroline's. I think maybe...maybe I was wrong to set my hopes on him. Caroline and he like to live too high. And that takes money. Plenty of it." She paused. "Oh, well, I was damn sure wrong to set any hopes on you. If you came back, you'd just hit the booze. There's a better chance of seeing an ice storm in hell than for you to straighten yourself out and me to ever change my mind and let you run this place."

Damn, she knew how to get under a man's hide. First his kid. Now she was throwing Maverick in his face.

Maverick was Chantal's first cousin, a favorite lover, too. He had been raised by his mother, the elegant Caroline Henley, Theodora's sister-in-law from the next ranch. Maverick had been sent East to prep school and college. He'd always looked down his snoot at Jack. Once he'd even called him border trash.

"Maverick's no rancher," Jack said, riled about being drawn in despite his best intentions.

"Well, he's blood kin. You're a con. Not that some cons can't change. I'll bet there's some that don't wallow in the gutter feeling sorry for themselves. Some men might say, 'I'm free now. I know the people and the land. I understand cattle and horses. I could help that old woman...that raised me, that set her hopes on me, that shared her dreams with me...if I took a mind to. She's too old to be facing all that she's facing.'"

Damn her. He didn't want to feel anything. She'd always been a controlling witch. What he needed was a drink. He didn't want to feel anything.

With cynical, self-deprecating humor he laughed.

She was easy to figure out. But then, so was he.

He was glad she couldn't see the neon-orange carrot flashing in his mind's eye. Glad she couldn't know he felt as hungry for a nibble of that carrot as any half-starved jackrabbit in a drought-stricken pasture.

"Yeah. Sure you'll let me run the ranch. You've used that line before, old woman, when you talked me into marrying Chantal and claiming Carla."

"I talked you into doing what was right. I'm trying to talk you into doing what's right now."

"Right for you, you mean."

"Right for the ranch."

They say that childhood forms us, that we are never free of it or of our boyhood dreams.

Maybe because his dark memories of going hungry in Mexico had haunted him, Jack had loved being a boy and growing into manhood on the ranch. Had loved the wide-open spaces and freedom he'd found in those endless pastures with their waving grasses so tall he could polish his boots by riding through them. Grass meant cows. Cows meant food.

Jack had loved the pastures even with their thistles and thorns, salt cedar and mesquite trees. He'd loved climbing windmills and staring out at the vast kingdom of prairie that seemed to stretch forever, loved imagining that he was king of it. Huge dreams for a poor Mexican boy who'd once starved and fought street gangs. Huge dreams for a bastard with no right to the land. Later he'd developed the same keen eye for cattle and horses his father had had, as well as a talent and dedication for land and livestock management.

Ranching was in his blood. Ranchers turned grass into meat. With the world's population exploding, meat was vital. The dream of being king had taken hold of Jack in his teens. And Theodora had always known it. Dreams of the ranch had kept him sane these past five years.

His memories of the endless range made the four walls of the motel room feel like a prison cell. Did Carla really need him?

He couldn't bear to think about the child he hadn't seen for five years. Then Jack's future loomed before him, meaningless and empty without the little girl. If he didn't go back to the ranch, would he ever feel whole again?

He thought of Mexico and other countries like it that were full of starving kids.

A good rancher helped feed starving kids.

Feelings. He didn't want them.

But he couldn't stop them.

As he lifted the receiver back to his ear, his fingers were clenched.

Theodora had raised him up from nothing. She'd taught him to dream her dreams. He would have been dead long ago but for her. Maybe he did owe her.

He hated owing anybody. Just as he hated looking back.

But he couldn't stop himself.

Good memories flooded his mind right along with bad ones. If he'd dreamed of being king, Theodora West had been born queen in her little corner of the world. When she'd gone down to Mexico and brought back a poor Mexican boy to raise, she had gone against the normal prejudices of her race and class, as well as against the desires of her husband and daughter. After Shanghai Dawes's death she'd found a letter from Jack's mother in Shanghai's cabin. Imelda had written pleadingly that she was bad sick and would die soon and that their boy would desperately need a home.

Theodora couldn't have known what Shanghai would have done if he'd lived. But she'd gone down to Mexico, snooped around in the barrio asking prying questions till she found the boy. His mother had just died. Even after Theodora had been told Jack was a very bad boy who stole liquor and food, she had arranged his mother's funeral mass and burial.

Jack's fingers tightened on the phone. He didn't believe in giving anybody a second chance, but he owed Theodora more than he owed anyone.

She had been a big-time rancher of the Old West. He had been the bastard son of the foreman who had gotten himself trampled during July roundup after a rattler had spooked Theodora's horse. She'd been thrown, her leg crushed, helpless when a bull had charged her. Shanghai had jumped under the bull.

Maybe she'd figured she owed Shanghai.

Plucking his bastard son out of that barrio had been her way of repaying him. Not that Jack believed Shanghai had ever given a damn one way or the other about him.

Jack remembered the first time he'd seen Theodora. Only his name hadn't been Jack West then. It had been Mocho Salinas.

His mother had lain in a cheap pine coffin in an impoverished Mexican church. The hot, Matamoros sun had streamed through the broken, stained-glass window in that tiny, airless chapel with its dirty, stucco walls, causing dust motes to sparkle as they sifted and came to rest on top the coffin.

There had been only two mourners at Imelda Salinas's funeral mass—the Mexican boy and the older, Anglo woman who'd been asking everybody about him. They'd sat as far from one another as possible, each nursing a festering terror and a resentment for the other.

Jack's thin, dark body had been as tight as a clenched fist in his ill-fitting, threadbare suit, a garment he'd stolen off a clothesline. He had never been inside a chapel before and wasn't sure how to act, so he sat glued to the front bench, too scared to fidget, sweating profusely and yet oblivious to the heavy, stifling heat.

But not oblivious to the woman behind him, the woman who was paying to bury his mother, even though he stubbornly refused to acknowledge her presence.

Instead of staring back at her through grief-ravaged eyes, he'd concentrated on his mother's coffin, as if by sheer force of will he could drag her back to life.

Even though he'd found no comfort from the crosses, the frosted chromolithographs, the flickering candles, the priest or from all the other religious images, he'd bowed his head and fervently whispered a solemn prayer. "*Por favor, Dios.* Please, God, I'll do anything. Just make her wake up so I can tell her I'm sorry."

He'd remembered his mother laughing, his mother whoring. He'd stared expectantly at her worn, young face, which had remained gray and frozen, her lifeless eyes closed.

Never had he felt so utterly alone and guilt stricken. Despair had opened inside him like a chasm. How many times had he prayed to the angels for some escape from his hateful childhood.

But he had not meant for his mother to die, to change into this pale, waxen creature.

If she couldn't live, maybe he could die, too, he'd thought.

He'd drawn a deep breath and clamped his lips shut, holding the air in his lungs till his cheeks and neck ached and his chest felt about to explode.

He had tried to imagine what it would be like to be dead. For his heart to stop and his blood to congeal. For his eyes to pop open and not be able to see.

When he conjured an image of a bloated dog he'd seen in the barrio, Mocho had exhaled in terror. It was no use. He'd gulped in a mouthful of air. Dying was too hard. Besides that...he'd stared down at his hand and imagined his own flesh rotting away like the dog's had. And death had seemed a mighty fearsome prospect.

Finally, he'd turned and dared a look at the other mourner.

On the last bench, her beak of a nose perched loftily, her thin lips pursed as if in distaste, Theodora West—not that Mocho had known her name then—had sat with the unhappy resignation of one forced to perform an unpleasant charitable duty.

He resented her for being the only one to come and for having the money to bury his mother. Who did she think she was, this woman with her nose in the air whose hair was steel gray, whose tanned face was lined from the sun? He hadn't noticed how small she was, for he'd been too awed by the terrifying power that had radiated from her like that of a fierce bull in a ring. He hadn't known then that she was still badly injured and in pain from the fall that had cost Shanghai his life, that she hated churches, that she longed for a drink from the flask she always carried but had left in her limousine.

If he wanted her gone, he wanted it no more than she.

But when he stared at her with cold dislike, she stared back at him unblinkingly. Then her bench creaked, her ivory cane tapping ominously as she rose.

Terrified, Mocho ducked. His muscles tightened when he heard the brisk clicks of her cane and the stiff rustling of her dress. With all his heart he wished he could turn himself into a wild creature, a wolf or an ocelot maybe. Then he would run away from this woman who dragged a leg, and would howl all night in the woods.

Abruptly the tapping stopped, too near him.

In the awful silence, Mocho's heart gave a leap of pure terror. Then he hunkered so low his unruly black mop shrank entirely from view.

Theodora stiffened. In cold flawless Spanish, without a trace of enthusiasm, she said, "Come, boy. Don't be afraid. I promised your father I would take care of you."

She had done no such thing. But he hadn't known that then. He'd learned it later. All he knew was that he couldn't allow himself to believe she could possibly want him. He was dirt. A whore's son. Nobody had ever wanted him.

"I don't have a father."

She didn't smile. He didn't know that she was touched by his proud grief. "Yes, you do."

Mocho's lips curled into an insolent sneer. "I don't like you. Go away and leave me alone."

"Nobody but me wants you, boy."

The coldness inside him expanded when her cane tapped his bench sharply, and she took another dragging step toward him. He shook his head and dived under the bench and then crawled up to his mother's coffin.

Theodora rapped her cane sharply on the coffin.

When he didn't come out, Theodora turned. As if on command, the doors at the back of the chapel swung open and a monstrous giant filled the narrow doorway.

"Boy, this is Ramón. If you don't come willingly, he'll carry you to my car."

When the tall, dark man lumbered up the aisle, Mocho bolted out from under the coffin, straight into the man's big belly. Mocho began biting and clawing and kicking, and the chauffeur bellowed. Maddened, he grabbed Mocho by the ear and cuffed him. Wrapping Mocho's wrists and crushing bone and flesh in his big fist, Ramón shoved Mocho to the wall and whispered in a voice too low for Theodora to hear, "Maybe you're Shanghai Dawes's son. Maybe you ain't. I liked Shanghai, though, same as *la Señora* liked him, so I'll give you the benefit of the doubt. If you're Shanghai's brat, I figure to like you, too. Stop kicking me, damn it, or I'll bite your ear off and break both your arms."

Immediately Mocho stopped fighting.

"Boy, Theodora don't mean you no harm—you do what she says."

Mocho, who by then had been beaten, shrank lower when Theodora frowned and began limping toward him. With great difficulty she knelt, so that she was on eye level with him.

Mocho stared at her sullenly. Then he saw his reflection in a windowpane.

His lip was cut and bleeding. The right side of his face was growing purple, the eye swelling shut.

He looked like a wild boy. But again Theodora seemed more impressed with his spirit and fierce determination than depressed by his appearance.

"For a small boy who has lost his mother, you have much courage," she said, pulling out a handkerchief and wiping the blood from his mouth. "They told me in the barrio that you are very bad, that you steal. But they told me, too, that you give the smaller children the food. A boy who thinks of others can't be all bad. Your father was like that. You've learned bad habits, boy, but you've got good blood in you. If you're half the man your father was, the ranch needs you."

Mocho drew back, startled by her kind touch and words. Startled to think of himself as having good blood, as being of value...to anyone. Before she'd said that, he'd seen himself only as an unwanted bastard and a thief. As nothing.

"If you obey me, I won't ever let anybody hurt you again," she said.

He didn't believe her because it was too scary somehow.

"If I go away, you'll just be another beggar. And Mexico has enough beggars."

Mocho glowered at the floor, not wanting to want what she offered.

"If Ramón lets your arms go, will you promise not to run?"

When Mocho fixed his bruised, coal black eye on her, she paled. Fearlessly, she persisted. "If you don't promise, Ramón will keep holding you. If you come with me, I'll send you to school."

Her Spanish was that of an educated woman.

She spoke his own language better than he.

He had never been to school.

He couldn't read or write. Once he had found a broken pencil in the dirt, and he had tried to draw the letters he'd seen on a license plate. But his efforts had been clumsy, and the bullies who'd gone to school had laughed at him. He'd felt stupid. The world belonged to those with knowledge.

Bitterness flashed in his heart at the unfairness of life—that some are born with so much and most with so little—but he was too tired to fight her.

The instant his forceful energy had abated, hers did, too. For a moment she looked so exhausted he almost pitied her.

She had known his father. He felt a dim glimmer of curiosity about the man he had never known.

"Why didn't my father come?"

"He died saving my life. I owe him. Maybe you do, too, a little." When an entire minute had gone by, she said, "It's a long drive to El Atascadero. We need to leave."

"I won't go till my mother's buried," Mocho said defiantly.

Her gaze ran over his high cheekbones, his aquiline nose, and lingered on the stubborn set of his strong jaw. Later he would watch her cull cattle with that same sure eye for bone-deep quality.

Maybe she sensed how desperate he felt to show her he was somebody, too. "I see more of Shanghai in you than your mother," she said at last. "If you didn't glower so, in the right clothes, with your hair cut, you know...you just might be an appealing boy."

"I won't go unless I see her—"

To his surprise Theodora suddenly relented. "All right." When he stared at her uncomprehendingly, she snapped, "Well, don't just stand there. Let's see her in the ground."

Stunned, he stared at her despite his swollen, black eye. He wasn't used to anybody ever considering his feelings.

This time when she looked down at him, she caught her breath at his smile. The sudden warmth in her gaze caused him to have a peculiar urge to touch her.

He forgot their racial differences, her wealth and his poverty. Even for a second, he forgot his pride. Briefly, he let his rough knuckles brush her wrist, but then, like a shy puppy making a new acquaintance, he pulled his hand away quickly.

Still, his simple gesture seemed to affect her. Just for a moment or two, her strong, sun-tanned fingers settled on top of his impossible hair.

They stared at each other in surprise, each wondering if somehow they had reached an uneasy truce. If so, it would be the first of many in what was to be for both of them a difficult relationship. For always, always she strove to control him and everybody and everything.

He hadn't known then how lonely she was. That with her plain face and bossy personality she had troubles with relationships; that she needed him as much as he needed her.

When Mocho had placed the last of his wilted wildflowers on top of the fresh dirt clods in the graveyard and Ramón had started the limousine, Theodora took the boy's hand and told him it was time to go.

He yanked free of her and flung himself across the withering flowers and howled like a trapped animal, his fingers digging into the dry earth. Finally, he stood up and walked to the car. When he got in, he pressed his thin face against the rear window glass and howled again. Even when she told him she had packed a picnic basket full of food, he kept his nose glued to the glass. Only when they'd driven out of the cemetery did his hoarse cries decrease.

He smelled meat, and his empty stomach grumbled, but when he opened the basket and unwrapped a sandwich, beggars raced up to the car. He shut his eyes, sinking his teeth into soft white bread and delicious ham. But he couldn't forget their desperate, dirty faces and the rancid garbage that would be their meal that day. He choked on the soft, sweet meat when he tried to swallow.

Through sobs, he said, "Stop the car...."

After he'd set the basket out, he began weeping again—this time over the loss of the ham.

"Tears don't ever change anything, boy. I wanted to be pretty when I was a girl...." Theodora stopped. It was not her manner to reveal herself.

Mocho squeezed his eyes shut.

"I lost my mother younger than you. I've hated funerals ever since," Theodora said, unscrewing the cap of a silver flask. "I don't like the sight of hungry children much, either. Life's hard—even for rich, old women."

He doubted that this willful woman who had a bully for a chauffeur and a big car and a full belly had a hard life.

"I keep this for just such depressing emergencies." When she thought he wasn't watching, she hastily sneaked three long swigs.

He watched her reflection in the window as she belted her liquor like a man, and wondered if she would get drunk and beat him.

After a while she said, "I have a daughter. Not an easy daughter, either. Chantal doesn't care about the ranch the way a boy would." Theodora drew a deep breath. "Maybe you and I will surprise ourselves. Shanghai and I saw eye to eye about most things."

She didn't tell him then of her loveless marriage to Ben West. Nor of Ben's long-term affair with a younger, fascinating beauty, Ivory Rose, who some said had bewitched him. Nor of Ben's other daughter, Cheyenne, who of late was so much sweeter and more appealing than Theodora's own daughter. Nor of Theodora's heavy ranching responsibilities.

Mocho's sobs died by fits and starts.

"Boy..." In sudden inspiration she offered him her flask. "Normally I wouldn't suggest this, but you're no ordinary child. Take a sip!" she ordered. "You'll feel better. All cowboys drink. Your father did."

She smiled. Mocho didn't know she was remembering the long nights she'd spent drinking with Shanghai while Ben stayed with his other woman.

Mocho wrinkled his nose. Just the smell of the liquor brought back the beatings he had endured in the barrio from his mother's drunken boyfriends. He had stolen liquor to sell it. "I'm no cowboy."

"Your father was the best that ever lived."

Mocho grew sullen as he thought of his father, who had never come for him.

Theodora pressed the flask to his lips, and Mocho

tipped his head back. She hadn't left much for him, but he swallowed, choking on what there was.

She patted his back, while he sputtered and smeared the back of his suit sleeve across his mouth. The stuff quit burning his throat after a minute or two. Then he found that she was right about it making him feel better.

A strange, relaxing warmth was soon spreading through him. His hunger lessened. Her brown face looked softer, blurrier—almost friendly now.

He began to feel very sleepy, so sleepy that the scary images of his mother's coffin and the bloated dog began to recede. When he rubbed his eyes and yawned, Theodora drew his black head down onto her lap as if he were her boy. As if it didn't matter that she was a rich Anglo and he a poor barrio brat.

"It was my fault that Mama died," he confessed guiltily, fixing her with his one good eye again. "I prayed that I wouldn't have to live in the barrio anymore. I wanted to go to *el norte.* I wanted to live like an Anglo. Now she is dead, and I'm with you."

"That's not your fault," Theodora stated in a tone that brooked no nonsense. "You know, since you're going to live in Texas, we're going to have to think up an English name for you."

He flinched, feeling sullen again.

"You must have a name that goes better with—"

"I won't take my father's name!"

"Then you can take mine." Her voice rang with even more authority. "West."

"Jack," he muttered swiftly, feeling defeated at the thought of giving up his own name even if she was willing to share hers. Jack was the name of an older kid he'd met at the river who'd once helped him fight a bully.

"Jack," she repeated, regarding him as she tested the name.

Jack. The name echoed inside his brain, an alien, hollow sound. It wasn't him. It never would be.

But he was too tired to worry about it.

Mocho wearily gulped in two ragged breaths and fell asleep.

He didn't wake up till Theodora ruffled his springy hair and said they were home.

"Here we are, Jack."

Jack? Who was she talking to? But he got up on wobbly legs and peered out the window.

Palm fronds that lined the drive roared in the Gulf breeze. The driveway made a graceful loop in front of a majestic main entrance, where the tall white walls of a red-roofed mansion loomed above gnarled mesquite and oak.

He muttered a Spanish curse word and shrank violently against Theodora. His new home felt even stranger and more alien than his new name.

Fresh panic surged through him as she opened the window and he saw the skinny little redheaded girl holding a fat, dozing snake. The girl's cold green eyes fastened on his face with fierce dislike. Then she smiled and hissed bad things about his mother and father.

Jack regarded the girl narrowly, knowing she'd probably always think she was better than he was. When he muttered the worst insult that he could think of, the girl laughed.

Theodora told them to stop fighting. "Get out of the car, boy. You behave, too, Chantal."

The second he jumped out, Chantal spat at him and then uncoiled the snake from her arm and threw it. When the thing had wrapped itself around his neck, he screamed like a girl.

Disgusted, Theodora pulled the snake off him. Later she'd said, "Don't worry about Chantal. She's been the ranch princess—till you came. Just give her time." But there was a strange hardness in her voice every time she spoke of her daughter.

Chantal was just a girl, he'd told himself. One stuck-up white girl who knew how to make snakes go to sleep. In the barrio he'd been outnumbered by dozens of thugs.

But this girl was rich and mean. So mean even her mother was uneasy around her.

He knew the girl would get meaner when she caught him alone.

Maybe his new house was a mansion.

Maybe he had a new Anglo name. Maybe he wouldn't have to beg or steal.

But nothing had changed. He was still dirt. He was still alone—with no friends. He was going to have to fight very hard for his place here. If Chantal made her mother hate him, Theodora would throw him out, and he'd be poor and alone in some garbage-strewn alley again.

Funny how he almost felt poorer and lonelier in this rich, Anglo world. At least in the barrio he had known the rules.

Later he found out that there were plenty of people besides Chantal on El Atascadero. Many despised him for his birth, but a few accepted him because he was Shanghai's son. Mario, the *caporal* of cow camp one, took him under his wing right along with his own son, Caesar, and taught him everything he knew, which made Caesar jealous.

Jack had had to work very hard to prove himself, and nobody had been more amazed than he at how fast he caught on to everything—school as well as cowboying. Theodora told him that he could be whatever he wanted. Not that he believed her. Not that he ever relaxed or stopped trying to better himself. But the higher he'd climbed, Chantal had always been there to bring him down and to tempt the dark side of him to wildness. And no matter how high he'd risen, he'd never felt sure. One false move and he'd be at the bottom again.

He'd been right, too.

Because of Chantal, a man had died in their barn, and Jack had served time for two murders.

Another ambulance rushed past Jack's motel on the San Antonio freeway. But Theodora's voice cut his bitter thoughts short.

"Come home, Jack. Maverick needs a wake-up call. We're in the middle of the worst drought of this century. We're burning the needles off prickly pears to feed our cattle. I've sold half the herd and leased land in east Texas to feed the rest."

"You threw me out. Why should I give a damn about your problems?"

"In four months, if she's still alive, Chantal will be thirty-five. I have been holding her shares of El Atascadero in trust while you were gone. On her birthday her shares revert to me if she's dead or if she doesn't claim them. I can give them to anybody. If you stay sober and prove you're better at running things than Maverick, I could will them to Carla and give you control till she comes of age. It'd look better if Chantal's alive, by your side. She's your wife. The shares would then legally belong to the two of you." Theodora paused. "I need you. The ranch needs you. Carla needs—"

"Leave Carla out of this!"

Carla. He remembered the last time he'd seen her, the afternoon he'd tried to tell her goodbye.

He'd been drunk, not so it showed, but she'd run away from him and climbed *her* tree. He had watched the branches bend with her weight as she'd scampered to the top. Then she'd sat on a skinny branch high above him and rocked back and forth, staring down at him as white-faced as she'd been that night in the barn. He'd stood there, under her, scared out of his wits she'd fall. But he'd just stayed where he was, watching that limb rock, thinking about how he'd once climbed windmills, thinking about how he might never see her again. The very next day they'd found him guilty and sentenced him to life.

Carla.

Little girls change a lot in five years.

Jack felt as if all the air in the room had been sucked out. "You're not promising me anything really—"

"Life's always a gamble."

Pain tightened his lungs.

He wasn't used to choices. He didn't want them.

"This is as close as you'll get, Jack, to having a chance to get back everything you lost—your daughter, the ranch, your good name."

"My good name? That's a laugh if ever there was one. You don't care about me. All you care about is controlling your ranch."

"I need you...for that. Mario and the others—they want you back, too."

Mario. Jack had too many tender memories of the tough old man who had been so kind to him, who was disappointed in his own son.

Carla, the ranch...

Jack wanted to yell, to bang his head against the wall.

He didn't want feelings. He didn't want this hollowness in the pit of his stomach, either.

"What about Chantal? What if she's alive and I find her? What makes you think she's changed? What if she starts lavishing Carla with expensive gifts instead of her attention again? Aren't you scared of what the two of us might do to each other the next time?"

"Hell, yes. But not nearly as scared as you are."

The hollow feeling was expanding inside him. "I'm not scared."

"Jack, maybe it's January, but, hell, you know how the weather is down here. Most days it's as warm as May. A few wildflowers are already in bloom—bluebonnets, pink primroses. A few hummers stayed instead of migrating south. They feed outside my window. You know how pretty it can be here when it's warm, and all the scissortails and Mexican eagles are flying about. I expect you'd feel mighty free if you got back in the saddle and just rode off as far as you pleased toward the horizon. You could take your guitar, and sometime, maybe... I got a mighty big hankering to hear you sing again, Jack. Remember how we used to sit out on the verandah and you'd strum your guitar? All you ever wanted to do was grow grass and cows and help feed the poor. Remember how it was to go hungry...?"

Damn.

Her voice died away. It was a habit of hers, letting her words trail into nothing like smoke in the wind.

His freedom hadn't meant much till she said all that. He could camp out. He could build a fire. He could watch the stars, roam the endless prairies. He hadn't sung in years. His life would have a purpose.

He was a rancher. That was all he knew. All he wanted to know. The work meant something to him. He had a daughter.

His throat constricted. When he couldn't speak, she didn't bother, either. He imagined her sitting back, taking a swig or two, giving her hooks time to settle deep inside his hide. She had him, and she knew it.

"Why don't you come home," she persisted. "Stay awhile. And then decide."

"Okay," he rasped. "You win." His voice grew more hoarse and shaky. "I lose. Like always."

When she broke the connection without saying goodbye, unwanted pain flashed through him.

Why the hell was he opening himself up to her again? He'd sworn he'd never...

He squeezed his eyes shut and opened them. Then he threw back the covers. His bare feet made contact with the threadbare carpet.

Slowly, step by step, he padded to the window. Pulling the curtain to one side, he looked out, his eyes straining, his dark face hard as he studied the freeway.

Chantal could be anywhere.

Whether she was dead or alive, he'd find her.

But if he brought her back to the ranch, it would be on his terms.

Not Chantal's.
Not Theodora's, either.
He had a score to settle.

Chapter 3

Jimmy was running down the driveway with his skateboard and shouting excitedly to his friend, Ronnie. The sun was shining through the trees, backlighting leaves and branches with shimmering golden light. Backlighting Jimmy's hair so that it looked like it was on fire.

Bronte called after him.

He never looked back.

Then it started raining, and he was lying there. And she was holding him and weeping, not knowing what to do.

Jimmy's bright head began to dissolve.

Tires whirred softly outside on the gravel drive of Webster's Connecticut farmhouse. The diesel engine of a big Mercedes pinged and went silent.

She called to Jimmy, but he vanished into a red, misty haze of raindrops and sunlight.

Bronte's new reality was the hollow feeling in her

soul and a charming bedroom with a slanting ceiling papered with tiny yellow flowers, and dormer windows that looked out onto rolling dark hills and shadowy trees.

The screen of her television set was flickering from across the room as she awakened slowly, feeling strange and lost. She had no idea that Webster's car had awakened her, but she guessed that she'd overslept by nearly an hour.

For one thing, the thick aroma of the chicken browning in thyme and sherry now filled Webster's farmhouse. Thank heavens the bird didn't smell like it was charred to a crisp this time. For another thing, moonlight and starlight were glimmering off the windows of the loft in the barn where Webster's mysterious study was.

As her gaze wandered to the distant trees, a bolt of lightning forked. Then thunder echoed, sounding faraway.

The front door beneath her bedroom was cautiously opened and shut.

Webster was late, much later than usual.

"A-a-a-choo! A-a-a-choo!" His hard, masculine sneezes erupted as soon as he stepped inside. Next came his curse. "Damn it!"

Bronte sprang up guiltily, knocking her gardening book and botanical catalogue from the bed. Two Garth Brown movie videos fell, too.

Oh, dear. Why had she brought the lilacs inside? And why did a man of such invincible ego and ferocious will have to be allergic to every flower in Connecticut? Why was she beginning to dread his dark moods the way she had once dreaded her mother's?

Not that he had discouraged her from her passion for planting, which had been her chief pastime during the spring while she had convalesced. No. Thank goodness. So long as she followed his medical advice, he was arrogantly indifferent about her other interests.

Webster sneezed and cursed again. He put on the highlights of *Madama Butterfly.* Then he yelled Bronte's name, and she raced out to the landing—only to linger there like a naughty child, reluctant to go down because he made her so nervous. Maybe it was the soaring opera lyrics, but Bronte felt like she was a little girl in her mother's house again. Webster had rules for everything just as her mother had had, and Bronte could never remember them all.

It was April. Which meant the pastures and the woods and the rolling hills and the stone cliffs and ledges were green and beautiful, especially with the lilacs in bloom.

It had been almost six months since Bronte's accident, and other than that one occasion after her second operation, when she'd looked at herself and then been terrified by how ugly she was with the swelling and bruises, she still had almost no idea what she looked like. She didn't care much, either. A lot of things had ceased to matter to her. A couple of times when she'd been mildly curious, Webster had intimidated her by hinting that any interference from her might jinx the outcome. She had decided maintaining his enthusiasm was more important than satisfying her curiosity.

Bronte had tried to tell herself that the main thing, after all, was that she was so much better. Maybe she was all alone in the world. Maybe she didn't understand Webster as well as she would have liked to.

Maybe Jimmy was dead, but her grief had abated when she'd felt his presence in the emergency room.

Perhaps he had really been there. Or perhaps coming so close to death had taught her that her life might be precious to her again. She still didn't feel much, but these months had been a time of healing and waiting. Gone were the hateful respirator, the casts, the crutches. Dental implants had replaced the three teeth that had been knocked out. He had cleaned out the dead tissue, put bones back together, and done trauma repair.

Still, Webster, ever the perfectionist, wasn't quite satisfied despite all he'd done.

Bronte felt guilty that she couldn't feel closer to Webster. He had saved her life and her face. In the beginning, he had even stayed at her bedside day and night.

Now Webster held himself aloof. He asked only one thing of her—that she live with him and not look at her face till he was through.

She had been told that Webster usually charged outrageous fees, money she didn't have. In her case, he had generously waived his fees and paid her other bills, too.

"Oh, I don't want your money," he had said, his eyes burning bluer than a laser, his voice scaring her a little. "Your case is unique."

She had given him pictures of herself. He had barely glanced at them.

"Oh, I won't need these."

"But I want to look like me..." Not that she had cared then all that much. She had been too ill.

He had turned away. "When you were a little girl, who did you want to look like?"

"My mother."

Webster had gone very still. "What was she like?"

"She sang. She was very beautiful. Everyone…loved her."

He had sighed a deep sigh. "Yes. There. You see?"

"No. You don't understand." She had stopped. She had never liked talking about her mother.

She hadn't told him about her early life, and he hadn't asked. She knew how she wanted to look, and it bothered her that Webster seemed so intent on his own agenda.

In the beginning Bronte had been too weak and too injured to tell Webster anything or to ask for anything. She had felt thankful that he seemed so directed and sure, that he saw her as a fascinating case. She had signed the informed consent without even reading it. She had been all too thankful that he let her retreat inside herself. Besides, she hadn't had anyone else she could turn to.

Slowly Webster had begun trying to perfect more than her face. He had given her a perfume that smelled of gardenias and insisted that she wear it. Like a robot with no will of her own, she had let him teach her to walk differently. What had anything mattered? He had changed her speech patterns. She was too skinny, but he had insisted she diet. He'd been bossy about her clothes also, as bossy as her long-dead mother, demanding that she wear clingy, silk dresses. The only colors he allowed her to wear were red and black. It seemed eerie that those had been her mother's favorites, too.

Bronte had begun to wonder a little about Webster's motives. She tried to reason with herself, knowing that surgeons were not wishy-washy people. Altering reality was Webster's job.

As it had been her mother's.

All of Bronte's doctors, even Webster's enemies, had been amazed by her quick recovery. Webster's nurse, Susan, the only member of his staff to ever see Bronte, was equally amazed.

Only Webster remained unsatisfied. "The nose isn't quite right. I think...just another session with the laser, my dear. We won't do much this time. Just shave the edge of a tiny scar. A little peel may work wonders."

"Webster, I'm tired—"

"Soon you can rest. I promise—just one more procedure."

He had refused to discuss the matter further.

Bronte was beginning to feel alive again, beginning to think that maybe she should have found the strength and the will to argue more. Now that she was no longer an injured caterpillar content to convalesce in her cocoon, she was weary of Webster's endless procedures, of the painful healing afterward.

She was growing tired of living with Webster. Sometimes she remembered old Dr. Montrose warning her not to go to Costa Rica.

"Miss Devlin—" dear old Dr. Montrose had hesitated "—do be careful. There are appropriate boundaries between a patient and a doctor—"

"Whatever do you mean, Doctor?"

He'd stared at her, groping for words. "What I'm trying to say...is that Dr. Quinn is not like other doctors. He seems so intense about you. I understand you're living with—"

"It's not like that."

"Forget it. I can see you're quite smitten."

"I am *not* smitten. It's quite the opposite. I don't care much about anything. And I have been told by so many that he has achieved miracles."

"Yes. *His* miracles. Not his patients' miracles."

Dr. Montrose's concern haunted her. Somewhere in the back of her mind, a vague foreboding had begun.

She was worrying more since their return from Costa Rica and their move to his charming house on his hundred-acre property in Connecticut. Except for those rare occasions when he took her to the opera, he had cut her off from everyone. Not that the physical isolation bothered Bronte. Bryan and she had lived on a small ranch several miles from Wimberley, a small town in the Texas hill country.

It was that Webster made her feel like a laboratory experiment. The snow had been deep in Connecticut, his house isolated on its hill. Even though she and Webster spent every night together and their bedrooms were side by side, he avoided her. It seemed strange that after every new procedure, when he studied her face and proclaimed his operation a success, he withdrew even more. And now that she was stronger and wanted to meet people, he didn't want anyone to see her.

Two days ago in his office, when he had once again insisted on shaving another scar, she had challenged him. "Susan says I'm pretty enough. I want a mirror. I want to decide. If I'm too pretty, I won't be me."

He had said nothing, but the fierce blue light that had burned in his eyes as he brushed the tip of her nose with a proprietary finger had silenced her.

Webster had removed all the mirrors at his farm.

Once Bronte had teased him that he was like a painter who wanted to realize his vision before he revealed his creation.

She was too upset to tease now. Last night at dinner she had asked him, "Has my face become your obsession?"

His blue eyes had stared straight into hers. "You flatter yourself."

"How come you scare me a little?"

"You are highly imaginative. You have suffered severe trauma. You are theatrical like..."

"Like...like what? Like who?"

He was silent. "Forget it." He stood up. Without another word, he strode out of the room.

She had watched his tall form move through the dark kitchen. Then the kitchen door had slammed, and he had disappeared.

Bronte knew Webster had gone to his study in the loft of his barn—a place that he always kept locked and had forbidden her to enter. It was this one mysterious place beyond that dark fringe of trees—like Pandora's locked box—that intrigued her more than anything on his farm.

Once or twice after dinner she had begged him to let her spend time with him in his study. Each time, he had refused, saying only that his experiments could mean a lot to other women, many of them more badly injured than she.

Once she had read him an unflattering article about his work from a newspaper. The writer had made the allegation that he had given several infamous criminals new faces.

"My jealous colleagues exaggerate my ability to

perform miracles,'' Webster had replied with uncharacteristic modesty.

But did they?

''A-a-a-choo!'' She heard him pacing downstairs in the living room. When he got close to the stairway, where she was hiding, he saw her. ''Bronte?'' He expelled a long, nervous breath. ''Bronte...''

''Yes?''

He relaxed visibly. Almost it seemed that, before he recognized *her* voice, he had thought she was somebody else.

Somebody whose existence electrified him.

She could not imagine Webster passionately involved with anyone.

''What on earth were you doing up there—hiding in the shadows?''

''I—I, er...just thinking.''

When Bronte dashed down from the landing and into the living room, Webster's blue gaze sharpened. ''Slowly!''

Instantly she obeyed, gliding toward him with long, graceful strides like a runway model.

''Better,'' he said. ''Now where are they?'' He forced a smile.

She arched her brows and innocently scanned the small tables and shelves.

He cupped his nose with his hands again to ward off a sneeze.

''I thought surely that just one small vase of lilacs could do no harm.''

He sneezed again—this time so deafeningly her ears rang.

''Would you please get those damn flowers out of here!''

"All right." She seized the offending vase and rushed back upstairs, spilling water everywhere. Her hands were still sopping when she returned a minute or two later.

He made no comment this time when she remembered to glide down the stairs. He sank into his leather chair and opened a thin black volume on plastic surgery. Bronte had scanned the book once and read of several cases where the doctor had made mothers look like their twenty-year-old daughters.

Flipping the illustrated pages, Webster pushed his glasses up his nose and bent his sculpted, silver head so low over the book she felt completely shut out.

He was so self-contained. So utterly controlled.

At fifty, despite the deep lines in his face, Webster had an ageless brand of masculine good looks that were bone deep. His athletic physique was that of a man of thirty. He hadn't the slightest interest in clothes, but his wardrobe was stunning. Even at home he always wore custom-made suits and silk ties. Yet nobody ever called him. He never dated; he never spoke of other women. He was so different from the hard-living, hard-drinking cowboys who had been Bryan's friends.

Bronte left him to check on the chicken she was preparing for dinner and found it so tantalizingly brown and tender, the meat was falling off the drumsticks. She took the clay pot out of the oven to cool. Then she walked outside to the swimming pool and the sculpture garden.

Lightning flared above a nearby stand of towering maples and changed the sculptures to frightening, spidery shapes. Webster's isolated house, even the beautiful woods, had never seemed a sanctuary. The peace and solitude that should have comforted her made her feel isolated and alone.

She turned and saw that Webster was watching her from a lighted window, as he often did when he didn't think she knew.

His moving away quickly when she saw him made her uneasy. It was strange how his farm and his house felt so much like a prison. Strange how he seemed like her jailer instead of her doctor.

When Webster stepped out onto the porch and called her, she ran away from him.

She was hungry, but she walked farther than she'd ever walked in the dark, even though the air now felt dense and heavy with the promise of rain. Past the pool and the bizarre modern sculptures. Through the mysterious, aromatic pine forest. Down to the stagnant marshes that reeked of dead, wet foliage. Across the lush fields of corn and alfalfa. Through a field of waist-high clover that smelled fresh and green and moist.

She didn't stop till she got to the lane. Her bad knee was throbbing by then, so she stood for a while and watched the bright headlights of the cars whizzing past. Dark clouds were massing to the north, and lightning blinked behind them. She longed for the day when she would leave Webster and this farm forever.

But she had promised him she would wait—till he was finished.

And he had promised, too—only one more procedure.

Soon. No more than a month or so. Then she would be free. Reluctantly she turned and walked back to the house.

When she passed the barn, she lingered in the long

shadow of a maple and looked up at the brightly lit rooms of the loft where Webster worked. She heard the faint strains of the opera *Carmen*. The soprano was some new star. When Webster's tall shadow loomed against a window, Bronte bit her lips and stifled the impulse to go up there and confront him.

Instead she returned to her attic room, which was cold in the winter and hot in the summer but pleasantly cool that April night.

There she undressed and went to bed.

But she couldn't sleep.

Not after it began to rain and the branches of the large oak tree by her window scratched the roof of the house.

Not when the sensitive skin on her face itched and her bad knee continued to throb. Not when the lights from the barn twinkled through the raindrops. Not even when the lights in the barn went out and she heard Webster climb the stairs and close his door.

She felt uneasy as she listened to him undress. He had never made a pass at her or expressed the slightest sexual interest in her. Still, she didn't like living alone with him now.

Something was wrong, really wrong between them. At first she had been too ill to understand that theirs had never been a normal doctor-patient relationship.

Webster wasn't telling her everything.

Why had he helped her?

Why was he so possessive?

He was a brilliant doctor, but he was a less-than-insightful human being.

Maybe she had made a mistake to put herself so completely in his hands.

But she was in too deep to simply cut and run.

Still, the sooner she got away from him, the better.

Chapter 4

Jack hadn't expected to like France.

He'd been told that the French were snooty and rude. Not so. Except for his Parisian taxicab driver, who'd tried to short-change him and had insulted his French.

The French sure knew how to dress. Americans all ran around in their kindergarten clothes. Jack, whose idea of dressing up was to wear a tie or a corduroy jacket with jeans, was pretty casual himself.

The French ate well, too, if you had time for two-hour meals. They had excellent wines, so he'd been told. It had been a struggle, but so far he'd stuck to lime water.

He'd figured he'd get homesick. But Provence, with its limestone cliffs and clear cool springs and green rivers and woodsy smells and golden light, was just like the Texas hill country.

Not that he felt easy here.

Not this close to such dangerous prey.

Suddenly the world-famous model who'd been strutting back and forth on top of the ancient aqueduct like an angry cat paled. Then she whirled and made wild gestures in Jack's direction. "Over there! Down there...!"

Damn! Damn!

Jack dove into brambles that scratched his face as the shoot's entire crew stared down into the trees.

Maybe she smelled him, Jack thought as he wiped blood off his cheek.

It wouldn't be the first time.

Chantal had strange powers, just like her sweeter half sister, Cheyenne, whose moods had made flowers bloom out of season. Cheyenne, whom he'd once loved...

Whatever. Quickly he hunkered lower in the dense foliage.

The air was cooler and smelled mustier under the trees. Contrasting shadows and light flickered over him.

A second or two later he aimed his binoculars back at the long-legged woman standing on the topmost limestone tier of the first-century Roman aqueduct. He had come all the way from south Texas to get a good look at her.

The woman atop the Pont du Gard calmed down. She wasn't quite as white underneath all those layers of professionally applied makeup. She wasn't pointing his way anymore, either. Still, the husky Italian photographer everybody called Edmondo had stopped the shoot and was demanding the rouge pot. The makeup artist was brushing the woman's high cheekbones frantically as Edmondo yelled that the light was fading.

Was she? Or wasn't she?

Jack squinted, focusing on the triangular face.

Damn. He needed to get closer, but the shoot was under tight security.

He felt pretty desperate. It was April. The four months Theodora had given him to find Chantal were nearly up. Things hadn't been going too well for him back at the ranch. For one thing, Theodora had aged greatly in the past five years. She had grown stooped, as if some weight rested on her heavily. Even though conditions were tough, he wasn't sure it was just the ranch bothering her.

Corn prices were up, cow prices were down, and they hadn't had any rain. The calf crop percentages were down as well. There had been more than the usual number of accidents and other problems, too. He and Theodora couldn't seem to get along even as well as they had in the past. She was determined to keep to the old ways, to the old ranch traditions, even though to survive and be competitive they needed to change. With workman's comp as high as it was, they needed fewer permanent cowboys and more contract labor.

More than one *vaquero* had hinted things had been smoother before Jack had come back. And even though Maverick had returned to the ranch as soon as he'd heard Jack was there, he'd been more of an aggravation than a help. He always sided with Theodora. He always found a way to lay every accident and every problem at Jack's door. Right before Jack had left for France, Maverick had noticed some cash shortages and taken the books to Theodora, who'd promised to show them to their accountant.

Theodora had ordered Jack home but had given him almost no support. One cowboy had been injured by a combine. Then the night of Jack's departure to France, when she'd sided with Maverick and blamed Jack for Caesar getting hurt in a tractor accident, he and Maverick had nearly come to blows. The truth was Caesar had gotten hurt due to his own damn carelessness. The only person who routinely took Jack's side was a distant cousin of Chantal's, Becky, but Becky lived in Houston and owned only a small percentage of the ranch holdings.

The dozen detectives Jack had hired to find Chantal had come up with zip. Then last Tuesday, when reaching for his wallet to pay for the more than twenty bags of groceries, he'd suddenly noticed Carla staring at the cover girl on a magazine.

Carla, who had begun to thaw a little, who even smiled at him every now and then, had quickly glanced away.

But not before he'd seen her tears.

Not before the model's glacial green gaze had riveted him, too.

He'd gone cold as he'd ripped the magazine off the shelf.

"No, Dad!"

Holding the magazine above Carla's outstretched hands, he hadn't heard the checker tell him how much he owed.

The man behind them slung a six-pack onto the checkout counter. "That's Mischief Jones. Get a load of those chi-chis. They say she prowls New York in her limo looking for men. She goes for dark young Latin types. Like you and me."

Jack had flushed.

"We've gotta go, Dad." When Carla jumped and grabbed at the magazine, the model's face tore in half.

"That'll be an additional $5.59, sir."

Jack's hand had remained frozen on his wallet.

Was she? Or wasn't she?

A powerful chill of recognition swept him.

The model had a classic-looking face. Her narrow, feline features were savage. She had huge slanting eyes, a delicate nose, prominent cheekbones and full red lips. She didn't look much like Chantal.

Yet he had known with an instinct that was needle sharp and true. His hand had shaken. He'd have given anything for a double shot of gin.

Chantal was alive.

And she was going to pay.

For what she'd done to him.

For what she'd done to Carla.

"It's not her, Dad!"

He'd stared at Carla. "Yeah. Right."

She'd screamed when he'd pitched the magazine into a grocery sack.

Theodora was always getting on his back because he never talked or explained himself to Carla. Hell, how could he when he was too afraid of damaging their new, fragile relationship? In the past she had always sided with her mother, making excuses for Chantal, saying she was perfect, blaming him for Chantal's neglect. Not being able to explain how he felt to Carla made him feel tight and all wound up inside.

When they had gotten back to the ranch and unloaded the pickup, he'd waited till Carla sulkily grabbed her sketchbook and raced outside to climb that damned tree of hers. Then he'd called his P.I. and asked him to check out the model.

B. J. Smith called him back within an hour. "Mischief Jones ain't as lily-white as she claims."

"So what did you come up with?"

"Not much. She became an instant celebrity four years ago when she hit Paris. Mostly because the most famous supermodel in the world, Beauty Washington, took her under her wing. But your girl's pretty wild."

"Tell me about it."

"Last spring at one of her parties, this friend, Beauty, fell ten stories to her death. Mischief got some bad press, but nothing was proved against her. The publicity pushed her to the top.

"Your Mischief's fed the press a clever line of crap from day one. She says her daddy is a French viscount. Wrong. The guy's dead, and so is his only daughter. Their château has been made into condos. She says she studied art history in Paris. Nobody over there ever heard of her. None of her other lies checked out, either."

"So whoever this lady is, she completely reinvented herself?"

"Yeah. By day she models classy clothes and lives like a queen. By night she screws bikers and losers she picks up on the street or in bars. She's got a soft spot for kids, though. Every single child model in the agency is crazy about her. Seems she wows them with presents from her shoots."

Chantal had always given Carla gifts instead of love.

"She's Chantal."

"You don't know that."

"I'm bringing her in, B.J."

"Hey—that could be dangerous. The lady has two bodyguards with records a mile long."

"My kind of guys."

"Why don't you just forget her? Theodora will come around."

"I have to because of Carla. It's hard to explain..."

Edmondo began barking orders, and just for a second Jack aimed his binoculars on him. Then the gorgeous young woman threw her head back so that her trademark masses of curling red hair tumbled down her back.

She was thinner. Much thinner. Bone skinny, in fact. But she had a long, swanlike neck and a sculpted, feline face. She moved like a cat.

Or a snake.

But this woman was different from Chantal. So different, he never would have known her...if he hadn't sensed her.

The woman thrust her legs apart, her stance that of a conqueror. Chantal used to do that. Right before she told him how much better she was than he.

Still, he had to get closer, much closer—to be sure.

Tonight he'd find a way.

Mischief had put on a CD of *Carmen.* But not even the soaring voice of Webster's favorite diva, Madame Devlin, could soothe her tonight.

Disappear or die.

Those were the same choices Mischief had faced five years ago in the barn. Only now the stakes were higher.

All her life other people had forced her to do terrible things. She hadn't wanted anybody to die that night in the barn anymore than she had meant to push Beauty. All she had wanted was what was hers.

The gilt-edged mirror loomed above the frightened woman in red. Feral green eyes devoured her own reflection. Dozens of Webster's facial creams, which were like a religion to her, lined the marble counter beneath the mirror, but Mischief had been too filled with dread to use any of them tonight.

A beautiful woman dies twice. A coward dies many times.

Webster had whispered those bitter truths to her after they'd made wild, vicious love the last time. He'd known those sentiments would fester and hurt far longer than his slap. Her terror of getting old only increased his power over her.

Mischief had the shower running in the luxurious marble bathroom in her six-room suite at the renowned George V in Paris. Madame Devlin's soprano voice swelled passionately. Thus, Mischief didn't hear the slight sound of a stolen key turning in the latch of her living room door.

Nor did she hear the hushed footsteps of a large man padding across her huge, elegantly furnished salon and bedrooms.

Mischief was naked beneath her red silk dressing gown with a golden dragon emblazoned on the front. As she stared into that misty bathroom mirror at her beautiful, triangular face, she did not see her beauty.

She saw only the faint, feathery lines beneath her eyes. Lines that would grow deeper and longer, and crueler. Until her lovely face would melt into those crevices like wax.

Mischief prized beauty because it was her source

of power. She had no other, for her father had taught her not to trust love.

Her father had said he loved her more than anybody in the world. But he'd lied.

He had had another little girl—a secret daughter, a usurper.

Chantal had been ten years old when she'd followed him to a strange shack in the marshes. She'd seen him hug that pretty witch, Ivory Rose. She'd seen him sweep another little redheaded witch girl named Cheyenne into his arms and kiss her and laugh with her as he carried her inside, where he stayed all night. When he had closed the door, night flowers had begun to bloom.

Chantal had vowed that night never to love any man again.

If she loved her new face, it was because it gave her fame and power over men. She loved the wild sex with boys who seemed to get younger and more in awe of her every year. She loved the limos, the clothes and the money. Or she would have loved such a life if the bastards who hounded her would leave her alone. And if she hadn't left behind a little girl she couldn't forget no matter how hard she tried.

Who was stalking her?

Beauty's big bad boyfriend who'd written Chantal threatening letters from prison because he blamed her for Beauty's death?

Rumor had it that José Hernando hadn't drowned in Costa Rica after she'd sicced him on her sister whom he'd almost killed. Had he figured out who Mischief Jones really was and where she was and sent his thugs after her?

Modeling was competitive. She'd made plenty of enemies getting where she was.

Then she remembered that last night in the barn...when she'd barely escaped with her life.

Whoever her stalker was, Mischief had damn sure felt him in Provence this morning.

But despite the dangers surrounding her, she was just as worried about the way her life was rushing by so fast, like grains of sand streaming through an hourglass.

Her beauty had been her ticket to the extraordinary life she had always wanted to live.

She was nearly thirty-five. Soon, too soon, she would look old. Her life-style was taking its toll.

She worked so hard and still she never had the energy to do all that was demanded of her. She had to wear the right clothes, entertain the right people. She loved the brilliant, glamorous life of Mischief Jones, daughter of a French viscount, internationally famous supermodel. Still, even though she was on top, Mischief could feel herself slipping.

All too soon, younger models would take her place.

Suddenly Madame Devlin's soaring voice stopped in midnote.

In the next instant a hard male drawl broke into Mischief's unhappy reverie.

"Chantal!"

Stunned, Mischief Jones whirled.

A tall, dark man stood in the shadowy doorway with the bedroom light behind him. He had massive shoulders and a dangerous face.

Her green eyes narrowed to slits.

Her husband.

Her heart beat madly. She felt herself blanch.

She had not expected Jack.

The long scratch that marred his tanned cheek made him look even tougher than usual. Tough the way she liked a bedmate to look. But too steely eyed. And too sober.

Like characters in a ballet, they stood poised, frozen, their gazes locked.

The roof of Mischief's mouth went dry.

"I thought they locked you up and threw away the key," she taunted in a low tone.

"You hoped."

Another piece of her past had suddenly caught up with her. So had more of her lies.

Jack would tell the world who she was. He would ruin her. *Who back at the ranch knew that he had found her?*

"Where are my bodyguards?" she whispered.

His slow, white smile was insolent, his laugh hard. "Those two overweight goons?"

Jack's educated voice was only faintly accented. If she hadn't known, she would never have guessed he came from squalor and whores and gang-infested streets or that he'd spent the last five years behind bars. He was tougher and harder than anyone she'd ever known. His memories were worse than most people's nightmares. He'd probably taken care of her bodyguards as easily as another man might knot his tie.

"Strip. I want to see you naked," Jack commanded in that dark growl that had once electrified her with lust.

Now, because there was nothing sexual in his request, she was momentarily at a loss as to how to handle him. If only he had been drunk. If only there had been even the slightest hint of a sexual demand.

In that other, almost-forgotten lifetime when they had been young, they had been good that way.

How she had despised and yet been fascinated by him when he'd been dirty and poor and illiterate. And wild. Uncontrollable. So wild, nobody had been wilder or made her feel wilder than he. He hadn't been afraid of anything. Not even of Theodora. Then he'd come up in the world. Gotten those damned college degrees. She had married him, so Cheyenne couldn't have him.

They'd had their darling little girl, Carla Ann.

Carla.

Carla, who had adored her. Carla, who would forgive her anything. Carla, who with her magic pencil could draw anything. Carla, who climbed trees and hid and did all the glorious things Chantal had done as a child before her father's cruel betrayal.

Oh, Carla.

Chantal remembered standing over the crib, willing herself to hate their little girl and then weeping uncontrollably at the thought of such a darling baby girl with downy red curls being born to a mother who hated her. She remembered how her hands had shaken as she'd lifted her precious baby into her arms and comforted her till she quieted. She remembered how only she had had that effect on the child. How, at last, she'd been first with someone again.

But not even her adorable little girl, not even Jack's proficiency in bed had been enough to satisfy her. She'd grown restless for more. For more men. For more of everything. Her dreams had been so much bigger than the ranch and motherhood.

Not once in the past five years had she ever allowed herself to think of Jack. Not true. She had thought of him the night she'd met his brother, Garth, at that film festival in Cannes. It had been weirdly thrilling to seduce the world-famous movie star even though his performance in bed wasn't even a close match to Jack's.

Still, her marriage was dead and cold. And even though she had missed her daughter unbearably, she had told herself Carla was better off without her.

"What do *you* want?" Chantal whispered. "Why are you here?"

Jack just stood there like he had when they'd been together in the burning barn. When he'd laced his large brown hands around her slim neck and tightened them very slowly, all the time staring into her eyes.

She hadn't been afraid even when his fingers had dug into her windpipe for that fraction of a second before he'd released her. He had a temper, but he wouldn't ever hurt a woman—even her. He would have let her go even if Carla hadn't wandered into the barn. But he had seen their child's stricken face. He had backed quietly away from her as Carla had hurled herself sobbing into her mother's arms. And Chantal had played the part to the hilt by screaming that he would have murdered her.

But Chantal hadn't run away from him. She'd run away from someone else, from that person who had set her up and sent Jack down to the barn that night, from that person who had tried to finish what Jack had lacked the guts to finish.

Jack's harshly carved face was silhouetted against the elegance of the Pompeian inlaid-marble wall.

Chantal shivered. His body was as heavy with muscle as she remembered. She knew the power in his hands. His black eyes burned her with a censorious and malicious fire.

Anyone else would have been afraid.

But Chantal's blood was pulsing with an unnatural, raw, animal excitement. Once she had liked his hating her and his wanting her at the same time. She remembered his rough hands on her soft skin. Maybe prison had given him a taste for the things she had always tried to push him to do.

"Strip!"

"Why? Do you still want me?" she asked.

His black glare flamed hotter.

She smiled. She kept smiling as she lowered the red silk dressing gown over her shoulder. The rippling silk felt cool and soft against her hot skin.

"Did you miss me?" she whispered. "You and I—we were pretty incredible."

"Shut up." His voice was deeper, gruffer.

"What was it like for a man like you—doing without for five years?" Her voice lowered huskily as she bared her breast and ran her fingertips over her nipple.

The color left his dark face; profound emptiness dulled his eyes.

"It beat marriage to you."

"I hope they hurt you."

"Oh, they tried." His dark face drained of color. He looked gray and sick suddenly.

"I wish I could have watched."

"Come here," he demanded, seething.

"Sure, baby," she purred, wanting to push him till he went wild.

At the last moment she rushed at him, claws extended, thinking she might somehow get past him. He grabbed her arm, shredding her dressing gown. And even as she thrilled to the brutal power of his hands on her skin, they gentled.

Just for a second she felt the old keen, wild wanting as his glittering gaze stared down at her naked body.

Then she read the true emotion in his eyes.

Too late she realized that he didn't desire her. That all he felt was cold, icy contempt. "Are you even human, Chantal?"

He continued in a strange, disembodied voice. "You have the body of a beautiful woman. But you're sick. If you weren't so dangerous, I might even feel sorry for you."

He'd told her once that for him their marriage had been like a roller-coaster ride. After a few cheap thrills, he'd been tired of it. He'd told her he'd only stuck it out because of Carla.

The last thing she'd ever wanted from any man was pity.

Suddenly Chantal could barely hear him. It was as though he were speaking from the bottom of the sea.

He forced her to turn around. She shivered as his callused palms traced down that jagged white scar on her back.

Then he released her and let her fall gently onto the Aubusson carpet.

And she knew.

Her fingernails, which would have clawed his flesh, raked the worn wool pile as she snaked away from him. He hadn't been sure who she really was. He was merely identifying her. Checking the scar on her left shoulder the way he'd check a brand to see if an animal belonged to him.

"Bastard!" she hissed, humiliated. "I wish you'd

burned to death in the barn that night. You were supposed to die then. So was I.''

"Get dressed,'' he snarled, helping her to her feet, throwing her dressing gown at her. "You have a plane to catch. You're going home. Back where you belong. To Texas.''

Hadn't he learned anything? Hadn't he figured out what had happened? If he took her back to the ranch, she would die. But so would he.

"I'm not going anywhere with you.''

"You're my wife—remember?''

"In name only. Our marriage is dead. I want a divorce.''

"Ditto, honey. But first we go home—together. You have a hell of a lot to answer for. We both do. Carla, for one thing. It's time people down there know what you are.''

Oh, Jack, somebody does.

As he pushed her into the bedroom, Chantal realized she needed to use her brains—fast.

On the edge of panic, she turned. "What about Carla?''

"She can't get over you. She runs away. She doesn't go to school. She's flunking math—''

I aced math. My daughter can't flunk—

"Carla blames... Hey, why am I telling you this as if you care?''

Chantal saw two white-faced lumps sprawled beside her bed—her bodyguards. How had Jack done that without making a sound?

"I—I do care about Carla. But she's better off with me gone.''

"Carla won't go to school unless I chase her down and put her in my truck and drive her. Carla and I are closer, but she still blames me for your absence from her life. She doesn't say much, but without you there...she feels all alone."

An odd desperation coiled around her heart as she thought of her little girl having problems. Of Jack dying. But fear for her own safety swamped all other anxieties. "Okay. You win. I'll do what you want."

Inside, Chantal was like a lava-filled volcano, ready to burst. She felt bad about Carla, but guilt couldn't compare to her fears and fury. She had a new life now. Big problems. Going back now would ruin everything. She felt crazy, absolutely crazy as she always did anytime anybody forced her do something she didn't want to do.

Jack was blind. Stupid.

Pretend. Pretend to go along with him.

She was moving past him into the bedroom, grinding her pretty white teeth, fighting for self-control as her wild gaze raked the silk draperies, the woodwork ornamented with gold leaf, the polished marble, seeking a weapon. The door to the terraced balcony was open, revealing its summer furniture and urns overflowing with red geraniums. Too far away. He'd catch her for sure. And the urns might be too heavy. Besides, the balcony overlooked a courtyard; she might be seen.

Nearer, she spotted the magnificent bookends on the antique table behind the sofa. They were made of heavy dark stone carved into the graceful shapes of big-earred Egyptian cats.

She lunged toward them, seizing one by the neck. As leather-backed books tumbled off the table, she whirled on one foot like a dancer and struck Jack square in the jaw.

She sidestepped gracefully as he toppled toward her.

She hadn't wanted to hit him. He had made her do it. He should have known better than to push her.

She knelt beside his massive, sprawled body to make sure he was unconscious and not...

With a fingertip she tenderly wiped away the blood that oozed from his mouth. There were deeper grooves running from his handsome nose to his well-remembered lips, a faint webbing beneath his black lashes. He, too, had grown older. He might have been happy if only she had not seduced...

But Cheyenne had stolen her father.

So she had stolen Jack from Cheyenne.

Suddenly the hotel maid assigned to her stepped into the room. "What are your men doing on the floor, *madame?*"

Mischief froze. Fear and guilty regret died instantly. She couldn't afford them. Couldn't afford to think about what Jack had said about Carla needing her, either. Couldn't afford to remember her own father abandoning...or Beauty's terrified face before she'd fallen...or the face in the barn that night....

Mischief had been forced to do all the things she'd done.

Forget the past. Forget Carla. Think.

She had to think. She stayed at the George V because of its excellent service. The hotel maid assigned to her was multilingual and impeccably trained. The traits that made her such a treasure would make her a perfect witness.

Mischief remembered the police and their questions after Beauty's death. The investigation had gone on for months. The newspaper stories had lasted even longer. She had to make up something that the maid would believe, so she could escape.

"Monique, this man is an intruder," she said softly in a robotic tone, forcing herself to let the bookend fall onto the carpet. "He attacked me. It was… terrifying." The stone cat landed with a dull thud. "Call the police, you little idiot! Now!"

This was Jack's fault. He had had no right to come here. No right…

He could have been followed.

She had to get out of here—fast.

All the designer clothes in Mischief's closet were either red or black. She ripped dress after dress off its hangers. Evening gowns as well as skirts were all thrown onto a heap onto the floor until she found…

With a smile she ran her hand down a favorite, black silk shantung jacket.

She got dressed quickly, methodically, in a severely cut suit that accentuated her voluptuous curves. She pinned a circle of diamonds onto her lapel.

When Monique wasn't looking, Mischief scooped up her purse and a long red scarf and walked out of the room, down the long corridor, letting the scarf whirl behind her so that it licked the carpet like a tongue of flame, letting it trail all the way down the wide, sweeping staircase that led to the public rooms and lobby that, with their rich old tapestries and paintings from the eighteenth and nineteenth centuries, were masterpieces of understated elegance. As she was.

Without bothering to check out, she stepped outside onto the tree-lined avenue, hailed a taxi and quickly vanished into the Paris night.

It was almost midnight. The city was dark and quiet

beneath a black sky as she sped past the Arc de Triomphe. Other cars glided past her cab on the wide avenue as silently as fish scurrying in an ebony sea.

She lost interest in the city with its lighted buildings and monuments and stared at her reflection in the window. In the dark glass, the tiny lines beneath her eyes were no longer visible. Her face appeared as flawless as it had five years ago after Webster's first procedure.

Not that she found pleasure in her beauty. She was filled with a deep and burning anger that was so all-consuming that it left no room for anything else. Why couldn't Jack have left well enough alone? Why had he cornered her? Why hadn't he seen that she couldn't allow him or that part of her life to threaten her again?

If he came back he would force her to—

Jack knew who she was and where she lived.

If he stayed sober, he would be relentless.

She would have to change all her carefully made plans.

Fast.

He was far more dangerous than the others.

He would come after her again.

If she didn't stop him, he would bring her down.

She didn't want to hurt him, but she would.

Part 2
BEAUTIFUL CHILD

Chapter 5

A dark-faced Papual fertility figure smiled mockingly from its fastening on the wall beside a boldly modern painting by Basquiat.

Later Bronte would look back on this night and wonder how she could have ever been so naive.

But then her mood was almost as eager as a child's during that last hour of kindergarten before being released for a holiday.

A heat wave had struck the Northeast. The May evening that was to bring revelation, ecstasy and so much despair was a blistering ninety degrees.

Not that she and Webster felt the heat in the immense, cool, ivory-tiled master suite's spa. Swathed in white towels, she sat on a three-legged stool with her long legs crossed in a lotus position while he hovered over her with powder and rouge. She had been taking turns staring out at the pool and sculpture garden or at the muted television screen every time her favorite star, Garth Brown, appeared.

Webster had turned off the television sound, muttering, "What garbage!" after a story about an attempt on a supermodel's life in Manhattan began. Then he'd played a CD—Mozart's *Magic Flute*.

"Close your eyes," Webster commanded in a raspy voice, setting powder and brush on the pink marble counter. "No. Don't squint."

All day his mood had been tense and more autocratic than usual.

When she relaxed, she felt the tip of the eyeliner brush flow expertly across her lids.

His brush tickled, and she wiggled her nose. "When can I look?"

"Hold still." A few minutes later, he said, "There! Now you can open your eyes."

But when she did so, Webster's intent, almost-angry stare alarmed her.

He gripped the sides of her stool and leaned closer. His unsmiling face was taut; the lines between his keen eyes furrowed. "I can't believe—" He broke off, looking appalled, dazzled.

With shaky fingertips she felt the warm, baby-smooth texture of her cheek.

His hands shook more violently as he traced the same cheek with a finger. "Magnificent."

Curious for the first time, she said, "I want to see..."

His dark smile died. "First I want us both to fortify ourselves with a glass of champagne."

"Why?"

"There is a great deal about me you do not know.

Why indeed?'' he asked ominously. ''The changes in your appearance are...radical.''

''But if I look pretty, why wouldn't I be pleased?''

''Because...'' His frown deepened. ''Because...'' His voice was low and hard. ''Go to your room and put on that red Dior I selected. And the perfume. Tonight I want you to look and be just like... Just perfect.''

''Webster, there's no need to make such a fuss.''

''Go!'' He waved her away impatiently.

She ran upstairs, wanting to get this unveiling over, wanting to get on with her life.

On her way back down, the phone rang. When he picked it up and said her name, Bronte stopped. He spoke in morose, cracked whispers. Still, she caught fragments of his side of the conversation.

''—I told you it's dangerous to call—''

''—yes, I saw it—''

''—the resemblance to you and—''

''—quite startling—''

''—upstairs—''

''—damn it—''

''—any minute...coming down—''

''—I don't give a damn about your husband—''

Only when he slammed down the phone did Bronte realize her heart was racing. With difficulty she resumed her composure and descent. She was halfway down the stairs when the telephone rang again.

Instead of answering it, Webster yanked it out of the wall. He was throwing it onto the couch and trying to untangle his legs from the wires when she glided through the doorway into the dining room.

''Webster, what's wrong?''

He whirled, gesturing grandly. "Nothing. Absolutely nothing. Where's the champagne?"

When she'd left the room, he'd put on a CD of *Rigoletto.* The passionate music made her remember her unhappy childhood, her beautiful mother, her own terrible self-doubts. Her first two lives. Her failures.

Jimmy's loss.

After her son's death she'd enrolled in a CPR class. Bryan had laughed at her for doing so. "A little late for that, Bronte, don't you think?"

She'd thought, he's right. She couldn't win ever again.

Bitter memories.

Don't look back.

Bronte smiled brightly, determined to put all that behind her. Webster hardly had drained a glass when he poured himself another. While the music soared, maneuvering toward a climax, Bronte sliced slim pieces of pink roast onto fine china plates.

He drank steadily through dinner. From time to time he would stare down the length of his gleaming table, his fierce blue eyes glowering moodily at her from behind the silver candelabra and its flickering red candles. Then he would look away as if deeply troubled.

"Webster, why are you so upset?"

"And why do you give a damn?" he growled.

What could she say when she understood him so little? She simply stared at him with compassion in her heart.

"I—I thought a woman like you could have no power over me. Not when she..." His eyes blazed. "But no..."

The soprano sang faster and faster, higher and higher.

Bronte recognized her mother's voice. Which was odd. Webster had never played any of her mother's performances before. She had believed he was only interested in the latest stars.

"She?"

"Forget it."

"I want to help you," Bronte said.

"You always want to help me," he said softly. "Damn it. You do everything I ask, don't you? You cook. You keep house. You're nice even when you are burdened with great pain. I've tried not to let it affect me. But I've never known anyone like you. And every day…as you grow more beautiful and look more like…"

Madame Devlin was singing the most haunting of arias.

Webster continued. "It would drive a sane man crazy—and I am hardly sane. To be in the house, night after night, alone with…with the daughter…with my goddess…" His eyes were wild as he sprang from the table. "Stay away from me. There's no help for me now—do you understand?" He heaved himself toward the kitchen. "No, of course, you don't. But, dear God, you will."

Madame Devlin's pure voice rose and held the final note in that last, dazzling crescendo. Then abruptly her angelic voice and the music ceased. But the silence that followed held even more dark, mysterious passion.

Suddenly Webster made an inarticulate, almost animal cry. Then he turned his back on her and left Bronte alone, staring at their ruined candlelit dinner.

When she heard the kitchen door bang, Bronte got up and, leaning over the polished table, blew out the candles one by one. She had found the opera disturbing, for it brought back the past. But she had found her conversation with Webster even more troubling.

For a moment she savored the darkness and the quiet of the dining room. Then she turned off the CD player and began to worry about Webster.

As always, he'd gone out to his study.

What was wrong?

She had thought he was cold, uncaring.

But he wasn't. He was afraid.

Of what, though?

Bronte's mind reeled. She knew what it was to be terrified. To feel all alone…and guilt stricken.

When she went into the kitchen with their plates, she nearly dropped them when she realized that the big carving knife with the sterling handle that she had used to slice the roast was gone. She rushed to the sink, but it wasn't there.

Then she remembered her mother's wild rampages after a bad performance. Had Webster taken the knife?

In a panic, Bronte rushed out into the sweltering night. A dog barked in the distance. Moonlight gilded the modern sculptures in the garden and made them appear to be twisted and oddly knotted as she raced past them.

Webster was nowhere to be seen until she reached the barn. Then she looked up and saw his black silhouette swell and then vanish against the blinds as he dashed back and forth furiously. The grotesquely elongated shadow of a huge knife arced and slashed. Next, the window shattered and a rectangular object fell and broke into pieces at Bronte's feet. He was playing music from the opera *Carmen.*

Wild panic surged through Bronte as she leaned down and picked up what was left of a broken frame and photograph of a girl with a lovely triangular face.

It was a face too like...

She recognized her mother's voice again, singing high and true—perfect as always.

No... No...

The world had suddenly gone crazy. Bronte was a child again, cowering in her mother's brownstone house during one of her rages.

When more glass broke, a thousand terrifying images flashed through Bronte's mind. Flinching at every violent, crashing sound, she forced herself to climb the stairs. For once, the loft door that Webster had always kept locked stood ajar. A narrow bar of pure yellow light spilled onto the first stair.

When she pushed the door wider, she nearly stepped on torn fragments of an immense photograph of the same beautiful girl who wore nothing but a silver fox fur. Her lovely cat-shaped face with its sculpted cheekbones and flowing spirals of long red hair had been slashed. Part of her lip lay in tatters. Her ample breasts had been shredded.

Webster raked a dozen framed pictures of her off his desk. His laughter was shrill when they smashed onto the oak floor.

Everywhere there were pictures of the same girl.

Then Bronte saw the huge poster of her mother costumed as Madame Butterfly.

This had something to do with her mother.

Bronte heard her mother's voice as she had heard it as a child, so many times, under glittering chandeliers with long gold mirrors reflecting the radiance of her mother's exquisite face and slender figure in glorious costume. The music and the voice surged toward Bronte in waves, hurtling her backward in time to her mother's brownstone where the original painting of that poster had hung, where gigantic photographs of her mother had graced every wall. The world had worshipped her mother's voice, her mother's beauty.

Nobody had cared that Madame Devlin had been dissatisfied with her child and unfaithful to her husband.

Bronte put her hands to her ears and forced herself back to the present.

Webster had known who Bronte was from the first.

The likeness between the girl in Webster's photographs and her own mother was uncanny.

How?

Webster had known all along about her mother.

Why did this model have her mother's face? How?

One of the photographs in Webster's loft was signed with the letters *M.J.* On another the model had signed her full name—Mischief Jones.

In one Mischief wore a black Chanel gown. In another red chiffon. In another she was painted gold and draped with gaudy silver jewelry. In one she stood on the deck of a ship in front of a wind machine. But in every shot, whether she was a waif or a siren, she looked incredibly feral and boldly haughty.

She had red hair, and it was the same startling shade as...

Mischief had slanting green eyes.

They were the same dazzling color, too.

Bronte was filled with a profound and growing confusion. Webster was watching her sympathetically. But comprehension dawned slowly.

Mischief's legs went on forever.

Just like—

Dear God. No!

Just like—her mother's. Just like her own.

Bronte sucked in huge lungfuls of air.

No! No!

What had he done?

She shook her head. He couldn't have... He wouldn't—

Bronte had longed to look like her mother. Until she had realized that it had been her mother who had longed for that. Not she.

As Bronte stared at the pictures, she struggled with a chaos of thoughts and long-suppressed emotions.

"Who are you obsessed with—my mother...or this model?"

"As a little boy, I adored your mother. She was like a goddess. I worshipped her. Then a woman came to me... I *made* Mischief Jones. I made you, too. I watched you at your mother's house. I followed you...before your accident."

"What?"

"Only you're even more beautiful than they were." His handsome face was strange and passive. "I never considered how your beautiful soul would enhance the perfect, ruthless facial structure so necessary for photography that *they* both had..." He swung around in a flash. He loomed over her, his thin face going in and out of focus.

Suddenly Bronte was absolutely certain. She didn't need a mirror. She knew what she looked like, *who* she looked like.

I want to be me. Not my mother. Not this look-alike Mischief Jones, either. I want to be Bronte Devlin.

I don't want to be beautiful. I don't want—

"You are a goddess now," he whispered, sinking to his knees.

For an instant the pain she felt in her heart was as cold as if an icicle had pierced it.

She stared down at him hopelessly. "You never cared about helping me. This was always about them. Which one are you obsessed with?"

His face went haggard.

"Why, Webster? Why did you do it?"

He just stared up at her.

"For vengeance?"

A low moan came from him. The knife fell from his hand with a clatter.

"Why?"

His gaunt face was gray, his blue eyes empty. "I—I wasn't sure I even could. I tried before. But this time, I used a three-dimensional CT scan. That's why I was able to get the facial bone proportions the same. I succeeded beyond even my wildest dreams."

As always, his plastic-surgery jargon was little more than gibberish.

"When Mischief became a famous model, did she jilt you? Did she crush your huge ego? Is this about my mother? Or did you do it to ruin Mischief? Well, if you did, I'll go to her and tell her that no matter how you threaten her, I'll never try to take her place. I'll make her know that all I'll ever want is to go home to Texas and get my own life back."

Webster got up, rushed toward her and, grabbing her arms, began to shake her. "If she sees you, you'll sure as hell never have your own life back. Stay away from her, do you hear me? Whatever you do, stay away from her. She's evil. Dangerous. She'll tear you to pieces. She'll destroy you—the way she destroyed me."

"Why should I believe you? You think you're a god. The way you play with other people's lives makes me sick. Well, you can't play with mine anymore."

Brave words.

"Don't go..."

Bronte felt hollow despair rising in her as his grip tightened.

"Bronte..."

Suddenly she was trembling as she stared at him and at the model's face behind him. And then at her mother's poster. Bronte's eyes glazed. "Why? Why did I let you do this? I've been such a fool."

Then Mischief's huge photograph with its slashed red lips blurred. So did her mother's poster. Bronte felt blank and empty. Almost like she had ceased to exist.

"Let me go," she said dully.

"Bronte, you've got to listen to me."

Her confusion was replaced by rage and fear when his fingers dug into her shoulders.

"Get your hands off of me!" When he just stood there, she pushed him away and ran, tears wetting her cheeks as she stumbled into the night.

He let out a cry of frustration.

"Bronte!"

At the sound of her name, she gave a sudden, anguished scream and ran faster.

"Bronte, I'm not a monster."

No. She was. She was the one with somebody else's face.

Chapter 6

Webster had replaced *her* face with another woman's.

"Oh God, oh God, oh God!"

And not just any woman's.

Bronte hadn't felt anything for so long. Now her feelings were swamping her.

She was shaking as she stared up at the Gothic turrets and gables, balconies and gargoyles that decorated the exterior of Mischief Jones's luxurious apartment building on Park Avenue.

"Not yet," Bronte whispered aloud to herself when one of Mischief's liveried doormen caught sight of her and waved, thinking he knew her. "I—I can't face her yet. Not when I don't even know who I am anymore."

Terrified, Bronte waved back at the doorman. Then she began backing away from the building. Not knowing where to go or what to do, she crossed the wide street and hurriedly walked two blocks to Central Park. She couldn't find a taxi so she strolled along Fifth Avenue.

Last night she had driven Webster's Mercedes to the train station and then taken a train to Grand Central. She'd watched the manicured Connecticut countryside give way to dirty, crumbling buildings spray-painted with graffiti. Then she'd caught a cab and checked into a nondescript hotel not far from the Museum of Natural History.

Why had Webster done it?

Bronte hadn't slept. She'd had nightmares about dozens of women, all who had the same lovely face she did.

Then she had a truly terrifying nightmare about her mother. Bronte had been a little girl again. She had sneaked into her mother's room and was standing in front of her gilt, floor-length mirrors, her young face garishly made up, her plump body zipped into a glittering gold costume. Then her mother had come in and had begun tearing the jewels and rich fabrics from her body.

Her mother had screamed, "Just look at yourself. You may be my daughter, but you can never be me! You're fat and pimply faced and...and just horrible!" In her dream, her mother's beautiful face had slowly melted into a death mask.

At first light Bronte had checked out of her hotel. Then she'd spent the next few hours wandering up and down Fifth Avenue, staring vacantly into shop windows. Finally she'd caught sight of her reflection and realized how much she really did look like her mother in the red chiffon gown she was wearing. New clothes would make her look more like herself, she'd decided, and she'd been the first customer to enter Macy's Department Store when it opened. There she'd stripped out of the evening gown and bought a pair of jeans and a white cotton blouse.

It had taken her that long to realize that she couldn't ever look remotely like herself again.

During her sleepless night in the hotel, she had carefully studied her strange and wondrously beautiful face in the hotel's many mirrors. Unable to accept that the incredible new face was really hers, she would touch her baby-soft flesh and then the cool mirror.

With such a face, it would be hard to hide.

How many others were there?

Where were they?

These questions haunted her.

Still, she did feel a little like Cinderella after the Fairy Godmother had magically changed her into a princess. Only this spell wouldn't end at midnight.

The slim, cat-like face with its delicately molded nose, with its tenderly voluptuous mouth and the seemingly high cheekbones was undeniably exquisite. A mad genius had taken her plain features and rearranged them to stunning effect. Her skin appeared fresh and golden, as if she'd bathed in honey. But while her bold features were smolderingly sensual, her huge green eyes made her look irresistibly innocent.

It was the face she had dreamed of having.

But now she would give anything to have her own face back.

Bronte didn't feel quite real. She wasn't sure who she was. And she was terrified.

Webster had told her numerous stories about nose jobs changing people's lives.

And she had this simply incredible new face.

Maybe Webster had made dozens of others.

"Oh God..."

Talking to God wasn't going to help. This wasn't *His* fault. This was Webster's.

Why had he turned her into a freak?

What could she do about it?

It was bad enough that she looked like her mother. But how was she ever going to work up the nerve to face the infamous Mischief Jones?

Webster's warnings haunted her.

She's evil. Dangerous. She'll tear you to pieces. She'll destroy you the same way she destroyed me.

Bronte had gone to the library and read about the woman. Her father was some sort of French viscount. Mischief had grown up in a château near Paris. After Mischief's meteoric rise in the fashion world, thanks to the help of an African-American model named Beauty, Mischief's sexual excesses had scandalized even the fashion world.

In Europe Mischief's lovers were older men who sported Italian suits and Riviera tans. In New York she went for young, leather-jacketed musicians and even younger Latins who hung out on street corners or bars at night. She was insanely jealous of younger models. When Beauty, her only friend, had mysteriously died, Mischief had been blamed.

Even though Mischief Jones didn't sound like a nice person, Bronte had tried to call her. When she'd failed to reach her, she'd gone to her building, but the mere sight of it had induced panic.

Bronte's plight wasn't made easier by the fact that

several male passersby on the street had propositioned her. Even though she had fluffed her hair so that she had as many spiraling red curls as possible to hide her face and was dressed plainly, everywhere she went, men stared at her.

Unused to so much attention, she didn't trust it.

In the hotel, the desk clerk had gasped, "Haven't I seen you before?"

She lowered her beautiful face. "No!"

"But aren't you—"

"Look, my name is Bronte Devlin. I used to teach kindergarten in Wimberley, Texas."

"I could swear..."

She was a freak.

This morning in the café where she had eaten a waffle and syrup, the waiter who had filled her coffee cup ten times had practically drooled with admiration every time he came to her table.

Suddenly, as Bronte was walking along the sidewalk, she felt a hot, prickly sensation race down the back of her neck. Next she heard hurried, yard-long masculine strides close behind her. When she tried walking faster and the purposeful footsteps quickened, she was terrified. Then she saw a cop nearby writing parking tickets and found new courage.

She whirled...and did a double take. Standing behind her in a black Stetson and a crisply starched, long-sleeved, white shirt was a man who looked almost exactly like her favorite movie star.

Garth.

No. This man was a bit broader in the shoulders, bigger boned. His skin was swarthier, his hair darker.

"What do you want from me, mister?" she demanded, shaken.

Bronte tilted her face to get a better look at him, remembering for some reason that Mischief had been attracted to dark Latin men.

As stunned as she, the man stopped. For a second she found herself staring into the fiercest black eyes—no, the most haunted eyes—she'd ever seen. His harsh features were tight with fury and disapproval.

He definitely thought he knew her. But he hated her.

Bronte's fear of him lessened because when he spotted the cop, he scowled at her and then veered quickly away. For a second she watched him race toward the street.

His boots and jeans and Stetson made her wonder if he was from around here. When she kept staring, he ducked his head quickly. Too quickly.

Who was he? The cop had scared him. Strange, since he didn't look like he'd scare easily.

Her confidence restored, she decided to give him a taste of his own medicine. "Hey! You there!"

When he didn't answer, she sidestepped so that she landed directly in front of him again. He had to either stop or run full-tilt into her. "You with the Garth Brown face and the linebacker's shoulders and the big black hat. And the attitude. I asked you a question, cowboy."

The tall cowboy opted for a collision course. When he hit her, his big hands clamped around her shoulders.

"Good morning to you, too, Mischief Jones!" he drawled through gritted teeth, despite his fury sounding pleasantly of Texas and wide-open skies.

His low tone was intimate as well as insolent.

His lips were so close, his warm breath tickled her neck and ear.

Bronte's racing heart` jolted when the hostile stranger's hands yanked her closer. She had a vague impression of being slammed against a wall of muscle and bone as her injured knee gave and she swayed on her feet. When he caught her and supported her, his hands and body felt so electric that her skin tingled.

Was he one of Mischief's lovers? Or just a wannabe?

She went still as she considered his long brown body lying over her, his hands roaming…

No. Still, she felt an unwanted tremor as she pushed the embarrassing vision from her mind. Still, her skin tingled and she flushed hotter.

Every sound in the city seemed to die, and the strikingly good-looking stranger became everything.

She didn't want to know this man, nor find him the least bit attractive.

Not now when she was so mixed up.

She saw a man whose eyes were dark and cold. A man who, for his own reasons, had given up on life, as she had. All these things she saw and knew yet didn't see and know at all. And didn't want to know. But she understood him without understanding him. And she studied him with more than the casual interest she would normally give to a stranger.

Somebody had broken his nose. But she marveled at the beauty of his hard, carved face under the wide black brim as it came into focus against a blur of blue sky and green trees.

His hair was Indian black, his skin burned to a permanent bronze. Or maybe his white cotton collar merely made him look so tanned. Still, there was something exotic about him, something foreign. When she met the haunted blackness of his eyes again, a wild tom-tom started in her chest.

She had been numb, dead at the center for so long. Maybe it was only because he looked like a movie star she lusted after, but the powerful wave of emotion she felt scared her so much she wanted to run.

This man both attracted and terrified her. He was not at all like Bryan or the other men she had dated in the past. There was nothing laid-back or casual about him. He was chased by demons. As she was.

The old Bronte would have withdrawn and gone deep inside herself until he let her go.

Sunlight beat down on him, tingeing the edges of his broad Stetson with a halo of gold. He held her in a tight, relentless grip. She didn't like the powerlessness of being held nor the feeling that he could have let her go and she would have stayed there still because he was like a sexual magnet compelling her into his orbit.

She didn't move or utter a sound when he snugged her hips against his. Nor when she felt her breasts, heavy and swollen, mashed into his solid chest.

"I—I'm not Mischief."

"Who are you today then?" he murmured tightly.

Oh, just the daughter of the diva a crazy plastic surgeon worshipped and made your friend, Mischief, look like. One day when he was feeling creative, he made another one. That's me. But you should know more about all this than most people, since you look like somebody famous also. Oh, hey, did Webster Quinn get ahold of you, too?

The stranger's eyes blazed with even more fury

when the cop looked up from his tablet and edged closer.

"I—I know I look a lot like your friend," she whispered. Why was she explaining anything to him? The smart move would be to get away from him.

"Yeah. Just like her." He glared cynically from the cop to her, his hard, glittering eyes clearly skeptical.

"How do we know each other?" she whispered.

His hands tensed. "Don't play games, honey. Okay?"

"Okay. I'm fixing to tell you the truth. *My* name is Bronte Devlin."

"Sure." He towered over her. His shoulders were so broad and thickly muscled she couldn't see anything but him. Not even the cop.

"It really *is* Bronte Devlin," she persisted. "This is going to sound implausible, but...but I had the same plastic surgeon as Mischief—"

"Hey, stop it," he interrupted. "What do you think—that after Paris, I would come after you here and just let you say sorry, stranger, and walk away?"

"Bronte... My name..." Too late, she realized she really shouldn't explain anything.

"Yeah. Right. *Bronte.*"

For an instant she wished she could have taken his arm and led him to a café where she could ask him questions about his real relationship with her look-alike. In the next instant that was the last thing she wanted.

"Just let me go," she whispered.

"Sure...*Bronte,*" he said with biting sarcasm. At the same time he kept a wary eye on the bulky man slapping tickets under windshield wipers. Then the stranger stared back at her, his ruthless face growing colder.

"I'll scream..."

There was a quick glimmer of hot emotion in the stranger's eyes that he couldn't quite conceal. "You'd do it, wouldn't you?"

"What?"

"Get me locked up in a cage again."

She stared at him blankly.

"You're damned good at this new act of yours." He broke the tension between them by barking an order. "So—go!"

She almost didn't hear the low rumble of sound that followed. And probably he didn't mean for her to.

"Run while you still can, honey."

She had felt the threat in his words all the way to her bones.

At the sound of children's laughter, she turned and fled toward a nearby playground. For a terrified second she felt the familiar prickle of heat at the back of her neck and was terrified he might chase her.

But when she turned, she saw he was still standing where she'd left him, with the sunlight gilding his hat and his large hands thrust deeply into the pockets of his jeans. He was watching her as intently and coldly as before. Why was his mere gaze, even long-range, enough to heat her skin?

Was it because he thought he'd slept with her?

No man had touched her for so long. She'd been dead to all that. For no reason, she thought of large brown hands shaping her body. Her skin burned at the thought.

Suddenly she turned and ran faster.

The next time she looked over her shoulder, he was gone.

What the hell was she trying to pull? He needed a drink.

Jack's black eyes blazed with censure and anger.

He didn't feel anything.

Nothing was changed.

Hell, yes, she was different.

He'd felt different, too—from that first second when he'd seen her.

She'd looked ingenuous and charmingly afraid. She was so radiantly beautiful she could have startled a blind man.

How could he think that after the way she'd led the cops to him in Paris? The bastards had thrown him in jail for three damned days.

She was working a number on him, dazzling him the way she dazzled Carla, softening him. Why? It had been years since she'd bothered to try to attract him. And even back then, he hadn't felt anything close to this.

His mind spun back to when they were kids. He remembered his first *corrida.* Theodora had cleverly assigned Mario, who'd worshipped Shanghai, to look after him, but Chantal had seen to it that Jack'd been given a bad rope and Potro, the oldest, clumsiest horse in the *remuda.* Then she'd chosen her moment when they'd been running in deep sand and had spooked his horse. Potro had stumbled right in front of the herd. Jack had been pinned under Potro as several steers rushed him.

He had been terrified. Chantal had laughed. Potro had been lying in the sand and kicking for all he was worth, and one hoof had nicked Jack's nose and broken it before Mario had jumped off his horse and pulled him out of danger. That misadventure had made Jack the joke of the cow camp, after Chantal and Caesar had told and retold that story.

"Damn the witch!" Jack whispered, coming back to the present. She'd never been so stunning. Her frightened, doe-eyed gaze had never been so soft. She was completely different than she'd been in Paris.

Maybe it was the fact he'd been raised by a whore that made him so sexually aware of feminine wiles and so determined not to be seduced. But he'd noticed all of Chantal's new tricks, the way her fingertips had skimmed his flesh so lightly, the way she'd smiled tremulously, the way she'd softened her voice.

Bronte?

What the hell was she up to? She'd recognized him instantly and then pretended not to know him, pretended to be some Bronte person with a plastic surgeon. And all the time she'd reeked of gardenias.

He had to remind himself that he'd found her standing in front of her own apartment building, that he'd seen her doorman wave to her.

Damn. If only she weren't Chantal....

Bronte. The name was soft and feminine and romantic.

In the sunlight her long red hair seemed a dozen gleaming shades as it fell in silky coils down her back. She was so much more than beautiful. She would have been striking in a room full of beautiful women. She exuded sweetness and innocence as well as a smoldering, vitally alive passion. Hell, her jeans were so tight, every man on the street had stopped to stare at her backside and mentally strip her... including him.

No matter how beautiful she was now, she was bad news.

Still, Jack felt shaken from their encounter.

Till he remembered the cop.

Nobody, no matter how pretty or supposedly nice, was going to get him locked up again. He would die before he got himself arrested, handcuffed, searched, fingerprinted and photographed again. Nobody was going to strip him of his clothes and pride and cage him like an animal.

Jack was still shaking as he watched the incandescent creature he believed to be his wife run toward the playground under the trees. He wasn't sure what had scared him more—thinking she was going to set the cops on him again—or holding her.

Chantal had damn sure never felt so good before. All soft skin and molten green eyes. Eyes that had stared into him and shared his pain and other things for a second or two.

Damn her for doing that when he knew what she was. He didn't like the way he'd reacted to her physically, either. Holding her had made his palms sweat and his groin swell with a need he'd thought she could never arouse again.

He'd better not let it happen, or the witch would sense her power over him.

He knew it had to be the plastic surgery and the new skills that came with her career. She'd deliberately reinvented herself. Still, he was stunned that her act was so effective that she could seem like such an entirely different woman.

For the first time ever, her beautiful green eyes had

felt fresh and compassionate, pure and alight with disarming warmth and tantalizing tenderness instead of evil. She'd even drawn his pain out of him for a second or two.

But he knew she wasn't like that. He'd already given her way too many chances.

He couldn't allow himself to forget again how dangerous she was.

Bronte was shocked by her forward behavior with a perfect stranger.

Why did he have to look so much like Garth?

Forget him.

But no matter how much Bronte wanted to forget Mischief's lover, she couldn't seem to put him out of her mind.

Thus, as she stood in the quiet of the sun-dappled playground, seeming to watch children play chase and throw balls and swing and ride seesaws, she saw instead the enigmatic stranger with the dangerous face whose haunted black eyes had burned her. She smelled him still—his clean fresh scent that was all-male and so pleasingly outdoorsy.

He had made her feel bold...and different. And most of all alive.

Suddenly Bronte was glad he was gone. Glad New York was such a big city. Glad he had refused to tell her his name. Glad she would never see him again.

Still, the brilliant sunshine seemed duller without him. The park, which to stressed-out city dwellers might have been a green oasis in the middle of looming steel and glass, felt like a prison to her.

The sky was the same serene blue. The soft greens of the grass still blended with the darker greens of the trees and the gray granite boulders pushing up through the earth. The light breezes still carried the wild, sweet fragrances as well as city smells. Beautiful couples still threw Frisbees. But Bronte felt alone and lost and unable to find joy in the children's creative antics at the playground.

A solitary little boy with copper curls, who looked just as alone and left out as she felt, was digging in a sandpile with a blue shovel. For want of anything better to do, she sat down and watched him build mighty castles and towers.

An hour later, when he got up and began kicking them to bits, she decided to leave.

"Don't go. Stay and watch me dig, miss."

She hadn't thought he'd even noticed her.

"But you're done."

His green eyes widened.

He had Jimmy's eyes.

"I'm starting over, miss."

He had been playing by himself, pretending not to see her. As she met his urgent green eyes, she realized how much her being there had meant to him. She remembered how Jimmy had liked her to watch him.

The little boy smiled shyly.

Jimmy's smile.

He said, "Please stay. I don't like playing alone."

It seemed to her suddenly that she had been alone her entire life, except for those brief years when she'd been Jimmy's mommy. After the little boy's request to stay, nothing could have made her leave, for nothing mattered more than her staying there and watching him.

So fascinated was she by the child that when the back of her neck prickled, she didn't think of the stranger. She merely brushed her hand through her red curls.

"Okay. I like watching you dig," she said.

The boy laughed when she climbed on the rock wall and asked him what he was going to build next.

"Disneyland."

"That'll take awhile."

"I'm fast," he bragged shamelessly. "Better than any of the other kids."

She stayed there until his pretty, blond mother pushed a stroller up and declared it was time to go.

He protested as all boys do, saying he wasn't finished, but his mother took him by the hand and led him away anyway. While Bronte watched them go, he shot her a backward glance. Waving, she felt a longing to have another child and to be a mother again. She wanted to be loved…

No. Quickly, very quickly, she suppressed those thoughts.

To love was to risk.

Never again.

When the boy and his mother vanished and Bronte was alone once more, she felt the warm, prickly feeling at the back of her neck again.

For no reason at all she thought of the handsome stranger with the Indian-dark hair and Garth Brown's carved face.

Terrified, she turned, half expecting, half hoping…

She saw only thick forest and a quiet pond.

Then a breeze blew sand all around the boy's buildings.

Her terror died. But so did that strangely expectant rush of unwanted excitement.

As she headed back to the sidewalk, a tall, rangy,

big-boned man watched her. His smile came and went, and somehow his face was left harder and meaner afterward. His skin was brown and tough and so tightly pulled across his forehead that she could see the shape of his skull. Beneath his collar hung a bright red tie.

When she shivered, the cruel smile came and went again. Then he ducked out of sight. She had the uneasy feeling he had been watching her.

It took her a minute to remember and reassure herself that she was arrestingly beautiful now. That she had the face of two promiscuous goddesses.

As she hurried past where the stranger had stood, she decided that perhaps she had overreacted. She was not used to the kinds of stares and interest her gorgeous new looks or possibly Mischief's reputation aroused.

What if she were disfigured instead of arrestingly beautiful? Suddenly she remembered all the patients she'd met in Webster's clinic in Costa Rica and felt ashamed for feeling sorry for herself. So many of them had been permanently maimed. When she had been a child she had prayed every night to grow up and look like her mother.

Be careful what you wish for.

At least her health had been restored.

At least she was beautiful.

She remembered the way her mother had walked down the streets of New York—head held high, a supremely confident smile lighting her exquisite face. Madame had expected admiration, craved it, demanded it. Trailing along behind her, Bronte had shyly noted the awed stares. Nobody had ever looked at her back then except with kindly tolerance and pity.

And she had dreamed, oh, how she had dreamed of growing up and being lovely and glamorous, too.

Well, now, miraculously, she was.

Bronte felt strangely confident as she hailed a cab and told the cabbie to take her to lower Manhattan and Trinity Church. As her taxi fought its way into the stream of jammed automobiles and buses, she thought that, as always, everybody in the city seemed to be in a frantic rush.

There were so many people, so many cars—all going so many places. Maybe that was why she didn't notice the man who stepped out of the trees and hailed a cab as soon as she got into hers. Nor did she notice when his cab stopped half a block behind her when she got out at Trinity Church.

The vaulted interior of the church seemed medieval. After the rush of the modern city, the solemn quiet inside those cool stone walls soothed her. She hadn't been in a church since Jimmy's funeral. She hadn't been able to pray since that day, either.

Immediately she knew she had been right to come here. She felt different. More open. She was grateful for her life. Maybe this time she wouldn't feel so dead inside when she asked for help.

Wrapped up in her concerns as she was, she never heard a man step inside, or his hushed footsteps behind her.

When she sat down near the front of the church, he took a back pew.

When she laced her slim fingers together and lowered her bright head to try to ask God to help her to accept her new face and teach her to confront the challenges in her life instead of letting them defeat her as they had in the past, the man's cynical eyes turned to shards of black ice.

Chantal at prayer?

Chantal with a look of serenity on her face after she left the church?

The whole afternoon had been damned odd. His response to her had been odder.

From the moment Jack had spotted Chantal lurking outside her own apartment, looking like a lost child who'd forgotten her key, everything she'd done and everything she'd said had surprised him.

Still, when she'd left the church and headed back uptown in another cab, Jack had no choice but to follow her.

Not that he wasn't getting sick of their cat-and-mouse game.

First they'd had their little chat on the sidewalk and she'd pretended not to know him. Then she'd watched the kid with the blue shovel.

Next Chantal had gone to Trinity Church. After that she'd made a dozen calls from public phones. Where the hell was her limo? Last he heard super-models lived on cellular phones.

What the hell would she pull next? he wondered, as raindrops began to splatter the windshield.

When her yellow cab reached fashionable Park Avenue once again, she jumped out a block or two short of her apartment. For a second she just stood there looking as lost and confused as that frightened child again, staring up at the black sky with those big eyes of hers and letting the rain soak her. Only when a laughing crowd of young people burst out of a fancy club across the street, their umbrellas exploding like brightly colored parachutes, did Chantal seem to decide what to do next.

She took a minute to read the neon sign above the exclusive bar. Then, after cautiously waiting for the light to change when there wasn't a car to be seen for a block, she ran lightly across the street and vanished into the club.

Jack felt a sudden, powerful thirst.

Why a bar?

She never went without sex long. No doubt this was where she picked up the men she took home.

Still, he was baffled.

So much about her seemed different.

Of course, he still wasn't used to her new face.

But she'd changed even more since she'd come back from France.

When he'd held her today, nothing about her except the color of her hair and eyes and her perfume had seemed like the old Chantal.

And what was she doing running around all day without bodyguards? How come she'd pounced on him like that and then acted terrified, all the while pretending not to know him?

He still couldn't get over the way she'd watched that little boy in the park, either. And Jack had never known her to pass out spare change to street people.

Hell, she'd stayed in the church for a damn hour, the whole time looking as pure and sweet as a troubled angel.

Nothing about her behavior today added up. She was like a completely changed person. If he hadn't stripped her naked in Paris and seen the scar, he'd never have believed she was Chantal.

All he knew for sure was that he was damned tired of trying to figure her out.

The bar would be dark and loud.

Before she could hit on a stranger or sic the cops on him, or he gave in to the temptation to drink, he'd grab her.

Chapter 7

Gone was the brave new Bronte who had emerged from Trinity Church. The Bronte who had felt spiritually inspired to accept her new face as a gift. And not to question it.

Panic surged in her as the rain beat down.

For rain always made her remember the day when she had lost everything.

Like a frightened animal seeking cover, she darted inside the mobbed bar, racing past half-a-dozen round tables of solitary men in an attempt to vanish quickly into the bar's neon-lighted, smoky depths.

She didn't know this was a frequent haunt of Mischief Jones. That sometimes when Mischief was on the prowl she came here to find men. That usually she headed straight for the pool tables.

Bronte didn't feel the dozen pairs of wolfish, male eyes devouring her body as she slipped past them.

She was early, the men thought. *She must be hot for it.*

A new tension wired every single one in the bar when she walked straight past the pool tables, past the men grouped there. Automatically they stood a little straighter; they stuffed wrinkled shirts back into their trousers; they finger-combed their hair. They lit cigarettes or squashed them out.

Not that Bronte felt the electric expectancy of their mood. She was still trying to absorb what Webster had done. She'd been robbed of her own identity and given someone else's. Every time she thought of Mischief, she felt so guilty she was glad she hadn't been able to reach her. The last time Bronte had called, a woman had answered and said Mischief was expecting guests tonight and would be far too busy to see her.

"Tell her Webster Quinn..." Bronte had lost her courage. "Never mind. I'll call back later."

Bronte needed to make that call. Instead, oblivious to her many admirers, she went to the bar and ordered a margarita. When a dark hand shot out and manacled her wrist, she cried out. The face leering into hers was thin and brown. The man's overlong, chopped tufts of black hair hung over his wire-rimmed glasses. When he smiled, his leathery skin made deep creases on either side of his mouth. His teeth were as yellow as old piano keys, and his breath stank of stale beer and cigarettes.

She shrank from him.

"I missed you, baby. We had some good times together, playing pool and other stuff—remember?"

"I don't play pool."

"You ran the table." He slid his stool closer and

slapped a crumpled five-dollar bill on the bar. "This one is on me, Miss Jones. For old times' sake."

She pushed his money away, shaking her head so fiercely that raindrops flew at him from her red hair.

"I never saw you before in my life, and if you don't leave me alone, I'll call the police." She turned away as the bartender set a frozen margarita in front of her.

Other men with heavy-lidded, smoke-stained eyes and teeth to match noted the little exchange with surprise. The woman they knew usually wasn't so choosy.

Bronte was cold and wet. When she started to shiver, a thin-faced man with a wispy goatee decided to try his luck. Shuffling behind her, he grinned boozily as he held out a limp jacket with a trembling hand. The jacket reeked of sweat and bourbon and cigarettes.

"What you looking for, baby?"

She shook her head, hating her new face more than ever. "Go, away. Please."

Suddenly she crossed her arms on the bar and laid her forehead on her wrist. The bartender signaled the bouncer.

She knew she should get out of here.

But she wasn't ready to face the city. Or the rain. Or herself. Or her mother's face.

A few minutes later the band began to play, and the female singer, who wore a long black gown, began to sing a particular song from Bronte's past. The first husky notes from the sultry brunette made Bronte forget her new face and admirers. Her fingers clenched tightly around her empty glass. With green eyes frozen in pain, she slowly lifted her head to stare at the singer.

Out of nowhere came the memory of that hospital aide's remark when she'd been stroking Jimmy's cool, waxen face after they told her he was gone.

All your kid had was a nick in his temporal artery. Why didn't you just apply pressure, lady?

Of all the bars in New York, why had she walked into this one? No other song could have brought back such bittersweet anguish. Bronte used to dance with Bryan and Jimmy to that tune every afternoon. Jimmy had had only to hear it to come running into her arms, demanding to be picked up and whirled about their living room.

He had been so full of life.

Bronte's face drained of color. She tried to swallow, but her throat was too tight. She put her hands over her ears and squeezed her eyes shut, but time ticked backward anyway.

Then a frightening sound—a hoarse sob—rose from deep inside her. She knew she'd lost all control. For the first time since her accident, scalding tears streamed down her cheeks.

Helplessly, Bronte saw Jimmy smiling up at her from the kitchen doorway as he'd picked up his skateboard that fatal afternoon, laughing mischievously when she'd chided him for wearing such ragged jeans and begged him not to go out because even though the sun was shining, the sidewalk might be too slippery.

When the notes of the familiar melody faded between stanzas, Bronte wept even harder as she remembered how she'd found his board lying upside down in the muddy gutter. As she remembered Bryan trying to force his way into the surgery suite hours later to see his little boy after the doctor told him he was gone. Most of all she remembered the way Bryan had tried to comfort her at the funeral as the casket lid was closed. He hadn't understood why she'd pushed him away and refused to let him hold her that day and for weeks afterward. She hadn't understood why grief wasn't harder for him.

Not that Bryan had ever done more than gently criticize. Not that she had hated him for being able to go on. But she had cut herself off from him, and the palpable silence had created an ever-expanding void until every intimacy of their fragile marriage had been devoured by it. Finally, Bryan, who was needy himself, had lost patience and turned to someone who hadn't given up on life as she had.

The lyrics expressed a deep and profound sadness for the lives of men and women who had loved and dreamed and hoped, who had made promises they couldn't keep. For men and women who had loved and lost and could never be whole again. As the singer's voice rose and grew more passionate and pain filled, Bronte's heart swelled with her own private grief. She'd loved her son and missed him more than anything.

Shrieks of male laughter erupted from a nearby table.

Bronte was sobbing, with no thought for where she was or who she was, when the thin man with the black bangs and yellow teeth put a familiar hand on her shoulder.

"Miss Jones, I've got just what you need."

"Please, would you just leave me alone?" she begged.

But when her would-be companion edged drunkenly closer and dug his hand into her waist, she pushed at him. "Please, I'll scream if you don't—"

"You needa shoulder to cry on—"

She couldn't stop sobbing even when she felt the presence of another man behind her.

They were like sharks.

"She's with me," drawled a deep voice.

Bronte stilled as a wave of heat warmed the back of her neck. For no reason at all she conjured Garth Brown's face as she had so many other lonely nights. Her knees went shaky; her stomach knotted. Slowly, as if in a dream, she turned.

Never in all her life had she wanted to be by herself so much as she had a few seconds before. Suddenly, even though she was terrified of the stranger from the park who stood there with his movie-star face, and of those eyes that held the same kind of dark pain she'd known, never had she felt such a fierce need to be with anybody else.

How could she feel such a profound desire to touch or be held—but only by *him?*

No matter how much he looked like a certain screen idol, this man was a stranger.

He had been fierce and terrifying on the sidewalk.

He still was—with his ice-black eyes and harsh face. And yet she sensed that underneath his anger, he was kind.

This man was intense as Bryan had not been.

He was her double's lover.

Through the thick blur of her tears she made out the same broad shoulders and lean hips and crisp black hair. The same white shirt and jeans. The same wonderfully carved features, which were rugged and hard and yet beautiful, too.

His shirtsleeves were rolled up now.

Their eyes met and locked. He frowned as if she confused him, too.

He was clean-cut compared to the other man beside her. Still, she suspected he was by far the more dangerous.

She knew she should run.

Blindly, she tried to rush past him, but he caught her and yanked her into his arms.

"Hey, hey—truce," he offered gently. "Go ahead and cry it out."

"Let me go."

His hands fell to his sides. "Okay."

Again she knew she should run. But she hesitated. Involuntarily she found herself grabbing handfuls of his starchy shirt with shaky fingertips and burying her face against his chest.

The man with the yellow teeth scowled as she sought comfort from the stranger.

Through soft cotton she felt the man's muscles. His skin was warm, his heart steady. He was so tall and so powerfully built that he made her feel small and infinitely feminine.

Swallowing tears that were thick and salty, she lifted her cheek from his shoulder and attempted a fluttery smile. "I feel like a fool. My grandmother used to tell me there wasn't any use crying over things that can't be changed."

"Somebody told me that once," he whispered, pulling her closer so that she could bury her face against his broad chest again and make big, wet, wrinkly splotches on his shirt. "Go ahead and cry. Who knows—maybe your grandmother will be wrong this time.''

His hands stroked her hair as she wept. When she was done, she levered herself away from his lean body.

As soon as she was free of him, she felt his heated gaze. What little light there was came from behind him. His white shirt glowed pink from a neon sign, emphasizing the width of his shoulders; the rest of him was in darkness.

She knew she probably looked awful, that her face must be red and swollen. Even though his carved features were hidden in darkness, she sensed the return of his grim mood.

But his stillness told her that he understood her pain.

''What's the matter?'' he demanded.

''I was thinking about the past. About all that went wrong. I was blaming myself for what happened—as usual.''

''That's damn sure a new one.''

He thought he knew her. But he didn't.

''Maybe for you. Not for me.'' She lapsed into an uneasy silence for a moment. ''I'm sorry. I probably ruined your shirt. What are you doing here, anyway? I didn't think I'd ever see you again.''

''You wish, don't you, baby?''

He ordered a whiskey for himself and another margarita for her. He brought his glass to his lips. Suddenly he slammed his drink back down on the bar and sent it flying away with a violence that startled her. And yet he never took his eyes off her—as if he was more afraid of her than he was of the contents in the glass.

Her margarita was strong. Too strong. Even as she lifted her glass again, she knew it was unwise to drink more.

"Thank you...for holding me a while ago."

"No problem."

"I lost it. You were kind."

His brows arched cynically as he ordered a lime water.

When the band struck the opening bars of another sad song, the flashing strobe light became a glistening ball that splashed the room with a million diamonds. The song was too sad to sit through. And suddenly he seemed less dangerous than a whole lot of other things—like loneliness and her new face and the real Mischief.

"Dance with me," Bronte whispered, desperately draining her drink. When he tossed his lime water down and shoved back from the bar, she laid her hand over his.

The minute her shy fingertips touched his, a shudder passed through them both. His callused hand coiled tightly around hers. "Hey, what is this?" he demanded warily.

"I just want to dance. That's all."

His eyes burned her. "Sure."

He yanked her closer, but not that close. How could the merest brush of her body against his be so electrifying?

He felt it, too.

"You're in a strange mood," he murmured with sudden huskiness. And yet with fury, too.

"I've had a really, really rough day. Then you come along looking like...a movie star."

Once again his grip relaxed, his mood, too. "Just

call me Hollywood." His other hand slid around her waist, imprisoning her against his body. She didn't like the way his manner was overtly familiar, but then he thought they'd been lovers. He was in for a surprise. She'd lose him—later.

"Okay," he said hoarsely, angrily. "I'll dance."

He snugged her tight against his thighs and pushed his jean-clad leg between hers. His gaze darkened.

He was holding her too close. Too late she realized that her confusion had made her too vulnerable and too forward.

She grew even more alarmed when he began to sway with her to the hot, pulsating music. Belly-to-belly. Hip-to-hip. Beneath the whirling lights, they undulated to the throbbing tempo like a jungle couple.

Bronte had never danced like this in her life. Not even with Bryan. She knew she should stop.

"Not here," she finally whispered. He laughed harshly and pulled her closer.

"The dance floor is over there," she whispered weakly, pointing to the wooden square of parquet tiles near the door. "Not like this—"

"I'm surprised you give a damn."

Dear God. What was Mischief like? What things did this man believe she was capable of?

The song got sadder and the beat stronger, and her memories made her cling to him despite her fears.

"You know I never was much of a dancer," he murmured as he wrapped her in his arms and led her with heavy, long strides toward the dance floor. "Nobody taught me the finer things down in Mexico."

Mexico?

"I don't know any such thing," she said.

His hand slid up her shoulder to her throat. Then

he lifted her chin, forcing her face closer to his. "You'd better watch yourself, baby. You used to know not to push it. This could get dangerous."

He was so right. Too much was happening too fast, but the two margaritas had gone to her head. So had the music and the man. She felt alive. Achingly, pulsatingly alive for the first time in years. Shy with him and yet bold, too.

Too late she remembered that she was in a very big city. That nice girls didn't drown their woes by drinking in bars and then coming on to a virtual stranger. A stranger who believed himself to be her lover. This anger-filled man who thought he knew her could be anybody and could want anything from her.

She felt hot.

He was hotter.

No matter how he might try to act like he wasn't.

She'd known so much pain. Was it so wrong to dance one dance with a handsome stranger in a public place?

The drums beat hard and fast, and as she melted into his body, she felt the electric tension between them quicken and wind tighter.

"Baby, you're playing with fire."

"Maybe you are, too."

"The difference is I have no choice."

"Neither do I," she said.

"We're crazy, you know that?"

"This city—what it does to people."

He'd lied when he'd said he couldn't dance. He shimmied with her, dipping her so low her red hair swept the floor and then easily pulling her up into his strong, hard arms again. The steady friction of his leg moving between hers caused the fierce explosive heat inside them both to flame hotter.

The music got faster.

Their bodies slowed.

Feeling the urge to touch him, she skimmed his face in the darkness with her fingertips. As she lightly traced the shape of his jaw, she heard his quick, indrawn breath.

"Don't push it." His voice was tight.

Her pointed nipples burned through her damp blouse and brushed his chest.

"I said stop," he whispered in that same urgent, tight tone. When she just stood there, swaying to the beat, his hands snaked into her wet, tangled hair, bringing her face and her lips within an inch of his.

When she wrapped his neck with her hands, she felt his pulse beating beneath her fingertips.

"You think you know all my weaknesses, and you're willing to use them against me. Since that first day when you called my mother a *puta* and threw that snake at me, you pushed. You knew I got started in the gutter, that I grew up with sex all around me. Sometimes my mother wouldn't even send me out when she had a customer. You knew I wanted to reject that kind of life, that I wanted my woman to mean more than just that. Still, you know I'm too damned primitive and too damned Mexican to ever be the kind of polished gentleman Maverick and his college friends were, the kind your mother wanted for you. You know I can't always cover my feelings with a civilized veneer. You knew that even though I'd lived so rough and wild, what I really wanted in a woman was gentleness and sweetness. So you've decided to tease me tonight and pretend—"

No. She hadn't known any of those things. She didn't know him.

"You probably even know I haven't had a woman since prison. I haven't even had a drink. That I'd get hot if you teased—"

Prison!

The cuffs of his long-sleeved shirt were rolled to his elbows. Too late Bronte saw the crudely tattooed hunting knife on his muscular forearm.

No commercial tattoo, that one. There was a raw, nasty power to it, a stark, unpolished simplicity. His tattoo had definitely been done on the inside.

He was an ex-con. He'd grown up in a whorehouse. He thought she was Mischief Jones, a woman who thought nothing of picking men up on street corners and in bars.

He and she existed in totally separate realities.

And yet...they didn't.

"Wait..." Little by little, reality was filtering in as she studied the slightly crooked, dark blue lines of the knife etched into his brown skin.

"You asked for this, baby..."

The strobe lights flashed, momentarily illuminating his hard, dark face and then casting it into shadow. His insolent black eyes burned deeply into her, down to some inner core that was real and true. And yet in that same moment, when Bronte felt her soul bonded to his, she knew how darkly she was hated.

But the knowledge came too late.

He was over the edge.

So was she.

As his mouth loomed closer, she felt dizzily bewildered and yet on fire with need, wanting nothing more than the intimate wetness of his lips on hers.

He could be taking her to heaven or to hell. She wasn't sure which, and she wasn't sure she cared.

She felt alive.

So alive that the furious impact of his hard mouth upon hers staggered them both.

The music ended. Not that they noticed.

The next song was wilder.

Spontaneous combustion consumed them. He stopped dancing and fused himself to her. She felt the dance floor tilt, so she clung to him.

His hard hands tightened around her. Desire made her weak and hot. With a carnal moan, she parted her lips and let his tongue come in.

Swift hot blood pounded through her in a deafening roar, blocking out her awareness of everything except him. Somehow her passion was all mixed-up with his hate. For a timeless moment, neither of them could stop devouring the other's mouth and tongue. His leg was still between hers, pushing tighter, closer. She parted her legs. The flimsy barrier of their jeans might as well have been nonexistent. She felt the heat of his skin pouring into her.

She wanted more. More. More. So much more. Everything from him.

So did he.

His kisses made her tremble as he half lifted and half backed her forcefully into a corner. When he imprisoned her there, her hands moved urgently down his back, over his waist, pulling him closer—if that was possible. Then she threw back her head and let his lips begin a heated journey from her mouth down her throat and then lower down the front of her damp blouse to her berry-tipped nipples protruding against wet cotton.

When she felt the warm gentleness of his mouth sucking at her breasts above the cups of her lacy brassiere, she wrapped his head with her hands and combed her fingers through his thick black hair.

Yes. Yes.

No. No.

Heaven and hell.

Shrouded in darkness as they were, no one could see them.

The tempo of the music got wilder and wilder.

She had forgotten where she was. Who she was. She became the wild, dark creature he imagined her to be. Someone she had never been before.

His tongue flicked roughly, hungrily, lustfully at the tips of her nipples. His kisses were like lightning bolts—sizzling bursts of sensations followed each one.

Her breathing became choppy and loud. Tears of joy and tenderness filled her.

"Say my name," he commanded. "Say Jack."

Jack? Jack who?

Funny how all she could do was obey him.

"Jack...Jack...Jack..."

Everything he did, everything he said was so erotic and suggestive that her emotions and needs were spiraling out of control.

She didn't care who he was. Or where he'd been. Or who he thought she was.

Underneath all his anger, underneath the dark torment of his soul, she sensed someone who was fragile and sweet and dear. Someone who was hard on the outside but gentle and good deep down. Someone who had known the same kind of terror and emptiness and loss that she had known. Someone who needed the same things she needed.

Someone who had been dead and was now, at least for this instant, excitingly alive.

All he'd done was kiss her. But she already wanted him so much.

She wanted him—forever. With his eyes and mouth and hands and body, he spoke to her on some deep, nonverbal and nonphysical level.

When she finally opened her eyes, he was gazing directly into them. For a fraction of a moment she lost her soul in that look.

Then his expression hardened.

"Damn you," he said. "Damn you to hell and back, Chantal."

His words and his glare were more brutal than a slap.

She remembered her new face and his prison tattoo.

And to be terrified of him.

Chapter 8

"Damn you," Jack muttered thickly again as he tore his mouth from her wet, soft flesh.

She was moaning like an animal in heat. Sex alone could never have aroused him so powerfully. But the sad music had opened his shuttered heart and exposed his bruised psyche. Music always made him yearn for love.

She was so sweet he could still taste her. Still, it had been the combination of that song and her tears, as well as the luminous pain lingering in her eyes, that had melted his anger for that insane time. He had seen so much sorrow and uncertainty and regret in those shining eyes. So much regret. All the things he'd felt and known and understood.

He should never have held her or danced with her. But he'd seen how the sad song had affected her. Music had a way of making his feelings bubble to the top, too. Images, buried deep and long forgotten, had seared his mind with startling clarity.

But it wasn't just the music. It was her, too. Incredibly, she had made him feel again.

The swollen ache between his legs was so hot and fierce he could barely stand. But the inexplicable tenderness he felt for this vulnerable-seeming woman he believed to be his wife was way more dangerous than his desire.

Never had he felt half so much for her, but his anger at himself overrode all else now as he fought a losing battle for control.

He was a dead man. Way past any hope of resurrection.

Nothing is changed. Nothing.

"Why did you stop?" she asked, backing away and looking so scared and uncertain he wanted to take her in his arms and reassure her.

He caught the faint fragrance of wild gardenias.

"One of us had to. We're in public—a fact that probably turns you on."

"No. I—I shouldn't have asked you to dance. It's just so much has happened to me. I needed..." Again she spoke in that soft voice he'd never heard her use before, the voice that twisted him into knots. That made him want to protect her. "Why am I telling you this?" Then she wet her lips with her tongue as if to taste what was left of him on her mouth.

As a kid he'd watched whores do that in bleak, dusty streets. He'd watched his mother do worse in that narrow bed beside his.

Chantal's licking her mouth that way sent his male hormones into overdrive. He wanted nothing more than to slam her against the wall and push himself into her and finish their rotten game. The same way people did it every day and every night in the barrios. Like animals.

Slam. Bam. No next time, ma'am.

"Damn it. Don't do that," he said.

"What?" she whispered looking nervous and scared again.

"The tongue bit..."

Her eyes widened. She stopped instantly, afraid.

That darling face of hers was tearing him in two. All he wanted was to hold her again, to savor the sweet, strange feelings she aroused, the first sweetness and tenderness he'd felt in years. The first he'd ever felt from her.

She was afraid; he wanted to protect her.

Damn. Reality check. This was Chantal. She'd slept with everybody. His friends. His enemies. Maverick. His cowboys. And that piece of slime who'd died in the barn, whose body had been charred to a crisp. She hadn't discriminated. Jack had stuck with her because of some idealistic, perverse, bulldog determination to save her or to change her and make their marriage work.

He'd spent five years in prison because of her. She'd cost him his soul. She could have come forward. But, no, she'd been too busy jetting to Europe. Too busy cruising for new lovers. He was through with her forever.

This whole trick today was a brilliant piece of modeling or acting.

He had to get a grip—fast. Before he really started believing there was a chance he could get from her all those things that were even more dangerous than sex—which was bad enough.

All he had ever wanted was to settle down with a woman he loved, have kids and work the ranch. But Chantal had been bored with all that. She had wanted sex from him, sure. The wilder the better. She had wanted him because she had thought he was low class. She had wanted lots of men. And maybe some part of him had thought he deserved no better than that.

Not that this beautiful girl with the loose, red tendrils falling against her rosily angelic face, this nymph in the damp white blouse and skintight jeans, seemed a thing like the old Chantal.

He knew he shouldn't stare, but he couldn't quit. Once, he would have sold his soul to have her kiss him like this. Instead, on their wedding night she had torn him with her claws and teeth—like an animal.

How the hell could she look like an angel when he knew how she'd lived?

He remembered how her face had been streaked with tears when he'd first come inside the bar. Damn it. He forced himself to remember the George V and how her eyes had glittered with hellfire when she'd smashed that black stone cat into his jaw.

How could she be so different? So different she seemed like someone else?

So different she could drive him crazier than ever before? Crazy with wanting, needing and hating—and all at once? New York City must have the finest acting schools in the whole damn world.

For his sanity's sake, he needed to get away from her.

But not for a second could he trust her out of his sight.

He needed a drink.

He didn't dare take one.

"How come you went to prison?" she asked fearfully in that soft, new voice that pretended to care.

"Oh, that's rich." Roughly he caught her wrists and yanked her toward the door.

"Where are we going?" she whispered, sounding frightened, as he tightened the grip on her hands.

"Home."

Her look of fear softened him.

Still, somehow he managed to make his voice hard and gruff. "Baby, you never used to go this far and say no."

She went as white as if he'd struck her.

"I'm not...who you think."

So sincere she sounded. So scared and uncertain.

A trick, he told himself. But when his hand clenched around her elbow, her low whimper of pain caught at his heart and gentled him.

He released her instantly. "I didn't mean to hurt you," he said, despising himself when his rough voice became velvet.

His obvious concern threw her off balance, too...as it never would have the old Chantal, who would have despised him even more.

"Look, this has all happened too fast. I like you...." She faltered. "I could like you a lot. At least I think I could. But this isn't what you think, and I've got something important to do now. I can't go anywhere with you. Not tonight, anyway. We need to slow this thing down. Maybe we could exchange phone numbers—"

"Phone numbers?" Careful to avoid her injured elbow, he circled her waist again and shoved her toward the door. "Cut the crap, Chantal, Mischief, whoever you say you are."

Still using that soft voice, she protested again. "I said I like you, but if you don't let me go, I'll scream."

"Scream and I'll give you what you gave me in Paris."

"Paris?" she squeaked, dumbfounded.

He kept half pushing, half hauling her through the cavernous bar.

Suddenly, in a milder tone, the kind she might use to calm a large, dangerous animal, she said, "You'd better let me go, or you're going to be in serious trouble. Look, I don't want this to get ugly. But you could end up in jail again."

"You get off on that, don't you?"

When she tried to twist free, he yanked her more tightly against his body. "I've been in trouble since the first time you sank your vicious little claws into me." He opened the door, pushed her out into the rain. He swore softly. "So what were you trying to prove back there by pretending to pray and to act so saintly in that church?"

His question made her whiten. "You were there, too? You've been following me all day?" she gasped, her pale face looking convincingly shocked. "I—I didn't see you."

"What did you think? Did you really think I wouldn't come after you when I knew where you were?"

The tears that glistened in her eyes only made her more beautiful as she began to struggle. When she opened her mouth to scream, Jack pinioned her against his body.

Two men stepped out of the bar.

Before she could react or make even the smallest sound or try to call for help, Jack's mouth crushed down on hers. His arms wrapped around her as he forced her against his long, lean body.

Again the taste of her both inflamed him and stole his wrath.

A cab skidded to a halt in front of the bar, spilling out a man and a woman, who rushed past them, laughing.

Only when the men and the couple had vanished did the pressure of Jack's mouth on hers ease. But by then, Bronte had sighed and raised her hands tentatively around his neck. Her breath was becoming uneven again, and she was gently quivering and going soft against him as she kissed him back.

Oblivious to the rain, he realized he could stop kissing her now.

Only somehow he couldn't.

Not when her fingertips were brushing the soft black hair on his neck, winding the short strands around her fingers. Not when the pain in his heart was dissolved by her tenderness. Not when his anger was gone, and so was her fear. Not when passion and new yearning for all that he had missed in his life consumed him.

He wanted more. Much more. Somehow nothing mattered but keeping his mouth fused to the soft, wet, responsive warmth of her lips.

Despising her, despising himself even more, he gave himself up and surrendered to what was the hottest, sexiest kiss he'd ever tasted. And the sweetest.

When he slid his tongue inside, she kissed him back with a silent desperation that matched his own, her small hands rushing over his back as she molded herself to him tightly.

He felt her fingertips slide from his collar up his neck to brush his damp face softly.

In the past she'd been wild and abandoned.

But never sweet and tender as she was now. She'd never sucked his heart out of him. She even tasted different.

In the past she would have bitten him when he kissed her. Now her gentle hand was gliding through his wet hair, stroking him in this new way she had never used before. Her mouth was warm velvet. She was moaning, and the emotional sound seemed torn from the depths of her soul.

Slowly and very reluctantly, he forced himself to let her go. But even as he eased her away, he found himself staring at her lovely face, his starved senses clamoring for more.

His confused gaze met and locked with hers. Even the way she looked at him was different. Her face was flushed crimson. Her eyes were as green as ever, but they didn't pierce him like cold daggers.

No. They were dark with fear and yet luminous and tender, too. Her cheeks were aflame.

Before today Chantal had never blushed in her whole damned life. Now she wouldn't quit.

He caught his breath. She made him feel young again, like he was a horny kid on the verge of falling in love with the innocent girl of his dreams.

His heart beat wildly as he remembered how delicious her flesh was to touch, how smooth and soft and warm.

What the hell was he doing? He knew any sexual involvement with Chantal was insane.

And this involvement was more than sexual. His needs were hopelessly profound. Longing with unkind intensity for what might have been filled him.

He brushed her hair back, saw the faintest trace of a scar at her hairline and was reminded of the plastic surgery she'd had, of who she really was and what she'd done.

Chantal had changed her face and let him rot in prison for her murder. She'd lived the high life while one dark night a gang of convicts had held him down and stripped him and tried to... Then Brickhouse had come at the last moment, and together, somehow, they'd fought them off.

But just barely. And all the while Chantal had continued her old tricks, but on a grander scale.

He remembered Paris. No matter how sweet she looked or acted tonight, she was the same.

"Damn it," he snarled, his voice harsh in his pain.

Remembering his purpose, he caught her arm, his hold as strong as a python's as he pushed her unresisting body toward the cab. After their kiss, the fight seemed to have gone out of her, too. She even opened the door and fell limply inside, without him having to force her.

He was about to slide in beside her, but she came to life like a dozing cat to sudden danger, slamming the door on his hand. Then, clubbing at the tips of his trapped fingers with her purse, she screamed, "Cabbie! This lunatic is trying to kidnap me!"

Pain knifed from his knuckles up his nerve endings as she squeezed the door harder.

"Let go, Jack," she pleaded. "I don't want to hurt you."

"She's my wife!" Jack yelled at the driver.

"I never saw him before in my life!"

"She's my wife, damn it!"

"I tell you, I don't know him!"

The cabbie, who had probably had more than his share of trouble with loonies, wasn't taking any chances.

He probably thought he could handle a tall, pretty girl.

But a powerfully built man with crazed eyes and hate-contorted features was a different matter.

"Step away from the car, buddy!"

"Hey, don't you dare drive off with my wife—"

"Please let go, Jack—"

The bulky driver stomped down hard on the accelerator and the cab shot forward into the darkness, swinging the door so hard onto Jack's hand that he fell back yelping in pain as tires spewed muddy water all over his jeans and boots.

He cursed violently and then stopped when he saw her beautiful, tear-ravaged face pressed against the back window. She was staring at him with those huge, bewildered eyes—as if she genuinely regretted hurting him.

Dear God. He felt all the pain and loss and longing in her soul as she stared at him.

His heart hammered in deep, aching beats. His palms were sweaty.

Damn her for making him feel so drawn to her all over again.

He tried to tell himself that she had sneaked up on his blind side because she was the only woman he'd held since he got out of prison. But that rationalization didn't play.

"Damn."

She'd outsmarted him again.

He opened and closed his bruised, aching fingers.

There were a few scratches on his knuckles, but no bones seemed to be broken.

At least all she'd hit him with was a purse. She probably could have crushed his hand with the door if she'd wanted to. But she hadn't. She'd begged him not to make her hurt him.

Begged.

In the past, Chantal had relished inflicting pain.

After Paris his jaws had been wired together for a month. He wouldn't soon forget the contorted, maniacal expression on her face right before she'd clipped him with that bookend.

Why was she so nice now?

Hell, he was through trying to figure her out.

He knew what she was and where she lived.

He'd catch her.

And when he did, she'd pay.

Chapter 9

She's my wife.

He had been so passionate and angry when he'd said that. So possessive.

And she…

She'd just met him.

She'd felt dead for years.

How could she feel anything for him?

But she did. Churning emotions.

Bronte was still hot and shaky all over. It was as if after being dead at the center so long, some pent-up life force had exploded inside her the moment she'd met him.

She was afraid of him and yet excited, too. She felt relief to know that she could still feel, that she was alive, and yet regret for all that had gone wrong before.

How was it possible that with a man she didn't

even know, she had felt something so rare, something so tender and fine and true?

It had been a gift.

A gift she wasn't really ready to receive.

Some irrational and wildly romantic part of her truly wished she had met him some other way. In some future time.

All he'd done was kiss her.

No. That wasn't all.

He'd stirred her soul.

He'd tried to kidnap her.

Because he thought she was his wife.

Stop defending him. He was Mischief's problem. Not hers.

Chantal? Mischief? Her mother? How many more...

When Bronte stepped out of the cab under the gold-tasseled canopy of Mischief Jones's apartment building, she was still stunned from his kiss and wrestling with her confused emotions.

Her stomach knotted.

Trembling, she brushed her knuckles across her lips. They felt raw and feverish.

Never ever had she been swept away so recklessly. He hated her. She had to remember that. He'd been rude and hostile. Maybe he looked like her favorite star, but he was dangerous.

No, *he* had a name. Jack.

Jack...

She had to put *Jack* completely out of her mind. Forever.

Right. Forget the unforgettable.

A limousine pulled up in front of her cab. A young blonde in white satin and wristfuls of diamonds got out and then helped an old man, who was probably immensely rich, out of the car, too.

As Bronte rummaged in her purse for cab fare, she knew she wasn't likely to forget Jack anytime soon. His effect on her had been more than anything she'd ever felt for Bryan. Maybe that was only because she was overwrought from all that had happened....

After paying the cabbie, Bronte strolled regally up the plush length of gold-trimmed, red carpet that led to the building's stone stairs. Her slim nose thrust self-consciously in the air, she moved with the hauteur and long-legged grace Webster had taught her.

Three doormen with gold collars and starched dickies rushed to help her up the stairs. A set of iron-grilled doors were thrown open for her.

"Good evening, Miss Jones. We thought you'd already gone up."

She barely acknowledged them. Stepping past them, she paused to clamp her purse shut and get her bearings.

"Some party you're throwing tonight," one of the doormen offered.

She didn't trust herself to speak for fear her voice might betray her. Instead she gave him a little condescending nod, the kind her mother used to give anyone she considered her inferior.

A second set of doors made of heavy glass and edged in polished brass were held open for her. Inside an opulent lobby of pink marble and crystal chandeliers, she felt even more like a fraud as two uniformed men waved her past security and video cameras toward a bank of elevators.

Her heart was racing like a rabbit's as she pushed the Up button and the doors opened.

The elevator was paneled in old mahogany that had been waxed till it glowed. Not that she had time to get used to the luxury. Within seconds she was whisked up ten floors.

When the brass doors opened into Mischief's opulent elevator vestibule, Bronte was hit by waves of throbbing music and high-pitched voices, punctuated by shrill laughter. The air itself seemed to pulse with frenetic energy. She saw the blonde and the old man again.

Mischief's dimly lit apartment, even the vestibule, was packed with the gaudily rich and the fun rich—famous actors and models, agents and photographers, as well as leading fashion editors and designers. Territorial people, fierce, self-absorbed people. Superficial people who loved fashion, who used clothes and interior design as an art form to define themselves and others. Rivals who fought like cats and dogs over every scrap of publicity, over every shoot, over every big-name model, every potential star, every assignment; petty people who pretended to love each other on nights such as this one, while they sought new means to gut each other professionally.

Naturally, nearly every woman was fashionably anorexic and dressed in some fashion absurdity with puffed sleeves or huge ruffles. Sexy nobodies had been invited to admire the rich and the famous. For how can one dazzle if there is no one to be dazzled?

Somebody had opened a vault. Slim wrists and throats and fingers flashed with fiery jewels. Everybody was drinking too much and shouting too loudly, each person wanting to stand out from the crowd.

Thankfully, nobody could hear half of what was being said, since the pulsing rock music drowned all of them out.

Bare-chested waiters with shaved heads and slave collars served sushi and champagne from silver trays.

When a thin man with intense gray-blue eyes and silver-rimmed glasses grabbed her elbow, Bronte had to fight the instinct to run.

As he leaned close and blew her a series of rapid-fire air kisses, the elevator closed behind her like a trap door. "Jeans? Ah, dah-ling, but *you* can wear anything."

Bronte smiled at him.

"You're looking so-o-o wonderful. Fresher, younger. Even better than you looked four years ago on our first shoot. You remember—the beaches? Normandy? You were so perfect. I'll never forget your skin, your neck, your legs...your breasts. And what we did in that cave. You have the most perverted sexual imagination of any woman I have ever met."

His voice was abrupt and yet speedy, but Bronte felt hot with embarrassment when his eyes flashed over her body and then stared pointedly at her breasts.

"You are still so exotic, so mysterious. And tonight you are quite exceptional. Simply sensational. If only I had my camera, I would ask you to strip for me the way you did that day in the cave—"

Bronte gasped.

"George..."

He shouted to the beauty who called to him, blew Bronte another series of air kisses and moved away.

Bronte had no idea who George was. He had made her blush and feel extremely uncomfortable.

A tall, African-American man with bronzed shoulders was staring holes through her. There was a disturbing blend of hostility and familiarity in his smoldering eyes as he set his tray of sushi down right beside her. Afraid he'd grab her or do worse, Bronte found an opening in the crowd and escaped.

When he tried to leap after her, a young woman threw her arms around him and licked his cheek with her long pink tongue. He was forced to stop. Bronte ran from them, knowing she was out of her element.

And always she searched the sea of garishly made-up faces and overdressed figures for a face whose savagely sculpted, cat-like features were identical to her own.

It was early, but the party's wild atmosphere held a dangerous, anything-goes edge. Bronte moved deeper into the starkly glamorous co-op. The apartment's trendy furnishings were in sharp contrast with the elegant French decor of the public rooms downstairs. Here the angular walls were covered in dark red and black silk. Heavy moldings framed high ceilings. The spare furnishings were a macabre blend of classic and modern. Huge paintings done in a style typical of Van Gogh were of tortured countenances and horrifying landscapes.

Candles burned from wall sconces and flickered in every window. Yet despite these bright, wavering flames that cast long dancing shadows, a feeling of soul-deep coldness permeated the rooms. The guests' cruel jokes bit without humor; their brittle laughter sounded cracked and cold. This was a house that exuded money, ambition and fine material things, but held no warmth or love.

In another room Catholic candelabra and antique silver picture frames covered the ebony surface of a miles-long grand piano. Dozens of pictures of Mischief wearing either red or black emblazoned the four walls. Above the fireplace was that last famous photograph of Bronte's mother, Madame, dressed entirely in red for her last performance as Carmen.

Bronte had seen most of these pictures before—only they had been slashed and had lain in curling fragments on the floor of Webster's study. Again she noticed how cold the lifeless eyes were as they followed her from room to room.

There were souvenirs from Mischief's shoots. Huge sabres and knives lay on tables draped in Indonesian fabric. Brass-handled daggers from Morocco filled another room covered by red satin wallpaper. Dead flowers were everywhere—both dried and silk—shimmering in the burnt orange glow of the candles.

When Bronte entered the last room, which had even higher ceilings, taller windows, towering oak bookshelves and a massive desk upon which sat a gilt phone, she barely noticed those details. Instead she caught the heavy scent of gardenias.

Like one caught in a spell, Bronte was suddenly held motionless, unable even to look away from the glare of green eyes.

A shock of recognition passed through Bronte's body. The woman in front of her had a fierce, triangular face. A face too like her own. Too like her mother's. And yet not like either of them at all. For this countenance was darker and crueler, like one of those weird, elongated reflections in a carnival mirror. And far, far scarier.

Against the candles, Mischief's shadow seemed to undulate in the middle of a brilliant kaleidoscope. Her dark brows lifted sharply and her lips curved.

As if caught in a witch's spell, Bronte could not move.

"What took you so long?" Mischief murmured from her stance near the fireplace. Her voice was low and deep and not at all friendly.

She wore a black silk pantsuit with huge cuffs and a wide belt and not a single jewel. She had a long, wonderful body. She was turning a wineglass around and around with her slim fingers, watching the flickering of candlelight in the bloodred liquid. Behind her, tall windows carved glittery, black rectangles out of the Manhattan sky.

Mischief had strange eyes. Eyes that drew one and yet repelled.

Webster had warned Bronte. *She's evil. Dangerous. She'll tear you to pieces.*

Bronte's boldness vanished. She felt tired suddenly, completely drained. Mischief had watched her move out of the elevator like the overconfident, naive little idiot she had been. Her ancient eyes had tracked her uncertain progress through each room with a deadly patience.

"I'm sorry. I don't know why Webster did this." Bronte's words sounded clumsy, ill thought out even to her.

"So, you're Madame's daughter." Mischief's voice was like ice and hideously calm. "She had a wonderful singing talent, but she was a very great actress as well. Do you have that special gift, too?"

"I—I don't know."

"Now is your chance to find out."

"I don't understand."

"I have a very special role in mind for you."

Bronte stared at her.

"My dear, the role you would play is...me."

"I—I just want to be myself."

"It would only be for a little while. I need to go away for a few weeks," Mischief said. "But no one can know I've left the city. Webster will escort you everywhere he normally escorts me. He tells me that you have made wonderful progress walking and that you will be able to keep my modeling assignments."

"I couldn't possibly do any of that. I—I just came by to tell you that I'm leaving New York. That you don't have to worry about me being Webster's pawn in whatever plot he's concocted, that I would never dream of trying to compete with you or hurt you in any way."

"You really don't have an inkling...I mean, about what this is all about." Mischief just stood there silently, like a spider in the center of a web. "Bronte Devlin, I need your help."

"Whatever do you mean?"

"It wasn't Webster's idea to give you your mother's face. It was mine."

Involuntarily, Bronte began backing away from her double. "I—I have to go. Now. I'm meeting someone."

"You're lying. Nobody knows you're here. You have no friends. No family. Webster made sure that you ceased to exist when you got that new face."

A premonition of dread struck Bronte as she turned to run.

But the black waiter with the smoldering eyes and the tattoo was suddenly standing in the door, his huge legs apart, blocking her flight.

"Shut the doors and get out of here, you big ape!" Mischief shrieked at him. And then she whirled on

Bronte. "Not so fast." Mischief's voice was sly as she slid toward her, a second glass of wine in her slim hand.

"I want to go home," Bronte whispered.

"In due time."

"Now!"

"Not till you listen to what I have to say."

Bronte felt some dark emotion that was as fierce and palpable as roaring flames.

"If it weren't for me, you would be a faceless monster. I, not Webster, paid for your operations. Now, I need your help...with a little project of mine. But first, why don't we relax and get to know each other? After all, we do have a great deal in common."

Bronte's heart was clamoring. "But—"

With a fluid gesture Mischief placed a wineglass into Bronte's shaking hand.

"I—I already had a margarita. Two in fact."

"Who's counting? The evening is young." Mischief's green eyes compelled her. "There's nothing faster than friendships made with wine. If you don't drink, I'll find a way to make you stay, anyway. And aren't you curious...to know why I did it?"

As if hypnotized by those cold eyes, Bronte nodded.

"Well, you just drink your wine like a good little girl, and I will tell you everything."

Bronte sipped, but something in the wine tasted so bitter that she gagged.

Almost immediately Mischief's face began to waver, as if she were under water.

"Enjoy," Mischief said maliciously.

"You were going to tell me... Where are you going?"

"Oh, I'll be back. We'll talk again...when you're in a more receptive mood." Mischief turned and walked away, her tall, black-clad body vanishing into the throng of revelers.

Bronte's thoughts seemed to fly around her like dark birds, but she couldn't organize them into anything coherent or call after her double. Suddenly the library tilted. The bookshelves leaned toward Bronte like the heavy limbs of trees. The candles seemed to be burning at a forty-five-degree angle.

When Bronte staggered, she barely made her way to the sofa before she fell. When she tried to get up, her brain would not tell the rest of her body what to do. Her legs and knees felt like they were made of spaghetti. Somehow she managed to reach across the desk and pick up the golden phone.

The desktop wavered. She leaned against the bookcase, and two biographies of her mother's life tumbled messily onto the desk.

One of them fell open to a picture of her mother's face. No. *Her* face. *Mischief's* face.

No. No. With sluggish, clumsy fingers Bronte dialed the first phone number her dulled brain could remember—Webster's office.

"I'm sorry but this number has been disconnected."

Dear God.

She slammed down the phone and dialed his house. No one answered.

Bronte felt sicker. She had begun to perspire so heavily her hair was plastered against her neck and face.

She put her hand to her damp forehead and would have wept, but she lacked the strength.

The receiver slipped through her fingers. The bookshelves began to spin. She fell to the floor and then crawled back onto the sofa, dragging herself up with her elbows as if there were no bones in her legs. When she pulled herself into a sitting position, she stared mindlessly down at her feet.

Around and around, her black leather pumps whirled against the gleaming cherry floor and throw rug. Her head fell back. The throbbing music died to a whisper and then vanished altogether in a void of utter blackness and silence.

She shivered, her body filled with an enormous lassitude. She tried to keep her eyes open, but they were like leaden weights, and the instant they closed, she slid deeper into the whirling blackness, but so slowly she had time to wonder with a sinking feeling of horror what Mischief had in mind for her.

A long time later Bronte was awakened by screams. Webster was there, smiling grimly down at her, a syringe in his hand. "It's all right," he said. "I'm here."

But it wasn't all right.

She could see the fear in his eyes. And the fierce determination in those of Mischief, who stood behind him.

Bronte lost consciousness again. When she opened her eyes once more, she had the vague feeling that something awful had happened in the apartment.

Even though her mind was hazy with exhaustion, she knew that Webster had been part of her nightmares. For no reason at all she remembered the huge black waiter with the golden face. Groggily she remembered Webster's voice tangled with Mischief's in a shouting match. Webster had wanted Mischief to release Bronte and abandon what he called her mad plan.

Then, suddenly, another dark figure had been there. Mischief had screamed. Bronte remembered Webster raising his hand to ward off a blow. No... He had leaned toward her with a syringe. She'd had a glimpse of a man's huge, bony hands. There had been a terrible fight, more screams. Webster had run.

Bronte was too confused to remember anything clearly.

Strangely, she kept seeing Mischief's white face, her neck twisted at an odd angle as she lay beside the library couch, her dead eyes staring wide-open at the spidery cracks in the ceiling with a look of horrible surprise, her long red hair flowing in a pool of dark purple liquid. Her face had been smooth, no lines marring its classical beauty, no expression of evil staining her loveliness, either. She had been wearing a black evening gown.

But when Bronte managed to sit up, she found that it was she who was sprawled awkwardly on the floor beside the couch. Her own clothes were gone, and it was she who was wearing a black evening gown with spaghetti straps. A wineglass had been knocked over, and there was a dark purple stain on the oak floor.

Bronte's skull throbbed as she clawed her way up the sofa. When she shook her head, her ears roared and her temples pounded, while bright stars whirred before her eyes.

She caught a shivering breath as she scanned the library for signs of violence and found none.

Where had everybody gone?

Was Mischief really dead?

Suddenly Bronte knew she had to get out of here before Mischief, if she was alive, or Webster returned. But when she lifted the telephone, there was no dial tone.

Most of the candles had burned out, and the vast, silent rooms were dark save for a tiny guttering flame in a candlestick or two.

Her heart beat wildly, in sharp contrast to her sluggish, heavy muscles. Her legs felt so numb and disconnected she could barely walk toward the library door.

When she finally opened it, she lurched into the next room like a sleepwalker and then into the next. Heading toward the elevators, she leaned on couches and tables and chairs, using them to keep her balance and to guide her.

But when she reached the massive oak doors to the vestibule, they were locked. Just as she was about to push against them, someone began to pound from the other side.

Terrified, she stretched onto her tiptoes and peered through the peephole and was riveted by a man's angry, golden face. She'd seen those fabulously sculpted, African-American features somewhere.

He was that waiter who had blocked her escape.

What did he want?

Like a child, she backed robotically away from the door.

She would lose, no matter what.

The waiter kept pounding, but the blows were muffled now.

A pulse in her temple beat a soundless rhythm as she sank to the wooden floor. Her sense of impending danger grew acute. She had to get out before he got in.

Fear propelled her. Using the same chairs and couches to guide her again, she stumbled back across the living room and out onto a balcony.

From the narrow ledge, she looked down and then rocked back dizzily. It was drizzling, but she was so glad to be out of the oppressive apartment that she welcomed the cool drops and lifted her pale face to the fresh, damp air. Uncaring that she was soon soaked, she continued to stand there, as if wanting to wash away some evil experience.

Her body weaved from the drug. Gripping the railing, she stared down to the faraway sidewalk, street and parked cars.

Two windows away on the same level as she, a metal fire escape gleamed wetly. She stared at it a long time, letting the rain soak her, until gradually she felt more alert.

But just when she decided she was strong enough to walk again, the lights went off in the apartment. She heard the creak of old wood flooring straining under pressure.

The pounding had ceased.

Was that waiter inside?

The single remaining candle was blown out.

The vestibule door must have been opened because cooler air raced against her damp skin. When the curtain billowed out onto the balcony and wrapped around her body, she screamed.

There was a crashing sound as a table fell over. A lamp smashed to the floor.

"Damn. Where are—" Suddenly a big-boned arm snaked out of the darkness and fastened around her waist like a steel band, dragging her back inside. A gloved hand cupped her under the armpit.

A circle of white light flashed on and off, blinding her.

"Mischief Jones!"

"No, I'm not her."

The barrel of a gun dug into her scalp.

"Scream, and I'll blow your brains all over the wall!" Another gloved hand closed around her windpipe.

Her assailant would kill her no matter what. He just preferred silence. Well, she wouldn't give it to him.

In terror and fury she lashed out at him with her feet and arms, clawing, scratching and kicking.

But the long, bony fingers around her throat tightened and dragged her down. Their bodies became entangled. Twisting together, they crashed onto the wooden floor. He ripped something from his neck and wrapped it around her throat.

She fought, determined that her life would not end like this.

But his gloved hands were a vise, winding the red coil of silk tighter around her slim throat.

Tighter.

"No! No! No..."

Bronte didn't want to die. Not before—

She tried to scream, but the strong hands increased their pressure.

He was pulling her down, down. Then she was drowning, sinking into a deep pool of endless darkness.

Part 3
LOOKALIKE CHILD

Chapter 10

Jack pulled a white windbreaker over his head.

When his black head popped through the neck hole, his face was shadowed and tense. He thought of Carla, who wanted to be a spy.

He'd never make it as a P.I.

For one thing, a stakeout or surveillance or whatever the hell you called it was a hell of a bore.

Damned uncomfortable, too, in the rain.

Jack's stomach growled. He was starved, but he couldn't leave. His jeans were wet, so his legs were cramping. But he couldn't sit down. The best he could do was lean further into his doorway.

He needed to take a leak, too.

But worst of all, he was thirsty.

Because of the emotional havoc Chantal had wrought, he wanted nothing more than to drown himself in drunken oblivion. For three months he'd fought the urge, staved it off.

Damn Chantal for being so nice today. For pushing him closer to some dangerous edge.

In the past she'd always thrown his low-class background in his face; never for a second did she let him forget that he came from dirt.

Theodora had tried to tell him that he was as good as anybody. But that first week after she had brought him home, when he'd clumsily nicked an antique highboy with a spur, Chantal had snickered and reminded everybody that he was used to old milk crates for furniture. When he'd tracked mud all over an Aubusson carpet, Chantal had found his muddy boots and carried them downstairs and told everyone that he should be made to live in the barn, that he was used to dirt floors and mud like pigs were.

Because of her, he'd damn near killed himself to prove himself to Theodora. But deep down, he'd believed Chantal.

Still, he had always made *A*'s in school, even if it had meant staying up nights to study subjects he hated. He had pored over books about ranch management, too. He remembered Chantal taunting him that it was his Mexican blood that made him so stupid he had to study so hard. She'd laughed at his accent, so he'd spent years practicing with tape recorders to get rid of it.

"If you were me, you would just know stuff," she'd said imperiously. "You're crazy to care about feeding the poor. What real good will that do? They'll just breed, and then there will be more to be miserable."

He'd been cynical enough to see her point, and yet the problem was too real for him simply to ignore it the way she could. He was in awe of her, though—

because she had been born higher than he. Because she took as her due all the things he had struggled to acquire.

His fatal mistake had been marrying her.

She'd driven him to drink. Funny how it only took a beer or two to make him feel almost as good as she. But the feeling always wore off.

Jack knew she was probably planning to shred him. She was just making sure to sink enough tantalizing hooks in his heart that she could tear out. He knew it, and still tonight her soft-hearted gazes and passionate kisses had stripped his soul bare.

The sky was a nondescript gray-black, streaked with wispy clouds. The damp air was so still he could hear his own ragged breathing.

Where the hell was Chantal, anyway? His neck had a crick from craning his head back at such a sharp angle for so long. And if that wasn't bad enough, the mist and rain made it damned hard to tell what was going on up there.

But something sure was.

Shortly after Chantal had gone upstairs, her party had broken up. Which was damned odd, since the doormen had told him it had just started and her parties usually lasted all night.

Jack had stood in a cramped, dark doorway across the street and watched suspicious-looking shadows of a man and a woman loom against the windows. Then the place had gone dark and quiet. But he hadn't seen Chantal or the man come out.

Jack was about to go mad with curiosity. Suddenly the drapes billowed out of one of the windows, and a fragile-looking woman in a black evening gown staggered out onto the balcony. She would have fallen if she hadn't grabbed the railing.

Chantal.

Jack stepped forward, into the rain. Chantal stood there weaving back and forth like a reed in the wind, letting herself get as thoroughly soaked as he was. She looked so lost and desperate, again so unlike the arrogant, hateful woman he knew. Jack felt an odd, unfamiliar ache in his heart. Sensing she was in some sort of danger, he was already loping across the street when he heard her cry out.

The guttural sound was low throated, terrified. A scream was formed, then swallowed.

A man was on the balcony with her.

The bastard got her by the throat. His hand closed over her mouth. She fought him as he dragged her inside.

All Jack knew as he raced across the street was that if he didn't get up there fast, she would die.

He'd never been more scared.

Not even in prison when they'd held him down. When they'd ripped his uniform off and tried to force him to play the part of a girl. When he'd known that if they had, they would have damned him forever to hell.

The red silk was a vise squeezing her larynx.

Bronte's eyes bulged. Her splayed hands clawed.

Her assailant fell heavily on top of her, the silk tie an ever-tightening band, cutting into her slim throat and windpipe until she stilled.

Dimly, ever so dimly, Bronte felt the band loosen. Too soon. Her attacker stood up and began methodically wrapping the tie around his big-boned fist. Then he inserted the roll into his pocket, as if he considered his business with her finished.

He moved, and a silver light from the window touched his hard features. For an instant she saw brown skin stretched tight over a huge skull. He had a prominent brow, a cruel mouth. Then his face dissolved into the darkness.

Whole but disoriented, she was dizzily aware of his quick movements about the room as he doused furniture and drapes with some sort of fluid.

She caught the reeking scent of gasoline.

A match flamed.

Above its golden flare she saw a deep wrinkle in his brow. His quick smile came and went, leaving his face crueler than before.

He relished his plan to burn her alive.

Bronte heard clanging footsteps on the metal fire escape outside. The sound of breaking glass elated her. A man shouted to her.

Boots crunched over glass. In the library a table was slammed into a wall. Books fell and were kicked aside.

"Damn."

The match was shaken out, the vestibule doors thrown open.

As her assailant rushed out, a man burst into the living room.

"Mischief..."

Bronte's eyes opened. Her gaze clung to his.

"Chantal..."

Through mists of pain and terror Bronte felt a large, warm hand close gently around hers. Next she felt him kneel beside her and lift her wrist. Then the hand was softly touching her face, tracing the line of her cheek, wet with her tears, and finally examining her bruised throat.

Jack seemed huge. His rain-wet hair stood wildly out from his head. She saw the knife tattoo on his arm.

He was savage. But beautiful.

When his finger grazed her windpipe gently, she moaned.

"That damned son of a bitch—"

She whimpered; his voice softened instantly. "Honey, try to put your arms around my neck."

Bronte tried to, but she was too weak. She barely lifted her arms before they fell limply.

"Never mind," he whispered as he slipped an arm under her shoulders and another under her knees.

She lost consciousness when he picked her up and carried her into the elevator. As they descended, he held her against his massive chest. She regained consciousness for a moment, and it was as if she were falling…falling in an endless, black sky.

Then the elevator stopped, and she was aware of blazing chandeliers, of him carrying her across the opulent lobby, past a dozen curious doormen, fielding their disruptive, shocked questions while he demanded that they clear a path and open doors, that they hail a taxi.

Motion.

He was carrying her hurriedly down wet stone steps.

Out into a wild dark night that was misty with rain.

Then she was in a cab, snug and warm, and he was beside her, holding her head in his lap, stroking her tangled hair.

For an instant she held his arm still and traced the vivid, blue lines of his tattoo.

When she raised her eyes, his black gaze locked with hers.

"I'm sorry you went to prison. I would never hurt you."

He went still, as if the word *prison* alone could resurrect the most terrible ghosts.

She knew all about ghosts.

In a flash of white she saw Jimmy's face, her mother's, Bryan's, too.

The back seat of the cab seemed suddenly too impersonal. Bronte's heart thudded painfully. A compulsion to touch him seized her, a compulsion to smooth the lines from between his brows, to caress the unruly hair that fell over his forehead. To make him know by touch alone that she understood the darkness that lay inside him. But she was too weak to lift a fingertip.

Turning away from her, he stared moodily out the window. And she felt cut off from him again by the terrible hatred he bore for his wife.

As they sped away in the darkness, she began to drift again, but the currents were gentler now, because Jack was there.

The killer heard the Mercedes engine ping to life. He watched the good doctor back carefully out of his space.

He was glad of the early morning hour. The traffic would be lighter. He wasn't used to big cities.

He was glad it was still raining.

Good night for a bad accident.

After the killer eased his rental car out of the parking garage, sirens sounded from the end of the street. A dozen police cars flew up to the co-op's entrance and squealed to a stop, their doors opening, slamming.

Rage—dizzying buzzes like sizzling currents—charged through his brain, fracturing him. He took a deep breath and concentrated while his windshield wipers slapped back and forth.

Easy does it, cowboy.

He sped out into the misting night.

When none of the cops pursued him, he shot a tense, lightning-fast smile toward his *date*, whose long red hair fanned out over her seat. He remembered how she'd laughed at him when she'd told him she'd found a new stud.

The killer chuckled.

"Bitch. Look who's propped up like a big dummy. Look whose slim neck is as twisted as some dumb chicken that got its neck wrung."

Chantal stared back, her icy eyes as big as green saucers and frozen in that queer, unblinking stare.

"You ain't nothin' but a big broken doll now."

He smiled when he remembered how she'd kicked and fought him. He wished he could've done it to her one last time. Her fear had turned him on.

There were two of them.

Maybe he could have some fun with the other one.

The Mercedes swerved sharply to the right, speeding onto an exit ramp that led out of Manhattan.

Skidding on the rain-slick street, the rental car veered across the same two lanes.

Webster Quinn was a boring target.

Men were no fun.

The smell and taste of a woman's fear gave the killer an erection.

When their hearts pumped wildly, his did, too.

When they died in his arms, his penis pumped as well.

Webster's stomach clenched when he saw the headlights behind him slew across two lanes and take the same exit ramp.

He was being followed.

Was it the same person who had broken into his car and stolen the before-and-after pictures?

While he'd been in Mischief's co-op and nearly gotten himself killed by Mischief's murderer, somebody had smashed his window and stolen Mischief's and Bronte's surgical pictures off the passenger seat of his Mercedes. He'd looked everywhere, but both manila envelopes were gone.

Mischief had asked him to bring them to her. She'd slapped him and screamed for him to go back down and get them when he'd arrived and told her he'd left them in his car.

Now somebody else had them.

Who?

That little mystery was the least of his problems.

A world-famous model had been murdered.

As her jealous lover, Webster could be a suspect.

Twenty party guests would be able to place him at the scene before she died.

He had to get out of the country—fast. With any luck, he'd be at his villa in Costa Rica by tomorrow, enjoying his tropical garden and waterfall in the mountains outside San José.

The traffic was heavy as Webster maneuvered the

Mercedes from lane to lane, speeding northward and finally along the tree-lined Merritt Parkway as fast as he could. But every time he checked his rearview mirror and saw the steady glare of those headlights, his heart thrummed faster.

Was the same horrifying bastard with the hideous smile, the one who'd strangled Mischief, on his tail?

Webster had tried to pull him off her, but the thug had punched him so hard that he'd been thrown halfway across the room. When he'd regained consciousness and staggered to his feet, the man had been pulling himself off Mischief's limp body.

When the guy had seen him get up, he'd lunged toward him with a maniacal smile.

Fortunately Bronte had cried out, and Webster had run.

Remorse struck him.

Why the hell had he played God? Why had he made her? At least he'd tried to warn her about Mischief.

He had no excuse. Mischief was a devil. She'd ordered him to do it.

His exit to Connecticut was next.

He was almost home.

There were no headlights in his rearview mirror now.

Just as he told himself he'd been paranoid, the little sedan was on his left, ramming him. Webster's steering wheel spun crazily. Fishtailing wildly, Webster pumped his brakes. The heavy car's tires squealed as the Mercedes whirled head-on into a van.

White streaks of paint that divided the lanes were rolling over and over, but the car landed upright. For a second he thought he was all right. Then the red car behind him rear-ended him.

Geysers of water and mist spuming around them, three vehicles skidded like out-of-control dancers onto the grassy median.

Back and forth Webster's windshield wipers swiped. Then the Mercedes hurtled into a pine tree. Webster was pitched forward. His forehead banged the steering wheel.

After that, all was still.

Webster was too numb to feel anything.

Then there was a muffled knock against his fogging window. A big-boned fist holding a jack crashed through the glass.

Briefly, in the white glare of headlights, a cruel smile lit the man's expressionless face.

Why was Mischief's murderer waving goodbye?

The face vanished. Webster heard breaking glass and an explosion like a bomb.

Flames filled the universe.

Clusters of people hung back in their cars, their worried faces brightening and darkening.

Webster tried to scream, but he couldn't make a sound.

They were shouting to him, but he couldn't hear them, either.

He was all alone, dying, already disconnected from them.

As he closed his eyes, the world seemed to dissolve a piece at a time until everything was still and blue and peaceful and painless.

Without breaking stride, the killer sauntered jauntily up to an old Volkswagen. The driver's baseball cap was turned backward. His jaw was slack as he gawked at the over-turned van and burning Mercedes.

The killer jerked the dented passenger door open. He was inside before the kid even knew he was there.

A gun was shoved under the baseball bill.

"Hit it, kid. Take off...slow. Real slow."

The killer turned around and watched the fire and wondered how long it would burn like that in the rain. He wished he could stay and see what was left of the bodies.

She wouldn't be much to look at now.

He should have felt happy.

But he hadn't been able to get the envelope with both women's medical records out of the car.

It wasn't over.

Jack had the other one.

Not for long.

No matter who she was, Chantal or her twin, she had to die.

Then the kid began to babble through choked sobs. "Just let me go, mister. Take my car. I don't want to die."

Tears streamed down his young, freckled face.

Fear.

The killer felt good.

"Shut up and drive, you blubbering sissy."

"You'll kill me."

The killer smiled. "Maybe." He twirled his gun with careless ease. "Maybe not."

Killing was an art.

He'd decide when it was time.

Jack cursed out loud as he stepped inside the bedroom of a charming, colonial, roadside inn with the sleeping woman in his arms.

He didn't want to stop. Not with the adrenaline pumping through him, wiring him. Not after he'd seen all those damned cops at the co-op. Not when his mood was to get as far from New York and whatever trouble was back there as soon as possible.

He had sensed a cold, deadly presence in Mischief's apartment. The fierce, sixth-sense premonition of danger had stayed with him. It was a gut-level instinct, something he couldn't put into words. Just a tightening inside him. But it was this instinct that had kept him alive in the barrio and alive for five years in prison.

This wasn't over.

That danger aside, he didn't want to spend the night with Chantal. He didn't want to share a strange bedroom with her. Nor a strange bed.

Not with her injured and higher than a kite.

Not with his own heart laid bare by her soft helplessness; not when he was so susceptible to her new tricks.

He'd wanted to drive south for at least another hundred miles. But Chantal had lain in the front seat of his pickup, shivering in her wet evening gown no matter how high he turned up the heater.

Sweat had poured off him, and not just because of the heat blasting out of the vents. Every time she dozed off, she'd awakened whimpering. He'd never seen such stark terror. The pupils of her eyes had been so dramatically dilated that they'd been all black with only rings of emerald encircling them. Her lips and skin were so bloodless she seemed only barely alive. Her fragility and terror scared the hell out of him.

Repeatedly he'd tried to reassure her. "Chantal, you're with me. You're safe now."

But were they?

"Chantal?" She had stared at him in dazed confusion, mispronouncing her name as if she'd never heard it before.

The things she said, the questions she asked made no sense. She was delirious. Finally he'd decided that he had no choice but to stop.

He'd bought burgers at a fast-food place, using the drive-in window so he could hold her head in his lap and stroke his hand through her hair. At the next corner he'd spotted a convenience store. He'd thought about buying beer, but he'd only jammed down the accelerator harder. Half a mile down the highway he'd found the inn. Weakening at the thought of spending the night alone with her, he'd made a U-turn and sped back to the convenience store, ripped the first case of beer he'd seen off a shelf and bought it.

He'd torn the carton open and pulled out a bottle, wanting to twist the cap off so bad he'd hurt. Then she'd moaned from the front seat and he'd driven back to the inn without touching the bottle.

Now he was in the tiny, dark bedroom, and she was shivering in his arms. She felt even softer and smaller and more helpless. Dear God...

Quickly he hurried across the room and laid her on the plump mattress of the high four-poster bed. She shuddered as her head fell back against the pillow.

He ripped the sheets back and tucked her into the bedding. But she continued to shake so violently he decided he had to get her out of her wet clothes.

Why had he let Theodora talk him into this?

"Undress!" His whisper was brusque and
"You're going to freeze to death if you don't
is your own damned fault, you know—for stan
out in the rain on the balcony."

She pushed weakly at a spaghetti strap. Then her hand fell to the pillow.

Her eyes were green pools of terror. "Can't. Oh, Jack..." Her voice slurred.

A surge of guilt swamped him. "Chantal..." His voice was grave, kinder. "Dear God, girl, take off your dress."

"Can't, Jack..."

His mouth tightened as he studied the supple curve of her smooth shoulder. Stripping her in Paris had been easy compared to this.

While he fought his demons, she stared wildly, mutely, pleading.

Maybe if he didn't look at her. Without bothering to turn on the lights, he rolled her over and unzipped her gown. But the second his rough palms rasped against the damp skin of her spine, he began to shake. His hands skimmed the straps from her shoulders. The silk clung to her buttocks as he pulled it downward along her curves.

She mumbled unintelligible sounds as he peeled the dress all the way off, discovering she wore no panties. No bra. Nothing underneath.

He shut his eyes, but his fingertips read her like a blind man's. She had creamy breasts, an hourglass waist, shapely hips and slim, long legs. She was too thin. Still, he felt thrills of warm sensation from her satin-soft body.

He was dizzy by the time he draped her dress over a chair. She curled herself into a tight ball and snuggled under the blankets. Determined to drink till he drowned out the memory of her, he strode outside and brought in the case of beer.

He set the case on the table and stared at it moodily. Finally, instead of a beer, he grabbed a cold hamburger from the sack, devouring the grease-soaked bun and then the limp fries almost angrily. He wadded up the empty burger sack. Leaning back in his chair, he read every word on the carton of beer while she continued to moan and shiver beneath her covers.

"Shut up, Chantal."

More kitten-soft moans.

He grabbed the phone. The manager yawned and said the heat couldn't be turned on this time of year and that no firewood was available for the fireplace, either.

Chantal kept shivering.

Jack's gaze splashed across the hype on the beer carton. He licked his lips, but he'd been down that particular road to hell. Too many times.

Maybe he should fill the bathtub with hot water and place her in it, but the thought of carrying her naked body anywhere made him break into a cold sweat.

And the last thing he wanted to do was get in bed with her or hold her. When her teeth clicked together louder than ever, he got up and grabbed the case of beer. In a rage at himself, at her, he cracked open the door and flung the case outside.

Glass exploded against concrete. Unnerved, he slammed the door.

He sat down quickly and bundled her shivering body into his arms, all the time wondering if every single bottle had broken.

Then she moaned. When her soft gaze roamed his

face, he felt an unbearable rush of heat. She seemed so helpless and innocent that he forgot the beer. He swallowed, his heart threatening to burst.

Stripping off his own wet jeans, he slid under the covers and eased her into his arms, hoping his body heat would warm her quickly so he could soon escape.

At first all the warmth in his body, as he held her shivering in his arms, felt inadequate to help her. The hardness of his chest gave her no softness upon which to lay her head. His muscled arms made an awkward cradle. Not that she seemed to mind. She nestled against him, burrowing her silken head into the hollow of his throat. Snuggling against his chest, seeking warmth more than softness, she was instantly asleep.

No more moans. Only contented little sighs rose from her injured throat now.

His skin burned beneath the soft swell of her breasts. He felt even warmer where her hips joined his.

Naked male flesh against fragrant woman flesh. Sober as he was, the sensations were too vivid—the floral-shampoo scent of her hair too sweet, the petal-soft texture of her skin too tempting. Nipples taut as berries were glued against his chest.

He wished he was drunk now. Maybe then lying with her wouldn't saturate him with such pleasure.

Did he really have to go through with this? Take her home? Didn't he have enough battles to fight already?

Then he remembered the haunted look in Carla's eyes when he'd tried to help her with decimals three nights ago. "My mother knows math. She'd come home if—"

He'd tried to stay calm. "Look, Carla, I know it's tough for you, not having a mom. Believe me, I know what that's like. But your mother and me..." What was the use of even trying to explain?

"Why do you drink?" she'd asked.

"I quit."

"You always start back. You used to get mean."

"I'm sorry. God, Carla, I'm so sorry."

She had thrown her arms around him.

He thought of the smashed bottles outside.

He was a drunk and a bad father.

Not anymore.

One day at a time. That was his mantra. Sometimes, like now, it got down to a minute at a time.

When Jack remembered what Carla had seen in the barn that night, he couldn't blame her for what she thought. But she didn't know what had gone down that night.

Somehow he had to bring Chantal home and keep her there until Carla and Theodora accepted him and saw once and forever how completely unfit she was as a mother or daughter or as his wife.

So he lay as stiffly as a post while Chantal slept, careful to keep his body rigid, careful to keep his hands to himself. But when she nestled deeper into the covers and her bottom rested against his thigh, he burned even hotter.

Motionless, soundless, sacrificial, he drew a tortured breath and then exhaled with a shuddering sigh.

He couldn't stand this.

He wanted to brush his lips against her hair, to kiss the velvet skin of her throat.

How was it possible to want a woman he hated?

Then she sobbed his name hoarsely, and he felt like he was flying to pieces.

The pillow crooked his neck at a bad angle. But she was so soft and warm curled against him. So he lay there as wide awake as a cat charmed by a bird. His mind hated her, but his body wanted her.

It seemed an eon before she finally stopped shivering.

He shot out of bed and stalked away. For a long time he stood in the door and let the night breeze cool and caress him. When he finally got a grip and began cleaning up the broken glass and pitching shards into a nearby garbage can, he discovered one unbroken bottle.

His seized the slim brown neck.

It was still cold.

Then Chantal cried out his name. He shut his eyes and flung the bottle at a nearby tree, hating the splintering sounds of glass breaking.

She was moaning when he stepped inside. He made sure she was okay and then went to the bathroom and shut the door. He sagged against it for a long time.

Then he stripped and took a long, icy shower.

His skin was blue, but he was cold sober when he stalked into the bedroom and got into his own bed. Next he called Theodora and told her he had Chantal. She was thrilled. She asked where they were. He asked about the ranch. She told him there was a problem with the sperm count of the new bulls. He told her to call the vet. Then he hung up.

He couldn't figure out the bull problem. He had had them tested at the cattle auction when he'd bought them. How could all eight be sterile?

He was too wired up to sleep, so he punched buttons on the television remote-control device and began to channel surf, determined not to worry about the bulls or Chantal.

But she moaned, her cries cutting him like a blade.

He swore softly and made the television louder.

He was all too human. He had needs, regrets. Not that he intended to reveal them.

Bronte was running through high-ceilinged dark rooms. Women imprisoned in square golden frames with golden bars across their faces were staring down at her with the trapped looks of exotic animals in cages, yet they did not try to save her from the tall, redheaded woman with the cat-shaped face and savage green eyes who chased her.

Then she saw that the women staring at her all had the same faces. And the same eyes as her pursuer.

Their faces were exactly like her mother's. Exactly like Chantal's.

Exactly like her own.

How many? How many were out there? Trapped as she was, in faces that weren't theirs? In lives that weren't…

Webster…

Next she saw a man whose skin was dry and dark and stretched too tight across his skull.

"Mommy?"

"Jimmy. Jimmy." Bronte stirred and began to thrash.

"Wake up," a terse male voice ordered.

"Jimmy?"

The leathery-faced man loomed above her. Gigantic hands stretched red silk around her neck and yanked.

She screamed.

"Hush up about Jimmy. It's me, Jack. I'm the only one here," that grimly melodious voice drawled. "You're safe."

Bronte's terror held her a moment longer in that state of tortured unconsciousness. Then, gradually, she grew aware of other voices that were distant, far-away. Rat-a-tat-tat sounds, too.

With painful slowness, Bronte opened her eyes.

The television was on.

Jimmy was gone. So were the triangular faces caged in golden frames. Her throat burned, and she remembered what had happened in Mischief's apartment.

Unfamiliar shapes came into focus. Bedposts with huge carved balls gleamed in golden lamplight. Unfamiliar sounds jarred her consciousness.

The television set cast bluish, otherworldly flickers into the room. Ancient-looking airplanes were bombing cities. Pilots in leather caps barked orders. It was a war documentary. The kind Bryan used to love.

On the double bed next to hers lay the silent viewer of this program. He was tall and massive, with only a thin sheet covering his lower body. His duskily tanned chest was exposed above crisp white sheets bunched at his waist.

His hair was blacker than Garth's, his shoulders broader. His dangerous, sinewy muscles rippled in the eerie bluish glow.

He hated her.

He had stalked her.

He had saved her life.

She remembered the gentleness of his warm hands when he'd undressed her.

But he could be so nasty and mean. He'd been to prison. He had that awful tattoo. And yet...

She knew without knowing how she knew that he would have fought to the death to save her. She had panicked when Jimmy had been hurt, and done nothing other than hold him in her arms. This man had nerves of steel and an incredible will. And he was kinder than he pretended.

She had lain beside him shivering on the front seat of his truck, staring up at his harsh, chiseled, dark face, which had whitened every time they met another car. Grimly he had tried to explain that she was Chantal West, his wife, and that he was taking her home to their Texas ranch. He had said he didn't want her back, but he had come for her because their little girl, Carla, wasn't going to school and wasn't passing math, and because of Theodora, her mother, who was growing old and wanted Chantal home for her thirty-fifth birthday. This birthday had something to do with who got control of the ranch, which was important because the ranch was in trouble.

Mischief was this man's wife. She had run away from him and changed her face so he couldn't find her.

Bronte had tried to tell him again that she wasn't Mischief, but he had refused to listen.

He had said she was going to live with him whether she wanted to or not—at least till Theodora saw that she wasn't fit to live on the ranch.

Bluish light flickered on black satin.

Her dress! Her black evening dress.

Every sensory receptor in Bronte's body went off as she eyed the glistening folds of cloth draped over the dinette chair behind Jack's bed.

She was naked. Completely naked. And he'd lain beside her. He probably thought nothing of it because he believed her to be his wife, a woman he had slept with for years and years.

Slowly she ran her hands beneath the soft cotton sheets till she touched bare nipples. With an indrawn breath she felt the curve of her belly and then lower.

He had stripped her. Then he'd lain beneath her as rigid and still as a statue, not taking advantage of her even though he'd been aroused and she'd been too weak to resist.

She remembered how wildly he'd kissed her in the bar. From the start she'd sensed a vein of ice in him that made being alone with him crazy and dangerous. Still, as Bronte's mind cleared, she knew she had to get away from New York fast.

Jack West, no matter how much he disliked her, thought he was her husband. He wanted his wife back.

Bronte was becoming quite calm. He was tough and frightening, but he was her only ticket away from the man with the big hands and tight brown skin. For now Bronte had to be Jack's despised wife—at least till she got better and could think of a superior plan.

"Jack?" Bronte whispered across the dimly lit room.

"Chantal?" he replied. "Feeling better?"

"A little."

His glittering, obsidian eyes were deep and dark and dangerous.

"So you finally admit who you are."

She shivered, momentarily afraid to lie. Then her coolheaded determination surprised her. "I should have known that I could never ever fool you for long, my own *dear* husband.''

His gorgeous mouth twisted. ''Stop it. I am not your *dear* anything. You know as well as I do that our marriage is a farce.''

His face was hard and set, his voice tight and dry.

Panic clawed through her. How could she know anything about their marriage?

She squeezed her eyes shut. Turning away, she stared at the wall quietly. ''Why did I ever marry you?''

''You got pregnant—on purpose—or have you conveniently forgotten about our daughter, too?''

''I didn't do that all by myself, now, did I, Jack?''

His heavy silence made her skin heat.

''No. You came to my bedroom, took off your clothes and got into my bed. You were all over me in the next breath. Hands and tongue everywhere. I was drunk. You said she was mine.''

''Was I supposed to be eternally grateful you married me?''

His laughter was brutal.

These awful events had nothing to do with her. She wasn't his wife. She was just using him. She didn't care what he thought or felt.

For no reason, she remembered how gentle his hands could be, and in a soft, thready voice, she said, ''Thank you for saving my life.''

Silence.

She held her breath and counted the cracks in the wall. Why couldn't she just fall asleep and forget him?

But she tossed and turned for what seemed like hours. When finally she did sleep, she dreamed Garth

Brown was kissing her. Then the characters and scenery changed, and Garth was Jack.

When she awoke, the memory of Jack's mouth on hers brought new panic. The television was blaring. He had fallen asleep, his brown hand frozen on the remote-control device.

With agonizing care not to wake him, she pushed her covers off and eased herself out of bed. The room was icy, so she wrapped herself in a blanket.

Gently she tiptoed over to him and, loosening the remote from his fingers, shut off the television.

For a long moment she studied the rise and fall of his dark chest. The room was so quiet, she heard only his breathing.

Sleep had erased the deep lines of exhaustion from between his brows. His black, curling lashes were inky crescents against his dark cheeks.

Again Bronte remembered how helpless she'd been, how he'd saved her. How tender he'd been, even though he disliked her. Hot new tears brimmed against her lashes. She didn't want to feel anything for him.

But she'd nearly died. The shattering experience had left her ego about as sturdy as an eggshell. So, on a sudden impulse, Bronte leaned down and brushed her lips against his with a kiss that held both gratitude and gentleness.

She drew back, slightly dazed from the kiss.

At least he was asleep and would never know.

Suddenly she swayed weakly. The walls swirled. Nausea crushed out her next breath.

The memory of those horrible bony hands throwing her onto the floor made her dizzy. She was shivering again from the aftermath of terror and pain. She told herself she was safe with Jack. That as soon as she recovered from the aftereffects of the drug in the wine and the assault, she'd be fine.

Then she remembered her new face. Maybe the killer was still after her.

Jack's truck keys glittered on the table. Jack was connected to Mischief. Which meant he was connected to her killer, too. Some part of her longed to seize his keys and bolt.

When she took an involuntary step toward them, Jack's eyes snapped open. "What the hell?"

"I—I couldn't sleep."

He pinned her with his darkly glittering gaze. "Get back in bed and stay put."

Chapter 11

Where the hell was she?

Jack was anxious to hit the road.

The premonition of danger had stayed with him even though he couldn't justify it. There was no sign they were being followed.

Still, Jack felt grim as he sipped his strong black coffee. He snapped his newspaper shut, drummed his fingers on the steering wheel of his truck and glared at the door of their motel room.

He wasn't just worried about unseen dangers, either.

He worried about her.

He couldn't concentrate with her around. He hadn't been able to sleep much, either.

Last night all he'd thought of was her in the next bed. Every damn thing she'd done from the first moment she'd seen him in Central Park baffled him.

When she'd sneaked over to his bed, he'd breathed

in the dizzying smell of gardenias and tensed, fearful she'd claw him.

Instead she'd brushed her mouth against his with exquisite tenderness. Nobody had ever done anything like that to him. His life, for all its passion, had been singularly lacking in gentle affection. She was shy and enchanting and utterly different from the hard, calculating woman he'd hated.

Just remembering had him edgily aroused. When he'd gotten up this morning, she'd been asleep.

Shivering no longer, she'd been tucked warmly beneath her covers. He'd studied her boneless, outstretched arm, her wild spray of red hair. Damn, but he'd wanted to get in bed with her, to fall back asleep wrapped in the silken heat of those arms and legs. He'd ached for her to kiss him again as tenderly as she had in the night.

Fortunately, the maid sweeping broken glass outside had distracted him. He'd tugged on his jeans and rushed out to tip her. Then he'd gone to the tree and gathered up the rest of the brown slivers.

After that he'd gone shopping. When he'd returned, he'd half expected Chantal to be gone. She'd been sleeping still—her cheeks rosier than ever, her hair the same riot of red waves spreading across the pillows.

He'd barked her name.

The lazy smile she gave him made him so hot he'd rudely chucked two sacks of clothes at her and ordered her to dress.

The sun was well up and shining brightly on a tall stand of maple trees behind the inn. He was on his third cup of coffee when their door opened and Chantal stepped serenely outside, her slim hips encased in skintight denim.

He was one lousy shopper. The blue cotton blouse was at least a size too small. The sight of her slim, but voluptuous body in that snug outfit made him bolt his coffee so fast he scalded his throat.

When she glanced into the trash can and smiled at all his beer bottles, he ducked sheepishly, cowering behind his paper while she struggled with the heavy door.

He didn't help. She was breathless by the time she climbed inside the pickup.

Her floral scent filled the cab. He fought to ignore it just as he fought to ignore her. Which was hard when her pretty face was framed with that bright aureole of shimmering curls. Again he remembered how silky those masses had felt on his shoulders.

Damn. She was so sexy. She made him feel needy.

He *felt.*

Feelings.

They scared the hell out of him.

Especially where she was concerned.

Nothing's changed.

Trapped with her in the cab, he felt his mood darken.

Think of anything else...anything at all.

He pitched his newspaper over his shoulder. With no more than a curt grunt, he started the ignition and swerved out of the parking lot, tires squealing.

The foam coffee cup she had forgotten on top of the cab flew onto the parking lot.

"Who broke all those bottles?"

He flushed. "Who tried to strangle you?"

"I—I asked first."

"I bet it thrills you to see how close you came to driving me to drink."

"You?" Her quiet voice seemed to hold both surprise and concern.

His eyes narrowed on the gritty black surface of the highway as they rushed past the suburbanized farm town and its enormous white colonial houses, into rolling, green country.

"Who tried to kill you?"

"I—I didn't see him clearly."

"You must have an idea."

"I don't have a clue."

Her voice sounded so painfully hollow he felt sorry for her. Then he caught himself—this was no time for misplaced sympathy.

He bit his lower lip till he tasted blood. Okay. She wasn't going to talk. Forget her. Drive.

But he couldn't forget her. She was too damned different. So different it was hard imagining anybody wanting to hurt her.

With an effort he reminded himself of the long years of their hellish marriage.

It was easier to note how her blouse and jeans snugly molded her slim figure.

He'd bought a blue bandanna to match the blouse. She'd carefully tied it around her throat to conceal the dark bruises. Jack remembered how scared he'd been when she'd lain across his lap barely whimpering. A suffocating despair had gripped him.

Jack turned on the radio. Music was a dangerous distraction, but he needed to take his mind off those buttons, which were about to pop open. She was a little bigger at the top than he remembered. Why wasn't there one damn thing that was the same?

There was! He remembered the jagged white scar on her left shoulder.

"Can I have a sip of your coffee? I lost my cup," she purred as a news commentator began to talk about a plane crash in the Indian Ocean.

"Sure," he muttered. Despite his best effort to sound indifferent, his rough voice was charged.

His hand shook as he extended his white cup. When her fingertips brushed his, he jerked back, sloshing lukewarm coffee all over his jeans.

"Damn."

The music was country and western, his favorite. Old Hank was crooning a melody about lost love and new love with way too much passion.

"Oh, dear," she said when she saw Jack's soaked jeans. "Did I burn you?" She touched his damp thigh and gave him one of those dazzling, worried looks of hers.

He jumped, his heart racing. "As if you give a damn!" he shouted like a man in the last stages of lunacy.

She closed her eyes as they sped south. "I do."

"I'm fine."

"Why is it so important that I be home for my, er, thirty…fifth birthday?"

"As if you don't know." He twisted the dial of the radio.

"No, leave it on," she said. "I sort of like it."

"Since when did you ever like… Well, I don't."

Liar. She could tell it was one of his favorites. It opened him up to her.

He spun the dial.

Jack wished he could remove himself, erase himself, as he had that first year in prison. Then the music and the woman wouldn't be able to get to him.

Nothing's changed.

"My, my. Aren't we grumpy? You remind me of a five-year-old. My specialty..."

Since when? he wanted to thunder.

But she laughed, and the silvery sound pulled him out of himself. Did he only imagine she sounded short of breath? Leaning toward him, her lips sipped from the same place on the coffee cup where his own mouth had been.

What the hell was wrong with him—to notice her lipstick smudges on a white cup? He hated her.

He had sex on the brain, the way his mother used to.

Suddenly he wished he'd bought airline tickets. They had too many miles to be stuck alone in this tiny cab together. But flying with her after she'd hit him in Paris had seemed risky.

"It's going to be a long trip." He leaned forward, hunching over the steering wheel, staring moodily at the flying white center stripes and black asphalt.

"Are you always this scared around girls? Or is it just me?"

"I'm not scared." *Like hell, West.*

"Why don't you tell me what's happened since I've been gone?"

She met his dark glance shamelessly.

"Do you really want small talk? All right then. I served five years of hard time because of you. I chopped cotton from dawn till dark with my ankles chained to other men's. When I wrote a letter, it'd take me fourteen days to get a single page done 'cause every night I was so damn tired all I could write was a line or two. I got stabbed. I nearly died, damn it. There were days I wished I could die. Like the night I nearly got raped...while you jetted around the world!"

Chantal's eyes were brilliant in her white face. "And the tattoo..."

"Oh, that. That was a gift from a buddy. I don't mind it so much. He saved me from those other guys."

"Jack..." Her voice was soft with remorse.

He gripped the steering wheel harder. "Shut up."

Jack turned the volume louder, so that the disk jockey's voice drowned her out when she tried to speak.

Five minutes later he spotted a roadside café. He jerked the wheel hard to the right, sending the pickup slewing into the parking lot. The horn of an eighteen-wheeler behind them blared wildly. Brakes screamed when Jack stopped.

More coffee spilled. This time all over her thighs.

She cried out. "You drive like a maniac. And you're rude and mean."

"Because you drive me crazy."

"This trip was your idea."

He flung open his door. "Get this. You and I have nothing, absolutely nothing, to say to each other."

She was dabbing at the coffee with a paper napkin as she slid out. "You want me to come home with you, to live with you as your wife, but you don't want anything to do with me. Have you thought this out at all, Jack? Here we are, stuck in this truck for however long it takes to get home.... Well, what's going to happen when we have to live in the same house and act like...husband and wife?"

The confines of the cab suddenly seemed stifling and close as he thought of those implied marital intimacies. Images of her naked body entwined with his, of her mouth parting in a gardenia-perfumed dark tormented him.

"That's why we're stopping now, girl. It's time I established some ground rules."

"I might want to establish a rule or two of my own," she said, shoving helplessly at her door.

"Very funny," he snarled as he came around and yanked it open.

He grabbed her arm and pulled her toward the restaurant.

But just the heat of her skin through her thin cotton shirt got him hot. After pushing her into the restaurant, he let her go.

She took one step across the threshold and froze. A dozen men had looked up and were staring straight at her. And why wouldn't they? She was drop-dead gorgeous. Her face was as beautiful as that mythic face of ancient Greece that launched a thousand ships. And not only her face. With every step, her hips swayed. Skintight denim seductively encased that curvaceous derriere and those forever legs.

A cowboy whistled.

She blushed.

Then she came running back to Jack, wrapping her arms around his waist.

"I don't want to go in."

"I'm hungry."

With an air of forced indifference, Jack shouldered his way through the door and led her to a booth near the jukebox. All the time, he was thinking that Chantal had never once run from male admiration and sought his protection like that.

The small café was reminiscent of restaurants from the 1950s, with old neon signs, plastic flowers and pool tables. The menu had low prices. Working men sat on stools and in booths, and more besides the one who'd whistled stared as she walked by.

But their stares just made her hold tighter to Jack. Watching her warily, he let her go and helped her into the red vinyl booth. He slid in across from her. After they ordered, she left him and went to clean up in the ladies' room.

Then she was back, and again, sitting across from her, he was as awkwardly spellbound as all the other men. He watched her every dainty sip of coffee, her every delicate bite of scrambled egg. Had she always been this sexy?

It had been a long time since he'd found such pleasure in just watching a woman, especially her—not holding, not even kissing, but simply watching.

Damn.

When she finished eating, she crossed her fork and knife across her plate on top of her two uneaten toast halves and beamed at him. "You said something about rules."

"Well, first, stop being so damned polite."

"So even that is a crime."

"Especially that."

"Did anybody ever tell you that you are rude and..." She looked away, out the window at a van flying north on the highway.

"And what?" he demanded, furious—and surprised, too—that he cared what she thought.

"And so insufferable. I—I see why Chantal, I

mean, I see why I left you. Why, any normal woman would. Didn't anybody raise you, Jack? What kind of mother did you have?"

His face blackened. "You always did love throwing her up at me." Planting his elbows on the table, he leaned forward. "Stop it. Cut that little-miss-purity act right now. You're not much better than she was, you know. She had to do what she did. You're not even normal. Our marriage was never a real marriage. At least I tried to make it work. You didn't."

"Oh, right. You're the saint. The way you act, that's getting harder and harder to believe, Jack."

"I was faithful. You weren't."

"I wonder why."

His mouth thinned. "Because you're insane." Red rage washed him. "And completely unreasonable." His hands knotted into tight fists. He made a low, animal sound and was further infuriated when she shrank from him.

"And did you ever hit me, Jack?"

"You begged me to," he exclaimed.

Her white face went still, her green eyes huge. "Did you?"

Why was she forcing all the bitter memories?

Too vividly he remembered finding her naked just days after their marriage in the bunkhouse with Maverick's massive, square body sprawled all over her on that narrow bunk. Jack had wanted to tear them apart, to see blood run. Instead he'd just stared, dying inside.

Blindly he'd stumbled out and gulped in fresh air. He'd felt the same violent urges when he'd watched his mother with men, but he'd learned as a boy how to shut down. He hadn't laid a hand on his pretty wife. Not even when she'd taunted him later.

"You know the answer, Chantal. You were my wife. I didn't like finding you with Maverick, but I never laid a hand on you. After him, you slept with every man on the ranch. How many times did I catch you in some bushy ravine or cheap motel with a wrangler? You did it everywhere. You wanted me to find you. The only time I came near hurting you was that last night.... But I didn't. I couldn't. But I've been through a lot since then. Don't push me."

Her hand lifted and fluttered uneasily to her bandanna. Her eyes were wary. "Is that a threat?"

"You're damned right it is."

He wrapped his fingers around her wrists and pulled her halfway across the table.

Big mistake. Her lips were too provocatively near. He didn't know which was hotter, his rage or the carnal flame licking through him.

His voice dropped and became more intimate. "I don't want you back. I don't want you for my wife. But damn it, this time you're going to be—"

"Excuse me, dears," their plump, motherly waitress interrupted, probably because she sensed trouble. "Hate to bother the two of you when you look so...wrapped up in each other...like a honeymooning couple. But could I borrow your salt, dears?"

Chantal yanked her hands free.

"Sure," Jack snapped, seizing the salt and pepper shakers and slamming them down in front of the pushy woman. "Here. Take them." He grabbed the napkin holder and pushed it forward. "Take everything on the table, why don't you?"

"You were saying?" Chantal prompted too politely, rubbing her bruised wrists.

"This has gone far enough. We're in a public place." He grabbed the check, crumpling the cheap paper in his fist. "Let's get the hell out of here."

"Wait." From beneath lowered lashes she looked up at Jack with that uncertain smile that made her look younger and more innocent than she ever had—even when she'd been a girl. "Jack, I want you to know something. I—I'm not going to sleep with those other men ever again."

Her sweetness only made his dark panic wind tighter. "I don't give a damn."

"Jack, I—I give you my word."

His skin felt like it was stretched too tight across his cheekbones. When he spoke, his voice was so low she strained forward to hear.

"Which never meant a damn thing in the past."

Her lovely eyes were wide with amazement. There was no way, however, that he could explain to her that his plan was to convince Theodora and Carla what an unfit wife, daughter and mother she was—so they would want her gone as much as he did. He wanted to use her to convince Theodora she had to trust him to run the ranch till Carla was older.

"I've changed."

Nothing's changed.

"You damn sure have." He admitted that before he thought that was the last thing he wanted to believe. "Your eyes are different. So damn different I sometimes can't believe it's you in there. Even your voice..."

Caution sprang into her eyes. Her incandescent smile died. "How?"

"It's deeper. Huskier. Not so sly. Everything about you is different. The way you look at me. The way I feel, too. I keep asking myself why? How?"

"Five years—"

"No. Since Paris. In one month you've changed completely."

She swallowed hard. Then she licked her lips as if they'd suddenly gone dry. "I have a sore throat. Last night—"

"No. You didn't talk the same in the bar, either. You didn't act the same. You've got some hidden agenda. I can feel it in my gut."

"Jack, I—I hardly know myself...who I am. Ever since my plastic—" Her voice broke. She swallowed. Suddenly she seemed unwilling to discuss the matter further.

"Well, I'm on to your little act," he said. "Nothing you can say or do will ever make me change my mind about you. You'll be packing your bags soon enough."

"Look, Jack..." Without thinking, she touched his sleeve. "If we're ever going to get to Texas, shouldn't we go?"

Her fingers burned through his cotton shirt like a brand. When she leaned closer, the scent of gardenias enveloped him.

Damn her. Was she trying to seduce him? Here? In front of all these men?

"Rule number one." His voice grated harshly as he jerked his arm away. "No more touching." He stared at her slim, trembling hand as if it were an obscene object. "You got that?"

"No objection here."

"No more kissing, either."

He was staring at her lips as she swallowed hard.

"Fine."

"I know you sneaked over to my bed last night and kissed me."

"That...was an accident."

Her gaze grew intense and dark, and she blushed as if she was struggling to fight down some foolish emotion. But her acting embarrassed and shy about it didn't fool him.

"Don't do it again."

"Any more rules?" she murmured tautly, staring at her plate now.

"Separate beds."

"Separate bedrooms, too?" she suggested, the charming blush creeping across her cheeks as that damn voice of hers deepened and grew huskier.

Jack felt thoroughly aroused. "Damn it. Separate houses."

"Great." She wet her mouth with her tongue. Her eyes flashed with defiant fire when she dared a glance his way. He could tell she was remembering he'd told her not to do that.

"Don't do *that,* either."

"Just testing. I'll be good." But she twirled her pink tongue one last time, making her lips so wet they glistened.

"I'm so glad we agree," he growled.

"Oh, me too." She paused. "Is that it?"

"That about covers it." But as he slid his wallet out of his back pocket, she snatched the crumpled check from him.

"Just a minute," she murmured in a low, sensual tone. "Maybe I want to make a rule, too."

He glared at her. "No way."

"Marriage means compromise."

His scowl darkened. "How would you know?"

She ignored him. "Here's my rule, Jack. You can be your rude, hateful self just as much as you like—when we're alone. But in front of our daughter and everybody else, I want you to treat me with courtesy and respect. I don't want you taking sides and ganging up with anybody else against me. In short, I want you to pretend you are a loving and supportive husband."

A stream of vivid Spanish curses mushroomed in his brain, but he bit them back. "No way."

"No. You prefer to wallow in misery like it's a religion. You want to feel sorry for yourself and punish me forever. Our marriage is nobody's business but ours."

His voice was rough. "You never gave a damn about our marriage before."

"Well, I won't follow your rules if you don't respect mine."

His whole point in bringing her home was to show everybody how miserable they were together. "I can't act nice to you," he muttered.

"I'm sure it would be a challenge for a man with your temperament to be pleasant to anyone," she agreed. Her saccharine voice grated. "You could still try." She squared her shoulders, which stretched the buttons of her blue shirt dangerously. Then she leaned back against the red vinyl booth as if she were prepared to camp there forever.

"We're getting off to a rotten start."

"Because you're stubborn."

"Me?" He was determined to run the show this time. Determined to be so hateful she'd be worse than ever. How else could he rid himself of her? But if she started playing the loving wife, even in public...

A cowboy put two quarters in the jukebox, and a sad golden oldie enveloped them. The lyrics and the singer took Jack back to their youth. To that time before he'd know for sure what she was. The warm, husky voice and a slow guitar worked sensual magic. For an instant the music bridged the distance that held them apart. Sadness they shared. Despair as well. He wanted to take her in his arms, to start over, to build instead of destroy. Then his anger rose up and smashed even that tenuous link.

"All right," Jack growled, yanking the check out of her slim fingers. "Satisfied?"

Her charming smile touched off an alarm in him. "For now."

The lyrics told of a man who couldn't live without love and made him ache with an unnamed need.

Jack had sung that song about a million times. How come he couldn't listen to it now with her? He raced toward the cash register.

She'd agreed to his every rule. How come he felt like she'd won?

Hell, she won every time she got close. Every time her eyes dilated. Every time a flush rose in her pretty cheeks. Every time he heard a melody.

His hands balled and stretched. He wanted to crush her against his body and make love to her.

He'd grown up with sex all around him. Hard as he fought his growing hunger, he just felt hotter.

He caught her uncertain glance.

They faced a long day on the road together.

An even longer night.

Chantal knew his weaknesses, especially his sexual weaknesses.

When a man didn't want to want her, she loved the power game of seducing him.

Nothing had changed.

Everything had.

Chapter 12

Three hundred strokes.

She had counted every single one.

Slowly, sensuously, rhythmically, she pulled the brush through her long hair as she sat at the mirror, her back to Jack. Her manner was calm as she pretended an indifference to him that she was far from feeling.

Suddenly the back of her neck prickled. Next she felt a tingle trace the length of her slim, straight-as-an-arrow back.

She didn't have to turn to know that Jack's smoldering black gaze was devouring her.

Never had a motel room felt tinier.

Or so dangerously intimate.

Not even when she'd been married.

As the hour grew later and the night sky blacker against the windowpanes, the atmosphere between them grew increasingly charged.

A shiver passed through her. How could his mere gaze, his mere presence, make her feel so alive? And yet so threatened, too?

Her fingers clenched spasmodically on the brush as she set it down.

Her skin burned. And not just the dark bruises that circled her throat.

He was Mischief's husband, and, thereby, connected to her killer.

She was his prisoner.

But he had saved her, too.

If their first day together on the road had seemed interminable, what would tonight bring?

No touching, he had sworn threateningly.

But he wanted it.

So did she.

Even though Bronte sat as far as possible from him, even though she struggled to ignore him, she felt inexorably drawn.

Her flesh was weak.

There was one bed.

No couch.

So where was *he* going to sleep?

For now, Jack sat rigidly hunched over a desk beside the windows. She was perched before the small dressing table, her slim back to him, the double bed between them.

She couldn't seem to stay still, though. She picked the brush up again and slid it through her hair, this time tangling the heavy strands more than smoothing them. No sooner did she set the brush down than she began chewing a fingernail. She'd already gnawed two down to their bloody quicks.

"Would you quit?" he demanded.

"Is that a new rule?" Her shiveringly soft question cut the silence.

The muscles in his jaw bunched.

She glanced at his mouth and remembered last night's tender kiss.

"Sorry." Her indrawn breath sounded faint. "You're right. Bad habit. I always get depressed and hate myself afterward."

He leaned over his map and pretended to ignore her.

Her gaze touched the raven darkness of his hair. She met his eyes.

He's not your husband.

He'll walk out of your life without a flicker of remorse.

He's not Garth Brown, either.

He hates you.

Use him. Don't think about him.

Suddenly she grabbed her purse and looked inside for an emery board. But as she rummaged, the soft leather pouch collapsed, spilling its contents. When her pen fell under the bed, rolling toward Jack, she gave a startled gasp. She couldn't help watching it in her mirror as it headed toward the scuffed toe of his boot.

Jack, who with a yellow marker was highlighting the shortest route to the ranch in a road atlas, jumped a foot when it struck him.

As if he felt her gaze, he leaned down, picked it up and made eye contact with her in the mirror.

With his glittering black eyes trained on her, Bronte felt caught in some cat-and-mouse scenario. He leaned back in his chair, his powerful, sinewy muscles rippling with tension in the artificial light. His savage countenance unnerved her.

She wished they were on the road. Then she could turn her back and distract herself with the constantly changing scenery.

He set her pen down too carefully on his desk. "How come you're always looking at yourself in that mirror?" His husky voice was precisely pitched and too controlled.

Because I don't see me. Because I see my mother. Or your wife. Or Mischief. Because I want to forget you.

"Am I?" she queried innocently, swiveling on her flimsy stool. "You do it, too." Her voice sounded false, too bright.

"Because I can't get used to your new face."

Tell me about it. "You will," she said aloud.

"Maybe. I don't know. You look younger."

"The magic of plastic surgery."

"Prettier, too." His lip curled cynically.

"How?"

"I don't know exactly. I just wish you didn't."

"You love to hate me, don't you?"

"It's easier." He paused. "That guy that tried to murder you must have hated you a lot. Who was he?"

His stare made her cheeks burn.

"Can't we be together five seconds without bickering?" she asked.

"You used to love fighting with me. It turned you on."

She turned her face away, her cheeks flaming again. "Is that what you're trying to do, Jack, turn me on? For God's sake, we have the whole night to get through."

"You think I don't know that?"

His fist slammed down so hard onto the wooden arm of his chair that his atlas crashed to the floor.

"Sorry. I shouldn't have said anything," she whispered.

When he grabbed her pen and bolted out of his chair toward her, she jumped up and scampered on bare feet to the bathroom.

His boots thudded heavily on the wooden floor as he stormed after her.

She barely managed to shut and lock the door before he hurled himself against it.

"Damn it, let me in! I was only going to return your pen."

Shaking, she leaned against the door. "Put it inside my purse—"

He beat on the door with his fist.

Sometimes two of her kindergartners had fought like this. But adults weren't supposed to...

"Jack, please, you're scaring me."

As the vibrations of his pounding raced through her body, she buried her face in her hands and wept. This wasn't her fault. Webster...

No use thinking of him.

Jack was her new reality, her new problem.

She'd only been with him a day. One agonizingly long day on the road. Now she felt like she'd been locked inside a powder keg.

How could she endure even one more night of this pseudomarriage? Of this tense, angry man who made her feel so scared...and yet so excited and bewilderingly oversexed too. Was she crazy? He was incredibly attractive, even when he stared at her with those hot, brooding eyes and accused her of all those lurid…

Bronte understood pain and betrayal, hurt and anger. On some deep level the pain that lay beneath his hatred drew her and made her want to heal him.

Crazy thought. Crazy impulse. Bury them.

He had to be a lost cause. If not, why had Chantal changed her face? Had this impossible man made her so desperate she'd abandoned her child? Her mother? Her home?

Why had Webster made Bronte look like this complicated woman? Had he worshipped her mother? Or Chantal?

Bronte felt the mystery expanding and growing more complex. She had so many questions. Already her charade was far more difficult than she'd bargained for. Jack despised her so much he could barely stand to be in the same room with her. He could barely endure the most impersonal conversation. Yet she sensed part of his anger had to do with a sort of baffled self-disgust that he found her attractive.

His constant hatred laced with desire exhausted and unnerved her. Never having been treated thus before, she hadn't realized how stressful such a relationship could be.

There were so many questions she wanted to ask him before they got to the ranch, but each time she was about to, she stopped, because she knew he'd just bite her head off again.

Who lived at the ranch? What were Mischief's habits? Did Mischief ride? How well? Did she work? If so, at what? Who were her friends? But how could Bronte ask him anything without making him even more suspicious?

Right now she had only him to fool. At the ranch there would be dozens of others. How many people lived there? What were their names?

She had a mother, Theodora. A daughter, Carla. A half sister named Cheyenne.

And all those unnamed lovers Jack had alluded to.

Bronte had yearned for a sister. She had been faithful to Bryan. She had never hated anybody in her life. How long could she possibly pretend to be this complicated woman? Mischief had given little away about herself in the few moments Bronte had been with her.

When Jack's pounding subsided to polite knocks, she wiped her tear-streaked face on a washcloth and opened the door.

She ignored the dangerous glitter in his eyes as she swept past him.

"I don't understand you anymore," he said.

How could he?

Hysterical laughter gurgled in her throat. She suppressed it. "Handle it."

"We've been married for years. We grew up together. But you're like a stranger. All day long I had this feeling that I have never been with you before. Why—"

"Handle it." Her voice sounded far colder and more impersonal than she really felt.

His dark gaze was leveled at her. "How, damn it?"

"This reconciliation was your idea," she reminded him in her calmest kindergarten-teacher voice.

"Not really." He grabbed her by the arm and spun her around.

Ah, that sullen, sensual, movie-star face of his. Not to mention his touch, which was all heat and sizzle.

Their gazes locked. Her nerves wound tauter. Suddenly she couldn't breathe. It had been years since she'd had sex. Forever.

Blood pounded in her ears like the roar of thunder.

"Remember rule number one," she whispered, her kindergarten tone shakier now.

"What?"

"No touching, wasn't that it?" She met his molten eyes.

"Yeah. Right. Right." Hardness edged his voice as he yanked her closer with surprising ferocity.

Her throat tightened.

So did his grip.

She went white when he snugged her against him. Whiter still when his hand slid roughly into her hair and a steel band circled her and made her his captive.

"You've never acted controlled or sweet a day in your life. Are you trying to make me love you and want you again? Is that why you're being so coy and ladylike—"

"No. I don't care what you think about me." *Liar.*

"No? Then why do you look so good? And feel so good?" His hand coiled a strand of her hair around two dark fingers. "Your hair is darker." His voice grew hoarse. "Thicker. Silkier. Even when you're quiet, I can't quit thinking about you. Even though you don't act bold the way you used to, you still..."

With the back of his hand he pushed the heavy lock back into place. His fingers were gentle against her ear and her cheek. Every nerve in her body was tingling in reaction to what he was saying and doing. She might have pushed him away, but she didn't. "Don't do this, Jack."

"You would never have said that in the past." A

derisive expression played across his face. ‘‘Is that your new come-on?’’

She shivered. ‘‘I hate you when you’re cynical and too knowing.’’

‘‘I know you.’’

‘‘Do you?’’

‘‘Hell yes.’’ Angrily, he caught her closer, holding her arm so hard his fingers would leave dark marks on her flesh. ‘‘One day—almost two—and you’re like a drug in my blood.’’ He glared down at her with profound bitterness. ‘‘I crave the taste and feel and scent of you.’’

His rippling muscles and his hard-edged masculinity were like an aphrodisiac. She craved all those things, too.

‘‘I want,’’ he continued, ‘‘things from you I thought I could never want again.’’

Her arms curled around his neck in artless abandon. *What was she doing?*

‘‘I felt dead to all women until I saw you in the park—’’

‘‘Oh, Jack…’’ Desire flickered through her—and a joy she had not allowed herself to hope for came back to her. Her blood pulsed.

He saw it. The urgency in her eyes was a reflection of his own.

His arms were iron bands crushing her to his chest. His brutal hands roughly forced her chin higher.

‘‘I…I was scared of you that day. I’m still scared—’’

‘‘You’re my wife. You’re not scared. So don’t play those games. You used to want it rough. You used to beg—’’

‘‘Not anymore—’’

"Bullshit. You still like your sex hot and wild, I bet."

With genuine panic, she stared into his fiery black eyes. Her breath came unevenly. Then his searing mouth ground down on hers. She wanted tenderness, kindness. And yet... Instantly, a feverish hunger swept through her, too.

He was forcing her down.

"You've driven me mad for years, Chantal. You chased after every man on the ranch while I did without—"

Bronte slid her fingers into his black hair. "I swear I didn't. I wouldn't—"

"I loved Cheyenne. You seduced me and got preg—"

"I would never ever do something so awful." But she was quivering like a frightened animal as his long, lean, manipulating fingers molded her to his length.

"If I drank, it was because—" his lips devoured hers "—because I couldn't stand the thought of you with another man. I kept thinking you'd change, and now that you have..." His hands ripped at the buttons of her blouse.

She trembled as his hands roamed her, shaping her naked woman flesh to his. Trembled when his breathing grew loud and harsh and his fingers closed gently over her breasts. Trembled when his body heat fused to hers.

Bronte moaned and fought to escape his plundering mouth and hands. "Don't... We mustn't..." But her thickening voice rasped more faintly.

"No, love." He knelt, bathing her nipples with his tongue till they became wet, erotic pebbles.

With a sigh, she closed her eyes and was still. She

would be who he thought she was for now. But, maybe someday, she could be herself.

A long time later, when she had quickened under his expert titillation, he stood up and pushed his delicious tongue into her mouth. With both hands, he stretched her tightly against his body, so that her breasts flattened against his chest. In the next moment, he prized a muscular thigh between her legs. She gasped, thrilled by the raw sensuality of this intimate cue.

At least he thought she was his wife.

She had no such excuse.

Still, eyelids fluttering, she clung, craving the mindless glory that only total knowledge of him could bring.

It had been too long. He made her feel sweet and feminine, and thrillingly alive. He was brave, and his bravery inspired her.

She would despise herself in the morning.

He would despise her even more. When he learned the truth, he would hate her for that, too.

For eight years she had been married to Bryan. She'd hardly known Jack two days.

Never once had she felt such insatiable and exquisite sensual pleasure.

She stared into his eyes and felt she'd known him always, wanted to know him always. There was pain inside this man. So much pain. What else could he feel for a woman...if he ever let himself go?

Jack ripped off her jeans.

She should have fought.

Instead she stood statue still, scarcely breathing, sighing as he did things she'd never let any man do, feeling strange and shy, and yet fully roused, too. She sank to her knees and unzipped him with fingers that shook.

In seconds he was naked from the waist down.

His body was long and lean and brown. His rigid manhood jutted toward her mouth.

When she kissed his bare thigh, he caught her closer with a groan.

She shifted, self-conscious suddenly as she gazed up at him, her torpid eyes both questioning and languorous.

He bent over her, his rough hands stroking gently through her hair, his fingers sliding down her neck as he pulled her face higher, guiding her mouth to the source of his maleness.

What might have been wrong with any other man was right with him. Still, her lips parted with a startled breath as he pushed inside.

He shuddered when her lips and tongue began to toy with him. She was shy and timid at first. With a groan of unadulterated pleasure, he used his hands to move her head back and forth. He was staring down at her, his black eyes cynical and hard and unyielding, shocked that she could arouse him so.

Yet when he reached that shattering, hair-trigger edge of control, he pulled out. Lifting her swiftly, he carried her to the bed. Then he lay down on top of her.

His arms circled her. In the velvet blackness, her eyes shone as brilliantly as emeralds.

"One of us is crazy," Jack muttered against her ear.

"Both of us." Desire swept the last vestiges of her guilt and fear away on its burning tide.

She caressed his inky hair. The sandpaper roughness of his carved cheek rasped beneath her exploring fingertips. His body felt heavy and huge and hot, but she twined her legs around him to keep him there.

He kissed each black bruise on her slender throat. "I'll kill the next bastard who hurts you."

Then the hot moistness of his breath brushed her scalp. His mouth nuzzled her warm skin and his hands fondled her breasts. He traced his mouth across her nipples till little moans rose from her throat.

"Open your legs."

Mindless with pleasure, she arched toward him so he could enter her. Instead, he stroked her wetly with long, deft fingers till her muted cries died completely.

"How beautiful you are, how soft and warm and sweet." His rough drawl was lazy and low with reverence and wonder. "You aren't the same at all." Then gently he thrust inside her and was still, enveloped by her warmth. When he began to move with a slow, passionate rhythm, gradually her desire built. Faster and faster, like dancers caught in the same spell, their bodies twisted together, till she was so hot she felt ready to spark. But when he felt her fully roused, he slowed, smiling down at her, drawling sexy endearments.

"Now," she pleaded as she felt the flame at the center of her being ignite. "Now."

He slammed into her, and she was moaning and writhing and soaring as he exploded, and the hot torrent poured into her womb.

Clinging. Sighing. Dying.

Together.

Too soon, the rush of emotion was over.

She wanted to lie quietly, enclosed in his strong

arms until long after the trembling of their bodies ceased.

She thought he did too.

He finished and rolled off her.

Her lovely eyes snapped open. Fully conscious, she stared at his handsomely aggressive profile as he lay on his back and glared at the ceiling.

His posture was rigid, his utter coldness like a slap, shocking her to her senses.

If only he would take her in his arms again... She had felt so warm and tender and alive. Crazy thought. She didn't really want that.

He lay beside her like a stone figure, hating what they had done together she supposed.

When she foolishly raised a hand and gently touched his face, the muscles of his jaw flexed. Violently he flung her hand away.

"Don't make it worse."

She shut her eyes so she wouldn't cry.

She had not meant for this to happen. She had tried to stop him.

She should have fought harder.

This cold, dark man was not hers to love.

Whatever her regrets were, his were more profound.

His ravaged face spoke volumes. When he finally spoke, his voice was solid ice. "This doesn't change a damn thing."

But it had. For him too. No matter how he tried to deny it.

"I—I tried to stop you." Her fragile voice was thready.

"Yeah. Sure. You said no, but you egged me on—with your hot eyes and your soft, willing body.

With that new pretty face that made me forget who and what you really are. I told you you were good, didn't I? You should be, honey. You've had a hell of a lot of practice. How many men have there been since me?"

When her hand flew toward his face, he seized it.

"That's more like the old you," he spat.

A tear welled out of the corner of her eye and rolled into her hair. Every muscle in Bronte's body hurt. He wasn't her husband. How could his words cut so deeply, shaming her to the core? As if she'd actually done all those terrible things he accused her of?

"I'll never touch you again, Chantal."

Bronte's stomach tightened. She felt numb.

"Who wants you to?" But she did. God help her, she did.

She bit her lips, and with a moan, twisted onto her side. Jerking the covers up to her neck, she closed her eyes again.

He hurled himself out of bed.

Through slitted lashes, she watched him.

With cold insolence, he stared down at her body, molded by the thin sheet. She watched him dress with desolate fascination. Watched him snap frayed, cotton buttonholes over every button.

She felt his determination to hate her. She tried to summon hatred for him, too. Instead the emptiness surrounding her dully pounding heart expanded into an aching void.

He yanked on briefs and jeans. Finishing swiftly, he flexed his hands into knotted fists and then unflexed them, as if every nerve in his body was lit by dark self-disgust and loathing for her.

"Jack?"

He jumped. "Damn it. I thought you were asleep."

"How could I possibly sleep after—"

"You always do. Tonight will be your last chance for a while because tomorrow's going to be longer than today 'cause I don't intend to risk another night in some motel room with you."

She curled her body into a tight, miserable ball.

He strode outside and slammed the door so hard the thin wall gave a convulsive shudder.

Or was it she who shuddered?

She didn't want to cry.

But the hot tears came anyway.

Later, when her sobs ceased, she knew what she had to do.

A red silk tie lay across the dusty, blue dashboard of the battered VW.

The killer got out and unzipped his fly.

Just as he frowned in tense concentration, a dark shadow appeared beneath *their* bathroom window across the highway.

Hot damn.

He whipped his rifle out of the back seat and raised his scope.

The bathroom window slid up.

A pair of pretty, long legs slid over the windowsill. Then a pretty, round butt wiggled in that golden square of light.

He got a hot tickle of lascivious excitement in his groin.

Get your head out of the window, bitch, so I can splatter your brains and red hair all over that wall.

A little song played in his head.

Kill. Kill. As fast as you can.

Yippee. He felt like a Wild West cowboy.

No way could he miss at such close range.

Her red head bobbed out.

His trigger finger quivered. She'd never know death was on its way. Her skull would pop just like a blood-filled watermelon.

He expelled a tense breath, took aim and squeezed the trigger. Damn! Suddenly Jack sprang out of the dark, quick like a cat, grabbing her and pulling her down into the dirt.

The bullet slammed into the wall. Pieces of wood splintered as a woman screamed.

The killer got off three more shots.

But his target was rolling over and over. When she got up and tried to scuttle away, Jack dragged her behind a tree by her hair.

Three motel doors opened.

The killer jumped into the VW and jammed his keys in the ignition. A minute later the center stripe was flying.

A hundred yards down the highway, he felt warm fluid gush between his legs.

Damn the bitch.

He'd peed on himself.

She'd pay for that.

He'd get up close to her. Take his time. Have some fun.

She'd die slowly while he came inside her.

Chapter 13

Bronte's heart was pounding so fast she had to think to breathe. Sharp rocks and tree roots ground painfully into her back. She couldn't move because Jack was sprawled on top of her, holding her down. The muscles of his arms and legs had her pinned helplessly. His breath rasped against her neck; his heart thudded like a voodoo drum. Worse, the bulge between his thighs was swelling bigger and bigger.

His angry gaze ran over her shrinking body with hot interest.

She closed her eyes in terror and despair.

Almost, almost, she'd escaped him—permanently.

Then he'd grabbed her and thrown her to the ground right before that bullet—

Bullet!

Again she felt the whisper of metal whizzing past her cheek. Again she saw pieces of wood splintering, felt flying slivers hit her face. Then Jack had her on the ground, and he'd rolled over and over with her. When she'd screamed at him to stop hurting her, he'd dragged her behind this tree and had thrown himself on top of her again, shielding her with his body.

"Get off me, you big lummox!" Bronte pushed at his broad chest with splayed fingertips.

He was enormous and as heavy as lead. All she could do was squirm helplessly under his long, muscular body as he looked up and peered past her toward that place where the gunshots had come from.

"Feels good," he growled, a nasty, tauntingly seductive sting in his low tone.

Instantly she was terrifyingly aware of the immense heat of his body, of the rippling muscles crushing her, of the rock hardness of his arousal. With an effort, she stopped moving and pushing at him.

"I said get off me!"

The expression on his face grew diabolical, so she quieted.

Jack didn't get up till he was good and ready. Then he stood up cautiously, brushed himself off, not caring that dust and small rocks rained down on her. When she tried to get to her feet, her ankle gave and she slipped back and fell heavily. She tried to get up again, but her arms were wobbly and her legs seemed to be made of jelly. Then Jack was there, yanking her up, his grip and expression so brutal that when she stared into his ruthless face, she screamed.

He clamped his hand over her mouth and slammed her against the tree. She fought him wildly, weeping and kicking. The rough bark tore her T-shirt and scratched her skin. He kept her pinned till she lost her strength and her hysteria played out.

"Hush."

When she finally quieted, sobbing still, but utterly exhausted, he removed his hand from her mouth. "You about done?"

"Did you see those bullet holes? Somebody tried to shoot me."

Perspiration stood out in beads on his brow, and his arms were damp with it. "I damned near got my ass blown off because of you."

"Is that all you care about?"

Other guests were outside their rooms shouting to each other, demanding to know what all the ruckus was about.

When Bronte started to answer them, Jack's big hand clamped over her mouth again.

"Shut up," he growled. "We've got to get out of here before the cops show up."

"I don't see why you're so afraid."

"You didn't spend five years in prison."

"I forgot about your record. This is all your fault, isn't it?"

His lips thinned. He grabbed her by the waist and hauled her bodily to his truck. "No, honey, it's yours. That trigger-happy slimeball is after you."

"No. It's not what you think."

"I'm sure it's a hell of a lot worse."

"Hey, you! Did you guys see anything?" a male voice called out to them from the dark.

Bronte whirled.

"Just get in the truck," Jack ordered.

"My things. They're all over the ground. I can't just leave—"

"Forget them."

His rudeness was making her mad. She'd nearly been shot, and he was blaming her!

When he opened the heavy truck door, she began to fight him again. He jammed her against the truck, imprisoning her with his body.

In that shadowy darkness everything about him—the muscles she felt bulging beneath his shirt and tight jeans, the hellish belligerence of his rugged features—shouted low class, barrio background, ex-con, dangerous.

"I—I don't want to go anywhere with you," she cried. "I'm sick of you."

"Ditto." Then with a dark scowl, he spanned her small waist with his hands and shoved her inside. He jumped in, too. She scooted across the slick seat and would have grabbed her door handle, but his hand manacled her wrist and yanked her back across the cab. "You gonna make me hog-tie you?" His voice was low and frighteningly intimate. He leaned closer, so close she felt that hot, unwanted prickle of awareness even before his warm breath hit the flesh of her throat. "Remember how you used to beg me to tie you?"

"No...." She didn't remember any of the sick, terrible things he was always alluding to. Shocked to the core, she didn't want to. She didn't want to have any more to do with him.

His face was an expressionless mask, his body perfectly still. With one hand he clamped her wrists together. His angry leer caused a freezing, burning sensation that held her motionless. "I could use my belt," he said. "I bet you'd like that."

"Just let me go."

His eyes smoldered for a long, charged moment, the dark irises almost entirely obliterated by the black of his pupils.

"Please," she whispered.

He released her wrists and started the ignition. "Stay put. Or I swear I'll do it."

"Jack..."

He turned. In the dark his heavy lids only half hid the blaze of those infinitely black pupils. With a lover's skill, he brushed his hand down the length of her arm. Then his fingers skimmed the undersides of her breasts, reminding her of the intimacies they had shared only a few hours ago. When he spoke, the chilling, sexual inflection was back in his husky voice. "Will you be good? Or do you want me to tie you? Like I said, I will..."

In that fraction of a second, before she got some of her nerve back and skittered to her side and began snapping on her seat belt, she began to burn with shame and some unnamed, never-suspected secret, sensual need.

A wild, thrilling shiver raced through her as she contemplated him tying her.

Then something cold curled deep inside her.

Terrified, she realized she didn't know who she was. Or what she felt for this man. Or where this dangerous relationship would lead.

He had bedded her. He had served time in prison for murder. What kind of man married a woman like Mischief? Even if he hadn't killed her, twelve people had believed him capable of it. Probably more than twelve. What else was he capable of?

Dear God. She had to get away from him as soon as possible.

Later, as Bronte stared moodily out her window at the flying scenery, she realized that if he hadn't yanked her out of that bathroom window when he had, the bullet would have lodged in her brain instead of that wooden wall.

Maybe he hated her.

Maybe she wanted to hate him.

But upon occasion, his timing was superb.

Jack's palms were embedded with gravel. His whole body was sweaty and his gut ached—and not from hunger.

He was in a state of acute agitation. Shock. He'd nearly died this morning because of her.

She wasn't worth it.

He had to send her packing—*pronto.*

Jack's window was rolled down, but the warm, early evening air that blew against his face and smelled of grass and cattle neither cooled him nor relaxed him.

His hands were clenched on the steering wheel. His spine throbbed from sitting so long, driving so long with her. He caught the scent of gardenias.

Texas.

The state was too damned big. At least it seemed so today, even though he'd driven like a madman.

Forget last night.

Forget her.

Nothing's changed.

Yeah. Right.

Forget the best lay of his life.

It had been more than that.

No.

Forget the hurt in her voice and eyes afterward when he'd been such a bastard.

Memories of her body joined to his flickered in and out of focus.

Forget how he'd felt when he'd seen that bullet hole in the wall and realized how close she'd come to dying.

He couldn't forget. Especially when she was sitting beside him, still looking hurt and lost and scared.

Not when he could still remember so vividly the feel of her naked, silky skin under his callused palms. Not when he could still remember how she'd arched up to meet his every thrust, how she'd gloved him so tightly again and again, pulling him deeper and deeper, her thighs closing tight around his hips.

Damn it.

She'd felt so right.

She'd never felt like that before.

He'd been married to her for years.

But only this once had the blending of their bodies ever included their souls.

How could he think that?

Early this morning she'd looked so pretty when she'd come into the bathroom when he'd been shaving. Her hair had been a bramble bush of disorganized curls, but her eyes had shone with that special tenderness that tore his heart out.

She'd been wearing his T-shirt, and she'd looked so damned sexy he'd remembered that sweet kiss she'd stolen in the dark. He'd almost pulled her into his arms and done it to her again right there against the bathroom wall.

Instead he'd pushed past her and stormed outside. He'd slept in the truck. The next time he'd seen her, she'd been backing out of the bathroom window.

God, she had him on the ragged edge.

All day they'd been in the truck together.

It seemed to Jack like it had taken them forever to cross Texas.

But here they were, barreling down the last ten-mile stretch of narrow blacktop.

He hadn't used anything last night. She could be pregnant again.

He was a fool. The worst sort of fool.

The narrow ranch road had never seemed this endless.

He wanted to be alone.

He needed to think about the ranch. About what Theodora would do once she had her precious daughter back. Who would she choose to run things now? Chantal? Maverick? Or him?

All he could think of was Chantal.

When he'd said they were nearly home, she'd put her terror and hurt aside and stared out at the view of sky and pasture and oil wells. She was looking up at the huge black buzzards that spiraled over the open pastures, riding the wind currents on their wide, seemingly motionless wings. When she tired of the vultures, she smiled at the red Santa Gertrudis cattle grazing on the sparse brown grass growing between the oak motts and rusting oil tanks.

South Texas was a land of mesquite and sand, of prickly pear and chaparral, of vast sky and brush country, of cowboys and cattle. It was hardly beautiful. At least not to the untrained eye.

But it was home and, therefore, beautiful to Jack.

The subtle lure of this wild, flat land drew him back again and again.

Chantal had always hated the ranch.

Until today.

He remembered the last night in the barn. Somebody had hit him from behind with a two-by-four, locked him inside and set the building on fire.

Until today he'd always thought it was her.

Today she looked innocent and guilt free.

She laughed when a flock of flustered wild turkeys ran back and forth in front of the truck, their tails fluttering like ballerinas' skirts. Jack slowed his pickup as they waited for one turkey to get up the gumption to fly. When one did, they all sailed clumsily over the low fence to safety. All except one lost Tom. This big bird ran back and forth along the fence line, too stupid and frantic to fly.

"Oh, Jack," Chantal said in a worried voice. "Stop! I want to see if he makes it!"

"Since when have you ever given a damn about wildlife?"

Confusion and hurt filled her eyes. She swallowed and looked down.

If she kept up this act, she would thwart his plan to convince Carla and Theodora that she was the last thing they needed.

Even though Chantal had insisted on sharing the driving, Jack was bone tired. He was sick to death of thinking about her and all the consequences her return might have.

He wanted the ranch.

He wanted her gone.

What was he going to do about this wife he didn't want to want? This wife who was besting him on every front? He felt all mixed-up.

Chantal probably knew she had him.

No touching, she'd reminded him.

Hell, he'd devoured her.

Hell, every time he looked at her, he was hungry for more of the same.

Odd how he couldn't think of one time when it had ever been like this between them before. Never once had he kept on craving her afterward.

He'd grown up in Mexico, despised because his mother was a whore. Even when Theodora had brought him to the ranch, he'd still been an outcast. Prison had been even worse. He'd begun to wonder if he'd ever belong anywhere.

Making love to Chantal last night had been like finally coming home—for the first time in his life. Finally he'd felt like he belonged somewhere—to someone. He had no clue that sex could be more than the satisfaction of a bodily itch, that it could be the touching and joining of two hearts.

Damn her.

He despised himself for wanting that feeling again.

Sitting beside her in the cab all day, acting grim and sullen every time she asked him the least little favor or question, had been sheer torture.

He wanted her tonight. Every night.

She was on the run from a killer.

They both had more important worries than sex. She'd let him bed her, too. She probably wanted to wind him tighter and tighter before she played him for a fool. He remembered her malevolent expression right before she'd hit him with that stone cat.

That was the real Chantal.

He had to stay away from her. Period.

The closer they got to the house, the more he thought about their living arrangements. In the past, they'd shared the large bedroom at the back of the big house. It had a wide balcony and a view of the lawns and pasture that swept down to the bay. He'd been living in it these past few months.

Separate bedrooms, she'd said. Separate houses.

He shoved his booted foot down hard on the accelerator. Chantal shifted in her seat with a look of surprise when they stopped in front of the gate. He leaned out and punched in ten numbers on the tiny keypad beside the road. As the gate backed away in slow motion, she stared up at the fifteen-foot-high stucco arch with the huge gold letters that read El Atascadero as if she'd never seen it before.

A guard came out of his trailer and waved them through.

Jack nodded. "*Buenas noches,* Bucho."

She waved at Bucho, too.

In the past she'd never done that.

So why this fake friendliness now?

How come she gave that little gasp of surprise and sat up taller when they topped a low rise, and the big house loomed above a thicket of mesquite like a Moorish castle?

He remembered that same look of surprise on her face that first day in New York when she'd claimed her name was Brooke or Bronte.

"What's the matter?"

"Oh, nothing," she said quietly. "It's been a long time."

"What has you so all-fired eager? Your family? Or your lovers?"

Her chin inched up a notch, and a haunted vagueness came into her luminous eyes. Suddenly he felt guilty again as he took a curve too fast.

The driveway arced around a planting of tall palms, a majestic live oak and the bell tower. He braked near the huge garage that stored tractors and cars and housed his office. Bougainvillea, scarlet and dense, bloomed from dozens of terra-cotta pots that marched up the staircase to the main house. Wide concrete steps that had been painted red led up to a screened verandah. Another set of stairs led down beneath a covered archway to the kitchen.

A short distance beyond the house a group of ragged, brown men stood in the deep shade of the palms. When they saw Jack, the tallest waved his dirty straw hat.

Good old Ernesto. He was an Indian of singular stature. A born leader, he was at least six feet tall, bullet-headed with a thatch of black hair, wide shouldered and reed thin. He swam the river at least half-a-dozen times a year. Jack didn't remember the others, but from the looks of the them, they'd probably walked all the way from central Mexico without a bite to eat.

Jack could empathize. He'd never forget how it felt to go hungry.

Desperate for work, they walked up from the border. The pipeline easement that ran north and south across El Atascadero was their highway, at least till they made it north of the Sarita checkpoint, where their friends could pick them up and carry them to the bigger cities and work in *el norte.* All over Mexico, at every post office, long lines of women dressed in black, their bowed heads draped in shawls, would be posting letters to these husbands and brothers and sons who had to leave them behind for months and years to work in *el norte.* Mexico's bad economy and young and exploding population made such illegal trafficking of human beings virtually a necessity.

Jack waved back to them. He'd deal with them later.

When Bronte saw them, her eyes grew huge with fear. Almost instantly, as she realized their desperate plight, her face softened, and with a timid smile, she waved, too.

When she grabbed her door handle, Jack caught her arm.

"Chantal..."

At his touch, stark pain glittered in her eyes. Then she composed herself and glared at his bruising hand. "Rule number one," she said very calmly.

His jaw clenched guiltily when he remembered what he'd done when she'd said that the night before. "Right."

With a supreme effort of will he relaxed his fingers.

White-faced, she stared back at him.

"If you so much as look," he began, "at another man—"

"Why would you care? The only reason you're bringing me home is because of the precious ranch."

"That's right." But his scowl deepened, and his blood beat violently in his temple. Suddenly he wanted to make love to her again. Right here in the cab. He didn't give a damn about the ranch. He didn't care that they were parked in front of the mansion and that anyone could see.

"I don't care what you do with other men," he stated. "Or which one of your rejected lovers is after you."

She hesitated, somehow sensing the true emotion beneath his words. "Look, I said I wouldn't..." Her voice shook. Almost, she seemed to be a real human being in that moment. Though she tried to hide it, her hand trembled on the handle.

"You will!"

"Are you jealous, Jack?"

"Jealous? Of you? No way." But her question stabbed him as sharply as a well-placed needle. "Nothing's changed!" he persisted. "And you'd better stay away from Carla. I won't have you playing your new tricks on her the way you're playing them on me."

Bronte cracked her door.

"I'm not finished with you. Don't be playing your tricks on anybody else around here, either."

Bronte ignored him and jumped clear of the truck. When she raced past the house, toward the clump of men under the palms, he watched her with a growing wariness.

What the hell was she up to now?

At first the men seemed hesitant with her. Then shy smiles broke out on their young, emaciated faces. They gestured toward the kitchen. She nodded, obviously promising them food.

Never before had Chantal taken the slightest interest in the plight of the starving Mexicans. She called them wetbacks. Once she'd even called the border patrol.

His estranged wife was surprising him at every turn.

Jack hurled himself out of the car.

She was speaking Spanish. He caught an awkward vowel pronunciation he had never heard before.

Even her Spanish was different.

Her syntax was formal, textbook Spanish. She had the typical, bad gringo accent that she used to mimic.

Chantal had grown up on the ranch where everybody spoke Tex-Mex. *Pocho,* the Mexicans derisively called it. Her grammar was horrendous, her vocabulary local slang.

Jack had hardly had time to recover from her shocking kindness and bizarre Castillian phrases before Guerro, Jack's golden lab, bounded toward her, barking ferociously. The Mexicans all cowered around Chantal for protection.

As if Chantal would protect them. She hated dogs. Guerro had detested her since she'd run over him when he'd been a puppy and then driven away.

Jack rushed to stop his dog. "Guerro! Stay, boy!"

"Shh," Bronte whispered. She turned calmly from the men and faced Guerro as he lunged. "Nobody's going to hurt you, big fella."

The dog's ears pricked up in confusion. As she continued to croon, his barking softened to a low whine. Although the hair on his neck remained spiked, his tail began to wag.

She'd charmed him the way she and Cheyenne had once charmed snakes.

Bronte extended her hand toward Guerro, all the while smiling. "Come on, big fella. Let's be friends."

"When have you ever wanted to be friends with my dog?" Jack yelled, letting go of his fury now as she petted the big dog behind his ears, reducing Guerro to slave-like adoration.

As she'd reduced him to submissive adoration last night.

Jack felt rage as the stupid dog sloppily licked Chantal's long, slim fingers.

Bronte laughed when Guerro's tail speeded up. Then she looked up at Jack, her beautiful face pert with triumph. "Today I want to be friends. And Guerro is smart enough to know it—even if you aren't."

She shot Jack a smile that would have melted the layer of ice around any other man's heart.

Damn her. She used sex, her beauty, even Guerro to best him at every turn.

She laughed when Guerro's big tongue lapped her nose. Her shining eyes, her bright hair, her glowing face—everything about her caught Jack's heart and charmed and enraged him.

Bronte's smile died. "Jack, these men are very hungry. Do we have some food?"

"You know damn well I always feed these men."

In rapid Spanish he told the men food would be forthcoming, but they were all looking at her.

Then, swearing beneath his breath, he grabbed Chantal's arm. "I said no more tricks, damn you."

"What's wrong now?"

"These men! My dog! You never liked dogs."

"Why do you want me to be as mean and bad as you say I used to be?"

"You may have a pretty new face, but people like you don't change. Not down deep, where it counts."

"Okay. I'm a witch." She flashed the Mexicans an ear-to-ear smile. *"Bruja."* Her warm green eyes sparkled mischievously.

The men shouted, *"No. No, Señorita Angel."*

"These men are starving," she said. "And so am I. Why wouldn't you stop on the road when I begged—"

"Because I didn't know who might be following us."

Because I didn't want to risk another night alone with you.

"Can we eat now?"

"Yes," Jack grumbled.

"How generous of you, darling."

The endearment stung. He was about to lash out at her, but she was quicker. "Do you remember our last rule, Jack darling? *My* rule?"

Suddenly the very air between them was electric.

Don't call me darling, he almost yelled. But he didn't want to make the starving men think he was mad at them.

While he glowered, Bronte said to the men in her peculiar and yet endearing Spanish, "He's my husband. This is our second honeymoon. If he wants me back, you'd think he would at least try to be nice."

"I don't want you back."

Gray-faced, Jack stomped down the kitchen stairs. Fast on his heels, Bronte followed him.

Suddenly, finding himself inside the house with her, he thought of his bedroom upstairs. They were husband and wife. Everybody would expect her to move in with him. He thought of waking up every morning to the sight of fiery red hair on the next pillow. To the smell of wild gardenias. To the knowledge that her satiny warm body lay next to his. To the knowledge that she was always hot for it and available any hour of the day or night.

He wanted that.

No way.

She was the same with every man.

The ranch was a big place.

Where...?

Shanghai's cabin.

Jack had never set foot in it because he'd never felt strong enough to deal with his misgivings about his father.

Years ago Theodora had boarded the shack up.

"Till you're ready to get to know Shanghai," Theodora had said once. "Nobody's going to touch the old place till then."

"What about Garth?" he had asked.

"Garth's mother made him hate Shanghai. You know he thinks he's too good..."

The shack was badly in need of repairs. Pieces of stucco had fallen loose. The porch was sagging. There was no phone. The weeds around it were neck high.

Upon occasion Theodora had tried to shake Jack with guilt. "You ought to take better car of your daddy's place. He'd want—"

"I don't give a damn what he'd want."

Everything was different now.

The shack was a palace compared to the hovel Jack had grown up in. Dealing with his father's ghost was nothing compared to living with Chantal.

Before they reached the kitchen, he grabbed her in the dark hall and shoved her against the wall.

"Why are you bothering to pretend?" His eyes narrowed contemptuously into ice-black slits.

She tipped her chin up and met his gaze.

Ruthlessly he scanned her guileless features. Then his expression grew even darker. "You don't give a damn about those men."

She bristled with outrage. It took all his determination to ignore the quivering in her quiet tone. "Maybe if you weren't determined to see me as a monster, you'd see the person I really am."

"What's that supposed to mean?"

"You figure it out." She pushed him in the ribs and backed three steps toward the kitchen.

"And what the hell's the matter with your Spanish? You sound like you learned it in grade school instead of—"

"It's a bit rusty," she snapped hastily. "I took a class. To improve my grammar."

Before he could reply, Eva was there, her body huge and ponderous, her glowing skin as golden-brown as maple syrup, her stained white apron carrying with it the smells of the kitchen. Someone had told her Chantal had returned—looking different, it was true—but still the same woman underneath the changed exterior.

"Hello." Bronte smiled dazzlingly at the ranch cook.

Eva frowned in confusion.

"There're a dozen hungry men outside. They've walked all the way from Mexico," Bronte said pleadingly.

That stopped Eva dead in her tracks. Chantal had always scorned her in the past, as she had the poor starving Mexicans on their way north. Eva, who was loyal to the mistress and the ranch, had kept her distance and her silence when it came to the mistress's daughter.

Eva flushed. But as she studied Bronte's sincere face and then the sudden tightness of Jack's jaw, a puzzled look softened her huge dark eyes.

Eva had had a hard life. She'd married a gambler of roguish charm whose loser's luck kept them broke. Eva found her joy by savoring the little things. She could stand a full minute with one of her cats, watching a bee buzz in a red bougainvillea blossom; she could stand longer than that in front of her oven to enjoy the scent of fresh rolls baking. She had raised a houseful of children and had more than a dozen grandchildren.

She liked the sparkle of sunlight in dish suds as much as a grander woman might admire the fire of a diamond. She found joy in feeding hungry men. Her father had been such a man.

And Eva saw something shining in this girl's face that was as true and beautiful as the pure love that always radiated from her favorite granddaughter.

"Well, I'll be. You're the last person I'd ever expect a kindness from. But maybe you got more than a new face, after all."

"I'm sorry, Eva, if I was—"

"Don't." More softly, she continued, "Your mama. She's been mighty worried. She's got the whole world on her shoulders. I expect you'll be a joy to her. Won't she be, Don Jack?"

"Oh, don't ask his opinion," his wife said. "He's determined to hate me forever."

"He brought you back, didn't he?" Eva said, disappearing into the kitchen.

"Not because he wanted to."

"Oh, you know Jack, he only pretends he's made of stone."

Jack didn't like them talking about him like he wasn't there. Maybe he should find Mario and get some details on those infertile bulls. Then his stomach growled, and he remembered he hadn't eaten, either.

Jack shook his head. He was crazy to risk another minute in Chantal's bewitching presence.

Hell's bells. He stomped into the kitchen and opened the refrigerator. Just as he was about to grab a drumstick off a pile of fried chicken, Chantal reached past him and grabbed the entire platter.

He ate a peanut butter sandwich in silence, gloomily pretending to ignore the generous spread of fried chicken and potato salad and beans that she piled onto tray after tray, pretending he wasn't the least bit interested in having a piece or two or a bowl or two of the beans and salad himself.

She could have at least offered him something.

All he had to do was ask, of course, but pride stopped him.

The Chantal of old would have begrudged those pitiful men every single bite.

This Chantal—

She was the same.

Nothing had changed.

Chapter 14

"She's trouble with a capital *T*. Nobody wants that bitch back but you!"

"What I want counts, and don't you forget it. I run this place. I was running El Atascadero when the rest of you were in diapers or living thousands of miles away."

"I want her back, too!" The indignant, childish cry pierced the quiet as well as Bronte's heart.

A long, smoldering silence followed. Bronte's blood ran hot and then cold as she climbed the stairs. The family sounded every bit as difficult as Jack.

It wasn't long before the angry outbursts resumed. The name Chantal rang out several more times.

"She's my daughter. I, and only I, will decide if she goes or stays."

Bronte froze. What had she done? What was she doing, walking into this minefield that had nothing to do with who she really was?

To save herself from the man who'd tried to kill her, she'd told a lie, and then lived that lie for two days and nights. She'd even slept with another woman's husband. And now...

Why couldn't it feel like an adventure? Why did she feel ashamed and a little afraid?

She dug her fingertips into the waxed wood railing. How could she face them?

Jack's hand found the small of her back. None too gently, he nudged her up the stairs. "Go on. You might as well get it over with. They'll settle down once they've seen you."

"But—"

"It isn't like you to be afraid," he jeered. "I'm sure you'll probably charm the socks off them—the same as you've—"

She whirled, wondering what he meant by that.

For a heartbeat they stared at each other.

Even that brief glance at his dark, movie-star face and long lean body had her skin prickling hotly. He tensed, too, as if he couldn't look at her, either, without a similar unwanted reaction.

"You have a funny way of acting charmed."

"I didn't mean it like it sounded!" But his explosive denial came too quickly and was followed by a rush of color to his face.

It was chemical. Inexplicable. Unwanted by both of them. Unimportant. Still, she found him too sexy for words.

He'd been equally sexy this morning when she'd stumbled into him in the bathroom as he'd been about to shave.

He'd whirled, and she'd gasped, some part of her longing to rush into his arms and confess the truth, hoping he'd stop hating her and want her. "I—I thought you were outside. I didn't hear you come back insi—"

His shirt had been off and his jaw dark from a night's growth of beard. Standing there, he'd seemed a symbol of dark, seductive passion. Her mesmerized gaze had fastened on the network of muscles across his brown chest.

"I'm going," he'd growled as he'd grabbed his shirt and raced past her. He'd flung the door open and forgotten to close it in his haste to get away from her. She'd heard his truck door open and slam.

She'd gone to the doorway and paused, one palm on the edge of the door, the other on the doorjamb as she stared at his slumped form in his pickup for a long moment. Then, sorrowfully, she'd returned to the bathroom. That time her gaze had flicked to the tiny window, and she'd known she had to use it to escape. She'd decided to leave him because she'd started to care too much.

Playing his awful wife when she found him attractive was getting harder and harder to do.

"Keep moving." His cold smile jolted her back to the present.

Her head drooped. "All right."

The upper floors were as cool and dark as the kitchen. Everything seemed immense and strange. The angry voices were a low rumble now, each person straining to outdramatize the other.

"The men don't want Jack back. He's got them running scared with his constant talk about labor costs, spreadsheets and net profit. They've watched all the other big ranchers around here go back on the promises their granddaddies made to their granddaddies. They've seen whole families of loyal ranch hands kicked out of homes their families have lived in for fifty years, homes they thought they would stay in for another fifty."

"The ranchers are fighting to survive. It's hard to give people rent-free housing forever these days."

"We could subdivide a few acres, sell off some of that worthless—"

"Over my dead body!"

Then Jack's drawl sounded behind Bronte. "High drama as usual. Funny how your folks can get along till you throw millions of dollars on the table or force them to face extreme economic realities. Every year is harder than the last one. I've been trying to make them see that things aren't the same as they used to be. That's a hard pill to swallow when you've been born and raised to do things a certain way. Then I go and bring you back from the dead to claim what some of them have been thinking might be theirs. So try to understand if they seem a little panicky, *darling.*"

Bronte's stomach knotted. "How do you feel, Jack?"

"My only claim is through you, *darling,* so my opinion doesn't count. But it sounds like your aunt Caroline, Maverick, Becky, Cheyenne and Theodora are plenty steamed up."

Bronte's pace had slowed on the stairs again. If only she'd been able to get away from Jack at the motel. These weren't her problems. This wasn't her life. He wasn't her husband. How long could she possibly fool Theodora and these other people? Why should she even try?

She walked slower and slower till finally, on the

second-story landing, Bronte came to a total standstill.

"Nervous? Or is it Theodora's renovations you can't get used to?"

Renovations? Everything looked and smelled old, Bronte thought.

"I'll go ahead," Jack said as he led her through a series of cool, dark rooms lit only by the fading afternoon light.

"You remember how your mother is so tight about spending her money?" Jack said. "Well, she's gotten worse."

The rooms were large and grandiose, but boxy and unimaginatively designed. In each, tall windows faced east to catch the prevailing breezes. Wide doors opened onto shady porches and balconies with views of the ranch and the bay.

Her mother's brownstone had been grander. As Bronte looked at the heavy antiques, at the sombre family portraits, the drapes, the Aubusson rugs, she tried to memorize every detail. At the same time she struggled to act as if she were familiar with the house and its routines.

Its strangeness oppressed her.

The house was dark and cold. Like her husband, it seemed reluctant to reveal its secrets to her.

"I've fought Theodora on some of the changes. But you know your mother. When she's set on a thing, she won't listen."

Bronte nodded.

Jack pointed toward the fireplace, where the grim portrait of a man with a long white beard hung. "Your great-grandfather was just as stubborn. Still, he was one hell of an empire builder even if he did have a rather limited imagination when it came to designing houses. He wanted to build something grandiose to impress the neighbors. He had this big ranch; he wanted a big house. You can't do all that much with a house like this. Not when it's so pure Victorian. Theodora went absolutely crazy when I suggested tearing it down and building something modern. She's equally determined to keep the ranch and its traditions the way that old man said they should be.''

Bronte nodded.

''I've fought her pretty hard, but he rules from the grave. Trouble is, no man's vision is all that keen once he's been underground a spell. Things change. His ideas were good in his time, but we can't keep this place going by following a dead man's dictates. She doesn't want to be the one to sell even one acre of land and let the family or the ranch down. His traditions are both her legacy and her burden.''

''But if the others want to sell—''

''She's in control. She cares more about him than she does about the modern family. When a powerful, hard-willed man with a vision takes you out on horseback before dawn when you're barely four, it's easy to be brainwashed. It doesn't mean a damn to her that we've got the government breathing down our neck at every turn—about everything from endangered-species laws and regulations about beef to the ranch's ever-increasing tax burdens. But back to his house. None of the modern family likes living in this old white elephant, and it's proved impossible to remodel.''

For once Bronte agreed with him. The house was too big and drafty. Suddenly she wanted to open the thick draperies and the windows, too. She wanted to run outside into the evening light, to climb that magnificent tree out back and be free.

Even as she longed for freedom, the library door swung open and a tall, elegantly dressed man with golden hair loomed on the threshold. An inch or two shorter than Jack, he was dressed Western-style in jeans and boots and a snow-white Stetson, but his boots shone and his clothes were crisp and new. He was not nearly so formidable or masculine as the rougher-cut Jack. No, this man's features were somehow too properly in place, his teeth too straight, his ears too flat against his well-shaped head. Only there were lines of dissipation beneath his eyes, and his mouth looked a little hard as if his boyish charm was wearing a bit thin as he aged.

He frowned when he saw her. Even so, he took a few steps toward her.

Bronte shrank into the darkest shadows and tried to hide from him.

"Well, who do we have here?" Maverick's too-hearty voice bellowed when he caught sight of her lurking under the stairwell. "Come out of that dark corner so your favorite kissing cousin can welcome you home."

A stillness descended upon her.

Cousins. Childhood playmates.

Lovers.

A sickening knot formed in Bronte's stomach. Even if Jack hadn't stared warningly at her as he gripped her elbow and steered her past the flirtatious Maverick, she would have wanted nothing to do with this overly familiar cousin.

Everyone except a redheaded little girl stood up as she entered.

Bronte felt their eyes on her face, and self-conscious guilt burned inside her, eating away at her natural friendliness, causing her posture to stiffen. They thought she belonged here. But she didn't.

On one wall there were tall oak bookshelves, on an opposite wall ten male heads. To avoid the living people's stares, Bronte studied the stern, bearded faces that hung, painted and friezelike, in heavy golden frames.

"Unbelievable," the tall, slim, redhead who had to be her half sister, Cheyenne, said.

"It can't be her, Jack," said a plump girl with a pretty face and shiny brown curls.

"Believe me, Becky, she's Chantal," Jack said heavily.

Bronte felt thick waves of dislike radiating from everyone except possibly Cheyenne, who merely studied her disbelievingly.

"New face or not, it's her," Jack asserted. "So she's got this beautiful new facade. Take a good long look till you get used to it. I know I had to. Then it'll come to you that underneath, she's still the same. This shouldn't be such a shock. After all, you sent me after her."

For a second or two longer, everyone stood frozen like actors in a bad play. Then a small, dark figure with a halo of silver hair detached itself from the group and hobbled toward Bronte.

Jack leaned closer to Bronte. "Now don't you be playing your tricks on your mother, either."

Theodora's sharp, curious eyes assessed Bronte and then Jack. "Don't just stand there, Chantal dear.

Come over here where I can see you. I'm afraid my old eyes aren't what they used to be. Neither are my legs."

Bronte turned quickly, but it took her a second to find the older woman's face in the gloom. She had instinctively aimed her gaze too high. The woman whose mere voice exuded raw power and authority was surprisingly small in size. Theodora had halted in the middle of a bar of purple light that one of the long, stained-glass windows splashed on the carpet, and in that merciless cascade, the lines on her weathered face seemed as harshly and unapologetically etched as those of a Plains Indian.

Although Bronte felt a strange reluctance to leave Jack, everyone gasped in amazement when she rushed to embrace the older woman.

Cheyenne quickly excused herself. "I have to go." She made a hasty exit after a word or two to Jack.

Only the little girl, who was scribbling wildly on her large tablet again, failed to watch Bronte.

The undemonstrative Theodora hugged Chantal as fiercely as she herself was being hugged.

Jack stared at them in amazement as the embrace went on and on. Finally, several minutes later, Theodora shot Jack a smile. "I never thought...I never dreamed you could find her."

Then she hugged her daughter again.

Something wasn't right, Jack thought. Mother and daughter had never been like this.

"You wonderful boy. It's a miracle, Jack. Too wonderful to believe," Theodora continued.

Yes, it was too wonderful to believe.

"But you did it." Theodora gripped Bronte's hand. "Welcome home, my dear. You are beautiful. Truly beautiful. But...your new face is going to take some getting used to. You are, as I'm sure you know, quite changed."

"Yes. I don't feel quite like I'm me, either."

"I've been lonely these past five years."

"I..." What could Bronte say? She knew all about loneliness. Suddenly she saw that pretending to be this woman's daughter was unforgivable. She had to tell her the truth. "You know, I—"

Theodora's grip tightened. Before Bronte could confess, she rushed to speak. "Everything I've ever endured has been worth it...to have you home. Safe and sound."

Jack shifted uneasily. He was thinking of the heat and drought and bad cattle prices, of the faithless husband and the wild, hell-bent daughter this old woman had endured. Not to mention the ungrateful half-Mexican boy she'd adopted and educated even when everybody, especially he, had fought her every step of the way.

Jack was willing to hide his misgivings about the ranch's future and this reunion and give Theodora a moment or two to celebrate. Still, he noted Maverick's sulky glare and Becky's jealous glances and Carla's frown as she scribbled more frantically.

"You used to call me Mama," Theodora was saying.

"Mama."

Suddenly, Carla shot the pair a furious, pain-glazed glance.

The bill of Carla's blue baseball cap was cocked at a defiant angle and turned sideways. She had a pugnacious nose, and her red hair was tied back in a tangled ponytail.

As the child stared at her, Bronte felt the years slide backwards, and an odd excitement began to churn inside her. Looking at Carla was like staring into a mirror when she herself had been ten. She saw Jimmy in the girl's face, too, and wondered if he wouldn't have looked something like her at the same age.

"Did you bring me a present?" Carla asked.

"I—I'm afraid I left New York in a hurry."

Without a word the little girl suddenly turned back to her drawing and began to chew her pencil tip.

Bronte flushed. "Maybe we could go shopping...together."

"You always brought me presents!"

"I'm sorry."

"Carla!" Jack said.

I have no right to be here. I don't belong here. These are real people. This is a real little girl. I've hurt her.

When Carla's pencil dug into the tablet again, her curly red tangles sparked like angry fire in the lamplight.

Just like Jimmy's had.

Carla's defiant eyes were like Jimmy's, too.

While Carla was pale, Jimmy had had rosy cheeks and a husky body. Jack's daughter was pathetically thin, and her jeans were so stained and rumpled Bronte wondered how long she'd been wearing them. And how long had it been since anyone had run a brush through that ponytail?

The child was *motherless.*

Bronte was *childless.*

They were a match.

No. Bronte was a fraud.

Maverick came up to hug and kiss her. As he bent

his perfectly combed, blond head to Bronte's, his firm dry lips claiming hers in a perfunctory kiss, she fought to squirm free. But Maverick caught her hands in his own and slid them down the front of his body in a too-suggestive manner. "We always were...kissing cousins," he whispered. "We shared a cradle, if you know what I mean."

Panic mixed with fury as she pushed at him.

"You never used to be this way," he said, his voice deceptively soft, his breath hot on her face for a second before his mouth closed over hers again.

"Take your hands off my wife before I break your neck."

Maverick released his supposed cousin in an instant. "I didn't mean anything. Why, hell, Jack, you never used to care."

"Well, I care now. Come here, Chantal."

Bronte scuttled back to Jack, who ruthlessly studied her innocent face before pushing her behind him. "You probably love me making a fool of myself over..."

She went white.

Jack jerked away from her. "I need some air." From the door, he said with self-derision, "Sorry. I almost lost it. I'd better check with Mario on how roundup is going. See about those infertile bulls. And the other stuff...while the rest of you enjoy getting reacquainted." Mockery and tension underlined his every word.

Then he stormed out into the hall, with Becky chasing after him.

And Bronte, her hands clenched at her sides, was left to deal with *her* family.

"Where's Eva? I thought she made fried chicken,"

Maverick said, sliding his arm around Bronte and daring a flirtatious smile.

"Right here, Don Maverick." Eva padded breathlessly toward him, carrying a silver tray loaded with peanut-butter-and-Ritz-cracker sandwiches. Becky returned to the library, carrying a second tray with drinks.

When Bronte, anxious to rid herself of Maverick, rushed forward to help Becky, everyone watched her as, together, the two women set the tray down without spilling a single drop of iced tea or coffee.

When Bronte started lifting plates and glasses and cups, Maverick edged her away. "What happened to the fried chicken, Eva?"

"Why, your cousin, Doña Chantal, fed it all to those starving men from Mexico—"

"She what?" Maverick sounded both shocked and alarmed.

Feeling hemmed in by all their questions and stares, Bronte lifted another glass from the tray. "I'm sorry, Maverick. They looked so pitiful and hungry."

With a withering glare of sour disapproval, he reached for a sandwich. "This is stale and soggy," Maverick complained sulkily.

"I'm sorry," Bronte repeated.

Her apology brought a long, grumpy stare.

Stifling a nervous yawn, Bronte moved across the room to the largest chair. Sinking into it, she laid her head back.

Their gazes followed, and their mild surprise was now shock.

For one paralyzing second Bronte wondered what she'd done wrong now. Since she had no idea that Theodora was most particular about where she sat or stood in any room, and that she had a particular chair or spot everywhere, Bronte didn't know that she had chosen *her* chair.

Without a word Theodora sank onto the sofa near Bronte. "I'm starved," the old woman said mildly.

The moment passed.

Still, Bronte felt the tensions around her mounting. She kept making mistakes at every turn.

Suddenly she wished for her own face. For Wimberley. Why couldn't she be sitting at her old dinette set in her kitchen with her calendars and lesson plans thumbtacked to the walls, with Pogo purring on her lap?

She almost wished for the numbness and grief she'd felt after Jimmy's funeral and the divorce.

"I remember how you used to love iced tea," Theodora said rather too quickly. "Carla, I said come over here and greet your mother. You're so skinny, she's gonna think we've been starving you."

"I'm not hungry."

Bronte's throat went dry, but when she lifted a glass, she suddenly paused, wondering what Chantal put in her tea. Sugar or lemon? Neither? Maybe a diet sweetener?

Just as she was about to set her glass back down, Theodora quickly handed her a pink envelope and a slice of lime.

Bronte tore the envelope and squeezed the lime, thanking Theodora silently for the clue as the older woman poured bourbon from a silver flask into a glass of tea.

"Carla..."

Carla threw down her scratch pad. "I won't sit by her! You can't make me!"

As the child was about to stomp past them, she saw a teaspoon on the carpet. On her way out, she picked it up and tossed it onto the table at Bronte.

Bronte picked up the spoon and then set it back down. Very slowly she got up and gathered the little girl's sketchbook and pencils.

Time faltered as she saw her own features and Theodora's scrawled on the white tablet. Bronte traced the vivid black lines with a shaky fingertip. With what cruel and yet clever talent had her lovely face been distorted into a merciless caricature. Theodora's likeness looked even worse.

She held the drawing up so everyone could see it.

The library grew soundless. Other than the ticking of the grandfather clock and the guilty beating of her own heart, Bronte heard nothing.

"I have to go see about her," Bronte said quietly.

"Why don't you give her time?" Theodora asked. "We've hardly—"

Bronte clutched the tablet. "Because she's...my daughter."

"She's been drawing those awful pictures ever since you left. She doesn't mean to be so unfriendly. Carla was very excited when Jack called her earlier. She's been running out to the verandah every five minutes. But when she saw your truck, she hid the way she used to when you first came home from one of your trips, dear—"

"She's upset. I have to see about her—"

"Why don't you let Chantal go, Theodora?" protested Caroline's kind, cultured voice. "I'm sure Carla needs her more than we do."

"Oh, all right." Theodora arose and sat in her own chair. Like a willful child she drained her iced tea laced with bourbon. "But come back as soon as you're done."

When Bronte was gone everybody smiled.

She was beautiful, one of them thought warily. And sweet. Still, her departure was a relief.

It was time to finish what had been started five years ago in the barn.

It was too bad about this lovely girl.

It was too bad about Jack.

Sometimes unpleasant necessities had to be rationalized.

Who was she, anyway?

She didn't belong here.

The girl's existence threatened everything.

That's why she had to die.

Chapter 15

"Chantal!" Jack's rough voice barked as Bronte raced out into the hall after Carla, who was bounding upstairs to the third floor.

Involuntarily Bronte stopped, her eyes searching a wall of grim portraits till she found Jack's tall, familiar form leaning negligently against a doorjamb. Relaxed though he appeared, she knew he was anything but calm.

"I told you to leave her alone." There was steel in his low tone.

"I thought you left to see about the ranch."

"Believe me, there're always plenty of emergencies around here. They'll keep." He straightened into a taut, upright position. "I decided my biggest problem was you."

"Or maybe," she taunted, her green eyes shining at him in the dimness, "maybe you like being around me...more than you're willing to admit."

He tensed with indignation. "I do not!"

"I remember how you looked at me this morning, when I surprised you in the bathroom," she whispered.

"You should have knocked. You caught me off guard."

"Your shirt was off." Her compelling gaze held his. "You looked...very sexy."

"Shut up."

"You were just as nasty then as you are now. But you couldn't take your eyes off me then...any more than you can now."

"I said shut—"

"Why are you always looking at me like that, Jack? Like you're starved? Like you want to eat me alive? I bet you could be sweet...if you weren't afraid to be."

"Your imagination is working overtime."

"You've given it lots of material."

"Don't flatter yourself. There's way too much wrong between us for sex to cure," he muttered savagely.

"Maybe you're not so sure of your feelings as you pretend. And...if I took a shine to you...I'd want way more than sex. I'd want you to treat me nice...all the time."

"Nice?" he sneered. "You'd be bored with nice in two seconds flat."

"Try me."

He lowered his voice significantly. "Just stay away from Carla."

For an instant longer, he stared at her. Then he walked away from her down the stairs.

She hugged herself, her feet rooted in the thick carpet. For no sane reason a secret, breathless longing filled her.

He'd dashed out of the bathroom just as abruptly.

He *was* afraid of her.

Why?

Maybe they didn't want to like each other or to appeal to each other. But maybe they did, anyway.

The front door slammed. She closed her eyes briefly against the aching emptiness that assailed her, knowing he had plunged out into the blackening night.

She leaned against the wall, alone in that dark hall.

This wasn't her life.

He wasn't her husband.

She felt ashamed that she'd lied to him. Ashamed that she'd slept with him.

Maybe their having sex had been wrong.

Maybe she wasn't who he thought she was. But her new emotions felt all too real.

Maybe she had a new face. Maybe she wasn't his wife. But he had saved her. And their sex had been wild and incredible, and unforgettable.

Everything that had happened, the whole fantastic situation, was totally out of control. But maybe that was the way life was. Maybe you had to take what came and make the best of it.

Maybe none of the other stuff had been her fault, either. Maybe it was okay that she hadn't ever been able to please her mother. Maybe she shouldn't blame herself for Jimmy's death so much, either.

Maybe things just happened. Bad things. Incredible things. But good things, too.

Like Jack finding her.

Maybe Jack was her new chance, her fresh start.

Maybe she was his.

Maybe they were both too blind and foolish to see it.

Suddenly she knew that if she didn't find the way to his stubborn, intractable heart soon, he was going to teach her an entirely new meaning for the word *heartbreak.*

Fight harder, she thought. *You've got to fight harder.*

Carla hunkered lower when she heard the whine of the screen door far below before the second door slammed. She watched her father storm down the steps and wondered why he was so mad. A few minutes later the trick stair near the third-floor landing groaned. Someone was approaching her bedroom on silent feet.

An angry flush crept up Carla's neck. Was it the impostor?

If so, what did she want?

Carla glanced up at the shelves stacked with lavish dolls and exotic stuffed animals and other useless gifts her mother had given her to buy her love. After a stretch of tense silence, Carla began scribbling again.

Who did this woman think she was fooling? Carla could see straight through her. Probably everybody else could, too. Except for Grandmother.

Why was Dad protecting her? Where was Mother? Had Dad really killed her this time?

Rage and fear engulfed Carla. Then she thought about how nice he'd been these past few months, taking her out with him to work cows, trying to talk to her, listening, too. He'd been nicer than she'd ever believed he could be.

Some people still said he was guilty of murder.

Lots of people hated him....

Later. She'd think about him later.

Carla wished she'd gone out and climbed *her* tree. Sick with worry about her mother, Carla made wild black marks on her sketchpad. Her red eyebrows screwed together. Her magic pencil froze. No!

This monster wasn't any good, either.

She ripped the sheet from the tablet and brought her pencil to her lips. It was very, very naughty, and she was ashamed of it for drawing so badly.

"I'll throw you on the floor and stomp on you till your lead is broken into millions of pieces," she threatened.

The pencil wiggled, frantic.

"Okay. One more chance. But just one."

When Carla began to draw again, the pencil shaped the hideous nose more adeptly.

Who was the woman her father had brought home? This woman whose hair and eyes were the right shade of red and green? Whose creamy complexion was flawless? Dad couldn't take his eyes off her; she did look exactly like the magazine pictures Carla had collected of Mischief Jones.

How was such a thing possible? Was she a clone, like the alien in *Starman* that had taken a single hair and made himself into a copy of the heroine's husband?

Carla had wished for a real mystery so she could be a real spy.

Be careful what you wish for.

Sometimes when Carla skipped school, she spent

the whole day by herself either under her bed or up in *her* tree. She could spy, and tell stories to her pencil, so it could draw its magic monster pictures.

El Atascadero was a big ranch. And it held lots of secrets. Secrets big people never told little people. Secrets Carla had to find out alone. Grandpa hadn't loved Grandmother. He'd kept a woman named Ivory Rose as his lover. Ivory had been a witch. That's why Cheyenne was her aunt but wasn't. Maverick was mad because he might not get the ranch if Mother was back....

So now the impostor was the biggest secret of all.

Carla was just a little girl.

She never said much, so the big people didn't think she knew much.

Except how to draw monsters.

Her monsters worried the big people. Whenever Dad saw one, he would get tight-lipped and act explosive. Once he had ripped up an entire tablet. Usually he didn't say or do anything. But even when he was nice, he scared her. She couldn't forget how he'd put his hands on her mother's throat that last night in the barn.

Grandmother didn't get mad about the monsters, though. But she had hauled her to a lady shrink. Carla had sat there in that big leather chair studded with gold buttons while Grandmother had told the lady shrink how she'd started drawing monsters after their barn had burned down and her daddy had nearly gotten burned up and her mother had disappeared.

"What really happened that night in the barn, Carla?" Dr. Lincoln had asked.

Horrible images had flashed in Carla's mind as she had stared silently and stubbornly past Dr. Lincoln.

Finally the doctor had told Grandmother the sessions were a waste of everybody's time and money.

Carla couldn't wait to get big enough to leave home. When she grew up she was going to be a spy and marry a spy. The ranch was boring. She wanted to travel all over the world. She wanted a glamorous life.

Like her mother's.

Her tree was the huge, old live oak her great-great-grandfather had planted nearly a hundred years ago behind the house.

Carla had planned her life in *her* tree.

Too bad her plans never worked out. Real life just seemed like a series of accidents.

She was always sifting through the mail looking for a letter or even a postcard from her mother. Even with Dad acting nicer, she had wanted her mother, too.

But Dad hadn't really wanted Mother back. He didn't like hearing that Carla looked like her, either.

When she grew up, Carla wanted to look exactly like her mother. Only she wanted to have lots of kids.

She would spoil them, too. She wouldn't just go off...

She didn't dwell on how staying home with her children would conflict with her career as a spy.

She left the window and her sketchbook and stretched back onto her bed.

Again she stared longingly at the high shelves that contained all the expensive dolls and stuffed animals her mother had given her. The house was ninety years old. Her walls had cracks and the room was shabby. But she hadn't let Grandmother change anything. She was staring at a crack that ran from the ceiling to the dull oak floor when a gentle tap made her spring up sharply.

"Carla?"

Carla clasped her fingers over her mouth and willed her to leave.

The door opened.

"You forgot your tablet." The impostor laid her tablet on a low, antique table.

"Go away. I don't want it."

"It's very good. Have you had drawing lessons?"

Nobody had ever complimented her monster pictures, especially not after she'd made that person resemble a monster.

Carla wadded her pillow up and then buried her face in it. "Go away."

"Why?"

"'Cause you're not her."

Silence.

Carla lowered her pillow and glared.

The woman sank down into a chair that needed a new slipcover and nervously studied the doll from China.

"Is my dad in on this?"

"No."

"You're lying to him, too, then."

"I'm going to tell him the truth."

"When?"

"Soon. When it's safe."

"Safe?"

"A man thought I was your mother and tried to strangle me."

She untied the bandanna at her throat, and Carla gasped at the black bruises on her neck.

"My dad?"

"No. He's been wonderful...at least in his own way."

"Then who?"

"I don't know."

"And Mother?"

The impostor went white. Then she turned and stared fixedly at the Chinese doll.

The silence expanded. Suddenly Carla was filled by a nameless, sickening panic.

Her nightmare was real.

Her mother would never come home.

In the next second she was denying her worst fears and telling herself the impostor was trying to trick her.

"She's dead, Carla."

"No!" But even as she denied it, Carla clutched her pencil so tightly that it snapped in two. "I don't want you here. I don't want to talk to you anymore! Not ever again!"

"Carla..." The impostor leaned down and picked up one end of the broken pencil. She said very quietly, "I know what it's like to lose somebody."

"Why don't you stop pretending you're so nice and just go away? Nobody wants you here."

Grief lapped around Carla like huge black waves. She stared helplessly at the woman who looked so heartbreakingly like her mother. "I don't want you here."

But the impostor sat down next to her, and her voice became grave and gentle, comforting, like her own mother's voice had never been.

"Years ago I—I lost... I probably shouldn't tell you this yet." The impostor's eyes were infinitely kind and sad and vulnerable, too. "Maybe we won't have all that much time together. You see, I know that if we did have time, we could be friends. Carla, I like children. I used to be a teacher."

"I hate teachers," Carla said defiantly. "They're stupid."

"Well, I like children. And I'd like you...if you'd let me." She hesitated. "What I'm trying to tell you is that my own little boy died." She grew paler than ever, and Carla felt a wave of pity.

"How old was—"

"Five. He died in my arms under a big ash tree in my front lawn. It was my fault. I—I didn't know what to do to save him. I just held him and rocked him and talked to him. Later, I found out that if I had only known some basic first aid... But that doesn't matter now." Tears brimmed on her lower lashes, and when she spoke again, her voice was thicker. "So I know what it's like to feel all alone...the way you feel. The way your dad feels, too. You're both afraid to love."

Silence.

Then slowly Carla asked, "What was his name?"

"Jimmy. He had lots of friends. He liked to ride his skateboard and his pony."

"I don't have any friends."

"I could be your friend."

Carla's lower lip trembled, and when she felt the woman's gentle hand ruffle her hair, she started to push it away. Instead, she sat very still, for the fingers felt nice. Almost they felt like a mother's touch.

"My dad hated my mother. They say he killed her. I used to hate him."

"He didn't do it. I saw your mother in New York. Why..."

"She was scared of him. That's why she ran away and left me behind."

The gentle hand caressed in soothing, circular strokes. "Maybe neither of them could help any of that. Your father saved my life. Carla, people can behave very differently around different people. Maybe your mother and father did the best they could. Maybe they just couldn't get along. Have you ever met a kid at school that you couldn't like no matter how hard you tried?"

"Lots of 'em."

"Well, sometimes no matter how hard you try, you just can't make things work. But you have to go on. To new things."

"What's your real name?"

"Bronte. Bronte Devlin."

"I want you to stay, at least for a while."

"I will if I can."

The impostor was at the door. About to go, when Carla remembered her overdue math assignment.

"Hey! Are you any good with decimals?"

"Math was my favorite subject."

"Then you've definitely got to stay…at least for a little while."

It was dark, and the shadows were long and deep in the wide hallway. Exhaustion was sweeping Bronte when she reached her bedroom door. But when she tried her crystal doorknob, her hand froze as something smooth slid through her fingers and rippled silently to her feet. When she opened the door, a bar of golden light flooded the hall.

In the next instant she was on the floor screaming.

For the silky thing she had seen coiled around her ankles like a snake was a man's red silk tie.

Her heart hammered as she picked it up.

The silk burned her fingertips.

She remembered large bony hands wrapping a similar tie around her neck.

Who had left it here? Was it a warning?

Was he here, too?

The red silk blurred.

She lay against the wall, unable to see or hear. She curled into a tight ball and again screamed.

She had no idea how long she lay curled like that in the dark, but suddenly she heard racing footsteps.

When she opened her eyes, Jack's arrogant face loomed out of the darkness.

Even as she tried to scramble away, he sprang toward her, his deep voice a kindly rumble.

"It's only me."

White-hot anger seared through her that he could be so calm. "Did you do this?" She held up the red tie.

"No!"

When he slid his hand down her arms to lift her to her feet, she fought to twist away from him. But he pulled her up gently, swearing to her, again in that soothing, velvet tone, that everything was okay.

Tears pooled in her eyes; she began to tremble.

"Have I ever hurt you?" he asked.

She fought harder to push him away.

"Hey, hey. Trust me," he whispered.

"How can I trust you or anybody here?"

He picked her up in his strong arms, carried her into the bedroom where he laid her down on a black satin, quilted spread.

"The killer is here. In this house."

"Okay," he said, sitting down beside her, folding her hands into his. "You found a red tie. You're scared." He wrapped his arms around her. Jack's voice softened to a caress that felt like velvet upon her skin. "But you're okay now."

And for some reason his saying that with such conviction helped her regain her calm.

"I'm okay." She bit her lower lip. "I'm okay."

Jack's eyes narrowed thoughtfully. "You're sure?"

"As okay as I can be...knowing he's here. But don't you go anywhere."

"I'm here." His reassuring grip tightened.

"You hate me."

"I wish."

The shadows of the bedroom and the rich black of the satin spread made his white shirt seem whiter and his dark skin darker. His features were so rugged that his potent, masculine virility struck her like a body blow.

Suddenly Bronte was aware that she was alone with him in their bedroom. With a little moan she pulled loose from him and buried her head in a pillow. "How can I trust you?"

"It feels odd, doesn't it?" A fleeting smile broke across his face. His usual dislike for her had vanished.

Then a thin gasp from the stairs broke the fragile moment of intimacy.

His smile died.

Bronte turned from him to the still, misshapen figure in the darkness.

Theodora.

Jack's face hardened when he saw the glass in Theodora's hand.

"Is everything all right?" Theodora demanded. "I heard a scream."

Jack's grim gaze was glued to the amber contents of her glass. "Everything's fine."

"Then I'd like to see my daughter—alone."

Chapter 16

Bronte took a deep breath as she stepped inside the library. The red tie had her so scared, all she wanted to do was confess everything to Theodora. She wanted nothing more than to run away from her pretend husband and false life as soon as possible.

But when Bronte tried to shut the doors so she and Theodora could be alone, Jack barged inside, too.

"Jack, I need to talk to Chantal alone."

"Later."

"Why don't you just go?" Bronte demanded. "There is no reason for you to act like you care about me."

"You're a most unusual wife. Most women would want a concerned—"

"Jack—"

After both women asked him to leave again, he finally said, "Okay, I'll give you a minute."

But he immediately returned with a huge laundry

basket full of mail, which he noisily emptied onto a polished library table. Then he plopped himself in front of the mess and grinned.

Both women glared at him, appalled.

He just smirked at them as though he relished the chance to be perverse. Like most men, knowing he wasn't wanted made him more determined to stay.

"You could do that in your office," Theodora said.

"I could. But I know how tough you can be." He slit an envelope with a theatrical gesture. "She's had a scare. I'm not sure she's up to what you have in mind."

"I'm fine." But Bronte's voice was weak.

"You look as pale as that lampshade. As your husband, my job is to protect you."

"From my own mother?"

"If necessary."

"Jack, don't be ridiculous."

"Humor me, *darling*."

As always his endearment had that cutting edge. Even though she was still scared, Bronte hated feeling safer because he was there. His stubborn insistence was hugely annoying. Determined to ignore him, she turned her back on him and sat down.

But she heard every single sound he made.

Her skin prickled every time he glanced her way.

Did he have to slash through those crisp envelopes so noisily? His chair groaned when he rocked back and forth on two spindly legs. He wadded up garbage, slinging each piece to his feet.

"Sorry," he whispered politely when an envelope struck her ankle.

He was as distracting as a splinter festering underneath a fingernail. No matter how hard she might want to pry him out, he delighted in wedging himself in more obnoxiously.

Bronte had come down to tell Theodora the truth, so she could be rid of him and all these lies forever.

Theodora drank steadily from her flask, scowling at him, too. But he cheerily dominated their conversation, reading newsworthy items to Theodora that she didn't care to hear. And, oddly, Bronte, who had been so anxious to talk to Theodora and escape this house and this man and this unwanted life, soon found herself fascinated as he talked to Theodora about ranching, their mutual friends, Mario, the jealous and problematic Caesar, cattle breeding and horse breaking, El Atascadero and town gossip. So fascinated that sometimes when he read something really funny, she actually forgot her fierce urgency to be gone and turned back to face him, laughing out loud.

Theodora relaxed, too, and began telling him what had happened while he was away. They discussed the bulls, and she demanded his opinion of that particular situation. Even Bronte could tell his answers and concerns were intelligent. When Jack mentioned that certain accounts were off, Theodora poured herself another drink and drank steadily in silence for a while.

Gradually Bronte relaxed. She forgot the red tie. When he read a letter from a Tad Jackson from Australia, describing the Aborigines' custom of sleeping naked together in a hole they dug, and then pulling their dogs inside on top of them as the night got colder, even Theodora looked interested. Tad wrote that the phrase "three dog night" referred to a very cold night indeed.

Bronte turned her chair all the way around so that

she could see Jack better. Slowly a man she didn't know began to emerge.

This Jack frowned at some of the things Theodora said, smiled at others, dismissed her next remark with no expression whatsoever. Gone was the angry, impossible man who'd hated Bronte these past two days and nights. Gone was the intense lover who'd made wild love to her and then despised her and himself for it.

This man was milder, lighter. He was quick and intelligent, well-educated. This man had a golden lab named Guerro, a willful daughter who spent her time spying on her family and the *vaqueros*. He had a family. A past. A life. Depth. Friends. And there was a fascinating richness and texture to his character.

But every time Theodora poured more whiskey from her flask, Bronte noticed how his hard features tightened, how he caught his breath or chewed his lip or stopped talking for a second or two.

She remembered the smashed beer bottles at their motel.

He had battles to fight, but he was a man of rare courage.

He had saved her life.

Even though he professed to want nothing more to do with her, he had come running when she had screamed a few moments ago. He had been gentle, reassuring. He was with her now....

She owed him.

No. She couldn't let herself think like that.

She wished him gone and herself alone with Theodora.

Still, a pleasant half hour passed before Mario interrupted them. Mario was a small, powerfully built man with a white streak in his black hair. He was most upset to have learned that Caesar had gotten drunk and torn up a bar and was now in jail in Val Verde where he was being held without bail. Bronte gathered that Val Verde was a border town eighty miles south of the ranch headquarters.

With a worried glance at Bronte, Jack picked up his Stetson and excused himself. Theodora's gaze sharpened on her daughter.

Bronte smiled, and for a few moments longer, the surface politeness between them remained untroubled. But with Jack gone, the tension level rose, and Bronte soon felt a good deal more insecure about all the lies she had told.

She was sure that somehow Theodora knew. Still, there was no telling how long she might have waited before confessing, had not Theodora made it easier.

"Jack is different with you. I've never seen him joke or laugh around you before." Theodora poured herself still another drink. When she spoke again, her voice was deceptively soft. "My daughter put lime...two slices...in her tea. She didn't use sweetener. She knew better than to sit in my chair, too. Except for your face, you are nothing like her. I'm surprised Jack can't see it."

"What?"

The two women stared at one another.

"So why did you pretend I was...your daughter?"

"Because I could expose you anytime...as I am doing now."

"I don't understand."

"How could you? But soon you will. For years I have sacrificed everything for the good of the ranch. I lived for the ranch. Chantal didn't understand that.

She was my daughter, but she took after Ben more than she took after me. She opposed me on every important issue."

"Why did you want her back?"

"She is the next generation. The ranch should rightfully be hers. I had to know for sure what had happened to her. Where is she? And why do you look like her?"

"She's dead."

Theodora took this news calmly, with only the slightest tremor passing through her.

"She was murdered, and I'm truly sorry. Two days ago. The man who killed her almost killed me, too. That's why—"

"Did you see him?"

"I couldn't see him, but I'd know him if..."

"Did Jack see—"

"No. The man was gone when Jack got there."

"I was afraid of this." Again Theodora's voice was only a trifle thinner. "For five years I've feared her death. Chantal led a wild, fast life that could only end one way. Did you talk to the police?"

"No." Bronte got up. "The killer's dark. He has big bones. Large hands. Strong hands. He tried to strangle me with a red tie. That's all I know...."

"Sit down," Theodora whispered shakily. "I need to think."

Bronte sank back into her chair. "Nothing you say will make the slightest difference. I'm leaving."

"It's not that simple."

"I'm not your daughter. It was selfish of me to pretend I was. My only excuse is that I was so scared. I was hurt. Terrified for my life. Scared of my new face, too. Jack saved me, but I knew he wouldn't take me with him if I didn't lie. But I could have a real life of my own, you know. I used to be a kindergarten teacher. My real name is Bronte...."

"I accepted you, Bronte, knowing you weren't her...to get to the truth."

"Well, this is the truth. I'm not Carla's mother. I'm not Jack's wife. I don't belong here. This face you see—it's not mine, either. It's a cross between my mother's and your daughter's. And...there was a red tie on my doorknob tonight."

"There are millions of red ties in the world."

"But somebody here knew what such a tie would signify to me. I can't keep pretending I'm Chantal. I don't want to die."

"You've told me who you aren't. Now tell me who you are."

For a long moment, Bronte was silent. "My mother was an opera star. I was a teacher. I'm divorced. But who I am doesn't matter."

"Tell me what matters more."

"I'm not sure."

"I've seen the way you look at Jack. Doesn't he matter?"

Bronte's eyes filled with tears. "No! We've only just met. Nothing is real between us."

"He's in love with you, you little fool. And you're in love with him. Even I can see that."

"I don't care what you think you see."

"So, you're a coward? A quitter?"

"No!"

"What about Carla?"

"My little boy died...because I couldn't save him. I'd probably hurt her more than I could ever help her. She's not my responsibility."

"If you love Jack, she is. You pretended you were Chantal, but he reacted to *you.* He fell in love with you. He never loved Chantal. He married her because she seduced him and tricked him. He stayed with her because he's stubborn. He sticks with anything longer than anybody I've ever known. He served five years for her murder because everybody knew he hated her. He loves you."

"He acts like he hates me."

"He's never loved anybody else. If you leave him, I don't know what will happen to him."

"He's stronger than you think."

"Becky's after him."

"Becky?"

"Chantal's plump little cousin. She's even got a small stake in the ranch. She lives in Houston, but since Jack's been home, she's come down every weekend. She's always out at the pens. He lets her work the gates."

Jealousy filled Bronte at the vision of Jack and Becky together. Bronte lowered her lashes against her pale cheeks, so Theodora wouldn't see. "Maybe they belong together."

"She'll get him, but Jack doesn't want Becky. He wants you."

"No...."

"If you leave, you'll smash him to pieces. I'm going to tell you a few things about Jack, because I know he won't."

"Please don't—"

"Jack's tired. Real tired. When you get as old as I am, you'll know that a man can only fight so much, for so long. First, there was the barrio and the shame of being a whore's son. He's stuck on the notion that his daddy deserted him without a backward thought. His father was the most talented cattleman I ever knew. He would have been so proud of Jack. Then Jack married Chantal, and she was his whoring mother all over again. He went to prison and nearly died because of her. He's different with you. Alive, almost human. If he loses you, he's going to start drinking—''

''He'll hate me when he finds out I lied.''

''Jack saved your life. Maybe you owe him the benefit of the doubt. I bet he cares...enough to forgive.''

Bronte thought of all the things they'd done and said together, of the glorious sex they'd shared. All he had to do was look at her and she felt special, like she belonged to him.

Theodora rose and lifted a heavy book from a shelf. When she returned, she sat closer to Bronte and opened the huge photograph album. After the first picture of Jack, Bronte had to see the rest.

The childhood photos were brown and faded. Jack had grown up overshadowed by Maverick, who was golden and gifted and beloved. In every picture Maverick sat on his horse ramrod straight, his handsome chin high and proud, while Jack sat slouched in his saddle, his dark head down, his overlarge cowboy hat propped low over his ears. There wasn't a single early picture of Jack smiling.

Silently Bronte flipped more pages.

''You say that the man who killed my daughter is here,'' Theodora murmured. ''If you don't stay just for a little while and help us nail him, he might kill Jack...or Carla. You don't know what he's after.''

Bronte paused on a page. ''I can't stay. Nothing

you can say will make me change my mind.'' But even as she spoke, she realized there was nowhere else she wanted to go. And out of that knowledge came the fierce longing to know if she really was so special to Jack.

No. She wasn't.

Wordlessly, Bronte flipped more pages. In all of them Jack was such an unhappy-looking little boy.

Soundlessly, she turned the final page and found herself staring at a black-and-white studio glossy of Garth Jones.

Her movie star.

She'd barely given him a thought in the excitement of the past few days. Garth grinned at her insolently. He had signed his name in a flourish of swirling black ink.

A fragile stillness descended upon Bronte. Garth Brown was connected to these people.

''What's his picture doing in here?'' she whispered. ''How do you know him?''

''Jack and Garth Brown are half brothers.''

''I—I didn't realize—''

''Garth is Shanghai's older, legitimate son. I think Jack's always figured that Shanghai didn't need him because he had Garth. Only Garth took his mother's side and never came near Shanghai or the ranch.''

Bronte hurt for Jack.

''Jack's never had anybody to call his own. Unless you change your mind, he never will. Stay.''

''I can't,'' Bronte said. ''I'm really really sorry, but I just can't.''

Chapter 17

Bronte closed her bathroom door and stripped out of the jeans and blue blouse she'd worn the past two days. Bubbles foamed in the bath tub.

She was leaving tomorrow.

In her mind's eye she saw again the yellowed photographs of Jack slouching and looking so forlorn. At the thought of leaving him forever, a surging ache rose from deep inside her.

She cared about Jack. Even though he wasn't hers to care about.

How could she have fallen in love in such a short time? When he had been so awful to her at times?

But so much had happened so fast. He had saved her. He had that way of looking at her. Was it really such a wonder?

A lonely old woman had asked her to stay, even though she knew Bronte was a fake. But it was the little girl with tangled red curls and sorrowful eyes—a child who looked so much like her own darling Jimmy—who tempted Bronte to stay almost as much as her love for Jack did.

Still, no matter how much she cared for them, they weren't hers to love. She wished Theodora hadn't told her about Jack's childhood or about his feeling put down by his famous brother and Maverick and Chantal. Seeing him as a vulnerable human being only made her feel more attached to him. She wished she didn't feel that, beneath his anger, his soul was bound to hers.

Dropping her towel onto the sheepskin rug, Bronte sank into a huge, antique, white bathtub with claw-and-ball feet.

Who was she?

She didn't know herself anymore.

There were too many riddles to be solved. Both in her own life and in Chantal's.

For now, Bronte wanted to take a long bath and go to bed. In the morning perhaps her resolve to go would be stronger.

The warm, foaming bubbles rose high against the porcelain sides. The water felt soothing after what seemed the longest day of her life.

The lights were turned off in the bathroom, but she didn't need them. Her body ached from the long drive. And her head from all the tension with Jack, as well as from what Theodora had told her.

Bronte couldn't quit thinking about Carla, who reminded her of Jimmy. Carla had Jimmy's pure sweet face and Jack's fierce pain and anger. The child was motherless, but she might lose her father, too.

Bronte remembered sitting out on the balcony of her own mother's brownstone, staring sulkily down at the street because she hadn't wanted to be inside around her mother or her mother's friends.

Bronte wished that she could stay and teach the little girl to laugh and smile, to make friends—as Jimmy had. For Bronte, who adored children so much that she had made them her career, Jack's daughter had added an appealing new dimension to her role as Jack's pretend wife.

She couldn't stay.

Thank goodness, Jack had gone out with Mario. Stunned and yet relieved by Theodora's acceptance, Bronte hadn't wanted the map the older woman had drawn of the house and the ranch. Still, Bronte had brought it upstairs to study. Theodora had shown her several more photograph albums as well. She had explained all the family portraits and the ranch's long history. She had told her how each generation kept the name West even if control was held by a female. Theodora had written names of key employees on the back of the map, too. She had told her about Carla and how she'd been traumatized that last terrible night in the barn, when she'd thought her daddy had murdered her mother.

In all the photographs, Carla's hair had been tangled and her clothes torn. She had stood apart, looking motherless and defiant and as heartbreakingly isolated as Jack looked in his pictures.

Bronte had poured over the pictures. But those of Jack as a boy had tugged at her heart more than any. He'd been so thin and dark. So much rougher and poorer looking than Maverick and Chantal. In every picture he'd glowered at those other, more fashionably dressed children, scowling just like Carla.

Theodora had described the appalling conditions he'd grown up in.

"I don't want to hear any more," Bronte had pleaded.

"His house was four pieces of tin stapled to pallets stolen from loading docks. You wouldn't believe the flies. He wore rags. He'd never been to school. He ate garbage. His mother slept with men in the cot next to his. Why, he was more wild animal than boy. But he took the best from both his parents—his mother's beauty and his daddy's brains and character. I brought him back, determined to tame him. He fought me every step of the way.

"The girls always chased Jack, but he distrusted his sex appeal. Then he married Chantal. She took lovers. Maybe because my solution to a similar problem was the bottle, he turned to the same solution. Every new lover made his drinking worse."

Theodora had gone on to other subjects, but Bronte had barely listened. Theodora had said that her grandfather had installed a bizarre and antiquated security system in the big house that had included safes under the kitchens and gun towers on the roof and a maze of underground tunnels to out buildings, where the family could hide from Mexican bandits.

She told her an old ranch tale about how this same grandfather, the ranch founder, Samson West, had been murdered by a hired hand. How the murder had been made to look like an accident with a rope and a horse. How Samson had been dragged to his death across the prairie.

Well, at least with Jack out of the house, Bronte could finally relax. She wouldn't think of murder or sex or her new face, or of anything else that had to do with this whole fantastic scenario. She would just enjoy being deliciously alone in the glorious antique tub filled to the brim with floating islands of silvery bubbles. Above the tub, steamy, delicious scents of lavender and gardenia blossoms wafted in the humid darkness toward the beamed, wallpapered ceiling.

Bronte's hair was twisted high above her head in a thick, clumsily shaped knot from which thick tendrils curled in damp strands against her forehead and neck.

Drowsily she leaned back against the tub. The warm water with its mounds of bubbles rose dangerously higher as she sank deeper. With a washcloth she lazily rubbed her neck, her shoulders, and dabbed at her flat belly.

She sank deeper still, wishing she could stay there forever. Thinking that if she only could, maybe she should stop worrying about Jack. Maybe then she could stop caring about the rightness or wrongness of leaving.

Deeper she sank, until even her ears were submerged. The walls of the bath and the bedroom were nearly two feet thick, so she didn't hear Jack's skeleton key turn in the bedroom door, which she had so carefully locked. She didn't hear his easy, long-legged strides as he crossed hard floors and Persian carpets. Nor did she hear him making boxes, taping them; pulling his suitcases out of closets. Nor did she know when he began opening and slamming drawers, emptying his clothes sloppily into the half-dozen cardboard boxes and suitcases, so that sleeves were left hanging out and thin black combs and shoes and socks thrown in on top of them.

She lay in a meditative trance in the semidark bathroom, a warm washcloth plastered across her eyes. Slowly, the tension from her long drive with Jack eased. Forgotten, too, were the bruises on her neck. Suddenly she was daydreaming about her other life. She was on her screened porch, listening to wind chimes, watching Jimmy climb on his first pony.

For a while she'd been happy. Had Jack ever known anything approaching fulfillment or peace?

Bronte never heard Jack's quiet approach when he'd finished emptying the drawers and closet. The well-oiled hinges made no sound as the big, white bathroom door swung halfway open. She didn't feel the whisper of cool air as he stepped inside.

But she smiled seductively.

Almost as if she sensed him, a bittersweet ache blossomed inside her.

The door opened into the shadowy bathroom.

One minute Jack felt cool and collected and very determined about packing his things and moving out to Shanghai's cabin as soon as possible.

In the next minute his gaze had sharpened with dark, laser intensity as he found himself captivated by the sweetest half smile on his wife's lovely face. His jaw tightened as he raged an inner battle with himself to go.

Her heavy-lidded eyes were closed, her lush, cupid mouth slightly open. In invitation. Or so it seemed. She seemed to glow in that semidarkness like the rarest of jewels. Like a desert flower beneath a moonless sky.

Her skin was creamy except for those cruel yellow-black finger marks on her slender throat. Softly swelling breasts with pert pink nipples broke the sparkling surface of the water.

He'd spent five years in a cell with nothing nearly as lovely or as alive to look at.

There had been graffiti on the walls. The stench of sweat and urine everywhere. He remembered the hellish loneliness of being caged. The hell of thinking he'd never get out. And then when he'd gotten out, he'd still felt as if invisible prison walls were encircling him, cutting him off from everybody else.

Blood pounded in his ears like primitive drums.

He was free now. Around her, he didn't feel quite so lonely.

Again he studied the purple ring around her throat. Odd how just the thought of her dying had made him feel more helpless than he'd felt even in prison when those men had held him down on cold concrete and tried to rape him.

Odd how those bruises brought back the pure, raw fear of being beaten; he felt some danger even here, tonight.

They were home.

He remembered her piercing screams, her claim that she'd found the red tie.

He believed her. He didn't feel safe.

Suddenly his pulse was beating violently, and he was frozen stock-still. He'd wanted her all day. Maybe that's why he couldn't tear his gaze from her lips and her delectably slim body, the body that was so tantalizingly exposed to his view by those drifting mounds of silvery bubbles.

A minute before, his big black boots had been planted on terra firma.

Now he was sinking into a vat of delicious femininity.

Of all the abominable luck.

Chivalry dictated that he withdraw silently.

But he hadn't learned chivalry in the barrio. He had learned other things, all the wild things that men like him, men who had an easy way with women, could do to pleasure a woman.

Hungrily, Jack's eyes wandered over her breasts and hips.

Even the sight of her slim toes turned him on.

Perhaps he made some sound.

Perhaps she just sensed him.

Or smelled him.

Whatever.

Her emerald eyes fluttered open.

And in those torpid orbs he saw some strange emotion as she slowly focused on his face.

Warmth flooded him.

Forgive me, he should say, like some elegant gentleman.

But he had bad blood. He came from a bad background. He was no gentleman.

She was no lady, either.

He should forget the boxes, his need to pack, and simply run.

Instead he shut the door behind him, shot the bolt and joined her in the humid darkness. His scuffed black boots were soon rooted in the soft sheepskin rug by the tub, and he couldn't quit staring at her. He'd spent the whole damned day dreaming about her.

When had he felt like this about a woman before?

Not even with Cheyenne.

Never with Chantal.

But everything was different now.

In the velvet darkness, the warm invitation in her gentle gaze compelled him. As if in a trance, she got up slowly, the curves of her body glistening, bubbles threading from the silken tendrils of her hair and trailing down to her nipples.

"Hadn't you better go, Jack?"

Oh, yes.

But he lacked the will.

Or, rather, his will was to stay.

Like Venus rising from her pink shell, this flesh-and-blood creature was infinitely more beautiful and magical than Botticelli's love goddess. Her face was illuminated with desire and the need to be loved. At the same time she warred against those things, too. In her gentle eyes he saw wisdom and desire wrestle with a soul-deep pain.

Warm water splashed the cuff of his jeans as she lifted a long, shapely leg gracefully over the edge of the tub.

She reached for a thick, soft towel.

But he was faster, leaping toward her, ripping the terry-cloth rectangle from the bar, handing it to her.

She began to pat herself dry with the fluffy cotton. She made slower strokes across the curve of her belly.

Watching every stroke, he felt like a man felled by surprise from behind.

Then he groaned aloud, took the towel from her and began to dry her skin caressingly, like a man worshipping at the altar of his goddess.

Long before he was done, he dropped the towel, and his hands were all over her damp, velvet skin. So was his mouth. He pulled her against his body until every muscular inch was pressed burningly against her soft, naked flesh.

He was lost.

So was she.

She was moaning as he trailed fervent, destroying kisses down her vulnerable throat. She turned her head toward his, sighing. It was as if she couldn't say no any more than he could to this dream...to this miracle that they alone shared. To this coming home.

He tore off his clothes. His belt with the huge buckle snapped through jean loops and clunked when he tossed it to the floor. Next came his boots, his jeans. She ripped the buttons of his shirt apart.

There was almost no light in the bathroom now, and they were naked together like living phantoms in some wondrous love poem. Her slick wet stomach skin fit against his dryer flesh. Thigh to thigh. Only the murmur of her husky love words, the light skimming of her fingertips and the spiraling warmth of erotic feelings were real. Her smooth, soft woman skin was real, too. Whatever was happening between them was beyond either one of them to stop.

His tongue slid inside her mouth, and she made a low, feminine murmur of desire. Her arms circled his neck and tightened beneath his crisp dark hair.

The fire inside him burned out of control. This was beyond hatred. Beyond love. Beyond anything he had ever known. His fingers closed around the swollen underside of her breast and his palm filled with her soft flesh. Her nipples budded.

Were they animals, bound by instinct to couple on sight?

Or simply too human?

Or just too damned lonely and too damned weak?

He didn't know. And he didn't much care as he sank to the sheepskin rugs and lay very still, staring up into her warm, glowing eyes as she began tearing off his shirt with eager, light fingers that thrilled him.

When she was done, he caught her by the waist and rolled her over, so that he lay on top of her. His hands slid into her hair. He seized her wrists, raised them above her head and pinned her on that litter of soft animal hides imported from Tad Jackson's sheep station in Australia.

She shifted, her whole body quivering as she arched to meet him, molding her body to his. The heat of her damp skin fused them even before he thrust into her.

Tightly sheathed, with his heart thundering in his chest, he stared deeply into her eyes and knew a mindless glory. Slowly their bodies began to rise and fall.

Perfect harmony. Perfect rhythm.

Man to woman.

Eternal. Forever.

She drew him deeper and deeper inside her.

He moved faster and faster.

Until their hearts beat like the wildest jungle drum.

Drinking in her exquisite beauty, drowning in it, he closed his eyes.

She was heaven.

Sweet precious heaven.

An angel.

Not wanting to look at her, he kept his eyes shut.

Blind as he now was, the sensations of touch only became more exquisite.

He wished he could be soft and gentle, but found he couldn't hold back.

If he was hungry, she was hungrier. One leg came up and wrapped around him.

They devoured one another, moving more rapidly in a fierce, fantastic rhythm that rocked them in flaming surges ever upward toward the shattering conclusion.

And afterward, when they lay panting and breathless together after that explosion and dying of selves, she touched her hand to where his heart throbbed beneath his ribs like it still might burst. Even later, long after their bodies had quieted and cooled, her hand remained over his heart. He closed his eyes and held her close, unable to let her go.

For that moment his isolation was gone. Usually only a drink helped, but she was better than liquor.

He didn't dare look at her. He was too afraid that she would see tenderness shining in his eyes.

He wanted to hate her. But even now when he was done with her, he burned for her on a soul-deep level like a man delirious with fever. Sweat popped out everywhere on him, drenching his head, his black hair, his shoulders.

Hatred was simple compared to this.

Then he forced himself to remember the long, dark years of their marriage. Her mockery of his low-class birth. His despair, black and bottomless, over her numerous infidelities. She had taunted him with man after man. Every time he had caught her with a new lover, she had said that he was a whore's bastard and had laughed at him for thinking he deserved a faithful wife. Later, of course, she had always apologized and promised she would never do it again.

He remembered the long, whiskey-filled nights, the sinking into that sour, bleary, soul-destroying oblivion. How he had hated himself and her when he'd awakened in filthy rooms with coarse strangers beside him. More than once he'd landed in jail.

The same determination in his character that had driven him to overcome the obstacles of his birth and achieve goal after goal had proved to be his undoing in his marriage to Chantal. He had stayed with her and put up with her abuse far longer than he should have. Foolishly, he had thought his patience might reform her. Once when he'd gotten drunk with a shrink in a bar, the bastard had told him that he was trying to save his mother by saving Chantal. Jack had given up after that.

Yes, he had hated her. But he'd loathed himself more. There had been other reasons he'd stayed. Maybe deep down he'd thought she was the only kind of wife who would have him.

How could he want such misery back?

Too much was riding on him now.

If he were to have any chance with Carla...

If he were to solve any of the very real problems of running the ranch, he couldn't let her do this to him.

How could he stop her?

"That was one hell of a performance," he growled, his voice bitter. "You knew I'd come. You were just lying in that tub with the light out and the door unlocked, waiting—"

"You bastard," she whispered with a strangled sob. Frantically she unlocked her legs from his waist. "Get off me, you mean-hearted bastard." She had used that word to taunt him in the past, but tonight her broken voice was stark, pain filled.

Her beautiful face made him remember her lovers,

and he was filled with the old, smothering darkness that made him crave liquor. "With pleasure, honey," he sneered.

Even though her eyes glistened with sorrow and her soft, stricken face tore him apart, his chiseled features grew fierce and dark and ever more remorseless.

She snatched her clothes from the floor and held them in front of her body. She grabbed some sort of crude drawing that had been lying under her bandanna.

"I'm leaving you! And I'm never coming back! I don't want to be your wife anymore!" Then she ran to the door, stumbling blindly.

Her hoarse sobs tore at him. Then he caught a glimpse of her back. Of her smooth, unblemished shoulders.

Unblemished.

No scar!

What the hell—

No wonder his mind refused to accept this Chantal who was afraid, who he could hurt with a cruel word or two.

This gentle woman was a stranger.

He didn't even know her.

She wasn't real. And if that was so, nothing they'd shared could be real.

His dark face turned to stone. For a moment he was too stunned to react. Then he felt a violent building rage as he listened to her pull on her clothes.

He grew too furious to trust himself to deal with her, so he didn't get up until she had finished and had run out into the hall.

Slowly, methodically, he dressed and finished

packing. Except for his record collection, he took every other item that was his.

He slung his guitar over his shoulder.

No way was he ever sharing a bedroom or a bed with such a liar again.

If she was a liar, what did that make him?

A damned fool!

Who was she? What was she after? Why did he even give a damn?

He saw her exquisite face beneath his on that rug, her hot emerald gaze, adoring him.

Even though he hated her, he still wanted her.

Way more than he ever had before.

Because she wasn't Chantal.

Chapter 18

By the time Bronte climbed the stairs to her bedroom again, she'd replayed the seduction scene on the sheepskin rug a thousand times.

One minute he loved her, the next he hated her. Who was Jack, really? What did he want from her?

He'd ripped off his clothes as if he'd die without her. Afterward he'd turned dark and hostile.

Her emotional turmoil had left her exhausted. All she wanted now was to do a free fall across her bed and sleep forever.

Hesitantly, she pushed her bedroom door open. Except for the faint glow of a night-light, the room was dark. Jack's cardboard boxes and his black guitar case were gone. She stepped inside and walked toward the bed.

That was one hell of a performance.

Scalding tears slipped from her eyes as his cutting words hurt her all over again. She was even worse than he thought. She had slept with him under false pretenses.

Suddenly her tearful gaze fell on a long, thin envelope lying on top of the black satin spread. Bewildered, she picked it up and read the name Chantal. The slanting handwriting was unknown to her. Still, her heart began to pulse when she tore the envelope open and shook several newspaper clippings and a piece of white, lined notepaper onto the bedspread.

A bold black headline blazed up at her: Supermodel Mischief Jones And Lover Dead In Two-Car Pileup. There was a black-and-white picture of Webster's burned-out Mercedes and several large close-ups of Mischief.

"No...." Bronte pushed herself away from the bed and sprang to a nearby lamp and then to another, snapping the little chains under the shades and flipping wall switches until the room was ablaze.

Then she sank onto the bed and spread the articles out before her. Lifting them one by one, she read in horror. The second clipping was Webster's obituary, the third Mischief's.

They were dead.

Murdered?

On the lined paper, a handwritten note in a childish scrawl read, "Nothing is what you think. Leave or die. A friend."

Bronte wadded up the clippings and the note, stuffed them back into the envelope and shoved them as far as possible under her mattress. Then she got up and began to pace back and forth.

Who had left the red tie and sent her these clippings?

Were they trying to warn her or to threaten her?

Without bothering to undress or brush her teeth, Bronte got into bed. She propped her pillows behind her head and stared blankly at the tall, shadowy walls.

Whole minutes ticked by. She felt too paralyzed to move.

When she began to shiver, she slowly drew the blankets and black satin spread on top of her. Then she wrapped her arms around herself.

But soon a coldness that had more to do with mindless dread than with the temperature of her bedroom seeped through. She couldn't stop shaking.

There were no stars. A thick cloud layer blanketed a moonless sky. A wild breeze tore through the brush and mesquite trees and prickly pear cactus that grew right up to the cabin.

Shanghai's dark, stucco shack seemed to reject Jack and his cardboard boxes just like the old man would have done. Jack's stomach twisted into a cold, hard knot like it always did when he thought about his father.

"I'm here to stay, old man. Whether you like it or not."

Jack forced himself up the stairs a step at a time, walking gingerly, testing each of the spongy boards before trusting his full weight on it.

When he'd crossed the porch, Jack set his guitar down and regarded Shanghai's cabin for a long, tense moment. It struck him as odd that Garth, the legitimate son, had never bothered to come home, not even for his father's funeral. Theodora had told him Garth was ashamed of his father.

When Jack swung his flashlight around, fleeting arcs of white light floated across the boarded-up windows, broken shutters and the wooden door, which had been nailed shut. There were holes in the stucco. Still, compared to his mother's tin shack in Mexico, where the floor had been dirt and the walls unsupported by mortar or cement or nails, Shanghai's shack looked sound. At least Jack's bed wouldn't float away on a river of mud or a wall collapse the first night it rained. He'd get the *vaqueros* up here first thing tomorrow to clean and patch the old place up.

As his flashlight bobbed, a white envelope gleamed on the porch floor near the door.

Jack aimed the cone of light downward and then knelt and picked it up. He read his name rendered in bold, childish, block letters. Then he ripped it open.

A cryptic note read, "Nothing is what you think. *Un amigo.*"

Too true. Furious, Jack wadded it up and stuffed it in his jeans pocket. He had to get inside and find some place clean enough to throw his bedroll. Mario and the men would be up at first light working cattle. He had to supervise them.

Jack set his flashlight down and went to work on the door, using his hammer to claw and rip at the rusty nails that secured the boards across the doorway. Panting heavily after removing the first board, he heaved it into a clump of prickly pear cactus. Then he began straining to remove the second board, prying the nails out and letting them clatter across the uneven planking.

He was about to set to work on the third board when the snap of a twig a little distance from the house penetrated his consciousness. When his gaze flew toward the darkness, he sensed unseen eyes staring at him. He turned on his own light and waved it

For years he'd hoped and prayed she'd change, but she never had.

Until now.

The girl was beautiful, naive. She made love like an eager virgin. She made him feel special, cherished.

Jack was thinking about how different she was in every way when he heard another footfall in the dry yard.

His mind cleared instantly.

Somebody really was out there.

In a single fluid movement he retrieved his long metal flashlight. Another stealthy footstep sounded in the dry grass closer to the cabin. Again Jack felt the pull of an unseen gaze.

"Hey? Who's there? You'd better answer." He hunkered low and slipped off the side of the porch, dropping as stealthily as a shadow into the soft sand behind a mesquite trunk just as a man's heavy work shoe rang on the first step.

"Hey there yourself, Hollywood," boomed a gravelly, all-too-familiar voice.

"Brickhouse?"

"Did I scare you, my man?"

Jack flashed his light onto a wide, bronzed face, a pair of bold black eyes that crinkled at the unexpected brilliance. Damned if Brickhouse didn't have the whitest smile in the entire universe.

"Shut that damn thing off. You had some manners in the stir, boy."

Jack doused his light. In the next instant they gripped each other in a bear hug.

"Sorry about sneaking up on you."

"I guess I was a bit jumpy."

"This place is spooky, man. Whatcha out here all alone for, anyway?"

"Long story."

"Here. I'll give you a hand." Brickhouse picked up the hammer and attacked the board Jack had been working on.

"When did they let you out?"

"I been out awhile." Brickhouse set his hammer down and pulled out a bottle of bourbon. "I thought maybe we could celebrate."

"Let's get inside first."

Brickhouse went back to work. Two more boards fell at their feet. Soon they were inside.

Jack lit a Coleman lantern and set it on a dusty chest of drawers. Draperies of cobwebs hung from the ceiling. A mouse skittered frantically along one wall.

Except for the dust that covered the two single beds, the rag rugs and the handmade furniture, the cabin was surprisingly orderly. Dingy, red-flowered curtains hung at the boarded windows on sagging rods. There was a picture of Garth on the bureau.

"Who's that?"

"This was my old man's place."

Brickhouse picked up Garth's picture. "This you or your famous brother?"

"It's him."

Brickhouse blew the dust off the photo and set it back facedown. "The real thing?"

Jack was furiously wiping dust off a chest of drawers. When he'd finished, he opened a drawer. It was full of neatly folded shirts, but the next contained tidy stacks of bundled letters.

"Man, this is giving me the creeps," Brickhouse said from over his shoulder as Jack read the envelopes. "How come nobody cleaned his stuff out before now?"

"'Cause Theodora wanted me—"

Jack broke off. The third drawer contained bundles of yellowed letters tied with a red ribbon like those his mother had always worn. They were written in Spanish and addressed to his mother in Piedras Negras. Jack slowly sat down on a bed and read the first letter.

"Whose are those?"

"My father's."

"Oh, man, I'm going outside to get drunk. You ain't supposed to read dead people's letters."

Jack was glad to have the cabin to himself. His dark face became a mask as he silently skimmed a dozen or so pages. In every letter his father had begged his mother to let him come down and get his boy.

Shanghai had wanted him.

The same as he'd wanted Garth.

With an indifferent air, Jack pitched the letters back into the drawer. What did they prove?

He went outside and picked up his guitar and then his boxes. He began throwing boxes into the house. He untied his bedroll and pitched it across a bed.

But all the time his mind whirled. How come his mother had said his father hadn't wanted him?

The unsavory answer came.

His mother had used everybody—her customers, her landlord, her neighbors—for all they were worth. She'd extorted money from Shanghai. She'd forced Jack to beg and steal for her.

Jack couldn't blame her.

She'd lived on the edge. She'd had to survive the

only way she knew how. Why would a whore who exploited herself hesitate to exploit her son or the man who'd fathered him?

Theodora had tried to tell Jack the truth, but he'd been too damned stubborn to listen.

Maybe Shanghai would have loved him.

No.

This didn't mean anything.

He couldn't let it.

"What'd those letters say?" Brickhouse demanded when Jack stepped out onto the porch again.

"Not a damned thing."

"You're in a foul mood."

"Shut up."

"You're too uptight. Why don't you play something on that guitar of yours? Loosen up. I need to relax."

"I don't mind if I do."

Bronte's breath sobbed, her heartbeats hammered as she whispered a silly little prayer. She would suffocate if she stayed inside the big bedroom a second longer.

Opening and then closing her French doors firmly behind her, she stepped out on the wide verandah and began to pace back and forth just as she had inside.

Waist-high ground fog swirled up from the lawns, blanketing the shrubs and the potted plants eerily so that she couldn't see much from the balcony.

Webster and Mischief were dead.

She couldn't be sure that their deaths were not accidents. And yet...

Jack had saved her life and then brought her home. He had made love to her. He didn't want her to stay.

With a longing that bordered on pain, she thought of the hard, accusing way he'd looked at her and insulted her when he'd sent her out of the bathroom.

And the red tie on her doorknob?

Bronte couldn't forget that red tie any more than she could forget those large bony hands winding a similar length of silk around her neck and nearly strangling the life out of her.

Jack had saved her.

He didn't want her.

Still, every time she thought of him, she flushed with a strange heat that told her no matter what he'd said or done to hurt her, she wanted him.

To go or to stay...?

As Bronte moved away from her lighted doorway down the shadowy verandah, she felt torn between love for Jack and Carla and her terror. The mists swirled up and enveloped her as she glided in utter silence past a tall grouping of wicker chairs and tables and potted ferns that were clustered beneath a ceiling fan.

"Chantal." Caroline's voice was soft, but the slim white hand that snaked out of a shadowy wicker chair and captured Bronte's arm when she was about to pass was surprisingly strong.

"Oh!" Bronte gasped. Her heart tripped faster as she made out the familiar face and shape of the older woman in the darkness. "I—I didn't see you sitting there."

"You looked like a ghost yourself. I had to touch you...to make sure you were real."

Caroline's dark eyes were wide, too, but she was as lovely as she'd been in the library. Her thick, golden hair was loose about her shoulders. For her age, she was astoundingly beautiful. Her feminine, heart-shaped face was as unlined as Theodora's was wrinkled.

"I—I should have said something when you first came out, but you took me by surprise, too. You may remember that I come up here and sit quite often this time of night. I hope I didn't frighten you, my dear."

"No. I couldn't sleep. But I thought you lived in that other house at the end of the drive."

"I do. With Maverick. But as you know, I often have trouble sleeping. I walk from my house past my husband's grave and then down to the big house and around it and back. I often come up here and sit and stare out at the ranch awhile."

"You're not afraid...?"

"Of what?" She sounded surprised.

"Oh, I don't know."

"It's quite safe, really. There's a guard at the gate. Then there's nothing but empty pasture and brush country and the Gulf for miles and miles on all sides of us. We know everybody who lives out here."

"It just seems like such wild country. Especially at night."

"Nights always seem softer to me."

"It's so isolated and so near Mexico."

"Well, there are dangers. Just a month back a *vaquero* got his leg caught in a combine, and Jack had to apply a tourniquet and give him first aid for nearly forty minutes till he could be airlifted to a hospital in Corpus Christi."

Jack was fast on his feet in an emergency.

"Is he okay?"

"He's back at work. But things like that don't happen too often. So except for drug runners..."

"Dopers?"

"They're a dangerous bunch. You don't want to catch them by surprise. But that's not too likely. They want to get out of your way as much as you want to avoid them. For the most part the wetbacks are harmless, too. More pitiful than anything. Now, we do get more dope planes flying over us than we used to. A few years back—when you were still in Houston—a plane crashed near the big house. It was chock-full of marijuana. By the time Jack got to it, the pilot and crew had run off like they always do."

"What happened?"

"Jack called the DEA. They sent some officers down to pick up the pot. The plane was registered to a Mexican citizen in Guadalajara. Not that he'd claim it when Jack notified him. So Jack just lassoed the tail and hauled the plane up to the house. It sat around here for a month. Then he sold it."

"So stuff can happen."

"There's no doubt dope smugglers are a dangerous breed. I wouldn't want to surprise one. They've been known to shoot and ask questions later. So you do have to exercise some caution out here. But then, of course, you know that. You were born here. You didn't used to be afraid of anything. You just hated it out here because it's so boring. I never told you...but I used to sympathize when you'd say that and Theodora would get so furious. At least I had a life *before* I married. I never blamed you for wanting more than this."

Jack knew a powerful thirst as Brickhouse threw his head back and swigged lustily from his bottle. Brickhouse drank once and then again and again.

"You gonna stand there looking at me like you're dying of thirst?"

"Give me that bottle. If anybody ever deserved a drink, I do."

"It's about time...."

Jack lifted the bottle. "To you, Brickhouse. To us. To freedom. We should be happy men."

"I don't put much stock in happiness no more."

"Yeah. This is the only true happiness."

Jack took a long pull. He liked the way the bourbon burned all the way down and then made him feel a little light-headed, wild.

"No woman's ever going to own me again." Jack took another long pull. "No woman—"

"Sounds like she's on your mind, though." Brickhouse's gaze darkened. "I gotta talk to you about that girl you brought home."

"She's the last thing I want to think about tonight."

"You wanna hear something crazy, man."

"I said shut up about her."

"That pretty white gal—she ain't your wife."

Jack's face went gray.

"Here, man. I can prove it." Brickhouse pulled out two folded manila envelopes. "That same night you were in New York to get your wife, I was there, too. I had my own agenda. I hired on as a waiter at Mischief Jones's party. Some job. I served raw fish and watched rich, phony weirdos gobble it down like that slimy shit was good to eat. Then this girl who looked exactly like your wife showed up. She looked me straight in the eye like she knew me and was afraid of me. Man, if I hadn't seen them both together..."

The liquor filled Jack with a strange lightness of

being, making him feel loose, relaxed for the first time in years. He wanted Brickhouse to shut up.

"Jack, there was two of them."

Jack closed his eyes and felt the light breeze ruffle his hair and caress his face. He was so tired, and yet his temples were pounding. The liquor that only moments before had had him feeling good and free and happy, now made him feel tense and confused.

A strange mist was rising from the ground and swirling around them, so that they seemed to be the only two people in the world. But the stars had come out above them, and when Jack leaned his head back against the railing, he could see the constellation Orion blinking down at him.

"You listen to me, man."

Jack saw Mischief Jones, her green eyes maniacal right before the stone cat slammed into his jaw.

He saw the girl in the park again, her beautiful face aglow, her eyes tender as she talked to a little boy.

Jack nodded dizzily as he threw his head back to take another long pull from the bottle. But this time Brickhouse's large fist closed over his wrist. He grabbed the bottle and threw it out into the darkness.

Glass shattered.

Jack jumped up drunkenly. "Now what did you go and do a damn fool thing like that for?"

"You've had enough, man. Damn it. Look at these envelopes. I got them out of Webster Quinn's car. Quinn was the plastic surgeon who turned your wife into a goddess five years ago. He made her so beautiful she became a model. For some damn reason six months ago he made this girl named Bronte Devlin look just like her."

Another piece of the puzzle.

Bronte.

Jack sagged to the floor, the name striking him like a blow. With a shudder Jack was back in Central Park. The girl with long red hair and glowing green eyes had run straight into him when she'd seen that cop.

Foggily he remembered her exact words.

I—I'm not Mischief. My real name is Bronte Devlin.

Like a damn fool, he'd played along with her. Because of the cop. He hadn't believed her, though.

She'd been telling him the truth. In the park. In the bar.

She'd run from him. She'd been scared and sweet. And *different.*

Jack's hand shook as he aimed a flashlight at her before-and-after pictures.

"She was pretty messed up," Brickhouse said needlessly. "These were taken in the E.R. She damn near died."

The pictures made Jack sick. As long as he lived, he was never going to forget them.

"Quinn took care of her for six months. When she found out what he'd done, she ran straight to Mischief. I was there, see, 'cause your Mischief had something to do with my Beauty's death. I wanted answers. Only somebody else got the bitch first."

"What the hell are you talking about now?"

"It's a long story. Forget it, man. I saved your ass in the stir because I wanted answers about Beauty. Only you hated the bitch more than I did. Then somebody else got to her before either of us could."

Brickhouse's words whirled queasily in Jack's brain.

Her name was Bronte.

He'd made love to Bronte Devlin.

Bronte Devlin had tricked him and seduced him.

Why?

Jack's stomach wrenched, and he swallowed the bitter bile in his throat. She'd used him. She'd made him care. She'd opened him up to the kind of pain he'd been running from.

"She's okay, man."

"No." Jack's face was hard and set. A cold, killing rage filled him. "She's a whore. Same as all women. She's faithless. Like my mother was. Like Chantal. She tricked me. I don't give a damn about her. She doesn't give a damn about me. She's been lying and pretending the whole damned time."

"You're too drunk to think straight."

"And whose fault is that?" Jack stood up. With a sickening lurch, he lunged at Brickhouse. His aim was off, and he weaved off balance. Staggering, he pitched forward, straight into Brickhouse's strong, waiting arms.

"You can't hold your liquor anymore, white boy."

The sharp tone made Jack's thoughts spin in a red haze.

Bronte. Hot tears burned close to the surface.

Once he had yearned for love. The bitter years with Chantal came back to him. The hopelessness and despair of prison was with him again. Old memories. Bad memories. He had too many of them.

Then he saw Bronte's shining face as she'd looked at him before he'd made love to her on that sheepskin rug. There had been so much hope and trust and adoration in those eyes.

Dear God.

"Bronte," he rasped with a choked sob.

"You got it bad, man."

Jack's cold, black eyes glared at his friend. The expression on Jack's face was just shy of frightening.

"I don't give a damn about her. Not really."

"You're too drunk and too stubborn to know what you want, boy. I expect you'll know in the morning, though."

Jack closed his eyes. "Shut up then, so I can sleep."

Chapter 19

Gossip was flying about the ranch as wildly as lightning in a summer thunderstorm.

Everybody knew long before Jack crawled off Shanghai's porch at dawn and splashed himself with an icy bucket of water that he'd brought Chantal home, only to desert her up at the big house and go and get himself roaring drunk with a fearsome, black prison buddy.

Everybody wanted to know what Chantal had done, or who she'd done it with, to drive Jack back to booze so fast.

Chantal had always been trouble, big trouble.

The bets were on that she'd done it with Maverick right under Jack's nose. The *vaqueros* as well as the foremen and their families couldn't talk about anything else except her numerous exploits, naming cowboys, naming places. Next to hunting, Chantal's exploits had been everybody's favorite topic of gossip for as long as anybody could remember.

Eva said Chantal was nicer now. She said the witch had grown herself a heart.

Then why was Jack so sore?

The smarter hands were sorry she was back. Sorry to hear that Jack had lost out to his demons. If Jack was finished, so was the ranch. The old señora was past her prime, and Maverick was no rancher. He'd sell the place first chance he got to city folk. He'd take his profits, fire the cowboys and live in Europe.

"Mark my words. The ranch is done for," said old Joe Crocker. "So are we. Chantal's trouble. She'll bring Jack down. She did before."

The sky was dark above the cattle pens. The dusty air that floated above the herd held a dampness that smelled tantalizingly of rain.

Every muscle in Jack's body ached, and his eyes burned from too little sleep, too much booze and a foggy tangle of lust and guilt. The sun seemed over-bright and his spurs, chaps and boots too heavy. The red bandanna tied like a mask over his mouth and nose choked him almost as badly as the dust.

He was glad of the deafening sounds. Glad of the horses that were neighing and sputtering and pawing the deep sand. Glad of the cattle in full voice, bawling up and down the register as gates sorted them into different pens, separating mothers from calves, steers from heifers.

Only the *vaqueros* were quiet. Especially Mario, whose all-seeing eyes darted everywhere.

Jack knew that the men had their minds on more than cattle, that they were curious about his love life.

across the trees. When nobody spoke, he decided it was probably a steer or a buck and went back to work on the third board, yanking at it till he was again drenched in sweat. Still it didn't loosen.

Chantal, or rather her lookalike, came into his thoughts in vivid, full-color images that he couldn't fully control. She was lying beneath him on a sheepskin rug, her green eyes hotly ablaze. Next he saw the shape of her body as she'd walked away from him toward Ernesto and his starving troop.

The visions blended into fantasy, and she was suddenly there with him in the darkness, sliding toward him, smelling of gardenias, her moist lips parted, inviting his kisses as eagerly as she had in the bathroom.

Jack swore and hurled himself at the third board in a frenzy, swearing a blue streak in Spanish and English when it still didn't budge.

"She's not worth it," an inner voice taunted. "Hell, she's easy—you can have her any old time. So what if she's a liar, take her till you get your fill."

Restlessly he picked up his hammer again and hooked two more nails, yanking them out and throwing them onto the porch with a vengeance.

He didn't want to think about her, but the more he tried to put her aside, the more he remembered how she'd felt like molten satin, how she'd quivered at his lightest touch. She'd never been so sweet. So perfect.

He thought of how she'd smiled at Carla. She'd been friendly to Eva and to Theodora. She hadn't even flirted with Maverick.

No wonder nothing about the new Chantal had added up.

The new Chantal.

Not that Jack planned to set the nosy bunch straight. He'd stick to the business of branding and vaccinating and neutering, of sorting and readying steers and barren cows. The hands had better do the same.

He scarcely noticed the smell of mesquite smoke, burning hide and manure that rose with the dust to his nostrils. His jaw was hard beneath his Stetson. His brown hands were folded across his saddle horn, and he slumped forward on Dom, studying the herd, fighting to squelch his visions of *her* as he concentrated on each animal.

From long hours and long years of assessing animals on roundup grounds, he'd imprinted a picture in his mind of the perfect animal. He was always looking for that exceptional heifer or bull that would stand out from a thousand others.

"You look kinda green about the gills, Jack." Dr. K. North, the ranch's veterinarian had to shout to make himself heard. "You gonna sit in that saddle by this here chute and cull cattle all the damned day when you're sick as dog? You oughta be back in the big house in bed with your pretty wife."

Bronte.

Jack's eyes narrowed; his lips thinned as he imagined her naked body tangled in cotton sheets, her red hair spreading away from her flushed cheeks.

He saw her bewitching smile and look of stricken hurt last night after...

Just thinking about her got him as hot and hard as a brick.

Dear God.

Without half trying, she'd wound him around her little finger.

She must despise him for bedding her and scorning

her twice. Who could blame her? Why should he care?

She was a stranger and a liar.

Maybe she looked like an angel.

Maybe sinking into her body had been as close to heaven as he was likely to get.

She was a fake.

If and when she knew where he'd come from and what he was, she'd find him as disgusting as Chantal had.

For a moment he forgot Bronte and remembered the poor, desperate wretch he'd once been. He saw his mother's emaciated face, the helplessness and pain in her huge, dark eyes as she'd lain in that oven-like hovel under a cloud of flies. When he hadn't been out stealing scraps of garbage to feed her, he'd been home fanning her hot face and swatting flies. There'd been a man who'd paid him to sing for coins the *norte-americanos* threw. Only the man had stolen the dimes and laughed when Jack had begged for them because his mother was dying.

Jack had prayed for a way out of that hell. He didn't deserve Bronte. Who was he fooling? He was a thief, trash, unworthy....

Still, he *had* to know for sure if she was as bad as he kept telling himself she was. He needed to go to her and talk to her. To ask her dozens of questions. He wanted to know who she was and what her life had been like.

Damn it, he wouldn't do that. Something was wrong with her if she was mixed up with Chantal. It'd be a cold day in hell before he set foot in the big house again. At least not till she went back to wherever she'd come from.

What would Theodora do to him when she figured out the girl was a fake? Jack's plan to manage the ranch till Carla grew up was coming apart at the seams. Well, he didn't have time to worry about that.

"The work getting to you, K?"

"No, sir."

"Then don't go sticking your nose where it don't belong." Jack's black mood caused his voice to come out harsh and loud. It was an effort to speak with so much tearing at him.

"That girl got you drinking again, Jack?"

"It was only a slip."

"More than a slip by the looks of you."

"I went a little crazy. But that doesn't mean... Damn it. I'm not starting back. Don't you go blaming her, either."

"That's a new one." K.'s voice was sassier than ever.

"What?"

"Your defending her."

"If you say so, old man."

"One day at a time, young feller."

K. was a reformed alcoholic himself.

"You got that right, K."

Then Jack touched his Stetson and gave a grim nod toward a particular shiny-coated, auburn heifer in the chute. K. North scribbled something on his papers, and Mario herded the prized animal into the pen for Jack's experimental herd.

Jack had been up since dawn, working cattle with Mario and Brickhouse and the rest of his men. He forced himself to sit straighter in his saddle even though he still felt queasy. Despite two aspirins, a violent headache throbbed behind his fiery eyelids. He had a hell of a hangover.

Four hundred bawling cattle didn't help his headache. Neither did K.'s reports that confirmed the bulls were indeed sterile. Since Jack had tested the bulls at the auction house, how was such an error possible?

Ranching in south Texas was a hard business. Over half the land of El Atascadero was heavy sand, dunes left over from the receding Gulf of Mexico. During times of adequate rainfall, cattle could survive on the rolling dunes amidst shin oak and mesquite. Ranchers could make a small profit. In times of drought, like now, making money was damn near impossible. Still, the problems Jack had experienced since he'd come home from prison were worse than the norm.

Somebody was setting him up. There was more to these problems and accidents than could be seen on the surface. How come every mistake could be laid at his door?

Somebody wanted him gone.

Who?

At two, when the day's roundup was half over and the cowboys broke for lunch, tension filled the cow camp. In a grove of mesquite and ebony trees, Mario had stretched a couple of tarps to make more shade. Rough wooden tables had been set up under them. A side of beef, slaughtered that morning, hung from a limb. The other half gave off the tantalizing aroma of barbecue as it cooked over an open fire.

The men kept to themselves, avoiding Jack. Not that he minded. His touchy stomach rebelled at the thought of ribs and sausage and sliced tenderloin, and he wasn't in the mood for conversation.

There were refried beans, tomatoes and onions. While the *vaqueros* ate heartily together of roasted calf testicles and saddle strings, which were long, thin strips of grilled meat pulled from the ribs, Jack sat alone and consumed only a bowl of rice and beans, and a platter of thin camp bread, which he washed down with five glasses of sweet tea.

When the men were done, Jack could feels their eyes on him. In the cattle pens beyond, the dust and bawling seemed to be more intense. Jack stood up to try to see what had the animals so riled.

White horns bobbed up and down like waves in a stormy red sea, but he couldn't figure out why they were so jumpy.

"The cattle and the men are getting restless," K. said. "Let's get back to it."

Jack sat awhile longer with K. in the deep shade of a live oak. Something didn't feel right.

Thoughtfully he watched his men set their plates down and start poking their branding irons back into the fire until the ends were white-hot. Still he hesitated before he gave the signal to go back to work.

Above the low murmur of the men's voices, Jack heard someone say something about marrying a ranch and getting more than he bargained on. Then Greg Cassidy's voice rose even higher. "I was glad she kicked the greedy bastard out 'cause it won't be long before she gets the itch and comes looking for it. You ever dipped your wick in that honey pot? She's juicy and tight, and she don't lay still. She kicks and screams and bucks better than the wildest bull I ever rode in a rodeo."

"If you ain't careful, she'll bite it off like a wildcat, Cassidy."

Violence swelled inside Jack even before the men laughed. In a blinding flash, he was on his feet and lunging toward them, swinging a fist into Cassidy's jaw and kicking a boot heel into his shin. Cassidy was taller and heavier, but he hadn't seen the blows coming. He reeled backward, sprawling clumsily into the dirt. Jack threw himself on top of him. Before Cassidy could get his breath, Jack rolled him over and planted a boot on his stomach and leaned heavily on it.

"You say one more word about my wife and I'll kill you."

Cassidy's eyes bulged.

"Enough," K. yelled. "Break 'em up...before somebody gets himself kicked to death."

Rough hands grabbed Jack's shoulders and pulled him off. He didn't fight the men who grabbed him, but his deadly expression didn't relax much, either.

"Get the hell off this place." Jack leaned down and picked up his Stetson. "And any other man who has something to say about my wife better get, too."

Bronte.

No wonder they wanted her.

Jack remembered her naked body and how soft and sweet she'd felt beneath his hands. He remembered the warm honey of her kisses. The kindness in her voice.

He wanted to hate her. He was determined to hate her. But the fierce emotion that made him want to kill any man who so much as thought about touching her was not hate.

The day got no better for Jack as it wore on; if anything, it got worse. Thunder rumbled. Not that so much as a drop of rain fell. At four, a gate latch broke, and one hundred cattle burst free, nearly crushing Mario as they stampeded into the brush.

When Jack discovered that the latch had been deliberately tampered with, he again sensed his unseen enemy. Thoughtfully, he ordered six cowboys to round up the cattle and secure the pen. Then he told Mario to tell Maverick he wanted to see him in his office.

Maverick sent word back that he was way too busy.

Doing what—making more mischief? Jack wondered. He damn sure hadn't showed his face at roundup.

Jack had been sitting in his tiny office off the garage for an hour, with bills, ledgers and spreadsheets stacked around him sky-high, when Maverick finally saw fit to show up.

He was wearing a white linen suit and a red silk tie.

"You wanted to see me?"

Jack's gaze fastened on the strip of scarlet silk. "Nice tie."

Maverick leaned heavily against the huge gun safe for a minute. Then he bent over and tossed aside several neatly labeled files that had been stacked on a chair. With a casual air, he sprawled lazily into the high-backed, leather chair, which was opposite Jack's desk. "Heard about the fight."

Jack ignored the comment. "Somebody used bolt shears on that latch today."

"Don't look at me. I wasn't anywhere near—"

"Maybe I could have used your help."

"That's a first." Their gazes connected and held.

Jack handed him the accountant's latest monthly

report. "Somebody's stealing, too. Got any ideas who that might be?"

A cool recklessness flashed across Maverick's aristocratic features. "You don't want my guess." As always, his voice was oddly pleasant to the ear. It was the well-educated voice of a gentleman, overlaid with the flat, casual drawl of a south Texas rancher. His air of utter assurance irritated Jack almost as much as it had when he'd been poor and illiterate and Maverick a snot-nosed, sissy brat.

Maverick's mouth curled with cynical humor when Jack remained stern-faced and silent. "Because I'd say it's you."

"Somebody's damn sure trying to make it look that way," Jack agreed tightly.

Maverick's eyes twinkled. "Who was a thief in Mexico?" Jack's tanned face darkened. "Settle down. Bear with me now. You know, there's a saying that goes like this—if you hear hoofbeats in Texas, don't think of zebras. When I hear the word *thief*, I think of the only one I personally know."

"I only stole when I had to—"

"How reassuring."

Jack rose out of his leather chair. "Now—"

"You asked!" Maverick's full red lips parted in a cool smile. "Why, everybody knows you only married my cousin for the ranch, not for Carla. I never shed any tears thinking about you losing Cheyenne, either. Cheyenne was too poor back then. You loved this ranch way more than any woman."

That got him—the way Maverick knew it would. But Maverick didn't stop there. No, sirree. Jack was determined to grit his teeth and hear him out.

Maverick sat up boldly, pushing him to the edge,

going too far, the way he could sometimes. "From the second you set foot on this place, you wanted it. You haven't changed, either. Why else did you go after Chantal as soon as you got out of prison? Why did you bring her back?"

"You tell me."

"Have it your way. I think you're hiding something, Jack. Chantal's acting strange. She's nothing like she used to be. I can't put my finger on what's wrong between you two, but something damn sure is. Don't try to make me think she's gone sweet on you. She only married you because she got knocked up and nobody else would have her. She wanted me...way more than she ever wanted you...even after she married you. She told me so lots of times. You saw the truth for yourself that day in the bunkhouse."

Suddenly Maverick paled as Jack's features grew wolfish, and it was mighty satisfying to see just how fast his rival could wilt when he felt he'd overreached himself and was cornered.

"If she's sweet on me now, that's our business. You stay away from her."

"I never chase women. Unless they encourage... With her, I don't imagine it'll take too long...."

"If you're smart, you'll ignore her encouragement," Jack warned icily. "Now, back to the subject at hand. Unless things change, this ranch is going under. Bulls are going sterile. Men are falling into combines. Money is missing.... Somebody's behind all this."

Maverick leaned forward. "I wonder who."

The anger in Jack's gaze matched the insolence in Maverick's.

"None of this was a problem till you came home,

Jack. That makes it easy, at least for me, to figure out what's going on. Not many of the men trust you. Why don't you quit trying to blame me? Why don't you take your bottle and crawl into some hole? Do us all a favor—stay there till you drink yourself to death. I'll take care of the ranch and Chantal."

"You'd drive this place into the ground the same you did Caroline's. If you lay a hand on...my wife, I'll kill you."

Maverick got up. "I've heard enough for one day."

"Ditto. But I warn you, I'm going to talk to Theodora."

Maverick grinned nastily. "I've got nothing to hide. You're the one with the record." At the door he paused. "If you're gonna attack every man that wants to do it with Chantal, you're gonna have to wage a one-man war."

"That's my business."

Late that afternoon the wind was rising. Thickening dust whirled beneath a black sky. Wranglers were once more hard at work on the herd, which was newly secured in the largest and strongest of the holding lots.

Jack could have quit, but it wouldn't be good for his men's morale. Besides, he didn't want to chance a run-in with *her*. So he waved to his cowboys as he rode past them, shouting he'd double-check the pastures and make sure the sandy stretches and dense brush were clean of strays. Cows could be ingenious at hiding themselves and their calves in dense brush or a gully until the line of the corrida swept by them.

Jack rode for a mile or two without seeing a single animal. Soon he was alone in a particularly brushy pasture. As was his custom, he had one end of his rope tightly knotted to the pommel of his saddle, while its coils, tied by a horn string, dangled loosely at his knee.

He kept a watchful eye on the thick line of brush as well as on the heavy, dark clouds that skimmed low and fast across the blackening sky. Suddenly lightning flashed against the horizon, and a startled calf, small but feisty, spurted out of the brush and raced away from him.

Dom shot after the calf. Jack bent forward and kept the stallion's head high. He neither urged nor spurred. Dom flew, his tail flicking in the wind. Jack hung on tightly to the reins. Fire ant mounds and thick clumps of *zacahuista* sped past pounding hooves. Mesquite and huisache blurred. Soon the poor little calf began to tire, and inch by precious inch, horse and rider started gaining on him.

Jack slipped the horn string off his pommel. With Dom racing over the uneven ground, Jack took the rope coils and the reins into his left hand. With his right, he made a small loop that he whirled and sent flying, but it landed short and fell into the tall dry grass. Jack held on to the rope, dragging it.

Dom never slowed as Jack coiled the rope and made a second loop, this one larger than the first.

The calf was slowing as Jack aimed for his head and threw. This time the loop closed neatly around his neck, and with an expert flick of his wrist, Jack pulled on the reins and the rope at the same time. Dom reared, yanking the calf around, dragging him, snorting and bawling, till he faced them.

When Dom quieted, the calf stood still, staring at them, wheezing and wild-eyed, the rope still strangling him. Sweat poured off Dom's flanks. He was panting even harder than the calf.

Jack dismounted. The calf was so tired, Jack figured the best thing was to carry him back to the herd over his saddle. But when he knelt to loosen the rope around his neck, the calf bawled and began kicking. So Jack just picked him up.

By the time Jack reached Dom, the tired calf was struggling and squalling only a little. But just as Jack was about to grab the reins and slip his foot into the stirrup, a powerful gust of wind stirred through the brush. Then a zigzag of white-hot lightning struck a hundred yards in front of Dom.

Dom's eyes rolled backward. Jack jumped away as the stallion reared.

"Easy, boy."

Thunder roared.

Dom didn't scare as easily as most horses, but like all of his kind, his instinct was flight. He'd trample anything or anybody in his frantic desire to escape.

Thoroughly spooked, the stallion broke into a hard gallop.

Jack's loose rope tensed. A single coil that Jack had inadvertently stepped through when he'd jumped away from Dom snapped tightly around his booted ankle.

"Hey, hey. Easy, Dom..." A cold sweat broke out on Jack's brow. He fought to hold the calf and twist his foot out of the noose-like coil.

But Dom continued forward, carrying the rope with him, and the loop wound tighter.

In the next instant Jack's foot was jerked out from under him. The calf kicked him in the chest and sprang to the ground. Hopping and then falling, Jack shouted to Dom as he felt himself being dragged.

But the stallion just raced faster.

They say that your life passes before you as you die.

Funny how all Jack thought of was *her.* Again he saw Bronte's luminous face as she'd lain beneath him on the sheepskin rug. Again he heard her soft sigh of surrender when he'd pushed himself inside her and been gloved by her exquisite warmth. Her shining gaze had locked to his as completely as her body, giving everything of herself to him—even her soul.

As Dom neighed loudly and lunged forward, the rope tightened and Jack's body bumped backward.

From a gallop, Dom broke into a hard run, dragging calf and man through mesquite, granjeno and brazil.

Jack's head cracked against a sharp rock, and everything went black.

Chapter 20

The sky whitened. Thunder crashed.

Guerro whined plaintively, thumping his tail against Bronte's ankle and looking up to her for reassurance.

A wild wet wind fanned Bronte as she sat on the verandah sipping hot tea with Carla and Theodora. An even stronger gust lifted Bronte's hair off her warm neck and tugged at her skirt.

Lightning flamed repeatedly, the sky flashing in bursts of green and livid white.

Bronte's fingers tightened on the wafer-thin handle of her china cup. A sudden uneasiness struck her. Jack was out in this violent weather.

Theodora pushed her chair back. "We'd better go inside."

Guerro loped to the door and looked up at the door handle expectantly, as if to suggest the same thing.

"But Jack's still working cattle."

"It won't be the first time he got a little wet," Theodora said.

Bronte set her cup down. She couldn't stop staring at the black sky. For a crazy moment she wanted to run out and search for him. Guerro padded back to her and put his head in her lap so she could idly stroke him behind his ears.

Why should she care so much about Jack? He wanted her gone. She would have gone, too; she would have left with Becky, who'd offered her a ride to Houston. Only Bronte had seen Carla sneaking out of an oak mott near the house with her lunch pail less than an hour after her orange school bus had driven away.

Bronte had told herself it wasn't any of her business if *his* daughter skipped school.

But an hour later she'd been standing under Carla's tree, coaxing her to come down. Then she'd driven the thirty-two miles round-trip to Carla's school and visited Carla's teachers and principal in an attempt to discover why she hated school. The reason had been logical; the solution was simple. Carla was unchallenged and bored.

So Bronte's excuse for staying was that a child's educational welfare was at stake.

Liar.

Maybe that was one of the reasons…

"How long do you think roundup will take?" Bronte asked casually.

"You never can tell," Theodora said. "Depends on how things go. I expect Jack'll put in a long day. One of the gates broke. Half the herd got loose. Jack's checking for strays. I reckon we ought to start dinner without him."

Bronte stood up slowly, her face brightening. Dom

was streaking toward them across the pasture. "No...look. Over there."

Thunder rolled.

Something wasn't right.

A sudden fear struck her, and she ran to the edge of the verandah, with Carla and Theodora close at her heels.

Dom was riderless.

He was galloping straight at them, dragging something so huge and heavy that it raked up spirals of dust behind him.

"Dad!" Carla yelled frantically.

Wild terror swept through Bronte as she remembered the story of Samson West being murdered and dragged by his horse to his death.

With a shiver Bronte grabbed the railing to steady her wobbly knees. Juan, a young *vaquero,* who was mowing the lawn, killed the engine, grabbed a coil of rope from his pickup bed and ran toward Dom. Juan's lean, brown arm was soon expertly twirling the rope, which fell in a perfect arc over Dom's head.

Enraged, Dom reared wildly. Juan dug his boot heels into the dirt and hung on, all the time talking in soothing Spanish until, finally, the stallion calmed a little.

Her face drained of color, Bronte ran toward them. Carla had seized hold of her hand, and Bronte hardly knew what she did as she dragged the child in her wake.

The rushing wind grew stronger around them, pushing against them, carrying the dark, voluminous clouds toward the house. The air blew damp and cool against their cheeks now.

Lightning flashed in a series of whizzing, white bolts, and Dom reared frantically again. Backing, prancing like a heavy, graceless dancer, the stallion lunged up and down repeatedly, his flying hooves crashing into the dirt and then flying at Juan's black head again as the *vaquero* hung on.

The sky had been equally dark and the weather equally violent the day Jimmy had died.

Jimmy.

Samson.

Bronte felt as if she stood on the crumbling ledge of a bottomless, black abyss. One false step and she would lose her balance and be sucked into the void.

Not Jack. Please, not Jack, too.

Before Bronte and Carla could reach the horse and the filthy, torn object that lay tangled and lifeless at the end of the rope, the rain began to beat down in torrents. Instantly Bronte's hair and dress were sodden.

"Oh, Jack."

"It's just a calf, *señorita,*" Juan said, his black eyes gentle, his breathless voice kind. "His neck's broke. The rocks, the rope…"

She knelt beside the still little animal that had been choked to death by being dragged across the pasture. Gently she removed the rope from its neck and laid the twisted hemp on the ground.

"Where's Jack? Where is he? I—I've got to find him…."

She stood up, but when she put her hand on Dom's slick reins, the stallion jerked his head away from her.

"He's too tired and wild to be ridden by anybody but Jack right now," Theodora said.

"Doña Theodora, she is right, Miss Chantal," Juan said.

"He could be hurt!" Bronte said fiercely.

"I'll go," Juan said. "You stay here with the old miss."

Bronte stared at them both. Her eyes grew dazed and unfocused as the rain gushed down.

"I have to go!"

Before they could protest, she blindly thrust her slim foot in the stirrup and swung herself up into the saddle.

Carla screamed, "Take me with you!"

"No!" Theodora tried to grab the reins. "You'll both break your necks."

Bronte reached down and pulled Carla up behind her.

"Hold on tight." Then Bronte dug her heels into the big horse's sides. Dom took off, streaking away from the house, into the storm that now fell in drenching sheets.

They were only a mile down the road when the sky whitened again, and a man screamed weakly, "Over here."

The sky went black again. The rain was so thick and violent, they might have still passed him by if he hadn't yelled a second time.

"Bronte!"

Her name.

He knew.

Bronte stopped immediately and dismounted.

Carla took one look at Jack, who'd been holding on to the fence as he hobbled back toward the big house, and then at Bronte. "I'll send someone with a truck." The girl sprinted away from them toward the house.

Jack's face was white; his eyes were ringed with black. His blood-soaked shirt clung to his shivering chest in ragged strips. A long laceration ran from his pale cheek down his jaw and neck, down the length of his torso.

She saw the clotted red line of gaping flesh. "Oh, Jack...."

He didn't smile when Bronte raced up to him and threw her arms around him. "You're wet and cold," she exclaimed. "Why, your skin's like ice. You're shaking. But you're alive. I was so afraid. I—I've got to get you home. Out of these clothes before you catch a chill." With gentle fingertips she probed the long wound. "It doesn't look too deep—"

He jerked away from her. "I thought you were leaving this morning. Why didn't you?"

The rain hammered them.

Rivulets ran the length of her cheek and dripped off her face like tears. "I was, but Carla..." Trembling from deep inside, Bronte took a step away from him. "She missed her bus. I drove her—"

"Quit playing the loving wife and mother. I know who you are now. You're not my wife. You may look like her, but—"

"I care about you, Jack."

"You're a liar, *Bronte.*"

"I—I tried to tell you who I was. That day on the street."

"You should have tried harder. I nearly got my ass shot off. You played the part of my wife to the hilt!"

"I didn't ask to look like Mischief. I—"

"Shut up. I wouldn't believe anything you said now."

She had to give him time. She shouldn't be surprised that he was furious. Still, his scathing insults, the mockery and harsh tone hurt.

"You played me for a fool," he said. "You're

worse than Chantal. You don't give a damn about me."

"How can I—" Bronte broke off abruptly. "When I saw Dom dragging that poor little calf... Oh, Jack, I was so afraid it was you."

"You don't know me. You don't know anything about me—how I was raised, who I really am. If you did—"

"Theodora told me. Everything. I'm sorry about what happened to you as a little boy. I'm sorry about Mexico. About your mother, too."

His dark face tightened. "We've known each other less than a week. We're nothing to each other now. Strangers...who shared a bed."

"Twice," she said softly.

His face looked startled for a second by the stark emotion shining in her too-brilliant eyes. Then he flushed darkly. "It didn't mean anything."

"Speak for yourself," she said tonelessly. "I love you, Jack."

"I don't want your love. I don't want anybody's love. You said you were leaving. So go! What the hell are you waiting for? I don't need you. I don't need anybody. Dom—"

"Jack..."

Jack gave a low whistle, and the big stallion ambled over as docilely as a lamb, trustingly sniffing his outstretched hand.

"It's about time you decided to settle down." Jack's voice was gentle now that he was speaking to his horse.

When he grabbed the long reins and put his good foot in the stirrup, Bronte hung on to his arm.

"No.... You're hurt. You can't ride. Carla's—"

He pushed her away. "You just watch me,

Bronte.'' With a groan of pure agony, he slung himself heavily into the saddle.

He gazed down at her in contemptuous triumph. ''See?''

''Jack, I really do love you.'' She didn't know her eyes had grown huge.

He clicked his tongue, and his stallion wheeled away from her.

''Quit acting like you give a damn one way or the other,'' he shouted down to her. ''Because I don't give a damn about you.'' He set his cold, insolent gaze on her one final time. ''If I did, I wouldn't ride off and leave you all by yourself in this storm. On this road. Where anybody could come...and anything could happen to you.''

More frightened by his callous indifference than she was of anything else, she took three running steps after him.

He scowled when he glanced over his shoulder and saw her still chasing after him in the rain. From under the brim of his hat, his eyes darkened when she ran faster.

''Jack!''

He raced away from her down the road.

Low clouds enveloped horse and rider, until they were almost completely hidden from her.

But she knew when he stopped.

She knew when he turned and saw that she was still coming toward him through the mist.

She could tell he was fighting a grim battle with himself. She understood, because it was the same battle she'd fought with herself earlier when she'd tried to force herself to leave him.

Even though he looked enraged, he must have been more moved by the fresh desolation in her eyes than he was willing to admit because suddenly, with a movement of his heels, he spurred Dom to a gallop and raced straight toward her.

Hooves splashed mud into her face and eyes.

Her scream of pure terror was cut short as Jack reached down and grabbed her by the waist and scooped her up. Without ever breaking stride, he slung her behind him.

Her legs clambered over the horse's back with fluid expertise. Quickly her arms circled Jack's waist, and she held on to him tightly, feeling foolishly joyous to suddenly find that he hadn't been able to gallop away and leave her as he'd so heartlessly threatened.

With a grim sigh, Jack turned Dom toward home. Bronte gasped with heady pleasure and buried her cheek against the middle of Jack's back and inhaled the musky warm scent of his damp shirt and skin.

When he felt her lips wantonly scorch his spine, he shuddered. Whether he knew it or not, whether he willed it or not, this was where she belonged and where she intended to stay.

Beside him. With him.

Always.

And she was willing to fight for their love and fight him every step of the way.

You can't win, no matter what you do.

Yes! Yes, I can! I have a new beautiful face. And this new, beautiful man. I am not an ugly duckling anymore. I am brave and strong.

As Dom walked back toward the house in the steady downpour, the whirling rain seemed less threatening to her than it ever had before.

Jack was alive and not too badly injured.

She loved him, and she was going to win him.

When the red-tiled roof of the mansion finally rose

over the tangle of mesquite, Bronte clung to him and pressed her cheek more tightly against his hard back. Again he trembled violently every time she touched him.

She wanted to share her life with him.

Not that she would tell him again just yet.

Not when he was so set against her.

Maybe, with such a stubborn man, it was necessary to play a rather perverse game to win him. She remembered her flirtatious mother playing hard-to-get with her many lovers. Always in the past, Bronte had spurned her mother's games. But she had her mother's face now. Perhaps just this once...

When Dom got to the drive that wound up to the house, Bronte jumped down and, with a pretense of spirited independence, ran from Jack toward the stairs.

Quick as a flash, Jack dismounted, too.

When she heard his boots ring on the concrete steps behind her, she tried to run up the stairs away from him, but he caught her slender wrist and spun her around.

His face was deeply lined, and his eyes were shadowed by fatigue. "Thanks...for coming after me," he said, his deep voice unsteady.

She swallowed, barely able to talk around the lump in her throat. "Jack...you—you should see a doctor."

"I'll be fine. I have to see about Dom now."

"I'll get Juan to do that. Your cut needs to be cleaned."

"I said no doctor."

"Then let me do it."

The muscles tightened in his throat. His expression grew fierce. "I said—"

She glanced up at him through her lashes, flirting

the way her mother had. "Why, Jack, did anybody around here ever dare to tell you that you're just about the most stubborn man alive?"

In his eyes, she saw some new emotion.

He looked away without answering.

She smiled gently—her own smile. "Well, I'm telling you then. I want to take care of you."

"There you are," a voice boomed. Maverick raced inside, drenched, grim-faced. "Carla sent me out to rescue you two."

Jack ignored Maverick and smiled at Bronte. "Looks like we did just fine without you."

"Thanks, Maverick," Bronte whispered softly, appeasing him. But she, too, was staring at Jack.

When his smile never wavered, she began to feel safe and warm. She almost felt she was beginning to belong in this house and to this man.

She was so beautiful that just staring at her made him feel euphoric.

And the minx knew it and was using it against him.

To shut her out, Jack closed his eyes and counted horses.

In the shelter of their bedroom, Bronte was gently bathing the jagged slash that ran from his neck to his midriff while he lay bonelessly sprawled in a large armchair. He didn't flinch even when the alcohol swabs Bronte dabbed at the cuts in his scalp and the long tear across his torso burned like hell.

Her breasts, swathed in damp, clinging cloth, pressed into his shoulder as she leaned over him, and her cool, trembly hands moved slowly through his thick, wet hair, down his neck and still lower.

He breathed in the dizzying smell of gardenias along with her own special scent and longed to touch that slim, luscious body that swayed so seductively over him.

The horses blurred, and she filled his imagination.

Bronte.

Was it really so essential to his pride that he stay mad at her forever?

No matter how hard he tried to maintain a sour expression, he couldn't stop thinking about how joyous she'd looked when she'd found him hobbling along that fence line in the rain, and realized he was alive. The memory of her bright smile and soft hands stirred him so hard that his longing for her bordered on agony. He clenched his fists to keep from grabbing her.

What was the matter with him? He was a lowborn barrio bastard. She would despise him for that alone.

She had said Theodora had told her everything. That she knew about his past. That she loved him anyway.

She had lied to him.

He'd been a thief. Who was he to judge? Nobody was perfect. And when, oh, when had anyone ever acted like they cared so much about him as she had this afternoon? In his whole damned life there had never been a single soul before Bronte.

She was touching his chest with those infinitely gentle fingertips, tending him with such care.

All night he had lain on Shanghai's porch in a drunken haze, dreaming of her. Remembering how huge and powerful he'd felt when he'd been tightly sheathed inside her. Wanting to find and kill the bastard who'd shot at her. Knowing he'd either die or explode if he couldn't ever have her again. Telling himself he wanted her gone. Knowing the whole damned night that he wanted her forever. Feeling scared and sick that she might still be in mortal danger.

He had never wanted anybody the way he wanted her. That's why she'd driven him crazy by being so sweet and kind to him when he'd thought she was Chantal.

Maybe he should back off his stubborn tack and compromise...just a bit. If it was a bad idea, he could play the bastard again later.

Then she smiled at him, like a golden sunbeam shining through a dark cloud. One glance, and he felt like she was staring straight into his soul.

As if he had a choice.

His steely black eyes narrowed. "Come here," he whispered, tenderly.

"Who, me?" Her voice was soft as she backed a step or two from him—deliberately flirting.

But her eyes held the connection, and as she began to understand his change of mood, her smile got bigger and brighter. The silence that stretched between them grew as taut as his nerves.

His mouth stretched into a slow grin. "I want to talk to you, Bronte Devlin," he said huskily.

"Kiss me first."

"How—if you won't come here?"

Her lashes fluttered, allowing him a final glimpse of emerald irises clouding with desire before she obeyed him.

Gently he wrapped his arms around her slim waist. He felt warm woman skin burning through wet cotton. Her slender fingers curled into the mat of crisp, dark chest hair, and when her hand stirred there, he felt his heart pound beneath her lightly caressing fingertips.

Slowly, gently, she lowered her face over his.

He kissed her mouth as she had kissed him that first night—sweetly, tenderly.

He closed his eyes as she returned his chaste kiss, her warm lips lingering gently.

"Bear with me," he murmured. "There's something I've got to see for myself."

With unsteady fingers he unfastened the top three buttons of her damp blouse and slid the fabric downward to expose her left shoulder.

"I knew who you were right after we made love in the bathroom," he said. At the sudden huskiness in his voice she looked up, bewildered.

He brushed the creamy, smooth skin with a reverent fingertip. His lips tasted the same sweet flesh. Then he sighed, deeply content, and began to rebutton her shirt.

"Jack, why did you do that?"

He felt like a cowboy checking a brand.

"Maybe I'll tell you someday."

She was his. Only his. He felt a rush of unwanted emotion.

No. Not yet. He wasn't ready to feel so much or to admit so much. Not even to himself.

"But why—"

"Later. Right now all I want to do is kiss you."

"Oh, I love you so much. I didn't think I could ever love anybody again."

"Do you honestly mean that?"

"Yes. And I love having sex with you."

He chuckled.

"I want it all the time. Every time I look at you." She blushed shyly. "Nobody ever made me feel like that. I just hope you don't mind my saying it."

He looked down at her, his eyes dark with unnamed emotion. "I don't mind." What she said was too wonderful to believe. "I just hope you don't mind if I can't say it yet." His voice cracked. "I don't know what I think anymore," he added a long time later when she broke free and nuzzled her cheek against his muscular shoulder. "Or what I feel. It's too soon to make promises. I would if I could...." Gently he traced the lines of her face.

"You don't have to," she uttered whimsically. "In my real life, I was a kindergarten teacher. Big changes...take time. I learned a long time ago to celebrate the small ones. So I don't expect anything. I just want this moment. It's enough...your acting nice for a change...."

He laughed. "I'm sorry. The situation has been a bit complicated. It still is. Maybe more than ever. Theodora sent me after her daughter. My wife."

"She's dead."

"I know. That's not what I mean."

"Does Chantal still matter so much?"

"Not like you might think she does. No. In that way, there's only you. I swear. But there's more to this whole situation than I first thought."

"What do you mean?"

"I'm not sure. I have a bad feeling about all this. I think we'd better be careful. Somebody nearly killed you—twice. I don't think that was an accident. Then you saw that red tie...here. Chantal is dead. So is Webster Quinn. I think they were murdered by the same person who tried to kill you. Nothing's been right since I got out of prison. Money's missing. We've had too many accidents. And I want to know why. Somebody's after something. I have a hunch we're blocking them—"

The phone rang downstairs. A couple of minutes later Theodora's shadowy form stood in their doorway. She gripped the cordless receiver in her thin, shaking fingers.

"It's Mario."

Mario was on a cellular phone. Static popped on the line, breaking his voice into incoherent fragments.

"A plane...down...pasture..."

"Where?"

Static crackled. "Three miles...pond...south...big house."

Rubbing his brow, Jack moved away from her.

"Jack, what is it?" Bronte whispered, frantic.

He told her.

"Who would fly in this weather?"

Mario was talking to him at the same time, so Jack lowered his head and strained to listen.

A second later Jack put his hand over the mouthpiece and looked up. "Mario says it's a private plane. He's not sure whether the pilot and crew got out. I have to go check—"

"No!"

"The *vaqueros* are afraid to go anywhere near it. They've heard too many stories about ranchers getting plugged in the head by dope runners. Two weeks ago a Mexican *federale* was shot a hundred times in front of his house and then run over with a car. I've got to go myself—"

Theodora shook her head grimly.

"Jack, no. You're hurt," Bronte whispered. "If they're dope smugglers, and they're still there, they'll be desperate. Caroline told me how dangerous—"

"I'll be okay."

"Jack, no—"

"Hey, maybe we'll get lucky. Maybe we'll be able to sell the plane. It'd make up for those bulls."

"Don't joke..."

Bronte knelt down before him. She threw her arms around him, pleading silently with wide, terrified eyes that showed the intensity of her feelings for him more clearly than any words ever could.

She loved him.

His hard face softened.

There was a roaring in his ears.

His heart drummed.

Tell her you love her.

His mouth was dry.

He whispered a garbled curse, and then he wrapped his arms around her, too. If he couldn't say it, he had to at least kiss her, even with Theodora standing there.

Gently he cupped Bronte's chin and brought her sweet face to his. His mouth met hers with an aching tenderness that soon deepened into something more. Their kiss was timeless, and yet for him it was fresh and new. The building pressure inside him was soon more than he could endure. He was as hot as a capped volcano when he let her go.

"No more," he whispered dizzily against her ear. "Later."

"Promise?"

A harsh shudder rocked him. He stared past her. At Theodora.

"I love you," Bronte said.

"I don't deserve you," he murmured.

"Yes, you do."

"You're too sweet and fine for a man like me."

"I've been such a coward in my life. I admire courage more than anything. You're the bravest man I've ever met."

"Do you really mean that?"

"With all my heart."

"Oh, my darling," he groaned, resealing their lips and then tearing himself reluctantly away again.

"Take me with you." Her whisper was low and hoarse, thready with need.

He wanted to push Theodora politely out of the room, to take Bronte to bed, to have her naked underneath him, to explore her warm, womanly softness, to forget the dope plane and all the other dangers swirling around them, to forget everything except losing himself in this beautiful woman again. To hold her in his arms for hours afterward—as he had not done before.

Wind and rain beat at the windows.

"No way can I risk anything happening to you. You stay here. Take care of Carla." Then he kissed her softly.

When he opened the front door several minutes later, Jack still felt dizzy and disoriented from their final kiss. Gently, very gently he loosened his hand from her slender, clinging fingers. Hurling himself out of the big house, he dashed down the stairs into the wild, wet rain.

He didn't look back.

Not even once.

He had no way of knowing how soon he would lie dying in her arms and regret that he hadn't.

Chapter 21

Never had Bronte hated rain more than tonight. It fell in gushing torrents. The wind roared in the palms, battered the shutters and screamed around the house, howling in the eaves. Thunder rolled incessantly, and the sky flashed like strobe lights.

Numb with fear, Bronte hugged herself and stared at the huge, sparkling raindrops slashing the long windows.

Jack was out there. Hurt, half-dead with exhaustion, he faced God alone knew what dangers in that wild storm.

"Why doesn't he call?"

"You've asked me that at least a dozen times," Theodora said impatiently. "He will."

"How can you know that?"

"He always does."

"Anything could happen to him."

"Not to Jack."

Still, when the phone rang, Theodora jumped, too.

"There! I told you!" she said as Bronte rushed past her to the library.

"Jack..."

The tense, male voice identified himself as Sheriff Ortiz from Val Verde, Texas.

"You've got a problem. Two convicts busted out of our jail down here tonight. They're armed and dangerous. We spotted them by helicopter not ten minutes south of your house. Lady, you'd better get your guns and your ammo. Lock your doors and windows. Get that cousin of yours and Caroline and everybody else into the cellar of your big house. Y'all stay put, till my deputy gets there. It's gonna take him an hour."

"But Jack's—"

She was speaking to a dial tone. The sheriff had hung up on her.

When she explained what he'd said to Theodora, the older woman's black eyes turned chillingly cold.

"We don't have much time."

"What about Jack?"

"Get Carla down here. Tell her to turn the lights off, both inside and out. Tell her to phone Caroline. You and I'll get the guns. Get Juan."

Bronte screamed up to Carla, who had no doubt been eavesdropping because for once she came flying.

"One more thing..." Theodora said to Bronte as Carla dialed.

"What?"

"The guns are outside in Jack's office."

"We'd better keep one," Theodora said, seizing a handheld automatic from Juan's pile.

"What for?" Bronte whispered.

"Just in case..." Theodora rammed bullets into the clip.

Bronte closed the steel door of Jack's huge gun safe as Juan rushed out into the wild night toward the house with the last sack load of pistols, revolvers, hunting rifles and shotguns.

Theodora offered her the loaded automatic, but Bronte, who was more terrified of the gun than the convicts, shook her head. "You keep it."

Bronte shut off the lights. With a pounding heart, she stepped outside.

Rain gushed from the gutters. Lightning streaked the sky.

Theodora followed as silently as a shadow.

A single light burned from a telephone pole.

Behind Bronte, Theodora lifted her automatic and took careful aim at the light. When she squeezed the trigger, the bulb exploded.

They were smothered in darkness as the rain beat around them as loudly as a drum. Bronte remembered how it had rained the night Jimmy died.

"We've got to make a run far it," Theodora said.

Sensing some uncanny difference in the atmosphere, Bronte hesitated. Suddenly the sky lit up again. She felt a gust of cool air as she raced out onto the drive toward the roaring palms. For an instant she was alone. Then thudding boot heels rang heavily on the asphalt drive behind her.

She whirled, only to be blinded by the rain. "Theodora?"

Silence.

Then a deadly male voice came out of the darkness. "It's me."

A scream rose and died in her throat. Before she could run from him, a large, bony hand manacled her wrist. "You'd better be good after the trouble you've put me to."

She tried to scream again, but rising terror made her throat catch. "Where...Theodora..."

He laughed. "You stupid little fool—"

"What did you do to her?"

Lightning lit his bony face. He looked haggard; his cheeks were sunken as if he hadn't slept in weeks. Then he smiled, that terrible, long-toothed smile that she'd first seen in Central Park.

He'd been there.

"Central Park? You—you were there...when I watched that little boy dig..."

Had he been stalking her then, too? Or...had he been after Jack?

"Who are you?"

"Caesar."

"Mario's son?"

"Not anymore. He liked Jack better than he ever liked me. Always throwing that bastard up at me. I'm sick of people thinking he was better than me. I took *his* woman. Now you're mine, too. Say my name—Caesar. It turns me on when a woman says it."

When she shoved at him, he slapped her.

Dizzily she reeled backward, her neck snapping as her skull cracked against the rough trunk of a palm. He ripped her skirt from the hem to her waist. With a laugh he pushed his body against hers.

"You're shaking. I like that."

Recovering a little, she fought him wildly.

"There you go! Wiggle against me! Scream! I like 'em wild...and scared. It'll be your last chance to get off for a while!"

Bronte froze as his hand crawled up her thigh.

Tears streamed down her face as he unfastened his belt buckle.

When he leaned forward to kiss her, she flailed her arms. Twisting her head from side to side, she clawed his face. His muscular body pressed against hers with an ever-strengthening purpose. She felt his hot, beery breath too near her lips.

He was about to kiss her when a hard voice behind him snapped, "Where's Nick?"

He turned. "Dead. Shot through the throat just like you wanted."

"Finish her."

"Not till—"

"Now!"

"In a minute—"

From out of nowhere a spurt of orange fire blossomed with an ear-splitting crack. In the next instant the big hands probing her breasts and thighs were lifeless. Bronte's would-be rapist slumped to the ground.

"He won't bother you again," Theodora said.

Bronte looked down at him. A neat, black bullet hole gaped from his forehead like a third eye.

The automatic jerked in Theodora's palsied hand.

"Where were you?"

That voice behind them.... "Finish her."

Theodora's face wore a sad-sweet expression as she raised the gun again.

Bronte's blood turned cold. Her mouth went dry.

"You!"

Theodora leveled the automatic at her heart.

"You're behind everything."

Still Theodora said nothing.

Bronte's teeth began to chatter. "But...why? Why

did you set Jack up? I—I don't understand. I thought you loved him."

"You're going to have a tragic accident. I will say that I was trying to save you, but my hand shook. I shot you first. Then him. I'll be so very sorry."

"But why?"

"It's a long story. Chantal lived recklessly, extravagantly. This ranch is worth millions and millions in land value alone...not to mention mineral rights. She wanted her part. She wanted me to break it up and destroy it. She didn't believe in the family or the ranch. She was no good...like her father who married me for money. She was always after me for money. Jack was just as bad...always wanting to modernize."

"But—"

"The ranch doesn't belong to anyone. It's sacred. Chantal couldn't see that, and finally she was so desperate she began to threaten me. That last night before she ran away, when she came here with those two murderers—with that cheap thug, Nick Busby—I think she wanted them to kill Jack and me. She slept with the boy in the barn to push Jack to the limit. He did get furious, but in the end he lost his nerve and backed down. But by then I saw a way to rid myself of all of them. I hit Jack in the head with a board. I shot that boy who died in the barn.... I shot Nick, too. Only, he and Chantal got away. I set the barn on fire. If Carla hadn't opened the barn doors and gotten help, if they hadn't pulled Jack out, everybody would've blamed him...."

"You sent an innocent man to prison. Your adopted..."

"I liked him, but he was always trying to change things. I had to put the ranch first. Jack wasn't the only one who suffered. I nearly went mad these past few years, wondering where Chantal and Nick were, wondering what Jack would do if he ever learned the truth. Then Nick started blackmailing me. He told me Chantal was alive. When he confessed to the cops that he'd killed that boy in the barn, he was setting me up. I nearly died of fright. He thought it was a grand joke bringing all those cops down here...while he taunted me the whole time that he'd tell them the truth. Then Jack was free, too. I couldn't let Jack out of my sight for fear Nick would talk to him. Nick kept hounding me, threatening that he'd set Jack on me. I kept paying him."

Bronte shut her eyes.

"Then Chantal called me. She needed money more than ever. Lots of it. Said she was coming here to get it, too. She said if I didn't give it to her, she'd go to the police, that she'd tell them I shot that boy. I didn't know who or where she was or what she even looked like. Then I saw a way to use Jack again...for the ranch's good, you see."

"The good?"

"I couldn't let them destroy what all of us have given our lives to build."

"But why me? Why kill me?"

"You saw Caesar. He couldn't hide out forever. He got himself locked up down in Val Verde to bust Nick out. Then he killed Nick. Caesar had bad, expensive habits. He'd do anything I told him to, as long as I paid him. He's always been jealous of Jack. If you die, I won't have to kill Jack. He'll never know...."

"I know everything, Theodora."

Bronte was thrilled and terrified when Jack's disembodied voice came out of the darkness.

"Put the gun down, Theodora."

Theodora swung around violently, staring in horror at the tall man in the blustery, rain-filled night.

"It's over," he said.

"Not quite, Jack."

He saw the insane hatred in Theodora's eyes and lunged.

In a blinding flash Bronte jumped toward Jack, trying to shield him as Theodora took aim.

But she wasn't fast enough.

A fiery spit of light exploded from the automatic.

Bronte screamed as Jack slumped toward her and fell unconscious to the ground.

The fabric of his shirt had been blown away. Theodora had shot him at point-blank range.

Bronte knelt, shielding his broken body from the downpour. His wet face was as pale as death.

She lifted him in her arms, but his head lolled just as Jimmy's had when she'd held him that last day.

Jack's eyes stared wildly, not seeing her.

"Jimmy...!" she screamed, for she imagined she was holding her dying son again.

No.... It was Jack....

She had to do something this time. Dimly she remembered what she'd learned in that CPR course. Desperately, mechanically, she wadded her shredded skirt and pressed it against his flowing wound.

"I need a blanket...something to cover him." She put her lips to his pale, purple-gray mouth and began to breathe for him.

"Breathe," she whispered. "Don't you die. Don't die, too."

"It's your turn to die now." Theodora lowered her gun to Bronte's temple.

The front door of the big house banged open.

"Grandmother!"

Framed in a square of golden light stood a little girl with tangled red hair. Maverick and Caroline raced out with shotguns.

"We heard shots—"

"Grandmother! What... No! No, don't! I—I saw you in the barn. I was spying that night. They told me to go the cellar, but I sneaked out. I—I remember what happened at the barn now...and it's not what you told me. I remember everything! You drove Mother away. She was scared of you! You tried to burn Daddy up!"

Carla streaked down the stairs toward them.

"She must've suppressed everything, all these years.... Those monsters she draws. I think she barely survived what you did that night in the barn," Bronte whispered. "If you shoot me in front of her, you'll destroy her, too. Are you going to kill that child? Is the ranch more sacred to you than your own flesh and blood?"

Theodora couldn't take her eyes off Carla. Slowly her ancient face crumpled with self-revulsion when Carla ran past her and threw her arms around Bronte and Jack.

"Daddy, Daddy.... I'm so sorry, so sorry I never wrote you. I read your letters before she sent them back. I read every single one."

The gun fell from Theodora's trembling hand.

Suddenly Maverick was there, picking it up. "Call 911. We've got to fly him out!"

Very slowly, with stooped posture and a shambling gait, Theodora turned away from all of them and shuffled toward the big house.

Hot, searing pain spread through his right shoulder, but Jack couldn't see or hear anything.

He knew *she* was there, gripping his hand, pressing something against his wound, pouring her warm breath into his aching lungs again and again.

He wished he'd looked back and seen her that last time when she'd stood at the door, watching until he'd disappeared in the rain.

Bronte loved him.

Something hard seemed to crack around his own heart. His chest throbbed.

He didn't want to feel such shattering need. He didn't want to want so badly to live. Not when his lifeblood oozed past Bronte's wadded skirt and flowed into the mud in thick red rivulets.

Not when he felt so weak and tired, and death yawned before him like a black chasm.

He loved her.

Why hadn't he told her when he could have?

The ranch didn't matter.

Nothing mattered but her…and Carla. He had always wanted to be part of a family. To have his *own* family. To be proud of the woman he loved.

He wanted to marry Bronte. He wanted her to be a mother to his lonely Carla. He wanted more children.

Their children. A whole houseful. He wanted to have a long, happy life with her.

Nothing was more sacred in Mexico than family. He had always envied people with families. But he was getting colder and sleepier.

A bubble seemed to close over him. Only dimly did he feel Bronte shudder. Her piercing sobs and Maverick's shouts grew louder. He barely heard them.

"I'm sorry, Jack," Maverick said. "I knew she was stealing. I knew what she did to those bulls, too. But I never thought…"

Jack wanted to look at Bronte one last time.

"Don't die, Daddy," Carla said. "Don't you leave me like Mommy did. I'll go to school. I just didn't want to because it was so easy. But Bronte told me I could go to a better school in Corpus. I'll be good if you get well. I'll love you forever. Only don't leave us."

"Open your eyes, Jack," Bronte whispered. "We love you. We need you."

It was too late.

He was too weak even to lift an eyelid.

He expelled a final breath, and the pain subsided.

Then he was free. Light as a feather. Floating above them. The rain stopped, and a warm lavender light pulsated around him. He was weightless. Flying. His being fused with that brilliant light. In the next instant he soared above that desperate little crowd huddled around his shattered body.

Higher and higher he rose, rushing far away from them.

Then, suddenly, a little boy with copper curls stood before him. He wore torn jeans, yet he glowed like an angel at the center of that blinding tunnel, blocking Jack's path like the fiercest sentinel. The boy had a skateboard tucked under one arm, but he held up his free hand and stopped Jack.

His strong, determined fingers closed around Jack's wrist.

Jack tried to shake himself loose. He felt an impatience to move higher, to fly faster, but the boy smiled a charming, lopsided smile and shook his head, pointing fiercely down to Bronte.

Slowly, Jack understood.

A leaden heaviness filled him. His shoulder began to throb again with splinter-sharp bursts of pain.

Then, hand in hand, the redheaded boy led Jack back through that glorious cavern of light.

Back to her.

Jack was on the ground again, helpless, his broken body pulsing as if metal blades stabbed him, his life-blood draining through her fingers.

"Open your eyes, Jack," she begged.

The boy squeezed his hand, and a new strength flowed into him.

Jack's inky lashes fluttered.

His soul had flown away when they'd locked him up in that cage and kept him there for five long, hell-ish years.

As he stared into Bronte's dazzling green eyes, his own soul rushed back to him.

"I love you," Jack whispered.

The boy looked from him to Bronte, his lopsided smile radiant. Then he was gone.

"I know," she said. "I love you, too. Don't try to talk."

Jack's perception of time was warped. How long he lay there swaddled in blankets and tarps, drinking in the sight of Bronte's exquisite, triangular face, he didn't know. He only knew she was beside him, holding his hand. He held her just as fiercely, determined never to let her go.

Then the helicopter was above them, a black, roaring, round bubble, its rotors sending out waves of blowing rain that beat down upon them. Everybody was screaming and running and ducking except her.

Then paramedics and cops jumped out, flung open a huge side door and scrambled anxiously toward him with a stretcher.

He heard one cop's voice, deep and calm. "Get him. Bring him in."

For once Jack wasn't afraid of a uniform. He knew he never would be again.

He was free of all the shackles that had ever bound him.

The rhythmic thumping of the rotors never slowed or stopped.

Jack and Bronte were airborn within seconds, circling overhead, rising above the big house into that violent night sky, like souls rising to heaven.

"A little boy led me back to you," Jack whispered, his voice low and choppy. "He had red hair. It was the same color as yours. He had your smile, too. And he looked a little bit like Carla."

Bronte's face lit with a tender, eager radiance that matched the little boy's. "That must have been Jimmy." Her eyes streamed with tears. "My Jimmy brought you back to me."

Epilogue

The bride wore white organdy; the groom wore jeans.

The redheaded flower girl wore jeans, too.

Bronte's feminine gown was styled with ruffles at the neck and hemline. She carried a bouquet of lily of the valley, gardenias and white tea roses. Her frequent smiles were as radiant as the golden sunshine outside.

The groom had pressed the razor-sharp creases into his jeans himself; his black, gleaming boots had been polished by the same hand.

The big house overflowed with guests and family. Carla wore a demure blouse of beige silk with her jeans, and her ponytail that was caught up in cascades of fresh lilies was neatly brushed for once. The pictures her magic pencil drew today were of flowers instead of monsters.

All the Jacksons were in attendance. Tad Jackson

had even come all the way from his home in Australia. Cheyenne and her husband had arrived from Houston, too.

Sterling-silver fountains bubbled with endless champagne, but the groom wouldn't drink anything but iced lime water. The wedding cake that had been flown in from Houston rose in graceful tiers nearly to the ceiling.

While members of the orchestra mingled with the wedding guests during the intermission, Madame Devlin's recorded voice soared to the highest rafters in the ballroom. Her daughter was as gorgeous as the diva.

Everyone was thrilled that Jack West, who had suffered poverty and unjust imprisonment, was marrying the beautiful daughter of the legendary opera star.

Except for Theodora West—who'd tied a rope around her neck and fired a single shot into the air, so that her beloved horse had bolted and dragged her to what she considered the most honorable death possible—everybody who was anybody had come to the wedding. Indeed, the same people who had followed Theodora's cortege and riderless horse to her grave site three weeks earlier had flocked to this wedding of the decade.

No one was listening to Madame Devlin, though. Nor were they paying much attention to the beautiful bride and handsome groom. No. The glittering throng had gathered at a far corner around Garth Brown, whom the groom had invited since his wife was an avid fan. The star had taken to his brother and was having the time of his life, autographing wedding napkins by the hundreds.

"You're being upstaged, Hollywood, by that scene-stealing, half brother of yours. At your own wedding reception,'' Brickhouse teased, lifting his drink as Jack pulled Bronte tighter.

''He's okay.''

''Yeah. He is,'' Brickhouse agreed.

No longer did Jack feel even the slightest bit jealous of his handsome brother. Instead he felt admiration and pride and joy at the fledgling bonds that had begun to form between them.

''You sure you don't want *his* autograph, Bronte?'' Brickhouse persisted.

''Why would I, when I am holding the real thing right here in my arms?'' Bronte whispered against her husband's lips.

''Why don't you go get her one anyway, amigo?'' Jack asked, for Brickhouse, he'd discovered, had been the one to leave the mysterious envelopes with the cryptic messages.

''Oh, I git you.'' Brickhouse smiled broadly. ''You two want to be alone...to get a headstart on your honeymoon.''

The three of them laughed. Then Brickhouse picked up a stack of napkins and headed toward the movie star.

''You stinker!'' Bronte's eyes shone. ''How come you didn't tell him you already had Garth autograph a dozen napkins for me?''

''Because I love you, Bronte Devlin West,'' Jack said, drawing her behind a potted palm. ''Because I want to kiss you...without him studying my technique. Because I don't want Garth to run out of napkins to sign any time soon and come over here and flirt with you again.''

''Jealous?''

''Never.''

''Liar.''

"I love you. And I don't feel like sharing."

Jack bent to kiss his wife, and, if ever a bridegroom had felt sheer joy to be alive and in love with his bride, if ever a man had passed beyond all doubt and uncertainty, it was Jack West on his wedding day.

Their mouths touched, clung. Time stopped, and they felt absolutely alone with each other even in that crowded ballroom.

It was a very long time before Jack let her go. Afterward Bronte stared up at him raptly.

"I adore you," he whispered hoarsely. "I wish we were already on our honeymoon so that I could make love to you for as long as I feel like it."

She could not speak, but her eyes said she adored him, too.

"You freed me from the past," he breathed softly. His gaze traveled across her face, as if memorizing every feature. "I didn't think I'd ever—"

"I love you, too. You and Carla gave me a new life. We have a future together now. I never thought..."

Jack knew she was remembering Jimmy.

"I'm going to give you children. Lots of children," he murmured.

"Jack...you...you already have."

"What?" His eyes scanned her slim waist.

She blushed and then nodded, smiling shyly. "I'm expecting your child."

Jack wrapped his arms around her.

"Don't squeeze...the baby."

The baby....

Jack remembered how quick-thinking and brave she'd been, how she'd sat beside him day and night at the hospital. How Brickhouse had been there almost as often. "I owe you everything. Even my life."

"No woman in the whole world is happier than I am."

He was going to have another child. With her.

Their child.

Bronte was exquisite. Her sweetness made up for everything. Jack would always love her. Even though Theodora had used him and betrayed him, because of Bronte, he believed in love and the goodness of life more than he ever had before.

Not that it was easy or pleasant for him to believe that Theodora had deliberately set him up. That she had sent him after Chantal. That, all the time, she had planned to use him to destroy her daughter a second time and then destroy him, too.

For the ranch.

She'd been crazy.

Forgive her.

Theodora had loved the ranch more than she could ever love anything or anyone, but at least, in the end, Theodora had set things right by changing her will and making Carla her principal heir. She had stated her wishes that Jack run the ranch, and he was thankful she'd written him a personal letter begging his forgiveness, too. As he had read her shaky handwriting and bizarre phrasing, Bronte had held his hand, and all his anger and bitterness toward her had flowed out of him.

At least Theodora had done right by him in the end.

That was all that mattered. He could live at the ranch he loved and manage it. Even Maverick seemed happy enough about the way everything had turned out. He had taken a job in Europe with an accounting firm, and leased Jack his land.

But the main thing was Bronte. He had always dreamed of having a family. Even in prison.

Now he had her. And their baby.

And Carla who was smiling and laughing and dashing after Cheyenne's son, Jeremy.

His wife and daughter and their baby were his new beginning.

Bronte was staring up at him with eyes so bright that they seemed to have invented the color green.

She was irresistible.

Gently, tenderly, Jack lowered his mouth to his bride's again. Her arms circled him, holding him close.

Marriage.

It meant family, love, and a houseful of children as well as a love that would last forever.

Their kiss went on and on.

Marriage.

The best part was that it meant having such a pretty, sweet wife to kiss every single day and night for the rest of his life.

"Bronte," he whispered a long time later.

"Yes, love."

"Who's going to tell Carla she's going to be a big sister?"

"You are. I'm going to break the news to your brother."

"You just want to make me jealous."

"And...are you...jealous, Jack?"

"No way."

"Liar."

Then he kissed her.

* * * * *

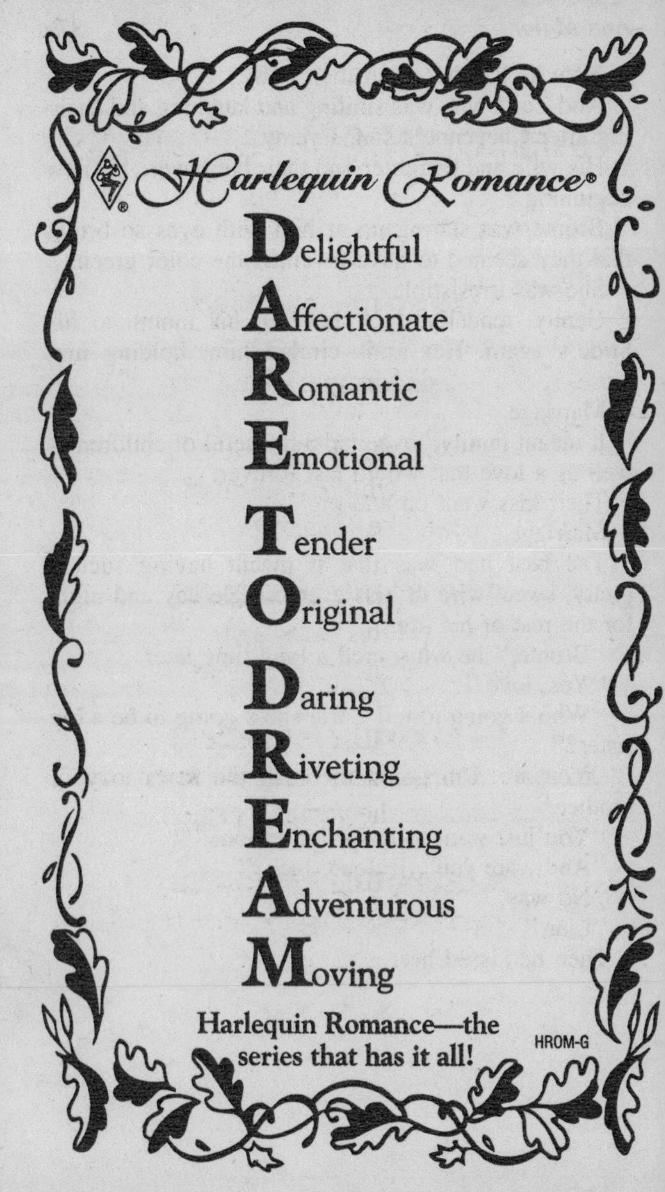
Harlequin Romance®
Delightful
Affectionate
Romantic
Emotional
Tender
Original
Daring
Riveting
Enchanting
Adventurous
Moving
Harlequin Romance—the
series that has it all!
HROM-G

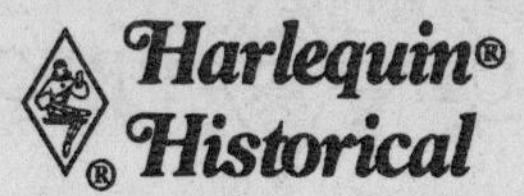
Harlequin®
Historical